PRA

THE MAN IN THE BUICK

"The grace of her writing, the intensity of her insights assert themselves in memory and won't let go."
—Colette Inez

"I'm telling you, this Kathy George can flat out write."

—Lewis Nordan

"   ghnessy

                                                              ensual,
                                                              lamour

                                                              para-
                                                              racters
                                                              so bril-

                                                              Livesey

"   es are
                                                              —and
                                                              o cope
                                                              , small
                                                              u and
                                                              a Paul

"*Fallen* is an absolute page-turner, as well it should be. Let's get that out of the way. But what really lifts this beautifully written book above any limitations of genre is its depth of characterization. The people George brings to life on the page are among the most interesting, complex, and frightening I have encountered anywhere. Never has evil been so seductive, even understandable, and, gasp, almost forgivable. That's what finally makes this wonderful novel so scary in the end. Forgive me, Lord, for I have rooted for the Devil, & Kathy George made me do it." —Chuck Kinder

AFTERIMAGE

"A gripping, gritty police procedural." —*Booklist*

"*Afterimage* sizzles with irony, tension, and surprise. . . . Nearly flawless in its plot and execution, Kathleen George's *Afterimage* is—we can hope—just one of many Colleen Greer adventures waiting for us in the future." —*Mystery News*

"Dark and gripping, Colleen Greer's progress in this top-notch police procedural is further enhanced by the author's deftly deployed humor and irony. Written with a noteworthy flair for plotting and a sharp eye for psychological details in her characters, author Kathleen George's *Afterimage* is a well-crafted and entertaining novel." —BookLoons Reviews

THE ODDS

"If anyone's writing better police thrillers than George, I don't know who it is." —*Entertainment Weekly*

"This very modern police procedural will not be easily forgotten." —*Library Journal*

"George is, above all else, a master storyteller."

HIDEOUT

"Kathleen George's *Hideout* is sharp, quick-paced, and thoroughly entertaining. Once again, George's characters come to life with all the complexities and complications of the world they live in. A smart and compelling read." —Gail Tsukiyama

"Not only could I not put *Hideout* down, I can't stop thinking about it now that I'm done. Kathleen George is not only a crack mystery writer, she is a crack writer. Period. Exciting and elegant. What a combination." —Robert Olen Butler

"*Hideout* barrels like a locomotive. The fast-paced suspense pulls you along for the ride." —Kathy Reichs

SIMPLE

"George's all-too-familiar story is so richly observed, subtly characterized, precisely written—her syncopated paragraphs are a special delight—and successful in its avoidance of genre clichés that you'd swear you were reading the first police procedural ever written."

—*Kirkus Reviews*

"Deft prose, skillful plotting, and winning characters." —*Booklist*

A MEASURE OF BLOOD

A MEASURE OF BLOOD

KATHLEEN GEORGE

MYSTERIOUSPRESS.COM

INTEGRATED MEDIA

NEW YORK

This is a work of fiction. Names, characters, places, events, and incidents either are the product of the author's imagination or are used fictitiously. Any resemblance to actual persons, living or dead, businesses, companies, events, or locales is entirely coincidental.

Copyright © 2013 Kathleen George

Cover design by Mauricio Díaz

ISBN 978-1-4804-4560-4

Published in 2013 by MysteriousPress.com/Open Road Integrated Media, Inc.
345 Hudson Street
New York, NY 10014
www.mysteriouspress.com
www.openroadmedia.com

For Hilary

A MEASURE OF BLOOD

To you, your father should be as a god;
One that compos'd your beauties, yea, and one
To whom you are but as a form in wax
By him imprinted, and within his power
To leave the figure or disfigure it.

Shakespeare, *A Midsummer Night's Dream*, 1.1.50–54

1.

SUNDAY

COMMANDER CHRISTIE AND HIS WIFE were sitting at lunch, surprised by the peace. They didn't have the kids this weekend. They were just about finished with the pasta and crusty bread, enjoying the Sunday, when the phone rang. Marina sprang up to get the call. She was lean and suntanned and full of vim and vigor these days, looking good.

In seconds her face fell. "Yes, he's here," she said. Then she handed the phone to him. "A new homicide. Colleen was there. She took the call."

Christie's police partner, Colleen Greer, was a workaholic. She had urged him to stay home, saying she would cover for him.

He accepted the phone. "Tell me."

"You're going to want to do this one, Boss. It's a homicide in Squirrel Hill. Very fresh. Just happened. I understand a child found his mother's body. I just got here."

By then he was digging in the bowl on the hallway table for his car keys. "Where's the father?"

"No father. Mother and son. That's it, I'm told."

"How old? The boy?"

"Seven. Going on eight."

Christie learned in quick sequence that it had happened at an apartment on Morrowfield Avenue, that an ambulance got there even before the patrol cops and called it in, that the patrol cops were there now, but the medics were talking about taking the body to Shadyside Hospital in spite of the fact that they couldn't get a pulse. The victim was a forty-seven-year-old woman, an art teacher. Margaret Brown, known as Maggie.

He paused, looked down at his clothes. He was wearing a blue T-shirt and jeans, far more casual than what he usually wore on a case. Marina, knowing how he thought, brought him the chino sports coat he'd flung on a living room chair the night before. He put it on as he made his way to the car.

Christie's house was in Bloomfield; he tended not to obey speed limits. He zoomed down Fifth, then up Wilkins. As he drove up Wilkins, he heard a siren; soon an ambulance passed him; he thought, *That's the one taking the body of the murdered woman to the hospital.* They had to try, of course, but it made investigating a bit harder. He avoided Murray Avenue because people would be sluggishly crossing the street with grocery bags or cups of coffee, wearing that stunned Sunday look. He took Shady, banking on its being faster.

When he got to Morrowfield, he parked half over a curb right across the street from the large apartment building where neighbors had gathered outside and in the downstairs hallway.

He had to hope patrol had taken good photographs.

He took the stairs to the second-floor apartment where the murder had happened. Greer was there all right. She wore sandals and she stepped carefully around the blood, which was just inside the door. Like Christie, she hated the booties and preferred to risk her shoes. There was a kitchen knife on the floor and it was bloody.

"Where's the boy?" was the first thing Christie asked.

"Next door. With neighbors. He knows them. They babysit him sometimes."

"You talked to him?"

"Briefly. It's . . . probably a domestic crime. He says a man came in to talk to his mother. He thinks the man was saying he was the father, the kid's father . . . and he wanted to see him. Apparently there was an argument. That's all we know."

"The boy witnessed it?"

"No. He ran out for help and then back. And he found her."

"You said he's seven."

"A couple of weeks from eight."

"Let's go see him. Hopefully there's some relative somewhere in the picture."

A boy that age was going to need something familiar to hang onto. When Christie's father took off, he had the house, his mother, his aunt. And still it was hard to accept the absence. He felt for the kid.

"You saw her? The mother?"

"I saw them loading her."

"Any chance she's going to make it?"

"No, Boss. The EMTs are playing angel games. You know, they want to deliver a miracle."

He sighed. "How many stab wounds?" He tipped his head toward the kitchen knife near the front door, where the body was found.

"It seemed like one stab wound. The heart. That's what the medics were saying. Boss, there's no chance. She was dead."

Greer was good at her work. Going to be great. He'd been her mentor but she was beyond rookie status now. Nobody doubted Colleen Greer these days.

Christie took in the one toppled pan in the kitchen—everything else in order—then the pool of blood by the door.

The patrol cop showed him four photographs on his digital camera. Christie had to keep tilting the camera to get good light. "I'll want these blown up," he said. What he saw in the small rectangle was a woman collapsed on the floor—shocked face, clutching her heart, her back to the door. No apparent wounds or bruises otherwise. Sudden. Impulsive. Effective.

"Let's go next door. You called anybody else?"

"The mobile unit."

"Good."

"And I called Potocki and Dolan. They're both available. In case you want them."

"Good. Call them back. Pull them in."

"I didn't call Child Services. I thought, like you said, we'd be hoping for a relative."

He nodded. "You can bet we hope for that. Who are these neighbors? You know anything about them?"

"The Panikkars. They own an Indian restaurant up on Baum. It's been there for about twelve years. Daughter lives with them. She has some degrees from Pitt. She apparently babysat many times over the last seven years, so she's taken care of the boy before. Likes him." Colleen straightened her dress apologetically. It was a beige thing, linen, he thought. She said, "My Sunday best. I was hoping for a slow day. How about you?" She smiled, gesturing toward his T-shirt. "Very hip."

The next-door apartment opened to a strong smell of spices. A middle-aged woman, red eyed and clearly extremely upset, appeared from behind the open door. Her hair was bound tightly and she was wearing a sari of orange and gold, a beautiful garment but surely uncomfortable in the heat. Christie could see past the woman and her living room into a kitchen where a lithe, good-looking boy with dark hair and dark eyes sat at the table. He was numbly eating a cookie and drinking milk while a young woman read to him.

Christie wanted to talk to the boy, but he made a decision to talk to the older woman first. Anything that calmed the boy right now was probably a good thing.

Mrs. Panikkar dabbed at her face with a paper towel. It was especially warm in her apartment.

"Could I speak to you in the hallway?" he asked.

Mrs. Panikkar looked behind her to where her husband was emerging from a back room. Christie became aware of the sound of a TV from where Mr. Panikkar came. He was hurriedly buttoning the last buttons of his guayabera. He looked as if he believed he should come to his wife's rescue.

"One at a time," Christie said firmly.

As soon as they got to the hallway, Colleen said, "We don't have to talk here. I've got a neighbor willing to give us his living room. Down the hall."

"You did a lot in seven minutes."

"I tried."

The fast command post Colleen had set up was the living room of a man who looked—by the piles of magazines and papers and the unfolded laundry in a basket next to the sofa in the living room—to be divorced. He had managed to clear a sofa and two chairs. It would do.

The man hovered in the passage to his inner rooms. He had an assortment of things in his arms from his cleaning up. Sweatpants, a book, a file folder. "Should I do anything else?" he asked.

"This is Mr. Holtzman," Colleen told Christie. "Anything else you want from him?"

Christie shook his head. "We'll be as efficient as possible. Has anyone talked to you about what you saw?"

"The cops first. Then her . . . Detective Greer? I told her I didn't see anything. Not a thing. I was in the back room reading."

"Hear anything?"

"No. I had my iPod on the dock and it—"

"Go back to it then. I'll check with you later."

Colleen ushered Mrs. Panikkar to a seat on the sofa.

Christie said, "Thank you for your time. We need to hear everything you know about what happened. Just tell it from the beginning."

She began to cry. "The little boy came knocking at my door. Calling for my husband. I said he wasn't home because he was in the shower and I didn't want to disturb him. The boy—his name is Matt, Matthew—pulled me to his doorway and I saw the blood. I screamed. I went to get my husband because . . . because the boy was crying, saying he needed a doctor."

"Your husband is a doctor?"

"Yes. A podiatrist. But I went to get him out of the shower and I also called 911. The boy ran back to his mother." She began to cry harder. "My husband is not the kind of doctor who saves lives."

"Detective Greer said something about a restaurant you own. Your husband owns it?"

"Yes. He does both."

Christie said, "Ah. Okay. Tell me what you saw, what you heard."

"Nothing. We had the television on because my husband watches the news. I was in my daughter's bedroom, putting clothes away and talking to her. The shower made noise, too. We didn't hear anything."

"Other times before today? Other disturbances."

"Never. If my door was open, I could hear the mother calling to her son or reprimanding him. But only the sound, not what she said."

Christie looked around at the building's good, thick walls that might have helped kill Margaret Brown. "Other visits. People visiting her?"

"Not many visitors and I don't know the names. Women friends, men friends with children. But I know the little boy will know who. He's very smart. My daughter tells me all the time he's smart."

"What did you see when the boy dragged you to the door?"

"A terrible sight." She put her hand over her eyes briefly but even when she removed them, her breathing was changed, panicked sounding. "I couldn't open the door the whole way. She was on the floor. She was dead. My husband said she was dead when he got there. I heard the policeman say she was dead. The boy wanted my husband to do something, and my husband looked at me to say it was no use, but the emergency doctors arrived. My husband sat down with the boy and he told him, 'She's gone. There is nothing I can do for her.' He said all those things people say. He said, 'She died and left this world. She is in heaven now and she is resting.' He thought it was important to tell the boy right away. I don't know."

Christie wished he'd been the one to break the news, but it was done now, too late. He would have left space in the conversation for the boy to ask, to talk, to come to understand it.

Colleen got a call and went out into the hallway to take it.

Christie watched her for evidence of what the call was about as he asked Mrs. Panikkar, "When you saw Ms. Brown—she was near the front door? Her back to the door?"

"Yes."

"I understand you volunteered to take care of the boy for a day."

"Oh, yes. My daughter is very fond of him."

"How well did you know Ms. Brown?"

"Not deeply. Only the way you know neighbors when you want to be private and you know they want to be private."

"Do you know who her relatives are?"

She shook her head. "I never saw or heard of a mother or father or sister or anything like that."

He got a deep pang of foreboding. It would be tough keeping the kid away from Child Services if there were no relatives.

Just then, Potocki and Dolan arrived. Christie trusted those two maybe beyond all others. John Potocki, a reliable, salt-of-the-earth Pole, forty years old, had amassed a solid history of good work, much of it from his expertise with computers. Artie Dolan, a tidy, muscular African American was the uncontested champ at getting confessions. He turned his dreamy brown eyes on suspects and they gave it up, whatever it was. Dolan had been around for almost as long as Christie. They went way back, sometimes partners, sometimes not, always friends.

He told Mrs. Panikkar she could go back to her place.

Dolan entered, saying, "This is going to be a big one."

Christie told him, "Yep. You start on this building. All the neighbors up and down. Somebody saw something. Potocki: Step around the lab techs. Pick up everything of interest. Datebooks, calendars, address books, computer, files. Whatever you can find. We need names. We don't know who was in this woman's life and we're going to need all the names we can get. Comb the place."

Colleen came back into the room. "DOA. It's official."

He told her, "Call Denman and Hurwitz and have them canvas the neighbors in nearby buildings."

Dolan made a half salute. He and Potocki moved on. Potocki touched Colleen's shoulder on the way out, the only acknowledgment that the bond between them ran deep and serious.

Christie noted his jealousy flare up at that touch. It was a human emotion and he had to live with it. He couldn't have all the women. He couldn't, being the person he was, even have two. And he couldn't help it that he and Colleen had some kind of connection. She was Marina's opposite in appearance with that tousled-on-purpose blonde hair. Marina was exotic with long, dark brown hair, almost black. He loved Marina, no question. But Colleen—also no question—crackled the air around her.

He'd been planning to call in Dr. Panikkar next, but he decided that a very smart kid was probably the better bet. He had the picture pretty clear. The doc was king in his household, not easily interrupted, watched CNN around the clock when he was home, expected his tea on time. Happened to be in the shower when he was called for and not so good at saving lives anyway. "Bring the boy. Matthew."

Colleen went out and came back with Matthew, accompanied by the young woman who had been reading to him. The young woman wore jeans and a cotton top that had probably been made in India—it had decorative stitching and tiny beads that sparkled. She was pretty, both westernized and not, interesting. "My name is Oopale," she said. "I've known Matt since he was born."

"Will you hang on over at your place? I'll want to talk to you."

"I will be there."

"Hi Matthew. How about you sit on the sofa with me? I'm a detective and I think you can be very helpful."

Matt came to him and slid up on the sofa. His face was tight. His hands were clenched tight. Christie wanted to hug him, to break through, and it was hard to hold back, but he needed to get the boy's trust first. "Your next-door neighbor seems pretty nice. Is she?" he began with Matt.

"Yes."

"Do you like staying with her?"

"It's okay."

Christie looked to Colleen Greer with a silent question: Am I gentle enough?

"Are you hanging in there all right?"

"Yes."

"Okay. You said a man came into your apartment this morning? Did you see him come in?"

"No. I was in my room."

"How did you know someone was there?"

"I could hear voices a little bit."

"Ah, good, okay. Is that when you came out of your room?"

"No. I was just playing a game on my TV. I didn't know anything was wrong."

"You kept playing? A video game?"

The boy winced and looked down. "Yes," he said in a low voice.

"Well, that's okay. You didn't know anything was wrong. Did you see the man later?"

"No. Well, I saw him just like from the back. My mother was yelling at me. She said to leave, run, and so I did."

"You were afraid of him?"

He hesitated. "I guess."

"Did you hear what he was saying?"

"No. But . . . he bothered my mother before. So I think it was the same thing."

"You saw him before?"

"Yes."

"You're sure it was the same guy?"

"I *think* so."

"How many times before?"

"Um . . . one time is all I know."

"Is that why you told Detective Greer the man said he was your father? Because that's what he said the other time?"

Matthew nodded.

"Do you know who he is? His name?"

"No."

"Do you remember when that was? That you saw him?"

"At the grocery store. He yelled at my mom."

"When? Can you remember?"

"I don't know."

"Long ago?"

"It was . . . it was nice weather out."

"This summer maybe?"

"I think I still had school."

"June?" He looked up at Greer. Some guesswork needed here. "What did this man say exactly? Can you remember?"

"Stuff like why didn't she tell him and he had a right to see me because I was his son."

"Was he angry when he said it?"

"Um . . . yeah, I guess."

"Tell me. Angry and what? Something else?"

"Surprised, like."

"Surprised. Was he looking for you, waiting for your mother, or was it—do you think it was an accidental meeting?"

Before he could revise the question, Matt answered, "He was surprised. Like shocked."

"Did your mom ever talk about him before?"

"No. Only after. She said he wasn't my father."

"Can you think of anything else?"

"She told him to do math."

"Uh-huh." Christie looked at Colleen. "Anything else?"

"She told him I wasn't even eight years old."

"Uh-huh. You seem to have a very good memory. Anything else that could help us?"

Matt shook his head. But then he said, "I think he had a reddish car. Dark red. I think it's called maroon."

"He was in a car? Driving?"

"He was leaning on it."

"Did you ever see him in the car?"

"No."

"Where did all this happen?"

"At the store."

"Do you happen to remember which store?" Christie saw suddenly that the boy was trying not to cry. "You're doing really well. You're helping us a lot. Do you want to take a break?"

"No. It was a grocery store. A big one. It's called . . . it's something fancier than our Giant Eagle here—"

"Whole Foods?" Colleen interrupted.

"No. The next one near it."

"Market District," she said calmly.

Matthew's face registered that that was correct.

Christie asked, "You never saw this man before or after?"

Matthew shook his head.

"Can you tell me what happened this morning? After you ran out?"

"I only ran out because my mother said to run."

"I know. That's okay. Did you happen to hear anything?"

"No. Just some kind of arguing and when I opened the door from my room, she said I should leave."

"How did she say it? Calmly or—"

" 'Run, Matt, go, leave!' stuff like that. She said I should go to a neighbor, but I didn't."

"Why?"

"I didn't feel like it." His face began to collapse.

"Okay. That's all right."

"Because I wanted to help. I took the phone on the way out."

"Where did you go?"

"Just down the steps. When I got outside, I called 911. I said, 'A man is bothering my mother.' Some lady said okay and she asked for our address. But it didn't feel like she was going to do anything. So, so I snuck back."

"Same way?"

"No, I came around the front."

"Were you afraid to come back?"

"Yeah. But I . . . didn't know what else to do."

"Did you see him again? When you came back?"

"No. He was gone."

Though it was excruciating to wait out the boy's struggle, to wait for what would come next, Christie allowed a silence to intervene.

After a while Matthew said, "She was on the floor and there was blood everywhere. I tried to talk to her, but she couldn't hear. Right away I called 911 again, because I knew the lady who answered didn't care when I called before. I asked for an ambulance."

Colleen took a step away. She was near tears.

"You didn't do anything wrong, Matt. It seems like you did just about everything right, okay?"

"Then I ran next door. Mrs. Panikkar didn't understand why I wanted her husband until I dragged her. Then she ran back to her place and I could hear her calling him in her language."

"That was a sensible thing to try," Christie said. "Wasn't it?"

Colleen, her voice raspy, said, "I think it was very smart."

Matthew twitched and looked down.

"Something else you want to say?"

"No," the boy said. "Yes. Was he my father?"

"I don't know. Your mother told you he wasn't?"

"Yes."

"Did she tell you anything else about your father? Where he was, anything?"

"Just away. He couldn't be with us."

"Is that . . . all?"

"She said he was a good person. She said he was smart. But we couldn't all be together."

"Matt. Tell me everything you can about the people in your mother's life. Tell us the names of relatives."

"We don't have any."

"None? Grandmother, uncle?"

"She said it was just the two of us."

Christie looked at Colleen, wondering if he could just keep at the boy. She seemed to nod. "Can you tell me who her friends were? Women friends, work friends, everybody you can think of. And anybody she was dating."

"She didn't go for dates."

"Okay. Other friends?"

"Sasha. Her friend Sasha."

Christie asked, "Did she keep phone numbers somewhere?"

"Near the phone."

17

"Good place. Who else was close to the two of you—other friends? Men friends especially. Take your time."

"I guess Sasha's boyfriend, Mikhail." He appeared to think of answers. "And Jason. He owns the coffee shop where she works. And the guy from the gallery where she works. Ben."

"How many jobs did she have?"

"Three."

"Can you explain how that worked?"

"Monday, Wednesday, Friday she had school."

"This was in the grade schools," Colleen told Christie. "That was her main job, teaching painting. Right, Matt?"

"Yeah."

"Other jobs were . . . what?"

"She worked in the coffee shop sometimes on other days."

"This would be on Tuesdays and Thursdays and Saturdays?"

"I think. When she wasn't needed at the gallery."

"That's a lot of work."

"Yeah."

"Where did you stay when she was working? With Oopale?"

"Sometimes. Or Jade, my friend. Or Grady. He's my other friend."

"Well, I'm glad you have these good friends. Hang tight, okay?" Christie said. "I'll check back with you."

Matt frowned and gave only the slightest nod.

Christie told Colleen, "Would you send in Oopale next and tell Dr. Panikkar he's on deck?"

They all walked to the door of Holtzman's apartment and Christie watched Colleen touching the boy's shoulder and talking to him as she walked him back down the hall. The techs had just arrived and were getting out of the elevator. Three methods of access: the utility stairway—the one Matt had apparently used—the front stairway, and the elevator. Christie began to lead the two men from the mobile crime unit down the hall to the Brown apartment. He kept his voice low and instructed the men not to open the door while Matt was still in sight. Then he told them what he needed in the way of photos and prints and the usual scouring for trace evidence. They opened the apartment door. Both techs stepped wide over the blood.

Moments later Colleen emerged from the Panikkars' door with Oopale. Christie told her, "I need you to go in there. Find that phone list. Call Sasha. Break the news. Bring her in. And anyone else you can get."

"Should we put anything out about the maroon car?"

He thought about it. "Too flimsy."

She mock-saluted him and stepped over the blood.

Oopale stood in the hallway waiting to be called to help Christie. She looked away from the open doorway. She was lovely and graceful.

"Come," he said.

Even though she still wore jeans, she moved as smoothly as if she wore a sari.

"Matt has been pretty clear on what happened. I won't keep you long. I think he probably needs you."

They entered Holtzman's apartment and sat. "Tell me everything you know about Maggie, her friends, her patterns."

Oopale brought her hands in prayer position to her mouth. "I don't know a lot. She worked a good number of hours. But she tried for the most part to be home when Matt was home."

"Did she have friends over?"

"I think, occasionally, a woman friend. I met her friend at the christening. Sasha. She was named the godmother of Matthew."

"Ah, good. Were there any *relatives* at the christening?"

She didn't have to think about it. "No, no, there weren't. Just local friends. I thought how different it was from Indian culture, where you can't get rid of family no matter what."

Christie smiled. "How about men who could have possibly been the father?"

Puzzlement crossed her face. "Nobody acted that way. Just, you know, friendliness. Modest gifts. It wasn't so much a real christening in the Christian sense as I understand it. Just little speeches and good wishes for Matt."

"What about dates? Men in Maggie Brown's life?"

"I didn't see any. I wondered if she was lonely. But many people are."

Christie stood and ran his hands through his hair. "Let me think."

"I'm wondering," Oopale said, "what will happen with Matt. Who will take him? I'm worried."

Christie turned to her. "You and me both. There's no evidence of a relative so far. Are you putting in a bid?"

"My parents wouldn't allow it, I'm sure. People would think he was mine and illegitimate. And it would be a huge responsibility."

"Definitely that."

"But if he goes to Child Services—"

"You know about all that?"

"I've interned there."

"Oh!"

"I know some of the people. Some are good. Some aren't. The red tape is terrible."

"That's for sure. But . . . but maybe you could help me through some of that tape tomorrow."

"I'm really not there anymore. Now I work with old folks. What could I—"

"Maybe this Sasha . . . Do you think she might make a claim? As godmother?"

Oopale began to seem as distressed as he was. "I don't know. I don't know."

But an idea, a good one, had been creeping up on Christie and now it revealed itself. "Look. I have an idea of something that might work. Can you keep him the rest of today? If I don't call Child Services right away, will you . . . support me in that, ease me through the system? It's Sunday, you know him, he wants to be with you, he knows you . . . Can you say all that?"

"Yes. Okay, yes. But after that, as soon as they get word, they're going to jump in."

"Right. Tell me about him. Is he generally well behaved?"

"More or less. He's rather addicted to computer and video games. And to sugar. A lot of parents don't let their kids have either, but Mrs. Brown didn't stop him."

"Oh. Would you say she was a bad mother?"

"No. She loved him. She was just . . . overwhelmed. So she let him make the rules sometimes."

"She didn't take charge?"

"Exactly. He was stronger than she was."

"Okay. I'm getting a picture. I've only met Matt today. Was he ever a happy child?"

Oopale paused. "Sometimes. More often nervous. Sometimes sad."

"Sad?"

"Not secure. Lonely. He asked a lot of questions about fathers. It was clear he wanted one."

When Oopale left, Christie took a call from his wife. He summarized quickly, then said, "Either the guy who did it is the father, and a nut, or the father is out there somewhere, nobody knows where or who he is. The mother told the kid the father was a fine guy and that he was just not available."

"She shouldn't have done that to him."

Something snapped like the twang of a guitar string in Christie's chest.

WHEN COLLEEN WENT into Maggie Brown's apartment, she saw the techs were busy in the kitchen and at the front door, examining the blood and the knife. Potocki was lining up boxes of papers in front of the sofa. Everyone was working fast. Potocki led Colleen straight to the table with Maggie's personal phone book and even to the entry for Sasha.

"In the back. Alphabetized by first name," he said as he handed the small phone book to her. His face was slightly flushed. They'd partnered in the past, but now that they were involved and thus *not* working as partners, there was the whole new problem of avoiding touch on the job. He started back to the mother's bedroom.

She took a deep breath, carried the phone book to the boy's bedroom—a messy space, books and toys, a nest. She made the call from there.

Sasha asked, "Who is this again?"

"Detective Colleen Greer." Then she made the announcement.

There was a silence. "Are you sure?" came a thin, reedy voice, then a sound of gasping and sobbing.

When Colleen told her what had happened, the best friend kept saying, "Oh my God, oh my God, are you sure?"

"Yes, I was here."

Colleen kept a detective's mind on the matter of Sasha's reaction. Bizarre and tabloid images flashed before she nixed them. She could imagine scenarios—Sasha's boyfriend messing with Maggie, Sasha getting furious, things like that, the worst of human behaviors.

Sasha was saying, "Oh my God. I can't . . . How could such a thing happen?"

"I'm sorry. I understand how shocking it is. But Sasha, we need to talk to you. Do you live very far away?"

"No. No, just Highland Park."

"We need for you to come here."

"To . . . to her place?"

"We're using the apartment down the hall, 2A. Will it take you long?"

22

"About . . . twenty minutes. I . . . have to bring my daughters."

"We'll find a place for them. Sasha. Let me ask you one thing now. Can you tell me the name of Matt's father?"

"Matt's father? No. I have no idea."

Twenty minutes, Colleen thought. Then we get to ask why nobody knows who this kid's father is.

Colleen went back to the boxes. Potocki had gone through everything including kitchen drawers for notes, pieces of paper. She could see him through an open doorway in Maggie's bedroom, working. Maggie had used a corner of her bedroom as an office, so the computer was there and Potocki was sitting at it.

"How's it going?" she asked from the doorway.

"She kept almost everything, sometimes very organized, other times not. Does Boss have a suspect?"

"Nope. I have to call a few other people to come in." She had her finger poised on the phone buttons. She moved farther into Maggie's bedroom for a moment. A whiff of perfume or soap. Suddenly the woman and her death were very real. Colleen stared at a bureau full of lotions and lipsticks. A good number of them were natural products of the kind sold in health food stores. Potocki, with a tuft of hair mussed, kept working at Maggie's computer.

"I'm in," Potocki was saying. "I'm in her email."

She wondered if it was true that Matt really had nobody. She knew the kid had already wrapped himself around Christie's heart.

MAGGIE'S FRIEND APPEARED at the fast command post. She was a tall, blonde woman, sturdy, with thick, curly, long hair. She wore no makeup and flushed easily. She brought to mind butter and cheese. Her gauzy skirt and shirt were a throwback to the '70s. She'd fit at a commune with a dairy farm and a good-sized vegetable garden.

Christie helped her walk her daughters to the Panikkar residence. Her eyes were red, but she was more in shock now than able to weep.

"My kids brought a DVD for Matt. I don't know if these people have a player . . ." she murmured.

"We can hope so."

Oopale opened the door and took the girls smoothly, saying, "I'll watch them, of course."

Christie guided Sasha back down the hall, explaining, "As Maggie's best friend, you are bound to be our best lead. You would know her other contacts."

"I still can't believe . . . I can't . . ." She looked about at the apartment she'd landed in, then focused on Christie again.

He decided to go at her sideways. "First, can you give us some insights about Matt?"

"He's a sweet kid. Oh, difficult sometimes . . ."

"Is he?"

"A little. Headstrong."

"Well, some kids just are. You told my colleague you don't know who his father is?"

"No."

"You mustn't keep that from us if you know. It's important."

"Why?"

"Someone was bothering Maggie about the boy. The person who killed her was, we believe, saying he was the father. So, you see . . ."

"Oh, some joker bothered her a few months ago . . . "

"Ah. Good. What do you know about that?"

"Only that she said some guy scared her and he was a nut."

"What else did she say? A name?"

"No. It sounded like someone from her past from a long time ago. She said he was always a bit odd."

"But *was* he Matt's father? Did she say?"

"Oh, no, he wouldn't have been. I knew her when she was trying to get pregnant. She opted for artificial insemination. I saw Matt the day he was born."

"It still could have been this guy as biological father."

"No . . . no she went to a clinic in New York. She wanted a choice of donors. And then she got pregnant."

"Can you be sure it was the artificial insemination that did it? And not another contact."

"Well . . . that's what she said. I believed her."

"She wasn't seeing someone?"

"No. No, she told me she was done with the whole dating scene. She'd been using some kind of dating service and she said she only met duds."

"The name of the dating service?"

"Oh, I don't know. She was disgusted with it and never said the name."

"Then straight to artificial insemination? So the goal was a baby all along?"

"Yes. She really wanted a baby. She was thirty-eight or thirty-nine. She knew a woman who had had luck with the clinic in New York. See, Maggie lived there for quite a while before moving here, so she—"

"She went the whole way there for the treatments?"

"She . . . made that decision." Sasha rubbed at her forehead as if that would help make sense of today. "I argued that with her. Pittsburgh is way up there medically. But she traveled to New York a couple of times and when she did get pregnant, she was ecstatic. It was what she wanted. She told me she'd made the right decision."

"But she didn't give you any details? Who she chose, why?"

"No."

"Nothing?"

"Only that she felt she had always loved men with dark hair and dark eyes. She chose dark hair and eyes, she said, on the guy's profile, but she never saw a picture. She said he was probably very smart too because of his college degrees."

"Which degrees?"

"He was starting on a master's."

"In what?"

"I don't know. She didn't say."

"What was the name of the clinic?"

"She never told me. She was very private." Sasha's eyes drifted, as if for the first time she had allowed herself to feel insulted by this withholding of information. She shook her head. "She always said the kid was enough for her."

"Tell me about men she worked with."

"She didn't date them. Jason is married. Ben is gay. Look. I don't like this—digging in her past when she's dead. We're just sitting here talking about her and, and criticizing her life."

"I'm not criticizing. I'm trying to find her killer. Please keep thinking. She's got to have leaked something."

Sasha swallowed hard and bit her lip.

"Tell me about the man who bothered her and Matt a couple months ago."

"She was freaked that he thought there was something between them. She said she only went out with him twice a long time ago."

"No name?"

"No."

Christie pressed. "Did she say what he did, where he lived?"

"No."

"Did *she* call him a joker?"

"No, she said he was sad, mixed up."

"Did she give you the location of the clinic in New York?"

"In the Village, I think, but I'm not sure."

"And she didn't think the guy *was* the father."

"She told me the father was a number in a book. Why don't you believe me? She was my best friend."

He had to stop. Sasha was getting shaky. Finally she said, "She was a good person. I just want you to know that. She cared about people. She loved her son."

"I sense that. I'm trying to figure out what it meant when she held back, didn't tell you things."

"She got embarrassed. She thought she made a mess of relationships." Sasha began to cry.

"I understand. You didn't probe because you could sense she was sensitive."

"Yes. Thank you."

"You spoke daily?"

"Pretty much."

"Phone calls?"

"Phone calls. Or in our studio. We shared a studio."

"I don't know about the studio. Explain."

"We're both painters. I teach school, too, but I'm a painter mostly—Maggie was starting to let painting go."

"Why? Did she say why?"

"She said her painting wasn't going anywhere and it was a waste of time." Sasha shook her head and dabbed at her eyes. "She was losing confidence that she could do something with it."

At that, she excused herself to go into the bathroom down the hall in the apartment they were using.

Christie paced. He was tired of badgering her. There was something stubborn in her, as there was with a lot of aging hippies who just wanted love and peace.

Colleen Greer came back in. Christie indicated with a pointed finger that Sasha was in the bathroom.

"It doesn't look great for leads," Colleen said in a low voice. "I have the two men friends coming over. They sounded truly shocked."

Sasha shuffled back into the room. He noticed her feet. Thick feet, thick sandals.

Colleen moved forward and introduced herself.

"We're almost finished," Christie told Sasha. "Just two more questions occur to me." He tried to keep pressure out of his voice. "What about Maggie's own family? Her parents?"

"Her father and his second wife were academics, not in the arts. And her mother and her stepfather were academics, too. Her mother was a musician."

Christie felt hopeful. "That's a lot of parents. Where are they?"

"Dead. All of them. It's why she wanted a child so badly."

"Brothers, sisters?"

"She didn't have any."

"Well, I have another kind of question, my second question. About Matt. Who would she have wanted to care for him? Did she make any legal plans?"

"I don't think so. She didn't, you know, think like that."

Christie flashed a look at Colleen, both of them aware that Sasha hadn't said anything about making a claim for Matt herself. After all, she was his godmother.

"You think he's a good kid."

"Rebellious sometimes, but smart, smart. And he's . . . yes, a good kid." She began crying again.

Finally Christie released her to go get her kids.

Colleen said, "I think I got a sense of her."

"Hmm. Talk to me."

"She's a 'let it be' kind of person. And Maggie wasn't telling her much. Both women are probably loving enough to their kids but they aren't *strong* mothers. Stubborn, uncertain, spacey."

"Yeah."

"How things change," she murmured. "In *olden times*," she said, mocking the phrase, "women just told the kid his father was dead."

MARINA WAS HOME, FEELING BLUE that her Sunday with Richard had ended so abruptly. He didn't even have time to change clothes.

He was upset about the little boy.

It had been almost two years and Richard was strong again, recovered from the chemo, in remission from the leukemia, totally . . . himself. Looking good.

He thought his looks were boring, ordinary—medium height, medium brown hair, olive skin, slightly crooked nose. Like some old boxer, he said of himself.

Marina could never in a million years find him or anything about him boring.

She'd spent the afternoon sitting in the sun, reading over the play she was about to be in. She was precast as Titania in the Shakespeare production at Pitt, about to go into auditions. The payback for being cast was that she taught two courses and she was expected to coach the student actors—a good deal, a great deal for an actress. She'd be out at rehearsals most evenings. So much for keeping a neat house, but she was not an especially eager homemaker.

Her phone rang and it was Richard again.

"I'm on thin ice here. The kid is, for all intents and purposes, an orphan. But I have an idea."

Was he going to bring the boy home? She got a quick stab of excitement and fear. And then she understood. Not them. The Morrises.

"Look. I want to try Arthur and Jan again."

"Oh, won't that be hard to pull off?"

"I'll have to do an end run. Do you have a phone number for them?"

"Yes, but Richard, they're in France. Let me think. Yes. Jan said she'd get back right before auditions, so I think that means they get back tomorrow."

"Get me the phone number. I'll make the first move now."

"I'm out in the yard," she said, "but I'm going in. This will take a sec. Only you should know Jan told me she and Arthur have given up on children. She said right before they went to France that she appreciates how rich their lives are, able to go to Europe, and all their time to themselves. They don't want to open up all that longing again."

Marina found her sheet of information. *Janet Gabriel, Professor. Robert Arthur Morris, SO.* Address. Email. Office number, home number. And the mobile listed below it. "Whether their cell works in France or not, I can't say." She gave the number.

"Call you later."

She worried about him. He got these ideas. It was as if he were a theatre director casting a play. Arranging lives. Looking for just the right chemistry, the right matches.

And she worried selfishly if Jan Gabriel would blame her for this no-doubt-false hope, another heartbreak come her way.

2.

WHEN JANET GABRIEL'S CELL PHONE RANG, it was ten at night in France, but still Sunday, and she was sitting with her husband, Arthur, on the terrace of the house they had rented. Their luggage was packed for the next morning's flight; this, their last evening, was something delicious—peace, food, wine, the sounds of creatures getting ready for the night.

She had to look for the phone and only just managed to find it.

When Christie identified himself, Janet walked back to where her husband was sitting. She couldn't imagine why the detective whom they knew, but not intimately, would call her in France.

"Look. This isn't for sure," he began. "I know you've given up and all that, but—"

Janet almost laughed then. "Richard. Please. No. Is it those four kids again?" She couldn't do it and she knew that—never even met the four kids he'd wanted to put with them two years ago.

"How about one?" His voice was serious.

"Oh. One of the four?" She looked at Arthur who was mouthing, "What? Who?"

Christie went on. "Here's the situation. Child Services will be involved tomorrow and they'll be looking for a foster home for this kid, Matthew. It's a new case. Matthew Brown. You're still officially registered as foster parents, right?"

Jan looked at her husband's worried face. She clicked the little megaphone that switched on the speakerphone. "Yes," she said.

"Well this is a kid—almost eight. His mother's been murdered. She was a single mother. I don't have to tell you he's going to do better with something familiar around him. His mother lived on Morrowfield—that's only, what, seven blocks from the two of you. He went to school at Minadeo. He has friends in the neighborhood. This could work out for him. . . . He's a handsome boy, and smart. Apparently has a nervous streak—I haven't seen it yet. He's in deep grief. He badly needs parents. He needs a strong mother and father. Will you meet him? If I can finagle the thing—which I hope I can."

Arthur looked stunned.

Jan thought: *a beautiful boy, smart, almost eight.* She had always wondered if something would happen when they were old, even older than this. Something. Some event. Just like that. And she would be a mother because in her heart she never really gave up. She always thought she and her husband were an Abraham and Sarah, waiting. She said, "We get home in the evening tomorrow."

"It isn't for sure. I'll fight for it."

It isn't for sure.

NADAL BROWN HAD PARKED HIS MAROON PONTIAC outside his mother's house in State College, Pennsylvania, earlier in the day and for most of the afternoon sat with his mother, watching TV. Pretending to watch. He'd poked out of the living room a couple of times to do laundry. For hours, his heart pounded so hard he thought she might see.

A glimpse. That's all he got of his son. Then he couldn't find him. He didn't remember the drive there. He did it in a dream.

At one point, his mother said, "Why is the washing machine taking so long?"

He shrugged that he didn't know. He'd run everything twice but he didn't say so. She fed him some sliced ham with cheese and bread and strong coffee. She drank coffee all day long, couldn't get enough of it, always smelled of it. She sat beside him, saying she'd watch anything he wanted to watch on the tube. He picked channels at random, trying not to surf at lightning speed (which she hated). When it was suppertime, she brought him a platter with two wraps, lots of hot sauce. The hot sauce shot another jolt through his system, making him feel shaky inside.

Now, it's nighttime and he's finally beginning to calm.

His mother asks, "Do you need money or something?"

"No."

"Just felt like visiting. Needs his mama," she says hopefully.

But he twists away from her. "I'm not a baby. Can't I just knock back for a couple of hours, be a vegetable? Okay with you?"

"I'm glad you're here. I always thought you didn't like this house." She indicates the dining room where his father spent his last weeks on a hospital bed and where the old man finally breathed his last. At least the hospital bed isn't sitting in the dining room anymore. "I thought I would never get you here again, just sitting with me."

"Well, here I am."

"I put the bed up in that little room, the one you liked. For a while I used it as my sewing room."

A strange little room—lock on the door, window that doesn't open. He chose it because he felt he could shut his father out, though his father never tried to come in.

They go quiet, in agreement not to talk about the father he hated, the man who had materialized only in the last years, when nobody needed *him* anymore and when he was sick and useless and he needed *them*.

"Tell me what else to get you."

"Nothing. Really."

His mother is plump and small. She doesn't think enough of herself, always serving people. She's too soft. And people use her.

He stares straight ahead at the TV.

"Do you like golf now?"

"Yeah."

All that. All that and he had only caught a glimpse of the boy and he didn't have him.

THE ROOM SMELLED LIKE SOME LADY'S PERFUME. He memorized everything in the room because he was excellent at memorizing. Dark wood bureau with one, two, three . . . eight photographs in frames. Incense burner. Funny decorated candles, little statues. A guy with a lot of arms and one guy with an elephant's trunk. Bedroom slippers on the floor in a row with shoes, shoes, then boots. The covers on him were red and gold, but so many layers, one thing after another. He hated covers.

He sat up in bed. He thought there was a good chance his mother was not dead.

The detective tried to tell him he did right, but he knew he didn't. He'd held his mother's hand. He was afraid to pump her chest because there was a lot of blood and he didn't want to touch the blood. But he should have done it. He saw it on television and knew what to do and could have done it. This was what bothered him.

He didn't do anything brave. Then Mrs. Panikkar and Oopale came to him and tried to pull him from his mother. The two women were crying. Mrs. P had lied at first and said her husband wasn't home.

Even if his mother was completely dead, he knew she could wake up, like in those TV shows where machines beep and doctors call out orders and the person comes back alive.

Dr. P told him his mother was dead but Matt thought he seemed odd, like maybe he was lying.

It was almost dark out but there was enough light from street lamps to see. He spied his clothing across the room—a few things the police had brought him, old pants and a T-shirt. He put them on. From somewhere in the apartment, he heard voices and also a TV. He opened the bedroom door. They were in the kitchen, eating, probably food from their restaurant, which he went to with his mother one time. "All these great spices!" his mother had said. "I love spices."

He tiptoed through the living room and out the front door. To his left there was yellow police tape making an *X* over his own door. To his right was the door to the stairway he took earlier today when he ran. Nobody was around to see him. He peered down the stairs. There was nobody in sight. He descended quickly and quietly.

Dead as a donut—that's what his mother used to say when they would find a stinkbug or some other insect with its feet up in the air. The expression made no sense. Why was a donut dead?

He trotted down the street in what he was pretty sure was the direction of the hospital.

One woman looked hard at him, and she even stopped walking to watch him, but she didn't stop him. He turned the corner and walked for a block before he decided it was better to get away from busy Murray Avenue and use the street a block over where there weren't so many people. He took Pocusset Street and kept walking. He often stayed up till midnight. He didn't like to sleep.

He passed a yard where older kids were playing basketball under outdoor lights.

He was good at fooling people.

Back in Oopale's room, when the door opened, through his pretend-closed eyes, he watched them—father, mother, daughter looking at him.

"He's sleeping," the foot doctor said.

And all the while he could see them.

They closed the door.

"What does *your* father do?" kids asked him at school. His mother said once, "Your father is far away and can't be with us. But you don't have to answer about that." He was supposed to say, "My mother is a painter. She takes care of me alone."

If it turned out she was really dead, maybe he could live with Grady. Or Jade.

He walked for a long time and passed a little store on Bartlett where older kids were shopping for sodas and chips. He didn't have any money with him, but he was winded, so he paused and sat on a stone wall.

"You okay, kid?" one boy asked.

"Yeah. Just going to meet my father."

A girl, quite heavy, with a bright, friendly face, said, "Honey, do you need any help?"

"Do you know where Shadyside Hospital is?" The ambulance men on their phones mentioned Presbyterian, Montefiore, Shadyside. He was pretty sure they decided Shadyside.

"Are you sick?"

"No, I just want to know where it is."

"Are you sure you're okay?"

"Yes. I know somebody in the hospital. I want to go tomorrow."

"How are you getting there?"

"I'll get my father to drive me tomorrow."

She began to recite directions, then dug in her purse and pulled out a phone. "Just a sec. I'll show you a map."

He watched her working Google and coming up with a map and a picture. "Pass Forbes, Wightman to Wilkins, left on Wilkins to Fifth Avenue, then left onto Aiken. Not too far. Follow the zigzags. Cool, huh?" She let him study the small picture on her phone.

"Very cool. I need one of these," he said.

She laughed. "I guess. Are you sure you're meeting your father?"

"He's just late. He's always late."

She frowned and lingered for just a little while but then she got into a car and drove off. He started walking again.

As he walked down Wightman, he saw a car that reminded him of the one the man had leaned on. It was maroon. He walked around it. *Corolla.* The color, the shape of the headlights, the shape of the grille—this is like the car he saw that day. Corolla.

That day. *My father,* he thought, happy at first. But his mother dropped her groceries. The applesauce jar broke. She cried out and cursed. When she stooped to pick the bag up, she said, "Help me, Matt."

"Matt? His name is Matt?" the man had asked.

"It's none of your business."

"Oh, yeah, it is. You owe me. Big time."

"Leave me alone. Leave us alone. What are you doing here?"

"I'm here in town now. I want to see my son."

"He isn't yours. You're wrong."

"Don't lie."

"I'm not lying." Then his mother got very calm. "Get in the car," she told Matt.

Matt did what she said, but he kept the door open so he could hear what they said.

"Bitches. Bitches. You think you can treat a man like dirt?"

"Look. I'm sorry. I'm really sorry. We didn't have a thing in common. I'm sorry. You can't keep bothering me."

"And my son?"

"Please. Do the math. He's not even eight years old. For God's sake, he's not yours. Leave us alone . . . or I'll call the police." Except she called him something now that he thinks of it. *Doll. Dull. Dal.*

When his mother drove away from the store, still very upset, Matt asked, "Is he my father?"

"I swear to you he's not."

"Then why did he say he was?"

"I don't know. He's wrong."

"Where is my father?"

"We don't know *where* he is, but he's not like that."

Why would she not *tell* him?

Then one day, not long ago, his mother came home upset. She kept hugging him and saying, "I'll always take care of you."

He knew she'd seen the man again.

Something is wrong. He's winded. The street he's on isn't Wilkins yet. It's still Wightman. He stands in front of a small apartment building. He tries the door and it opens. He stands inside and suddenly he's not sure, he wants to lie down and he's beginning to cry.

A man entering the apartment building stops in his tracks and says, "Hello. Never saw you here before. Are you all right?"

"Um . . ."

"Are you okay?"

"Um . . . I need a ride to the hospital. They took my mother earlier and I tried to walk there but it's taking too long. I need to see her."

"Oh. Is anyone with you?"

"No."

"What's your name?"

"Matt."

"Where do you live?"

"I just need to get to the hospital."

"Maybe we should get you home."

"There's nobody there." He starts to open the front door to leave.

"Wait. Wait. Okay, let me help you get to the hospital. One way or another, you shouldn't be alone."

The man eyes Matt warily. He puts a hand to his pocket, checking his wallet, then says abruptly, "Let's go. But I'm not going to just abandon you there. You have to be with someone. My car is outside. It's the silver Hyundai."

Matt follows him to the car. The man keeps looking at him, trying to figure him out.

A *LAW AND ORDER* EPISODE is on now but Nadal, not quite watching, is replaying what he has been replaying off and on all afternoon.

What are you doing here?

I came to see him. I have rights.

Don't you touch him, don't you go near him. He's not yours.

But I can see he is.

Oh, you're wrong, wrong, wrong.

He knew she was lying. *Well, I am going to get to know him. I'm taking him for a day, two days. A father and son should know each other.*

Matt! she cried. Matt, leave the house. Go. Go now. Run. Go to a neighbor. Just run.

He heard the door slam behind him. You bitch, telling him to run. From me.

She grabbed his arm, hard. Yes. *You're acting really funny. Are you . . . Are you on something?*

No. Stupid. Why can't I talk to him?

He's not yours.

I'll find him. I have rights. He shoved her and one of the pans on the counter behind her vibrated and fell to the floor. He moved to the door, thinking he would chase down his son wherever he went. She came after him. She was holding a kitchen knife.

Please leave us alone.

You're lying.

No. She looked to a table near the door where there was a cell phone charger. But he saw the phone wasn't there. She blocked the door. She still had the knife. *I went to New York. I went to a clinic.* He tried to grab at the knife hand because she was holding the knife out toward his gut. He grabbed the knife from her.

He got it, he got the knife.

The hateful way she looked at him—

Then he had blood on him. She slumped to the floor. He grabbed a kitchen towel and pulled at the stain on his shirt, wiped his hands. He had to get out of there. He descended the stairs from the second floor to the first floor and out the door. He wound around the building, all the while looking for his boy. He looked everywhere, quickly. Down the street maybe . . . He walked down Morrowfield, passing one man talking to his own little boy, passing an old woman pulling a wheeling cart of groceries.

He couldn't stay. His car had been parked around the corner on Murray in front of the Russian store that had caviar signs in the window. He got in, still wiping at his clothes.

Up ahead was a little boy. Matt. His head throbbed. He started up and drove down the block but when he got there, he saw it was another kid, older. He was so weak he wondered if he'd been stabbed, too. He drove a block to the parkway and found himself taking the Monroeville ramp. The car seemed to decide. Murraysville, Route 22, State College.

His mother looks at him, smiles, almost a question.

BEFORE THE ELEVEN O'CLOCK NEWS on Sunday night, Colleen is collapsing in front of a TV with John Potocki. They're at her place, exhausted, and she's cradled in his arms. They need to sleep soon so they can get back to it at five in the morning, fresh. There are no leads at all except what the little boy told them. They can't even be sure the killer is the same guy who bothered Maggie Brown at the grocery store.

Some cases aren't ever solved. Ever. The man might have been asking for her wallet.

Potocki sighs and changes position. He wants to resolve their living situation, either move in here or find a house they can both agree on. "I feel like I'm living out of a suitcase," he said last night. "I don't even know what shirts I have over here."

She still wants to have the possibility of her whole house to herself. He worries, she knows, that she's still in love with Christie. But that's done, that was fantasy, not real, just Christie having his Christie effect—the ultimate strong, square father figure, thoughtful and plain old charismatic. Her phone rings; she sees the ID and picks up. "Hey Boss. You must have something."

"The boy has disappeared."

"Oh . . . Oh my God."

"He's not at the Panikkar place. We're combing the neighborhood. I've called the kid's friends and he isn't there. I called Sasha. He isn't there. Apparently the kid has a thing about running off, according to Sasha. That's the hopeful part. But I'm going to need you to . . . help look."

"I can call the media."

"I already did that."

"I'm going for my car as I speak. I can take this part of Squirrel Hill. His grade school and all that. There might be other friends. Potocki can do other parts of Squirrel Hill." She breaks from the phone to say, "We have to look for the boy. He's gone." Then she tells Christie, "We're both on it," and hangs up.

Potocki is putting on his shoes. He has muted the TV. They leave it that way, don't even bother to turn if off. "Is it an abduction?" he asks Colleen.

"We don't know much of anything yet."

They go in two separate cars. Colleen leaves hers running to walk around the playground of Minadeo Elementary. She tries all the doors of the school building. Locked. She peers out at the neighborhood.

Would he just run off? Or has he been snatched? Such a beautiful little boy.

Hospital, Colleen thinks. Hospital. His mother.

She calls Christie to tell him to try the hospital.

"Great minds," he says. "I'm on my way there now. I called

Marina. She says it topped the eleven o'clock news. So the word is out. That's good."

She drives slowly through the neighborhood, looking, looking.

Her phone rings ten minutes later. "You were right. He . . . thought his mother might still be alive."

"I'll come to the hospital."

"Thanks."

She calls Potocki and tells him he might as well go back to his place, where he can at least find his remaining clothes.

"WOW," SAYS THE ANCHOR to the sub-anchor. The anchor is a woman with a tight cap of blonde hair. The new guy is a young man of extraordinary good looks—hazel eyes, dark hair, and a bone structure that would make anyone envious. They're on commercial break and she is fiddling with her earphone and making notes. "Yeah, yeah, yeah. I'm going to close with it. Wow. What a story. Heartrending."

"Heart rendering," the sub-anchor jokes. "What happened? Am I going to be in on this bit, too? Do I get to comment?"

"No, probably not enough time. I'll take it. No time to explain. It's a good ending. It's a happy note." She considers. "Happy-slash-sad."

HE STOOD UP and took out his car keys.

"Stay the night," his mother begged. "I'll make you a good breakfast."

"Gotta go. I have work tomorrow and I have to prepare for class."

"I thought class didn't start yet."

"I have to study anyway."

"But you'll be driving all night."

"Not all night."

"Nadal, Nadal," she said. She pulled his sleeve and hugged him as he pushed past her. He hated his name, hated, hated his stupid girl name. His father's idea. And when Nadal argued with him . . .

Of course I know you are Catalan. Your mother showed me Catalan names! I chose your name.

But in Puerto Rico, it was a girl's first name. Thank God for the tennis player giving it heft these last years.

It's melodious. Names are epicene these days anyway, said his father, stupid Arne Brown.

At school he signed everything Nate.

"Let me make you a care package. At least a sandwich." She hurried to the kitchen. He could hear her taking things out of the refrigerator.

He messed with the TV remote again. News. He froze before it.

"Good news on the case of the missing boy," said the anchor. "He was found only a few minutes ago. He had started to walk to the hospital, convinced his mother was still alive. When asked about it, he talked about the miracles he saw on television programs." The anchor made a sad face and paused for what felt like a long time. "There are no new developments in the homicide case. But police are working around the clock. And the child has been found. He's safe." She sighed, looking down.

He switched the channel.

His mother handed him a bag of food.

IT WAS A LITTLE AFTER MIDNIGHT when Christie opened the door to a hospital conference room and let Colleen in.

They'd been talking in the hallway about how to proceed.

"Unfortunately, it hit the news," he said. "The judge is going to jump all over us for not notifying Child Services from the start."

"He could have run away from anywhere."

"You know it. I know it. She might not. I thought to call the Pocusset Safe House for tonight, but I'm going to let Oopale Panikkar take him back. She's in our corner with Child Services. I can put a patrol cop outside their door. The kid isn't going anywhere tonight. Plus, he only came here to corroborate the reports that his mother is really dead. And pretty soon—"

Colleen wiped angrily at tears that had sprung up. "Sorry. I can't stand it."

"I know. Let's go in."

The room was pretty much a square with a rectangular table and six chairs. It was meant for the sort of conference doctors had with families when there was bad news to be delivered. In one corner of the room was a coffee machine, its carafe crusted and dirty. On the other end of the room was a small, square box of a TV, vintage 1980.

Oopale Panikkar was sitting with the boy.

Matthew squirmed.

"I understand you want to see your mother," Christie said.

Oopale looked worried.

"Yes."

"Matthew, you got yourself the whole way here, so I know how badly you must want to see her. I explained that to the doctors and they're going to allow it."

Matthew nodded.

"The doctor is going to come back for us. I think he was on his way down the hall. I'd like to come with you. Okay?"

Matt nodded again.

Moments later the doctor came into the room. "Okay, we're as ready as we can be."

What had they had to do? Tidy her up a bit, put her in one of their least messed-up rooms? "Show us the way," Christie said.

Christie walked with the boy down the hall. He wanted to put a hand on the boy's head, but he resisted.

A few moments later, the doctor halted in front of a room. He stooped down in front of Matt. "I want to be sure this is what you want. You'll be able to see her at the funeral home tomorrow or the next day," the doctor says.

"Where will that be?"

"Whatever funeral home your family chooses. Where people go to pay their respects. But I'll let you see her here if it's what you want."

"I want to," Matt says.

MATT FOLLOWS THE DOCTOR IN. The room is like the ones on TV with machines everywhere and trays with implements on them.

It's his mother all right, lying there. Some kind of padding makes the sheet lift up over her chest where the wound was.

"Can I go closer?" he asks the doctor.

"Yes," the doctor says.

It's just him and the doctor and that detective he talked to earlier. They all move closer. His mother's long hair is spread out as if she is sleeping. Her eyes are closed. She's still. Very still. Matt touches her arm. It's hard and cold and doesn't move back. Like a bug. Like the squirrel he poked at in their yard. But then he sees her breathe. Yes, her chest is moving. His own breath catches. The longer he looks, then, the more she might not be dead. He keeps holding her arm and then, bravely, shakes it a little, trying to see the movement again.

"Matt?" the detective says. He feels the detective's hands, strong, one on each shoulder.

"I think she moved."

"It sometimes looks like that. It isn't happening but our eyes trick us. Doctor, tell me, isn't that right?"

The doctor says, "It's exactly right."

Matt wants to be sure nobody is lying to him. "Mom?" He smooths his hand over her arm. "Mom?" She doesn't moan, nothing. "Can she hear me?" Matt looks to the doctor.

"No, I'm sorry," the doctor says. "She can't."

Finally, he lets them take him away.

The detective says, "You must be getting tired."

"No."

"We'd like to get you to bed."

Matt sits down in the conference room again. He wonders why they have a TV if isn't on. She breathed and then she didn't. They *said* she didn't. They said . . .

MATT WAS ASLEEP.

Christie lifted him. "It's okay. I'll take him in my car. If I don't remember how to lift a sleeping kid, I don't remember anything."

"Yours are that age?" Oopale asked.

"No. Older now." He lifted the boy and carried him out to the hallway. Colleen followed behind. She was on her phone. He said to Oopale, "I'll follow you, I'll carry him into your place."

"Thanks. Thank you."

They kept walking down the sterile hallway where a janitor paused, watching them to be sure he could bear witness if they were characters up to no good.

They got outside to the car.

Oopale pointed to a small red Nissan. "That's mine."

Christie laid the boy in the backseat of his car. Colleen caught up with him. She was looking at her watch. It was something close to one.

"Go home," he said.

"I said I'd start at five tomorrow."

He heard her asking for sleep. "Make it seven. This case has two aspects. Find the murderer. Take care of the kid. If we spend a lot of time on the second, it . . . can't be helped."

Christie calculated. He'd get the boy to bed and then he'd call Jan and Arthur. He needed to tell them before they heard it from some other source that the boy had run away but was now found.

THE BUILDING THAT OOPALE LIVED IN WITH HER FAMILY, and that Maggie Brown had lived in with her son, had a front door that didn't use a security lock or a phone system. Christie was glad to see a cop on duty at the entrance. "I probably need you inside, outside the apartment door," he grunted while holding Matt in the sack-of-potatoes position over his shoulder.

"We have another officer upstairs for that."

"Oh. Good, good." This kid wasn't getting out tonight. Christie mounted the stairs to the second floor.

"Are you all right?" Oopale asked.

"Almost there," he said.

She fumbled for a key while he looked at the police-taped door of Maggie Brown's place. Finally Oopale opened the door to the Panikkar apartment.

Sasha hadn't asked to take Matt nor had Grady's or Jade's parents. Well, maybe they all thought he was spoken for. Oopale led him to the room that Matt had run away from. It was colorful, pretty, and had a sweet smell. But it was also a smothering sort of room, not something a boy would like.

"Should we try to undress him?" she asked.

"I think he'll be happier if we leave him as he is. The room is hot."

"Yes. I think my parents turned off the air conditioner to save money. I'll put it back on." She did so and pulled one thin layer of cover up over Matt. And then they left him.

"Would you like something to eat?"

The spices he smelled alarmed him. His stomach couldn't take exotic foods. "No, thank you. I live just ten minutes away."

"Sure?"

He was almost dizzy with hunger. "Okay. Just a piece of toast."

"Toast?"

"If possible."

The elder Panikkars poked their heads out of a doorway.

Oopale said, "It's okay. Go to bed. It's the detective. He brought Matt back."

"Give him something to eat," her father croaked.

"I will, I will. Don't worry."

The parents went back to bed.

"We have to feed you something. It's tradition. *Atithi Devo Bhava.*" She smiled. "It means, 'The guest is truly your god.' "

"Oh, dear."

"We have okra in curry. And rice of course, and a chicken tandoori left over."

"Oh, toast sounds awfully good to me."

"Toast and an egg?"

"Perfect."

They sat in the kitchen speaking quietly.

"Was Margaret Brown unhappy, do you think?"

"I don't know. She didn't tell me things. I worried about her."

"Why?"

"Working two jobs or three and not too much money. Matt wants everything of course."

"What do you mean?"

"He wants everything he sees." She got the egg on the stove in a small pot of water, waited till it boiled, then started the toaster doing its thing with a piece of white sandwich bread.

Christie was totally grateful for the ordinary foods. "I have kids. I understand how they want things."

"You said you have somebody in mind for Matt—"

"Yes."

"Will they give him stability?"

"I think so. It's good of you to care."

"To be honest, I worry that nobody will know what to do with Matt. Not even me."

"What do you mean?"

"He's sweet, he definitely is sweet, but he never is content. Or lighthearted. Never."

"I'll let you know if there is anything you can do. Maybe help the Morrises with the transition—if I manage to get him placed with them."

"Yes, I'll do that. Do they work, the Morrises?"

"Oh, heavens yes. They're both professors. Robert—he goes by Arthur—teaches mostly poetry from what I understand. Not that I understand it. Janet is a theatre teacher. She teaches Shakespeare and things like that and she directs plays. In fact she's directing one starting in a couple of days, a Shakespeare play that my wife is going to be in."

"I'll have to see that."

"My wife is a teacher at Pitt, too. But I knew these folks, even from before my wife got to know them. They're kind and they want a child and they have two salaries."

"Oh, good. Good. Are they young?"

"Not too young. Why?"

"I just wondered."

The water boiled and the toast popped. He ate his middle-of-the-night meal and left, and then took out his phone to make a call from his car.

JAN AND ARTHUR ARE having coffee at the airport but in Jan's mind she is halfway home. She is thinking, praying, that she will know how to love Matt, to help him through a trauma her mind can hardly contain.

Her phone rings. She digs it out of her bag. "Christie again," she says nervously.

She listens to Christie tell about what has just happened. When she hangs up, she tells her husband the boy they want ran away to the hospital and scared everyone pretty badly for a couple of hours. She's not surprised that his face is full of worry.

It's the middle of the night in Pittsburgh, she thinks, everyone involved with Matt strained, exhausted, and just going to bed. In France, all is coming alive, a new day. Soon they will be in the air, collapsing the time difference between the two places.

In her mind, she is already there.

On the plane an hour later, she closes her eyes as other passengers bump on, trying to stash their carry-ons.

When the plane lifts, Arthur squeezes her hand. She falls into a half slumber to make up for last night, when she was too excited to sleep at all. Restless dreams toss her, images of the judge refusing to let them have Matt. Time leapfrogs all over the place and even in her half sleep, she can't keep up.

She wakes when they land in Frankfurt. Their flight is anything but direct. They are certainly not alone in that. Most people have to go out of their way to go where they want.

"We have an hour," Arthur notes.

The Frankfurt business-class lounge is humming with people, and there are used plates and glasses on most surfaces. It's like a well-appointed bus station with upscale clients, each with a laptop. Arthur wanders around to look at the available foods—good German breads and spreads. Good coffee. Jan pulls out her computer. When she gets a connection, she quickly logs in to her email.

Soon, Arthur is walking back toward their seats with plates of sandwiches and sweet rolls for both of them. He settles, looking for a place to put down their plates among the leavings of other travelers.

First she types in a message to Marina. *You probably know by now we're going to try to get Matthew. I just got this idea to put Matt in the play. He's going to be disoriented and grieving. It might help him to have something to look forward to. I need to be with him as much as possible, and what do I do about the fact of needing to be in rehearsals every night? So if I let him come to rehearsals and work with me . . . don't you think that might be good? I have this idea to actualize the changeling child. You'll have a scene with him then—a moment—a falling in love kind of moment. Or a being in love. What do you think? I have to do some other emails. More later. Jan*

People are franticly typing on laptops or talking on phones, gulping food. Anxiety everywhere . . .

Arthur hands her a plate of food. Brown bread with some kind of fish salad on it.

She imagines Matt traveling with them, holding on to them, trying the food, liking it.

3.

MONDAY

NADAL IS AWAKENED BY THE PHONE. He rolls over, confused, ignoring the phone and then it stops. Suddenly he remembers yesterday and he comes fully awake. His heart pounds unmercifully.

He's worried the ringing phone has bothered the others. His roommates—there are three of them—are Korean. He's money in the bank for them—his room is not a room, just a space meant to be storage or something. The bed barely fits. His choice though because he likes to be alone. He's not on the lease. He's their spending money.

They sleep in one bedroom while he has this other (very tiny) room to himself.

The phone begins ringing again. This time he answers. It's his mother.

"Dal?"

"What?"

"I thought you weren't there. I thought you didn't make it."

"I was *sleeping.*"

"I'm so sorry. It's just that I've been up."

"Doing what?"

"Worrying about you. Watching TV."

Does she know? It's as if she knows.

"Watching the news. There was a terrible murder in Pittsburgh. A nice woman in a good neighborhood. Just like that. Home on a Sunday and somebody comes in and kills her. It gives me the shivers. Are you still there?"

"I'm here." He waits.

"Just a woman with a young son. Same name as ours. It was very upsetting to hear about."

"Well, Mom, I have to go to work. Good thing you got me up. I don't want to lose my job."

"No, no. Don't lose your job."

When classes begin later this week, he will have only one and that one meets once a week. His mother thinks he's in graduate school, which is what he told her because she worships the whole university-intellect-learning thing. But he has only one class—to test him for provisional admission to the graduate program in computer science. He told his mother another lie—that he has an assistantship, when it's just a plain old job in the computer lab, answering desperate people's questions about what is wrong with their computers.

He knows a good bit, but not as much as some of the other computer consultants do. He has one very good answer for many inquiries. "Have you shut it down and restarted?"

He tiptoes to the bathroom and turns on the shower. He wishes his mother hadn't jarred him to consciousness. It's better to be asleep. Awake, he has to worry if anyone saw him leaving the building and going to his car. And if someone did, if that person saw the license plate . . . His heart won't quiet down.

The water always begins slow and lukewarm. His roommates buy soap and shampoo as cheaply as possible—large generic containers of the things needed to clean themselves. They never touch his Tone soap or his hair conditioner even though Shin talks about special personal products that he loved in Seoul, things he intends to afford in the future.

Seung, Shin, and Gab-do are not thieving sorts. They never hesitate to put their share in, or to show receipts, but for his own peace of mind, Nadal checks his money every time he goes into his room. No, nothing is ever missing.

The three roommates stick together of course—it's their chance to speak their language—plus they've had the place together since last year, so they know one another. Nadal's only been here since last May when he got his one course approved and snagged the job. Then he saw Maggie and his son, and at first he believed he would be able to visit them, eventually move in.

He listens through the splashing water for his roommates. No, not awake yet.

They are good enough guys to room with, but it's a business arrangement mainly. Right—what does he have in common with them? They cook. Rice and this. Rice and that. Other things. They always offer. He eats his frozen packets of burritos, his cans of beans. One night they wanted to go to a club on the South Side and asked him to go with them. He supposed they wanted to pick up American women and wanted his help. But when they got there, Seung told them all it was important from his experience not to look too eager. "Correct?" he asked Nadal.

"That's what I hear," Nadal said.

"It's the same in Seoul. Clubs, the same everywhere."

Nadal didn't like clubs and it galled him to spend so much money on a drink. Shin told him, "Always to drink slow, not spend too much."

The water finally comes hot. He scrubs himself.

His car. He must get rid of it. Step one.

As soon as he's dressed, he sits down to breakfast. He is aware now of early snufflings from the next room as he stirs milk into his cereal, generic corn flakes. Each month he will plunk down two hundred dollars cash for the rent and fifty dollars for groceries and supplies. That's the deal. The Koreans take care of the rest. Seung is the money manager. He buys chicken and cans of soup or beans for Nadal—Nate is how they know him here. He never even told them his last name—Brown.

Brown. How this whole thing started.

The supplies under the sink are pretty good—bleach and soap and glass cleaner and baking soda. His roommates are clean, anyway. His mother would surely approve of them for that. When they're not around, he will scrub the car. Again and again. Three times.

After breakfast, he forces himself to open his laptop and search for the news.

There it is.

Margaret Brown, 49, a single mother of a seven-year-old boy, was stabbed to death in her apartment on Morrowfield Avenue after noon on Sunday following an altercation with an unnamed man. Neighbors did not hear the disturbance but the child alerted them to the incident. Neighbors then discovered his mother, dead of her wounds. Police are investigating.

Ms. Brown was a well-liked teacher of art in the elementary schools. Employed by the ART-FIRST program, she was hired to give private tutoring to students who showed promise as painters. She had a studio and was a painter herself.

Commander Richard Christie of the Pittsburgh Police Homicide Division said it was early in the investigation. Police are working on the identity of the man reported to be arguing with Ms. Brown. The man allegedly believed himself to be the father of her son. Anyone with information about this person is asked to come forward.

Allegedly. Believed.

OOPALE AND HER MOTHER make him eat cereal and toast. They sit and murmur at him until he makes the food go down. "The detective is coming for you. He will take care of you today."

"Can I go home now?"

"No, it isn't allowed yet."

"Why?"

"Because there's an investigation. Nothing can be touched."

Yes, he's seen that on TV. He could go to Jade's house or Grady's house. They could play something anyway.

"Is there anything you want? Anything I can get you?" Oopale asks.

"No."

The two women look at each other. They clearly don't know what to say to him. After a while, Mrs. P smiles with a sad face and puts on the TV.

"TWO-PRONGED TASK," Christie repeats at the squad meeting. "To find the murderer and to keep the boy safe." Then he adds, "Two-pronged investigation also. Think of it as the two fathers—there is the person who stabbed her and who insisted he was the father. There is the man who supposedly fathered the child—artificial insemination, we're told, at a clinic in New York. We have to follow that up. We have Potocki going through all kinds of files. The two fathers very possibly could turn out to be one and the same, but we have to follow both avenues. Nothing so far on the clinic. Right?" He addresses Potocki. "Fill us in."

"She might have thrown away financial records from eight years ago. People do. I haven't found them yet. I'll try her current bank if nothing comes up today. One other thing: I asked a neighbor there if there was a storage unit in the basement. He said no, but I found this key on her ring that doesn't go to anything. So I called the super this morning and it turns out there *is* a storage unit in the basement. I'll get stuff from there today."

"Right. Good. So here we are, looking at three possibilities—One: The father is anonymous, from a clinic in New York. That's what the best friend says. If this is the case, the guy is probably not our killer.

Two: The father is very present and knows he's the father. He has a secret tempestuous history with the mother who didn't share it with her best friend. Or, Three: The guy who killed Margaret Brown thinks he's the father but he isn't. That information comes via the boy and the best friend who didn't really know much beyond the fact that some guy from way back reappeared lately. What do we believe?"

"The guy was probably in her life," says Coleson. "This is an angry killing."

"It is."

"Did we pick up any DNA from the guy? The knife or anything."

"There's going to be some DNA somewhere in the evidence they collected. They got some prints. They ran the prints locally. No matches. They are running the prints more widely today. We'll see about that. We'll test any DNA we have. Anything else? Ideas? Let me hear from you."

"Any chance," McGranahan begins, "that the kid is like some bad seed and he did it and made the whole thing up?"

"Always a chance," Christie says.

"Tabloid heaven," Colleen mutters.

"Were the prints on the knife good?" Coleson asks.

"Not very. But we got some bits."

"So do we have any notion of which prints at the apartment belong to the killer and which are those of innocent friends?"

"Not clear yet," Christie says.

"Whew," McGranahan says. "Not simple."

"So it's Potocki on paperwork and the storage unit at the apartment house, the rest of you canvassing—Dolan has the assignments. And Dolan has a list of friends and acquaintances he's working through with Hurwitz and Denman. Call me with anything. I'm off to get the kid squared away."

COLLEEN AND CHRISTIE take one car to the apartment where Matt is staying. Colleen answers her phone on the way. It's the Giant Eagle

Market District—the store where they think Maggie Brown was first accosted by the man—finally getting back to her.

"Is this the detective who wanted to know about tapes?"

"Yes."

"We don't keep them long."

"How long?"

"We don't have tapes over a month old."

"Oh." Not that she's surprised. Only disappointed. "I'll come by to see what you have anyway."

Christie says, "Small chance it would have caught an altercation in the lot anyway."

"Small chance, but a chance," she says. Then they approach the apartment house on Morrowfield. "Anything new happen last night when you got Matt back here?"

"I put Matt to bed. Oopale was very kind, fed me a little meal. I asked her if she'd ever seen male visitors to the apartment. She said no. Very, very consistent reports."

"Unfortunately."

They take the stairs one floor up.

The mother and daughter both come to the door to show them in. They all move quickly to the kitchen table where Matt sits, dawdling over his food. Christie chooses the seat across from him. "Matt. How are you this morning?"

Matt shrugs.

"Would you show us what you did yesterday? Would you help us?"

"Yes."

"Okay. Let's get up then. Let's pretend the living room over here is your apartment. You were where, again?"

"In my room. I was playing with my PlayStation."

"Okay, let's make this chair over here be your bedroom. And then?" Christie asks calmly.

"I heard a knock on the door. I heard my mother answer the door."

"Did you go to look at all?"

"No, I kept playing." He breathes hard. He is not okay with this part. "She gets deliveries sometimes, stuff like that."

"On Sunday morning, no deliveries, people are relaxing, who comes by?"

"Sunday." He looks frightened at his mistake about deliveries. "Maybe Sasha?"

"Anybody else?"

"No, I can't think of anybody."

"Okay. And then?"

"I was just playing. Then I heard, like, arguing."

"That's important. What were they saying?"

"Stuff like, 'Get out,' and 'You can't treat me like that.' "

"Good, good. Did they talk about you?"

"The guy said, 'I want to see him. I want to know him.' I peeked out of my room then because I could tell it was about me. I thought finally she would tell me who my father was and I would meet him."

"Could you see him?"

"Just from the back a little bit."

"Did you return to your room?"

"No, because she yelled."

"Okay. I know it's awful to have to repeat things, but tell us again what she said, okay?"

"Like, 'Matt. Leave. Just run. Leave. Go to a neighbor.' "

"But you couldn't see this man?"

"I was running."

"And the little bit you saw . . . what did he look like?"

"Just regular."

"Anything you can remember? Hair, how tall?"

"Dark hair. Taller than my mom but not real tall."

"Like me?" Christie asks.

"Yeah. I think."

"And he was wearing?"

"Blue jeans, sneakers, just a shirt."

"What kind of shirt?"

"I don't remember."

"That's okay."

"She was saying to run, so I ran."

"But you grabbed the phone. Stopped a little bit to grab it."

"I don't think I stopped. I just grabbed it."

"Okay. And then you used the stairs?"

"Yes."

"When did you use the phone?"

"When I got to the bottom."

"Inside, outside?"

"Outside."

"Show me how you left, where you were."

"The real stairs?"

"Why not?"

Matt leads them down the dark back stairs to the door with a crash bar that opens on the backyard.

"Here."

Christie says, "Now, you knew what number to call. Had you ever called before?"

"No."

"But you knew what to do. Good. Then?"

Matt's face collapses into a frown. "I . . . I could tell they weren't going to come. So I went back up."

"Show me?"

Christie makes him show them everything. He keeps checking his watch. "Did you pause? Did you wait before going up?"

"A little bit."

"Good. Smart. Show me how long?"

Matt pauses and then begins to move. Three seconds. Five. Ten.

"Was there a reason you went around front?"

"I thought I might find somebody who could help. A person walking in or out."

"Ah, makes sense. Did you see anybody?"

"Nobody was around, so I just went back up."

"Show us your movements."

Matt opens a gate and they all go around to the front.

"Did you see the man again?"

"No."

"How do you think he got away?"

"I guess the back stairs after I left. Or maybe the front before I went around. I don't know."

"Makes sense," Christie murmurs again. "I'm sorry to ask you all this but it could help. Could you tell me anything you saw when you went back up?"

"The door was partways open."

"About how much?"

"Only a little bit."

Christie nods. He doesn't ask anything for a while.

Finally the boy says, "I had to slide in because she was on the floor."

"Tell me, if you want to, what you were thinking then."

"I tried to make her talk. I had the phone so I called 911 again. I told them they had to come."

"Very good."

"Yeah. But then I ran next door to see if Dr. Panikkar was home."

"Because he's a doctor."

"Because . . . because . . . I was afraid to do that thing where you push the chest to make a person breathe."

"Did you know how to do it?"

"Kind of. From TV." Matt is breathing raggedly.

"That's a hard job. Almost impossible when there's an injury."

"I thought I would make it worse."

"That was correct. You didn't do anything wrong."

"I didn't?"

"Not a thing. You were great."

Colleen lets out a big breath of relief. This was hard, very hard, watching a kid wound tight, falling apart.

"Tell me, when you were outside, did you notice a car that was unfamiliar or anything like that?"

"No, I wasn't looking anywhere. I was thinking: should I go back up the stairs or just wait."

"You did fine," Christie says evenly.

When Matt gets ahead of them, Colleen asks, "Boss? Why did you make him go through it again?"

"Because Chief had the same idea as McGranahan. *Liked* the idea of a bad seed. I swore I'd check the kid out for consistency. I swore I'd have an expert witness it. You witnessed it. You've got the creds."

"Me?" she says with some surprise. She does have a master's in counseling, though she hasn't practiced formally for a few years.

Christie takes out a handkerchief and touches it to his face. He is shaking. "So I did it. What did you think?"

"I thought he was truthful and that he's been harboring some guilt about not doing even more."

"Right."

Matt turns on his heel and comes back to them. "I forgot to say last night that I know what kind of car the man had."

"I'm not sure what you mean," Christie says.

"When I was out last night, I looked for one like it. It was a Toyota."

"Are you sure?"

"Corolla."

"You saw the exact car, the man's car?"

"No, one like it."

"What clued you in?"

"Like the shapes. The way the lights go."

Corolla.

MATT LOOKS OUT THE WINDOWS of the detective's car from the backseat where he is riding with Oopale sitting next to him. She told him she took a day off work, a sick day. Nothing is normal today. People are quiet when they talk into their phones and he's not supposed to hear.

He told everything about not pumping her chest, and they didn't say he was to blame. He only shook her because he thought she might move, but she didn't. She shouldn't have let herself die. She should have fought it. He would have. He won't ever let himself die.

Today, later, he gets to see Jade for a play date.

The police are taking him to some place where they match up parents and children. But he doesn't want any of that. Jade or Grady, that would be okay.

Last night he thought she moved, but she didn't. They said she didn't.

Everybody lies. Grown-ups lie. Maybe the man was his father even if his mother said he wasn't.

"What do you think you'll do with Jade later today?" the woman detective asks him.

"Wii. Watch a movie. Play *Grand Theft Auto*."

"You like video games, right?"

"I'm good at them."

"You must have quick eyes."

"Yeah."

"He amazes me," Oopale says.

Quick eyes. Quick ears. "I remembered something else. When my mother yelled at the man in the parking lot, she used a name." The car pulls over to the curb and both detectives turn around to face the backseat. "It was something like Dol. Or Dal."

"Dol or Dal. Anything more?"

"No."

"What did she say exactly?"

"Something like, 'What are you doing here, Dal?' and he said, 'I live here now.'"

"Dal?"

"I think. Something like that."

WHEN HE FIRST MET HER, it was at a coffee shop and they only gave first names. She was pretty. Older than he was, and that threw him for a while, but mostly she was pretty. She said, "I can't date you. You're too young." He told her he was old in his soul.

Maggie smiled at him and told him she was a bit late in the game but that she wanted a family, at least one child.

He said, "I want that, too. I do."

She laughed. "Don't even think it."

He said, "We could go to Puerto Rico where I come from. Now that's a place to raise a kid. Kids are happy there."

"It's poor there."

"You don't need much there. It's poor but kids are happy."

"No, you're . . . too young."

"Let's go to a movie. Let's go get a hamburger."

"No foie gras with you."

"What's that? Food. Yeah, I heard of it. You're making fun of me because I said about living in Puerto Rico."

She looked dashed. "No, that's not true. We don't even know each other."

"Well, you could give me a chance. We could do something."

"Okay. A movie. A movie won't hurt anything."

They met the next time at a movie theatre. He didn't have a car. And didn't want her to know he had hitchhiked three hours to see her. He didn't have anything, hardly a penny, and she wanted that foie gras kind of life. He reached for her hand in the movie. She wouldn't hold hands at first and then she did. She had beautiful eyes and full curly hair. There was a little bit of gray coming into it, but he didn't care. She was very American.

"I'm so messed up," she said when they left the movie theatre, walking. "I got old without noticing. And I still want a baby."

He didn't understand why she didn't have one if she wanted one. He wasn't sure what to say to her.

"I have no savings. I live in an efficiency," she said. "I'm ridiculous. That's going to change. I'm working next year in the schools. At least I can get a bigger apartment."

He wanted to say he was ridiculous too. He didn't tell her *he* only had a cell of a room in his mother's house—or what was really his father's house, way up in State College. His childhood was in Puerto Rico, his high school in Florida where the stud guys pushed him around and where anybody was lucky to get home from school without being stabbed. And after that, everything was even worse when they moved up to State College so his mother could take care of his father, who was sick and dying.

He attended college halfheartedly. His father, a professor, got tuition benefits and couldn't see not using them. Nadal didn't mind learning, but papers, exams, teachers had stressed him almost to the breaking point.

"Let me see your apartment," he said to Maggie.

When they got to her building on Hobart Street and she fumbled with her key, he stood behind her, looking at the mailbox. What he saw blew his mind. It made him ecstatic. Her last name. Same as his. Same as the one he got from the professor. Brown.

"You don't know a Professor Arnett Brown, do you?" he asked, feeling giddy.

"No," she said. "Why?"

"Just checking. He's a prof I had. Same name as yours."

"And hundreds of others. It's a common name."

He smiled. "And mine. My name."

"You're kidding."

"You see! This was meant to be."

"I don't think so." But she laughed.

They kissed a little. She said, "For me, relationships keep not working out. It must be something about me. But what do I do about wanting a baby? I dream about being a mother. I really want to be a mother."

"That's a good feeling."

"What do you know about it?"

"Well, I want to be a father."

"Really? Most men don't want to."

He could only remember the strutting boys from his high school, counting off their conquests, their offspring. "It makes you a man," he said. "It makes you somebody."

"Oh, Lord."

"What?"

"Different worlds. I mean, I knew you were young, but . . . Thanks for the movie, Mr. Brown."

He kissed her. At first she didn't kiss back. Then she did. They started to mess around. She said, "We shouldn't be doing this. I can't get into a relationship."

"You said you wanted that."

"Sure, with the right person."

She looked right through him. They kept messing around. They even ended up on her bed. She made him stop short of intercourse, but he knew that one little drop could make its way up the river and end up getting her pregnant. He hoped it did.

When he got up to leave, Maggie's hair was wild. She looked very beautiful. "I'm sorry," she said.

"For what?"

"I don't want to lead you on."

"Didn't we have a good time?"

He waited to call her because he knew he was supposed to make her want him. He also had work at the Kinko's in Bellefonte and he had classes—all of which he hated. And then it rained for weeks and hitchhiking in the rain was a bummer.

Finally he did call her. He said, "We could just go for a hamburger." At that point he was in his fourth year and she had started teaching.

"I could use the company," she said.

He got himself to Pittsburgh and to her apartment with half a minute to spare. They walked up the street to the Squirrel Hill Cafe where burgers were cheap. She ordered a beer, so he did, too. He had to show a card, because the waiter didn't believe he was of age. She rolled her eyes. "See?" she said.

It turned out she wanted to talk about her work—how scared she was about being a good teacher. She also said she was still painting whenever she could get to it, but finding studio space and affording supplies was hard. She had a line on a studio she could share.

"What kind of paintings?"

"Oil. Text driven." He didn't know what that meant, but he nodded. "It's probably hopeless. For everyone who wants to be an artist, maybe one in a thousand, if that, can actually get a gallery show. So why I try, I don't know."

He wondered if she was the kind of person who smoked weed a lot. She seemed very dreamy. Her hair was tied up and knotted. He didn't like it that way. He reached across the table and untied it.

"Ouch," she cried.

"Sorry."

"What are you doing?"

"I like it when it—" He made wild curls with his fingers.

"And chauvinistic, too!"

He just kept smiling at her.

That time, they ended up in bed again. They did the whole number. Then again at two in the morning. She said, "You have to go. Back to your own place."

"Ah, no."

"I mean it."

He felt angry, but he got up. He didn't want to tell her his place was three hours away. When he went online for the dating service, he had lied and put down Pittsburgh because he liked the idea of a different life, a new life, somewhere away from his mother and the professor.

He went outside from her little place. It wasn't raining, but it was damp. He walked. He couldn't even find *people*. Finally he found a guy to ask, "What bus do I take to the Greyhound station? Are buses still running?"

"Hop in," the guy said.

He took a look at the guy and said, "Never mind." For two hours he huddled in a doorway. Then he walked to Oakland, to the university area where there was a modicum of activity. Finally a city bus came by.

He eventually got himself to the Greyhound station and went back to State College.

He had one more date with Maggie. This time, they didn't even go out. She made him dinner. They made love after dinner and she told him again that he had to go.

He said, "Why are you off and on?"

"I'm not very on. It's my fault. You shouldn't come anymore."

"Is it because I'm a foreigner?"

"No."

"Because I'm part Puerto Rican. You know we're Catalan, my family."

"No. That isn't it."

"But you love me."

She clapped a hand to her mouth for a moment. "I don't love you. I don't feel good about this. I'm a terrible person. I really am. I like how you look and I'm letting that be enough for me and that's . . . wrong. I'm so sorry."

"You said you like how I look."

"That isn't enough. You need to just forget about me."

"You're Brown. I'm Brown. It was meant to be."

"No, no, no."

"You want a baby. I want a baby. We both want a family."

"Right. And you want to put my hair down and take me to some farm in Puerto Rico."

"You think I'm nothing."

She sighed. "See, I can't even have a conversation with you. No more. That's it. I'm not dating ever again. Never. I'm finished."

But it wasn't true. He went back to her place unannounced and waited for her one afternoon. She walked up to her door with a guy.

"Oh-oh," she said when she saw him.

"Who's this kid?" the guy asked. He was not good looking. Older. A little bit bald.

She said, "A guy I know, that's all."

"You want me to dust the sidewalk with him?"

"No. Let's just go in."

She walked past him as if she hardly knew him.

He had never given his phone number, which meant she couldn't call him. So he called her from work.

"What are you doing?" he asked. "You treat me like shit. Who was that guy you started up with?"

"I was wrong," she said. "Look. Erase everything. We are no more. We are finished. No more. Don't call."

But he had an email for her. *Were you just using me?* he wrote.

She wrote back, *Yes. I'm sorry. I was. But I'm not the only one at fault. I got a new phone two weeks ago and when you called me, I saw the phone number on the screen. You were calling from Bellefonte. You said you were home. What's that all about?*

He admitted, *I live near there. I traveled to see you.*

She answered, *Don't travel. Don't call me. This is over and I will call the police, I swear. I'm sorry if I hurt you, but I don't want to see you ever again.*

Finally he let it go.

Various things intervened—work and brain-breaking classes and his dying father who hated him and his mother who adored him. Getting his degree took six years. And he'd started late. He floated after, doing a lot of nothing. Then he decided to move to Pittsburgh, where he got a provisional admission to graduate classes.

He found the Koreans. He thought, We'll be like brothers, like a family.

Then he saw Maggie in that grocery store parking lot.

She looked at him blankly, then unhappily.

He saw his son. His son.

She said, "What are you doing here, Dal?"

"I live here now."

"That doesn't change anything."

"My son. I want to know him."

She stood in his way. "He's not yours. Haven't you grown up one little bit? You're hopeless, Dal." She told the boy to go to their car.

When the kid had moved off a little, she said, "Do the math. Just do the math. He's not even eight."

He didn't believe her. Why should he believe her? People could say anything.

"He's mine."

"His father is another man. He's not yours. You need to get a life."

"You can't just get rid of me." He turned to get a glimpse of the boy. The boy looked like him.

"You leave us alone. We have nothing to do with each other. You're in your own world. We're not . . . we're not in the same world."

He didn't like her anymore. But his boy looked smart . . . looked athletic. Perfect. The perfect boy.

"You stay away or I'll call the authorities." She was shaking. She went to her car and drove away.

ARTHUR SLEEPS AND JAN works at her computer much of the way from Frankfurt to Philadelphia. How quickly her life has changed. She anticipated butterflies about *auditions*, about directing the play. Now that huge project seems like nothing. The play will happen. The young lovers will get mixed up in the forest, the fairies will arrange and botch, the royalty will live their lives of privilege, an audience will come or not, reviewers will like it or not, and hopefully, hopefully, Matt will be her son and Matt will play the non-speaking role of the beautiful changeling child.

Irony not lost. Not lost at all. Changeling children are the stuff of drama, fiction, no matter how they're defined. *Changeling*. Oh, she knows the definitions, having taught this sort of thing. Sometimes changelings turn out to be nasty children with bad tempers . . . the bane of parents. Often they're simply children of sadness, children who don't belong. Most often they're smart. Rare, special. Simplest definition: A changeling is a substitute for a natural child. A found child.

THE SUPERVISOR IS A TALL, comely woman who is probably Italian, perhaps Egyptian. "Oopale!" she greets Matt's friend, hugging her. "How nice to see you again. How are you?"

"Good. I like my new work."

"I'm happy to hear it." She allows herself to stop and think what to do. She asks Christie to sit and get comfortable, but she instructs Oopale to take the child into an adjoining room to play.

"Detective. This child has had a terrible loss."

"It's especially terrible. He was with his mother. He saw her. I hope to get him some help with the . . . grieving."

She nods. "You're right to do that. Even if he doesn't show it, he will be very disturbed for a while. You seem to have become attached."

He pauses. "Well, I have. There are no relatives, and I know how these things can be. So to explain, the reason I'm here . . . I think I know the next best thing for him."

"Would that be you?"

He's surprised. "No. No, I didn't mean that. I was thinking of people who are already on your books. I know them and they're very good."

"I'm not the head here. There are a bunch of rules about who gets called. Those who've been calling in, active, get the first call."

"But that's exactly what I'm worried about. Those people might not be best for him. Let's not kid each other. We know some of them aren't."

"They're not in it for love. I know."

"Please look up Janet Gabriel and Robert Arthur Morris. They had a tough experience with one foster child, but . . . I know what good people they are."

After she studies Christie, she leaves the room and comes back with a file folder and holds up a hand to silence him and sits there reading. "Their foster daughter kept running away."

"Yes."

"They didn't contact us after that."

"They were shaken by how difficult that girl was. After a while, they were trying to adopt."

"That didn't work out?"

"It was a foreign adoption that fizzled."

"I see. And you want me to bump them up on the list?"

"I do."

"I saw the news last night. This child ran away. How difficult is he?"

"When I'm with him, he seems . . . sweet, normal, but his circumstances aren't normal. I don't think he's ever been fully secure.

My police partner is trained as a counselor. She used to work with children. She agrees with me that he's wound tight, watchful. He needs to feel secure, we know that much."

She thinks for a long time. She even walks to the window. "No relatives. You're sure? The father?"

"Either a maniac or an anonymous donor. Believe me, we're following up. We just don't have the leads yet."

"You want me to go to Family Court with you tomorrow?"

"If you see my point."

She laughs. "All right. I'll go. And you think they are looking to adopt? These friends of yours?"

"I think so."

"Why aren't they here?"

"On their way back from Europe at this very minute. They're due at the airport after eight tonight. What with baggage claim and all that, I'd say after nine."

"At least you didn't say they're off playing golf."

"Good heavens, no."

"They should start getting an attorney for the paperwork right away. An attorney to be in their corner. We'll try to pull off temporary custody tomorrow. I'll come to put in a good word."

"Thank you!"

"I'll tell you one thing," she says. "You are very lucky this didn't happen in New York. They would have whisked him away and put him with foster parents of their choosing, no questions asked, no pleas answered. They have a system and they stick to it. By the time the kid gets a permanent arrangement, he is so traumatized—oh, don't get me started."

"I'm glad this isn't New York, then," he says.

"What's next today? For the boy?"

"We take him to a friend's house."

But when Christie goes to fetch Matt, the boy asks suspiciously, "Can I stay in my own apartment?"

Oopale, frowning worriedly, leaves Matt and goes to say her good-byes to her old supervisor.

"All that about apartments and where to live has to be worked out," Christie tells him. "But for now let's get you to Jade's house. Like we said."

Matt walks fast to the car ahead of Christie and Oopale.

JADE'S MOM LETS THEM HAVE pretzels and orange pop and they are allowed to play *Red Dead Redemption* in the den for as long as they want. The den is in the basement. It's just a room with wood walls. "Not real wood," Jade once told him. "My dad wants to rip all this out and make it really nice with the real thing."

Today Jade studies Matt with something like awe. "Did your mom really die?"

"I guess. They said."

"Did you see her die?"

"I think so. I don't know."

"We're not supposed to talk about it. My mom said I shouldn't. She didn't even want me to know. But I heard her talking and then she told me. What happens now?"

Matt shrugs. "They took me to some office. I'm not allowed to go back to my apartment."

"Why?"

"Could I come live here?"

"Sure." Jade hesitates. "We could use the sleeping bags or get bunk beds."

"I'll tell the detectives. I tried to tell them before that it would be okay, but nobody listens." He tries to imagine Jade's mom being his mom, putting them to bed, pouring milk on cereal. It wouldn't be so bad. Suddenly he can't remember what his mom looks like.

"We told my father."

"What?"

"About your mother getting killed. We had a phone call with him last night. And we told him. Ha!" Jade says, setting a virtual fire that scatters men who were holed up a second before. "Ha, ha, ha."

"Where was he?"

"China. It was already today there, Monday. They're way ahead."

"When does he come home?"

"Next week."

You don't need a father, his mom always told him. Lots of people don't have a father. I'll do everything for you that you need, she'd say.

"Ha!" Jade says again.

Matt tries to concentrate on the game. Jade is getting better at it. He's just killed about seven outlaws. Some were hiding in another shed, some getting on horses, two were fighting the fire.

He becomes aware of Jade's mom standing in the doorway. When he looks at her, she comes over to him and kneels a little and hugs him hard. "Oh, Matt, let me give you a squeeze. Hamburgers for dinner. I know you like hamburgers."

Her perfume is strong, like flowers. He hates to be hugged. She keeps holding on to him.

"He wants to come live here," Jade says.

She pulls away to look at him and taps him on the nose. "You can come visit any time. We love to have you here. But I know the detective has something else in mind for you. I talked to him yesterday. He's taking you to Child Services."

"We went today."

"Ah, you see."

"But if I want to stay here—"

"We could get bunk beds," Jade interjects.

Matt says, "We talked about it."

Jade's mom hugs him again. "Not really a sol— Like I said, you can come visit a lot. But we don't have the room or the beds."

"I don't care."

"You would. And there's clothes, food, all that. I'm so sorry."

Clothes. He has clothes. Food. He doesn't eat much.

"But visits. All the time. As much as you want."

The wooden walls seem ugly and the carpet smells like beer.

LATE AT THE OFFICE on Monday, Christie holds another squad meeting.

Dolan reports that a visitor to one of the tenants in Maggie's apartment building had come forth to say that she saw a man rushing from Morrowfield to Murray at about the time of the murder. "She described him as young and pretty nice looking. She said he was wiping his hands on something like a kitchen towel. She didn't see where he went after that."

"That's it?"

"Couldn't get anything else out of her. I asked for a further description. I said, 'Good looking means what?' She said, 'Neat. Neat clothes. Clean.' She wasn't a good witness but she's all we have."

Colleen says, "The surveillance tapes for the grocery store are tough going and probably too new to be much help. But I'm looking and I have some of our other guys looking. He might shop there all the time. Maroon Corolla, young man, nice looking or at least *clean*, and we'll try to get a license plate."

"Good."

Potocki says, "We haven't found any calendars or things of that sort that we didn't see right away. The storage bin was a bust. Camp stool and beach chairs. We're going back to the apartment tomorrow to see if there is anything we missed the first time around, hidden papers, old computer disks, something under floorboards, anything that might name the clinic. If there *was* a clinic. We need to corroborate."

"Like wouldn't a hidden diary be nice?" Coleson asks. He's one of the ones on surveillance tape duty.

"Certainly would. Yes."

Christie has two trusted detectives, Hurwitz and Denman,

checking dating services that were popular eight years ago and continuing to conduct interviews with people at the schools and the coffee shop where Maggie worked. They are an odd pair of partners but they get along well. Hurwitz, a small unkempt city boy, provides any necessary skepticism. Denman looks like the classic strapping country boy come to the big city. Together they make a kind of sense.

A picture has emerged of a sweet, well-liked woman who never overcame her uncertainties. She was that wistful, slightly bohemian type who never liked to take charge. Poor Matt.

Greer says, "I spent some time with the best friend, Sasha, making funeral arrangements." She makes a face and everyone laughs because by now they all know she keeps getting funeral duty and she hates it. "Coroner won't release the body just yet because Sasha chose cremation and that's . . . well as final as we get. It's going to be closed casket anyway. There's to be a memorial gathering at this Sasha's house in Highland Park. She's thinking Thursday or Friday. She's started calling Maggie's friends to work it out. She's sure it's what Maggie would have wanted."

Christie looks around at his people. He's ridiculous in a way, a soft, sentimental policeman, but he feels so much affection for these people. And he has favorites. His old partner, Artie Dolan, always well dressed, carries himself with dignity. Says what he says with that honey voice. Right now Artie doesn't have anybody to manipulate into a confession. That makes him restless. And Colleen—Greer he sometimes calls her—well, there she is, blonde, lively, and she does a pretty good job herself of winding people around her finger.

Christie writes new assignments for tomorrow on the board.

Re-examine checkbooks, bills, etc. Greer, Dolan
More hours on surveillance tapes. Coleson, McGranahan
Continued interviews with possible witnesses. Hurwitz, Denman
Databases for Dal and Dol. Potocki

Databases for registration of Maroon Corollas. Potocki

The last two assignments were needles in haystacks and Potocki always got those.

"Is this guy dangerous?" Hurwitz asks. "To the boy?"

Christie nods. "I'd say so. Two meetings and in both he's obsessed with the kid. Finally kills the mother. Yes."

Christie dismisses the squad. They haven't joked as much as usual today. Colleen looks depressed. She and Potocki walk down the hall together. Potocki puts an arm around her briefly.

Dolan hangs around, follows Christie into his office. "This is a bad one. Nobody knows beans about who this guy is."

"So far. What does it mean?"

"Secretive woman."

"I'd say so."

"Embarrassed she messed with him. Embarrassed is what I'd say."

"Why? Talk to me."

"If the witness on the street is right, he's young. So maybe the age difference. If he's crazy, too, well, that would explain why she didn't talk about it. People are messed up, they make mistakes, they don't want anybody to know how stupid they are. Were. You know what I mean?" He sits on the edge of Christie's desk.

"I do. I agree with you."

"Put it out about the Corolla?"

"I'm thinking. See what Potocki finds."

"I hear you're playing fairy godmother with the adoption thing."

Christie grunts. "I'm in plenty of hot water about it."

"What's happening?"

"Chief yelled a warning over the phone. Promising demotion and all that. 'Interfering with procedure.' So . . . so what? Let him try. I'm picking up Matt from his friend's house. Then we're meeting the new parents at the airport. Then Family Court tomorrow."

"Man, you are moving a few mountains."

"Yep. Trying. Tomorrow is a big day for the fairy godmother. Go on and get some sleep. One of us ought to."

MATT STANDS STIFFLY BESIDE Christie as passengers stream into baggage claim—on cell phones, pushy, tired; soon enough they are slamming carts into the legs of others. Christie has argued with himself this way and that. Where is the best place for Matt tonight? He has decided for sure to get him away from the apartment building where the police tape on the door is a reminder of trauma. He's considered Jade's house, Grady's house, Sasha's house—all those were possibilities. But they were also all fraught with the likely scenario of Matt asking if the arrangement could be permanent and then being told no and then being switched again. He considered seriously taking the boy to the Pocusset Safe House and he'd called Elizabeth Ross to ask about it.

She said, "Richard. I've been hearing your name. Or reading it on my computer. Jan Gabriel wrote me an email from the airport in Frankfurt I think it was."

"Well, I'm trying to make this thing happen."

"At least you didn't try to give them four kids at one time."

"That would have worked, I'm telling you. Now that was a brilliant match. They never had a chance to find out."

"Maybe. But this boy—is he coping?"

"Yes. Coping a little too much. I'm trying to figure out if I should bring him to you for the night—clean beds, chocolate cookies, the whole works your people do—or whether to introduce him to Jan and Robert right off."

"It's traumatic either way."

"Yes. They'll be rushed coming in. It'll be late. On the other hand, the kid told me he always stays up until midnight."

"That'll change soon, I hope. Why don't I call the Safe House and make sure they have a place for him. And you introduce him to Jan and Arthur. And you all play it by ear—where he'll stay tonight."

"It sure would go better in court tomorrow if they were used to each other, familiar. I can hope for that."

"I'll hope with you. For everyone's sake."

And soon Christie will know. There are two eager-looking people walking fast, fast toward them.

Christie takes Matt's hand. Stiff, tense. "Matt, here are the people I've been wanting you to meet. They sure want to meet you!" Earlier, he told Matt, "They have a big house right near your school and your friends and they have lots of room and they have a dog."

Again Christie tells himself this is right. These people should have a kid. This kid needs parents.

Jan and Arthur don't leap on the boy. They let him look at them for a moment. Then Jan leans over to say, "Hi, Matt. Hi. I've been thinking about you this whole trip home."

"Where were you?"

"In France."

He nods.

Arthur has stooped down beside him. "Hi. We were so eager to get here. We'd like to show you our house."

"Mr. Christie told me you have a dog."

"Oh, we do. He's a good one. Big and affectionate. Do you . . . do you like dogs?"

"We weren't allowed to have one in our apartment."

"That's the usual rule for apartments. Our dog is named Felix. We love the name."

"Felix. Why?"

"The name means happy. Oh, back in Roman times, anyway, the name comes from the word for *happy*. So we thought that was a good idea. How about we take you to meet him?"

Jan's face shines with hope. She's a smart-looking woman, medium-length hair with a slight wave, brown eyes, and an open face, eager to please. "We still have to get our luggage."

"We could meet you at the house," Christie volunteers. "We could go get us a milkshake and meet you in an hour or so."

Is he right? Is everyone relieved by the little break he has proposed?

TWO HOURS LATER, Matt is ready for bed in his new pajamas, bought for him by Christie. The dog is at the side of the bed—as thrown off course as all the humans are. He has just come home from the sitter. He is dog-angry that he has been left alone for two weeks. He is also ecstatic that his family is home again. And he's curious about the new person—a usurper of his place? Still Felix likes the size of the usurper and he likes the way the boy keeps wanting to pet him. The dog is deciding to be happy. He is Felix, after all.

Arthur watches the dog and the boy and his wife, wanting to understand everything and to savor it all, too. He watches this new life unfolding before him—Jan climbing into the bed next to Matt and reading (books lent by Christie). How patient she is. How she's needed this, being a mother. She has energy to spare. Not to mention love. He listens, almost asleep himself, as he sits in the room's only chair, the *Post-Gazette* on his lap. He allows himself to imagine many evenings like this. And some at PNC Park in summer. And trips to the zoo. He's a *teacher*. He'll be a teacher father; he's definitely not a coach father, strict-disciplinarian father, or preacher father. To watch someone learn and grow, it's his thing and he's good at it.

What happened to this boy's mother is unthinkable and he must not expect the child to get past it any time soon.

By their body clocks, which are still on French time, it is five in the morning. He slept on the plane, but Jan hardly slept at all. She never can when something's up.

By the time Jan is on the fourth book, Matt's eyes are beginning to stay in the half-closed position.

When Matt is asleep, Arthur shows the newspaper to Jan. The murder is front-page news. She puts her glasses on, reads.

They go to their room, just next door, but she's afraid to leave Matt alone. He may wake frightened, she thinks. So she drags a futon from the floor of a third room she uses as a study to the floor of Matt's room.

"Just for tonight," she says.

Arthur climbs down next to her. Sleep? Who needs it?

THE PHONE. HIS MOTHER AGAIN. "I keep thinking about that awful news—same last name as us . . ."

His heart starts pounding again. He stops at the bank and leans against the building to steady himself.

"What are those sounds?"

"Traffic. I'm on my way home."

"You should be careful."

Careful? "What's with you, Ma? You sound, like, restless."

"I am. I am. I think sometimes I ought to just pick up and travel. You know, see something different."

"You should. You should go. You took care of the old bastard forever."

"Don't call him that."

"You didn't find him foolish?"

"Sometimes."

"Well, I'm glad to hear it." He starts walking again.

She chatters on about plans she could make. He doesn't care that his mother is restless. He has bigger things on his mind now—what's going to happen to his son. He has tried to find out, but how to take the next step is not clear to him.

Earlier that day he drove down Morrowfield and looked toward the building where it happened but he did not see his son.

He parked way down on Murray where he couldn't be associated with his car and he walked back to the Golden Seal vitamin store. When he got inside, he pretended to browse the shelves for a long time.

"May I help you?"

"A general vitamin? My girlfriend wants a high-quality brand. "

"We carry pharmaceutical grade."

"Good, good. I mean we're moving up a couple of streets away. So this place is convenient. The only thing—we were wondering, is the neighborhood safe? I mean, isn't this where that woman was killed?"

"Just around the corner. Horrible."

"My girlfriend just kept wanting to know about the little boy. She saw it on the news and she just felt so bad for him."

"Everybody does."

"What happens to a kid like that?"

"I don't know. Foster care. Whatever."

"Foster care?"

"You know. People who make a few bucks taking on kids that need a home. It's a lousy life for the kid."

He had to buy the vitamins, still didn't know anything.

"Are you still there?" his mother asks.

"Yeah, Ma, but I have to hang up now."

He's made it through Monday, and when he arrives at his apartment, there are no police at the door and none inside the apartment, only the three Koreans drinking beers and talking, talking, talking.

"You wash car. It look new," Shin says.

"Have to keep things looking good."

"You hungry? We have vegetables, rice? Always make extra."

"No thanks."

Finally the Koreans go to bed. He's missed the news on TV, so he finds a video on his laptop. Is there anything? Yes. Yes. *Police say the perpetrator may be the owner of a maroon sedan, possibly a Corolla.*

Better not drive by the house again. They have the make wrong, but the color right.

Late, it's late, but he finds the website for the *Pitt News*. He's going to lose money, but he knows what he has to do, before they start looking at makes other than Corollas. *Beautiful '09 Pontiac, perfect condition. $9,500 or best offer.*

He'll take the loss.

His hands tremble as he types. On the upside, he'll have cash. His mother told him a new car was money very foolishly spent. She drove an old red VW Bug and it served her fine, she insisted.

He sleeps fitfully, with bad dreams.

4.

TUESDAY

TUESDAY MORNING AND Nadal eats his cereal and strides to work at the computer lab in Lawrence Hall. The whole lab has been torn up (as it always is when there is a school break), with some computers replaced. There will be glitches. Now that students are back, it seems most of the inquiries are about how to use the official Pitt email—some kids are swift but a few of them get irritable trying to get used to the new setup.

He takes his place behind the table. For the first four hours he just needs to monitor the printers and answer questions from walk-ins. He gets phone duty for the second four hours. Sometimes he gets phone duty at night and that's great because he can sleep for stretches between calls.

Josh, the night worker who is logging out, gives him a high five. "Got good classes this term?" he asks.

Nadal has only the one class, but he answers, "They're looking okay. You?"

"Terrible," Josh says cheerily. "I'm going to flunk three of them, I'm sure."

Nadal sits and tinkers. He checks his email to see if there's anything about his *Pitt News* ad. Yep, it didn't bounce back. Hopefully it will be in the paper tomorrow, Wednesday.

He is looking up notaries in the area so that he can do the sale as quickly and painlessly as possible, when a woman approaches the desk. "Could you help me?" She dips her head a little. "My computer just froze on me. I don't know what I did."

He guesses she is about forty. Her hair is long and straight, kept in place by a thin scarf tied at the back of the neck. She has a very Anglo face, not at all bad looking. Is she flirting? He can't tell.

He stands. "Show me what the problem is."

They walk to one of the computers where he can take a look at her screen. It's frozen but it's not her fault. Beginning of the term—always always problems with the new setups. "Ah," he says. "I'll have to work on this one later. Let's try another."

They move to the next one over. It behaves much better, giving her a log-in screen that then gets her into some Internet choices. She logs on with *ALA21*. "There you go."

"And if I, say, want to buy some of my books online, do you know the best sources? I'm sorry. I'm new to this. Just coming back to school."

He instructs her how to choose search words that will get her to used textbooks. She works on this while he fiddles with the machine that won't unfreeze, eventually taking his own advice and restarting—which works. He looks like a genius.

"You're just starting college?" he asks.

"Well, more or less. I finished freshman year a while back. Then I ran off and got married."

He tinkers for a while at the computer he got working, pretending to test various applications. When he looks up, she smiles at him.

"So that's romantic, to run away to get married."

She looks amused. "It was for a while. Then it went stale. Then it was over. And now I'm trying to make up for lost time." She shakes her head at her predicament. "I'm going to stick out in every class."

"No, no, it's okay. There are others."

"Like me?"

"Yes."

"That's good news. I feel very awkward."

"You'll see."

"Where do you come from?"

"Me?"

"I hear a little bit of an accent."

"Brazil."

"How totally exciting. São Paulo or Rio or where?"

"Rio. But a long time ago."

"Do you go back?"

"No. Not yet."

"I love Rio."

Well, now he can't talk to her until he researches Rio. There's always something to catch up on. But he needed this, her. She smiles at him as if he's somebody. "You're an undergrad?"

"Graduate school," he says.

"In what?"

"Computer science."

"Well, I certainly knew who to come to. Thanks." Her smile is quite beautiful.

COLLEEN SITS WITH ARTIE DOLAN sorting through folders full of bills or other papers at a small table in Potocki's cubicle while Potocki works on the computer. This way they all have company today. Conversation. She didn't much like her stint with the surveillance tapes yesterday.

"Anything?" Potocki asks after thirty minutes.

"Not so far," Dolan says. "Only thing is she kept decent records. So why would the records from the year she got pregnant not be here?"

"Exactly what I keep thinking," Potocki says. He's now looking at domestic abuse cases involving a Dal or Dol.

Dolan continues to study Visa bills that Potocki has already been through once. Colleen recognizes the name of a pediatrician in some canceled checks. "I'm going to make a call. She may have told the boy's doctor something."

"Medical records. Ha, good luck," Dolan exclaims.

Colleen wrangles with the pediatrician's office for a good long time. The woman there tells her *with* court orders, they might release the boy's records, but definitely not without.

Colleen tries, "But don't you understand? We're investigating a homicide." She hears papers rustling at the other end.

"I'm just going to say, simply, don't bother with the court order. There's nothing here. And I never said that."

"Are you telling me—?"

"One word. *Unknown.*"

Colleen puts down the phone and starts searching for the name of the gynecologist Margaret Brown had used in more recent years. The day wears on. Computer keys tap. Messages ding. Papers rustle.

"How's Boss?" Dolan asks, his question directed at Colleen. But that's what they're all wondering, because today he's in court, trying to get the kid fixed up with those people he likes—the professors. And court is not good for him. They know that. He gets tense.

They all stop working for a second.

She says, "Frantic, I think. He hasn't called. Late yesterday afternoon he ran home and got books for the kid. Then he went out and bought him new pajamas with cartoon figures. And he's got—guess who? Worst luck. Judge Gorcelik."

Judge Gorcelik already thinks Christie's a bit odd, his having tried so hard to place the four Philips kids with Jan Gabriel and Arthur Morris. What will she make of him today?

They sit for a minute, nobody wanting to criticize Christie further. Potocki finally turns back to his computer. About all they can do is clear the decks. They will have Maggie Brown's phone records for their commander by this afternoon, a treat for him when he's back from court.

GORCELIK IS AS TIDY AS EVER, molded hair. Christie knows that outside the courtroom, she's a chain smoker, one of those super-clean smoke-addicts who makes up for it with scrupulous attention to everything else. "Ah, Commander Christie," she says. "We meet again."

"We do." His voice catches a little.

"This is the case of Matthew Brown," she recites formally, looking at notes, "believed to be an orphan and a ward of the state. Have you engaged Child Services?"

"Yes, we have."

She looks at him hard. "I thought perhaps you had—from the battalion you brought with you."

They are a group, yes. Arthur and Jan, their lawyer, Blackman, Matthew, Oopale, and Ms. Aakil from Child Services.

"Matthew, I'm very much looking forward to talking to you. Would you wait outside for a moment? Can someone take him outside?"

Oopale raises a hand and everyone waits until she and Matt are outside the courtroom.

"My question is: Did you engage Child Services on Sunday when this child was orphaned?" Christie begins to speak. "Don't bother. I know the answer."

"The woman who just went out with him had worked for Child Services and she knew the boy and had babysat for him since he was an infant."

"I see. 'Had worked for?' "

"Yes. She had understanding."

"Nonetheless he ran away."

"Yes. It's not the first time. He has a bit of a habit. Wanting to be . . . free."

She studies Christie. She studies her records. "He's going to need counseling."

"We know that," Arthur says.

Gorcelik scrutinizes him and his wife. "You're the two our commander wanted as parents for those four kids a while back."

"Yes."

"You're married? Two different names?"

"I already had a career under my own name," Jan explains.

"No apologies necessary. I use my own name. I see you're on the approved list from Child Services. You have a stable marriage? Of course you're going to say yes, but I want you to be utterly honest. Did either of you ever start divorce proceedings?"

Jan is so taken aback, she starts to laugh. "Good God, no. We're normal enough. We bicker. But we're so together I think sometimes people envy us."

"Too together isn't good either."

"Oh."

"It leaves no room for the child."

"We understand," Jan says hurriedly. "There is room."

"Look, he's a beautiful boy, isn't he? He's going to be a heartbreaker for adults and peers. Did no one else come forward? Family friend or relative? The point is: I don't want to jerk this kid all over the place."

Christie then tells Gorcelik how they have searched for a relative but have found no evidence of one, how none of Maggie's friends know of a relative, and then he explains that the boy was supposedly the product of an artificial insemination but that they haven't yet found the clinic.

"Someone may come forward," she says soberly. "So here is the question: Should I place him somewhere he knows is temporary while this investigation proceeds or should I risk that he gets involved with these two friends of yours?"

Christie says, "We're working as fast as we can. I doubt we'll find any relatives or anyone else making a claim on him."

"You aren't getting paid under the table by these folks, are you?"

"Of course not."

"That was a joke. You clearly think highly of . . . Janet Gabriel and Arthur Morris." Gorcelik pauses, looks at the ceiling, and then turns back to Christie. "What is the current state of affairs with those four Philips kids you were backing? You were as involved with them as you are here."

"I think nothing has changed."

"Have you been back to visit them?"

"At first. I haven't been lately."

She considers him. "Lost interest?"

"No. Just busy. And I assume Child Services is keeping up."

"So you do trust Child Services to make decisions?"

A trap. He doesn't immediately answer. She waits him out. He throws up his hands. "When I can't do it myself."

She laughs. "Honesty at last." She addresses Ms. Aakil. "Do you agree with this temporary placement?"

"I do. The reasoning is very good. These foster parents are interested, they have financial means, they live in the neighborhood the boy is familiar with—he could keep his school."

"No other children?"

Regretful shakes of the head all around.

"Matthew could use some siblings. As he heals. Bring him in. Let's see what he has to say."

Ms. Aakil goes to get Oopale and Matthew. Judge Gorcelik asks to have him brought up close to her. "The rest of you stand back," she says.

When Matthew is beside her, she says quietly, "Matthew, I am very sorry for your loss. I want you to know I want the best thing for you. I want you to live a good, happy life. I understand you got to meet the two professors last night. Did they have a good room for you?"

"Yes . . ."

"But? What?"

"None of my things."

"That's fixable. They'll get them as soon as they become available, right?"

"Yes, yes," says the chorus from the corner. Gorcelik shoots them a look and goes back to her so-called private conversation with Matt.

"How was it, staying there?"

"Okay."

"But . . . what?"

"I thought I could stay with my friends. I thought—"

Christie shakes his head.

"What?" Gorcelik asks him.

"We checked the boy's godmother and the mothers of the friends, and I promise you we were thorough. They . . . " He looks at Matt while he searches for phrasing. "They felt their lives were extremely complicated and that they were unable to take on that new charge. They have all offered playtime, suppers, Saturdays. Whatever they can manage."

"I see. Matthew. Tell me something nice about the place you stayed last night. And the people who are going to take you. Anything you liked."

"The dog."

"Ah. They have a dog!"

"Felix." After a moment he adds, "His name means 'happy.' "

"It does indeed. Good, good."

"And they're going to put me in a play."

"Explain," Gorcelik asks the group in the corner.

"I'm directing *A Midsummer Night's Dream*. I would like to have him with me at rehearsals. So I've come up with a role for him. He likes the idea."

"Late nights?"

"Not for him."

"I can stay up," Matthew says. "I always stay up late."

Arthur shakes his head. "We'll work on that."

"You are ultimately interested in adoption. Is that correct?"

"Yes," Arthur and Jan both answer.

After a long silence, the judge says, "The court orders that Matthew Brown be placed with Janet Gabriel and Arthur Morris until and unless a suitable relative comes forward. And in the event that does not happen, and if the arrangement suits all parties, the assignment is to move to a more permanent arrangement."

Won one with Gorcelik. Christie can hardly believe it.

Jan and Arthur are holding each other and crying. Matt watches them curiously.

The judge summons the adults closer. "He must change schools, though. I insist. A dangerous man was looking for him. Do you have an option? Private schools?"

"Yes, yes, we know about other schools," Jan says. "Falk, maybe, would work."

"Commander? Let me see you alone."

When the others leave, she says to Christie. "You are trying to find the birth father?"

"We're trying to find the clinic."

"Try harder. I want a release from the father."

BY AFTERNOON, COLLEEN and Dolan and Potocki are working on sheets of phone records in the conference room. Each of them has a sheaf that represents a full year.

Dolan has ordered the last three years and then also seven and eight years ago.

They go through the recent years methodically, noting anybody they think they should follow up on. But if the son is right, the killer only came back into Maggie Brown's life a couple of months ago. The evidence will then be in Colleen's pile, but she hasn't found anything yet except calls to and from work or to the people they already know about. And Macy's or Home Depot or Verizon.

She hands her sheaf over to Dolan and takes his. Dolan says, "This is looking like the guy didn't stalk her by phone. He maybe was an in-person kind of guy."

They keep looking. Colleen puts the recent pages aside and takes up the pages from years ago. "Hmm. Here's something to go on, maybe. One single call from a Herb Katz, one from a Joseph Tokey. We gotta find these guys." The others move closer to her to look. "One from a Kinko's in Bellefonte, Pennsylvania. No, three from the Kinko's. Oh, and later she calls that number back once, no—twice."

"Maybe she was traveling and had something copied," Dolan suggests.

"Long calls?" Potocki asks.

"Short. Three minutes. I'm more interested in the fact that she might have been traveling up there. I'll call the Kinko's and ask Sasha. I'll give you guys the goodies. You can have Herb and Joe."

The young-sounding man who answers the phone says Kinko's has nobody there who has been there longer than three years. Their orders are in storage, but the young man tells Colleen he is willing to look up Margaret Brown to see what she might have ordered. "Meanwhile, I can look at recent statements for her name and charge card. Do you want me to?"

"Yes, please."

She listens to rapidly clicking keys.

"No, no payment from a Margaret Brown on any of the statements we have in the system."

Okay, people travel, they get calendars made up, and all that. But if she wasn't ordering something from Bellefonte, she might have been talking to someone there. After all, there were plenty of Kinko's closer by. "Can you get me a list of employees from back then?"

"Can try. It might take a couple days."

As she hangs up, Potocki is at his computer signaling them he's got contact information for Katz and Tokey. He throws up his hands in amazement that things are looking up. "Both have retained the same phone numbers. Good deal."

While they are giddy with hope, Boss calls with his good news.

ALL DAY TUESDAY, Nadal googled for entries about foster care and then narrowed it to Pittsburgh and read as much as he could. Finally, when it was almost five, he stoked his nerve to call Child Services. He walked across the street to the dorms and used a pay phone and the name of a girl who had left her computer logged on. He lightened his voice as much as he dared. "Hi. My name is Diane Estevez. I'm taking a Child Development class at Pitt and we have the assignment to write about child trauma. I was wondering if I could learn about that little boy whose mother got killed. How would I be able to find out—"

"I'm just an intern. I probably won't know whatever you need."

"I just have to research for a paper."

"I doubt if anybody is going to want to be a part of a school project."

"Oh."

"You're at Pitt?"

"Yes."

"The foster parents are at Pitt, but I doubt—"

At Pitt. What did that mean? His heart began to race. He worked to keep his voice light. "Well, I guess I'll have to find another project. I just . . . I saw this one on the news."

"You can try to talk to the fosters. I think the name was something Morgan. Or something Morris." Suddenly she stopped. She must have realized she'd said too much, broken a confidentiality. "Never mind. I'm sure I was wrong. What did you say your name wa—"

"Thanks anyway," he said brightly and hung up. He went and sat on a bench in case the phone rang again. What if she called and asked for a description of who had been on the phone? He'd be remembered. Nobody used pay phones anymore.

The phone didn't ring. When enough people had milled around and past him so that he could be forgotten, he—Diane Estevez, in case there was a trace of accent detected—walked out of the Towers Dorms.

MATT SITS ON THE FLOOR, leafing through one of two books Arthur has just bought him: *The Lion, the Witch and the Wardrobe* and *Harriet the Spy*. He has chosen the latter and is moving through it fast.

Arthur sits across from him in their living room, watching him. Jan has auditions tonight and is already gone. Later, in a little bit, Arthur will to take Matt to the theatre so Matt can get the lay of the land. Jan almost always puts a full meal on the table, but tonight it was pizza on the run for the two guys. It was fun. It felt normal, like other people's lives.

"Do you read fast?" Arthur asks gently.

Matt shrugs. "Pretty fast."

"I saw you reading the newspaper this morning. Can you read it?"

"Pretty good."

Arthur says then, "You got quiet after court. Are you okay? Any questions?"

"I didn't understand everything the judge said."

"Okay. Tell me what confused you."

"Not confused. Sometimes she whispered like."

"I know. Just ask me anything."

"What was the part about those other kids you were going to have?"

"That was an idea the detective had. We were in France and Italy and the time went by."

"You didn't want them?"

Arthur tries to think how to say it. "Well, we didn't know if we could have enough room. That was one thing since there were four of them. But by the time we got back, it was too late. The judge had made other arrangements. We want you. I hope you know that."

"Did you know my mother?"

"No. No, we didn't. We want to hear about her, though. We hope you'll tell us about her."

"I don't know what to say."

"She painted?"

"Yes."

"Tell me about her paintings, what she cooked, anything you think of."

"Spaghetti. Meatloaf. Toast."

It makes Arthur smile—toast.

"What did the judge whisper about my school?"

"Well, here's the thing. She wants you to go to a different school."

"But I want my old school."

"I'm afraid she made it a condition. She said we have to switch. I'm sorry about your old school."

"It was close. I could walk."

He can't frighten the boy by talking about danger from a man who claims to be his father. "She wants us to try a different school. It's a good one. Near our work. So we'd be close by. I know change is hard but we can do it. We'll work on it together. I promise that."

"Oh." Felix waddles in and settles down with his head on Matt's lap. Matt turns a few pages with the book held above Felix as if he's done it hundreds of times.

All those near misses, and now out of the blue comes this boy who sits in their living room, petting Felix. Felix makes a funny sound, something like a cry. He sticks his nose up into Matt's hand.

Sometimes life is empty and at other times overfull. Theirs right now is bursting with future. Arthur can hardly think, can only exist from one moment to the next. He understands facts one at a time: Matt likes the books. Matt liked the pizza. He loves the dog.

HE DOESN'T WANT TO shut himself up in his tiny room. He walks around, thinking, and then decides to go back to the computer lab.

His son . . . with strangers. Walking across the street, back to Lawrence Hall, he imagines himself in a different school for his master's degree, in a different city, with a job, his boy by his side. That's what he wants.

A long blast on a car horn jolts him. He's too slow crossing the road, wasn't looking. He picks up his pace and makes it to the sidewalk and then hops up the stairs to the computer lab.

Because he's not working, he has to fight for a seat just like anyone else. Finally he gets one and messes around, looking for his next move. Chicago. New York. Atlanta. Where does he want to live?

He pulls up the Pitt faculty pages. *Morris. R. Arthur.* Is that it? It must be. English Department. Married to Professor Janet Gabriel, Theatre Arts Department. That would be it. Yes.

"Will you be very long?"

He turns to see a skinny boy slinging down a backpack. "Wait your turn," he blurts. "Don't hang over me." He punches hard at the buttons to log out, hurries out to the street, and walks, walks, not ready to go home to the cheerful Koreans, who will no doubt be laughing and quaking in fear every time they mention the mean professor they keep hearing about.

MARINA SITS NEXT TO JAN as one student after another goes up to the stage to do two monologues—one sad and one glad, as they say in the business. These are the screening auditions; she and Jan will see a hundred hopefuls tonight, each with a two-minute presentation. There are thirty-second transitions on either end and a few longer breaks threaded in.

Marina gives Jan an encouraging smile that she hopes communicates the long night would beat up *anybody*, even a person without jetlag.

She watches the auditions, aware of all that wanting, hoping, even from those who are totally unschooled. She's been through it all herself as an actress, lessons learned. DO introduce yourself and your selections with a firm voice. DO prepare thoroughly so that there are no stops or glitches. DO know how to pronounce the words in your selection. DO choose materials that suggest you know what sort of play you are auditioning for. DO NOT assume the director is your enemy. DO NOT shuffle or otherwise dissipate your energy. DO NOT wear eccentric clothing (black capes, et cetera) or inflexible clothing (five-inch heels). DO NOT choose highly sexual material and proceed to straddle a chair or otherwise thrust your pelvis to show what a hot item you are.

Jan looks very tired.

"Anything I can do? Everything all right?" Marina manages to ask between auditions and the notes she's making.

"Well, of course, I keep thinking about Matt. Which do I do first? Do I help him remember his mother, you know, get him to talk about her? Or do I show him who I am?"

"Both probably."

"I know. We've already thrown so much new stuff at him. Now we have to change schools, put him in Falk. A new trauma for him." The next actor is ready to go. "Let me know who looks good to you," she says to Marina.

"Three so far." Marina shows her list with its checkmarks and stars. "Three good and two possible." Jan pushes her list across. Good. They noted the same people.

The young man on the stage has bad posture, partly a personality factor—he's a bit timid. "I'll do Angelo in *Measure* and Caliban in *Tempest*." He talks the talk, Marina thinks. And then he begins, and he's good. It's like a little blessing to watch him working the words, to see a kid in love with the material.

In the next hour, they neglect to take a break. The stage manager looks nervous, afraid to interrupt Jan, who keeps steaming ahead. Marina knows they're on Equity rules and they should be observing breaks.

There is a rustling sound to their left just as actor number fifty is taking the stage. A cup of mint chocolate-chip ice cream appears in Marina's peripheral vision. Arthur and Matt appear, each with cones in their hands. The stage managers were too intimidated to stop them. Arthur is smiling and moving slowly, a man and his boy on holiday.

"Shhh," Jan warns.

Man and boy sit noisily.

Number fifty barrels through a speech by Theseus. Not bad. Jan makes a checkmark and a note.

"We thought you'd both want ice cream," Arthur whispers. "We guessed at the flavors. I've been explaining about casting."

Matt moves restlessly behind Jan. "How many do you get to pick up?" Matt asks. He's thinking drafts, salary caps, sports.

"Altogether, oh, twenty-two."

"Will you have enough good ones?"

"That is a very good question," Jan whispers. "That is *the* question."

Number fifty-one is on the stage, waiting. "Helena," she announces, "from *Midsummer*."

Marina has a hard time pulling her gaze away from the boy. He is magical. Beautiful and . . . something. *Stirred up.*

The actress makes a face and then begins. She's not bad at all. And she has a sense of humor—she puts them, perhaps not in the palm of her hand, but in two hands, juggling sloppily.

She breezes down the house right aisle while number fifty-two starts up the left aisle.

Matt cranes his neck to watch the student actress. "Pick her," he says.

"I just might," Jan whispers.

The stage manager flaps his arms. "Ms. Gabriel. We need to take a break."

"Oh, yes, good. Thank you."

"You forgot earlier."

"I'm sorry. You just need to stop me when I get too involved. Sorry," she tells the auditioner. "We need to take ten."

The kid turns on his heel and reverses direction.

"When she's working, she even forgets to eat," Arthur tells Matt.

Jan laughs. "Hardly." She stands and squeezes Matt's hand.

The little group starts to move toward the lobby.

All the while, Matt, doing round licks of his chocolate cone, is turning in circles, taking in the Gothic ceilings, the chandelier, the stage. He must think he landed in a Harry Potter film. Interesting kid. Dreamy. Distressed. It will be *easy* to play falling in love with him onstage. He . . . pulls you to him. He's lovely to look at, with big, deep eyes and that thick head of dark hair. And the sorrow, beautiful, too.

Jan's student assistant, Beattie, has come up to them. She's this brilliant student they are all amazed by, good at absolutely everything.

"This is Matt," Jan tells Beattie. "Matt, this is Beatrice. She's my assistant. We call her Beattie for short."

Beattie puts up a hand in a shy salute hello to Matt. "Want to see the theatre?"

"Okay."

"Is it all right if I show him?"

"Yes."

"This goes to the balcony," she tells him, pointing to the carpeted stairs. "Let's check the sightlines, okay?"

"Going okay?" Arthur asks Jan. But her face falls as she watches Matt run off happily with Beattie. Marina understands. Matt is showing whoever longs for him that he doesn't need them. Telling himself the same thing.

"SEAT BELT."

"Can't I sit up front?"

"I wish. Afraid not. People in the know tell me I have to put you in the backseat."

"Oh."

He watches the kid slump. "You liked the theatre?"

"It was okay."

Arthur has wondered what it would be like to be a father. He wanted that in his first marriage—children, a whole brood really, but it didn't happen. He stayed married for twelve years and it didn't happen. He learned eventually that his wife, Eve, had a secret abortion. She would not tell him if the child was his or someone else's. After that, he knew the marriage was truly over. Eve never gave him a fight. He realized that work, his students, and his colleagues had been what kept him going all along. When he divorced, he was almost forty—and for the first year and a half, he didn't date, just worked all the time. He couldn't imagine wanting to try again.

He studies Matt in the rearview mirror. Ah. The sleep schedule may be improving. Matt's eyes are closed.

No.

"Did, um, Jan, always do directing?"

"Pretty much always. I met her at a conference when she was talking about it."

He tells Matt how he went to her talk at MLA, how he liked it, how he'd heard of her for years but never met her.

He *likes* remembering. He'd asked her for a drink and then that led to dinner and then talk, talk, talk . . . At first he had thought her pleasant looking only, but as they spoke, she became more beautiful to him. The way her bones shaped her face. The smartness in her eyes. She was a bit shy, one of those quiet theatre people, not at all dramatic in her own life.

"Meet you for breakfast tomorrow?" she asked. She had the most wonderful look in her eyes, acknowledging what was happening between them.

They married a year later.

They threw away birth control; they wanted the whole ball of wax, everything they'd missed. But Destiny, Fate, God, whatever you want to call it, didn't come through for them.

Matt sits up a little straighter in his seat. He says, "Grady lives near here. After this street and the next one, you turn left."

"Good. Got it. We'll do that tomorrow or the next day." I'm right here in the car with you, Arthur thinks; see *me*, see *me*. And he laughs to himself at his childish need.

After a few more blocks Matt says, "That big street back there, where there was a gas station, that was the one to Grady's house."

"So Grady is your *best* friend?"

"And Jade. Jade and Grady."

"We'll make sure you see them." Arthur is dismayed at the sound of his voice, the stiffness, and he's noticed it in Jan, too, as if they're amateur actors, he and Jan, taking on their new roles, trying their lines, but always with that layer of performance over them.

Time. It takes time.

NADAL GOES HOME where he watches TV late into Tuesday night with his roommates and eats chicken and rice prepared by them. They seem happy he is eating their food. "Good? Okay?"

"Very good," he says.

At every commercial break, they joke around in Korean, which unnerves him, but then they remember him and translate. It's nothing about him, all about how that guy, one of their professors, whom they haven't even had yet and won't until classes begin tomorrow, is reputedly so mean. They can't stop talking about him, even mocking themselves, quaking in fear.

Restless, Nadal announces he's going to his room to read.

"You work hard," Gab-do observes approvingly. They do, too; they have been studying the course texts before they even have class.

Shin's computer is open on the kitchen table. Nadal is tempted to say, "You mind?" and use it. But he forces himself not to. He goes to his room and tries to read, but he can't.

Then he chances it. He opens up his own computer and calls up *whitepages.com*, asking for Morris, Robert Arthur. On the Pitt website, there was no home address included, only a campus office. There are twelve men listed under Robert or R. A. He considers as unlikely the twenty-nine-year-old, the seventy-year-old, the ninety-two-year-old. The rest, thirty-five to sixty-two, are more in the possible range. Oh, it's easy, so easy, in the end. There it is, Robert Arthur, fifty-two, and listed in his household, Janet Gabriel.

That does it. Beacon Street. That's Squirrel Hill. That's . . . practically right around the corner.

He lies in bed for a long time before he can sleep.

5.

WEDNESDAY

THE SQUAD MEETING INCLUDES all the detectives working on three concurrent cases. Colleen and Potocki and Dolan and Christie report but only briefly—there is not a lot that is new and they're quick about it, explaining there are no answers as yet on either Tokey's or Katz's phones but that Potocki and Dolan will keep calling. Denman and Hurwitz give their summary reports, which include substantiation that Maggie Brown had no remaining relatives. After the squad meeting the six of them meet in Christie's office for a less formal talk.

"How does the new-parent situation for Matt seem to be taking?" Potocki asks.

"Well, he's got two parents now and neither one is crazy. That's to the good."

"I know this is obvious, but he's probably watching to see if they'll leave him," Colleen says.

Denman says, "Of all the people we talked to—you know we went back to the friends—there was one consistent theme. This kid, Matt, asked the guy from the gallery and the guy from the coffee shop and even a neighbor if they were his father—these guys were embarrassed to tell us and probably a little *scared* that we'd start suspecting them. But mostly they were sad."

"Did you pick up any relationship history there?"

"Did not," Denman says. "Didn't think so. It's always possible. I think the dating service is the better bet."

Potocki and Dolan wave their pieces of paper. They still have Tokey and Katz as possibles. Christie shakes his head. "Look, don't people get multiple contacts from a dating service . . . ? There might be several more men. If it isn't in the phone records, then her email?"

Potocki says, "See the thing with email—there are so many different applications. You know that. Lots of people use the free ones. And why not? I did everything I could with her computer and then I sent it on to a guy at CMU to see what he could dig up. He's the closest thing we have to an archaeologist, digging under and under for the hidden history."

"I wish I understood that stuff," Denman says.

Potocki sits forward. "Quick lesson?" he asks.

They all say yes.

"Well, there are three kinds of email servers—POP, IMAP, and Exchange. The possibilities of recovering email varies with each. POP—with this kind of server, the server receives the email and then pops it to the user's computer the next time that he/she connects, deleting it from the server. If it is downloaded to the user's computer, and if it is then deleted from there, there is a decent chance that it can be recovered from the hard drive using forensic tools; but recovery is not guaranteed."

"Oh," says Christie.

"This is what we have my guy at CMU doing. If you want to know about IMAP and cache servers, I can try to explain—"

Christie laughs. "You're giving me a headache."

Denman says, "I've got to learn that stuff at some point. It's the future."

"If not the present," Potocki smiles. "Anyway, our victim was on AOL and Hotmail eight years ago. What she deleted may just stay deleted. Or, with luck, there may be the shadow of something."

Christie shakes his head. "There's got to be a trail somewhere. The dating service she used?"

"We don't know what she used. She might have used a newspaper ad. Or a service that came and went. Or even Yahoo! when nobody was rigid about record keeping. But we're checking all of it."

Dolan adds, "And then people meet other people on the street, on trains, at airports and they ditch the dating service or lump it all together, as in, 'I'm done with dating services.' "

"Yeah," Potocki says. "Yeah."

"How maddening that she hid a whole segment of her life."

They sit around for a moment, thinking.

Potocki says, "We'll find Tokay and Katz. Hopefully today. But also I want to go back to Brown's apartment. There has got to be something else there. Has to be. She was private. She wasn't careless."

THERE WAS LITTLE CHOICE BUT TO TAKE MATT to work with them early in the day. Arthur had his first Shakespeare class, the first day, at ten, and Jan had a meeting at noon. So the plan was: She got him until eleven, the three of them would take a walk around the block together until noon, then Arthur would take Matt to lunch while Jan had her meeting. Then they all had to go see the attorney.

Last night, Jan had forced herself to sleep in her own room. It meant waking four times in the night to check on Matt. He appeared to sleep soundly.

"This is my office," she said.

It was crowded with bookcases, a small table with two chairs across from each other, her desk with computer and printer, and a sofa she'd gotten from surplus university furniture. She's weathered

KATHLEEN GEORGE

the usual jokes about the sofa being a casting couch. The sofa was great for taking naps before a long rehearsal.

She sat at a table with Matt and worked out her callback list, explaining all the while. "The important thing is to see people in combinations. There are times an actor doesn't do much with one partner and suddenly comes alive with another. And there's this thing we call chemistry—not the school subject. The way people are together, what lights them up. So I'll look for that. There are some actors I know what I want to do with—where I am likely to place them—and other ones that are talented but I'm not sure what is best. So anyway, that's what I'm up to. And . . . I'm putting you on the list—see? I have to post the list by noon."

He stretched up to look at his name and seemed to be pleased.

"Do you want to read?"

"Could I use your computer while you do that?"

"Yes, sure. You play games, you said?"

"All kinds of things."

"Okay."

She worked on her cast list while he played. When she took her jottings to the computer, she saw he'd been playing with Google Maps. "You know how to do that?"

"Kind of."

"How?"

"Some lady taught me."

"A teacher?"

He shrugged and nodded.

"What were you looking up?"

"Where we live. Where I used to live."

She looked at the long purple line that led to Shadyside. "And this?"

He didn't answer. The hospital. He'd been looking up where they took his mother on Sunday.

"Sweetheart . . . let's talk about your mother."

"We did yesterday."

"I know, but there's no limit. We can talk about her all we want."

"I thought she'd be buried. In the ground."

"I know. I know."

"Am I supposed to see her again?"

"If you want, I'm sure we could manage it. This is a holding period . . . for about a week." She couldn't bring herself to say *cremation*, though both Christie and Arthur have been preparing Matt.

He tightened his lips.

Jan toughened herself. "Are you asking why she preferred cremation?"

"Who would want to be burned?"

"A lot of people choose it. Because when a person has died, it doesn't hurt . . . and it's very pure and clean . . . and it allows the family to scatter the ashes in a place the person loved." He is listening, though he's heard it before. She is about ready to call the funeral home to tell them to disregard Sasha's word, to prepare Maggie for burial. Instead, she continues. "A lot of people choose the mountains. And a lot choose the sea. Beautiful places. We'll choose one with you." Sasha has said a park, maybe up north where the two families vacationed once.

Matt doesn't ask where or volunteer a suggestion.

Maggie is out there, floating with possibilities, feckless even in death.

KATZ IS AT HOME. He turns out to be a big, bald fellow looming in the doorway of a house in Squirrel Hill.

Dolan and Potocki introduce themselves and ask politely, "May we come in?"

"Yes." Katz frowns, puzzled or playing at it.

"You live alone?"

"Most of the time."

"What does that mean?"

"I have friends over from time to time."

"Relationships? Dates?"

"Yes. Are you going to tell me what this is about?"

"I am. Margaret Brown." The man collapses back onto his sofa. "We understand you knew her."

"I saw the news."

"Tell us about her. How often did you see her?" Dolan manages to say this in his honey voice.

"Not for many, many years. I ran into her at the Squirrel Hill Theatre once, oh, a couple of years ago."

"Who was she with?"

"Her little boy. She was taking him to some kid flick. She seemed happy."

"You dated her at one point."

"Two times. We went out two times. That was it."

"When was that?"

"A long time ago. It was before she had a kid, I'll tell you that."

"Your relationship didn't work out?"

"Look. I was up-front. I always am. I don't want any commitments. No marriage. I did it once. I don't want it ever again. She was in it for the long haul. She wanted a baby. Now that's a commitment if I ever heard of one. So I stopped seeing her."

"How did you meet her?"

"Dating service. Yahoo!. I've moved onto other ones since."

Dolan and Potocki look to each other. Good. They have the name of one service at least. "Yahoo! still operates the same service?" Dolan asks.

"Oh, yeah. I'm sure they've upgraded by now."

"Why do you say that?"

"Everybody has. Now these places check your name against your charge card, things like that."

"Do you know if Ms. Brown used more than one service?"

"I have no idea."

"You have any idea of anyone else she was seeing around then?"

"No. Well, yes. This young kid was hanging outside her place once when we came back from cocktails. He was clearly upset to see me with her. I'll tell you, I'm no prude, but I was surprised at what a cradle snatcher she was. He looked like trouble so I asked her if she wanted me to beat him up. I'd had a few Manhattans. I probably wouldn't offer today. But she just said no, not to pay him any mind."

"Did she say who he was?"

"No."

"No name? Anything about him?"

"No."

"Anything you noticed?"

"He didn't seem American."

"What does that mean?"

"I figured he came from somewhere else."

"An accent?"

"Possibly a little something."

"What kind?"

"I'm no good at accents."

"What month?"

"September. No, October."

"How do you know that?"

"She'd recently started teaching. Had put in several weeks."

"Where was she living?"

"She had a tiny little studio in a building on Hobart."

Accurate. They've checked out the place on Hobart where she once lived. Neighbors who were still there didn't remember her.

Dolan smiles. Potocki loves watching Dolan work a witness. "And where were you the morning of August twenty-sixth?"

"This year?"

"Yes."

"That was that day—you mean—"

Dolan nods, still very sweet.

"Sunday. I was at the house of a very nice widow who lives up on Darlington. Her name is Sarah Wetz. I'd spent the night."

"This no-commitment thing seems to work for you," Dolan says mildly.

"Sometimes."

"Jot down her address."

On the way out to their car, Dolan says, "He's not a looker. Doesn't pull in his pot. He must have a way about him. Not that I could see it."

"I don't see any motive. This fellow wouldn't *want* a kid. Thank God." Potocki gets into the passenger seat.

Dolan checks the address and soon they're on Darlington and at a door.

The woman who opens the door says she is Sarah Wetz. She is dressed nicely for the day. Expensive-looking pants and top. Necklace. Earrings. Makeup on.

"You were on your way out?" Dolan asks.

"No," she says, puzzled by the question.

"May we come in?"

"Oh, yes. Please. Sit down."

It's a scrupulously neat house, Potocki notes. Both house and her person, perfect, and time to spare.

Dolan doesn't sit. "We're checking the whereabouts of Herb Katz. He tells us he spent some time here. Do you remember when?"

She blanches. "You're investigating him?"

"We're just being thorough. Do you remember when he was here?"

"Saturday night. Last Saturday."

"And he stayed the next morning?"

"Yes, we went out to brunch."

"What time?"

"Noon. We went to the Grand Concourse."

"They do a nice brunch. You've talked to him since?"

"Never heard from him again. Said he was going to call me when he got home. Never called. I hope he's in trouble. I think he's probably a scumbag," she says.

Potocki can't help himself. He laughs and says, "I think you have his number."

THE FELLOW SITTING NEXT to Nadal at the command center in the computer lab is Sean, a pale guy with bad skin and an arrogant manner. He is likely to ask incredulously, "You don't know how to . . . ?" Fill in the blank. It's useful to sit next to him if you can get over the insults. Right now he's lecturing Nadal, "If the guy wants Yahoo!, let him have Yahoo!. They mostly go for Gmail."

Nadal knows about that. Large storage. Send twenty pictures of yourself at the beach and they all go through.

A fairly good-looking young woman with stylishly cut blonde hair—short in back, longer at her jaw—tiptoes to the desk and, voilà, presents a Starbucks coffee and a sandwich to Sean. There's a sign about not eating or drinking in the lab. Sean does anyway, sometimes. This time, he says, "Cover for me. I'm going out to the hall." And to the blonde, he says, "Hey, dudesse. I can't believe you knew I was hungry."

Bitterness rises in Nadal as he watches them leave.

He spies a *Pitt News* somebody has left behind. He leaves the desk to pick it up. It has coffee stains on it. He starts to page through it anyway on the way back to the desk. Yes, yes, his ad is there. He had to go to the newspaper office yesterday to add more detail and to pay cash. But it's in.

A tense kid with bad breath gets right in front of him. "I printed out something fifteen minutes ago," the kid says. He's very young, probably a freshman. "I don't think it went."

"Let me look. Your username?"

"Vickers."

"Vickers." He goes to the lab and finds that indeed Vickers' paper did print. It's titled *bio for freshman seminar.* There are seven other printouts on top of it, so he takes them all to the large table in the corner and sorts them alphabetically as he is supposed to do, ignoring Vickers who hovers.

Back at his desk, he wonders if there are any existing emails on any account from the time years ago when he knew Maggie Brown. He's pretty sure he was using Hotmail then. And he deleted that long ago. Did she delete? What did he call himself back then—captainspockonboard? And he always makes his numbers random. He remembers distinctly the messages he got from her. She had discovered he didn't live in Pittsburgh and she chewed him out.

He figured she dumped him because he had no money. And because of his foreignness. And his timidity. She said it was because he lied to her. He did lie but not . . . not big lies, little ones.

The first time he saw her, he didn't tell her he lived in State College because he worried she would say that was too far. He let her think he was local. He told her he worked as an engineer at Geo-Home, an inspection service for underground mines and land faults under residential properties because that was way more interesting than copying pages at Kinko's. She said he must have a very high IQ and he told her he didn't know his number but that he had high grades. The truth was, most terms he barely scraped by.

Back then, when he lied, because he lied, there were good moments. In the beginning they had a chance.

"I'm a lot older than you," she said.

He was twenty-three. He said, "I'm thirty-one," which is what he is now.

She said, "Oh. You seem younger."

When they went back to her place, she began to cry. She said, "I'm almost forty. Sorry. I don't know why I'm crying."

He liked her then. He loved her. "It's okay. Everybody cries."

"You?"

"Yes."

"I like that. I'm getting older. Fast. And I . . . still want to have a baby."

"You seem like somebody who should have children."

"You think so?"

He shakes his head, shakes off the memory. She wasn't worth it. She was a bitch who thought nothing of him, used him, got what she wanted, and dumped him and never told him he had a son.

Sean has still not returned to his job. Nadal is starving. It's past his time for a break, but no Sean. He goes to the laser printers and gathers the new material to be sorted—which he does slowly, slowly because he hates everyone who treats him like shit, students hovering to grab what is theirs.

JOSEPH TOKEY ISN'T HOME but Dolan and Potocki learn from neighbors that he runs a Uni-Mart in Shadyside and works long hours.

"Good chance he's there, then," Dolan says. "Your turn, pal."

The store looks newly painted; the lot has been paved; there are few customers; and the clerk points the detectives to the back office, where Tokey sits with a computer plus an old-fashioned adding machine.

The first thing that strikes Potocki is that Tokey looks like a guy who has not had a lucky deck. He once had terrible acne; his hair is thin; he has jug ears. There is a photo of a woman and children on his desk, though.

Potocki does the introductions.

"Is this your wife and kids?"

"My sister and her kids. I'm close to them."

Potocki takes a breath. "We're here about Margaret Brown. We understand you knew her."

"Briefly," Tokey says. "Very sad."

"Tell us about how you met her."

He flushes. "Dating service."

"Which service?"

"Yahoo!."

"And you saw her for how long?"

"We never did. We met for coffee once and I called her but she didn't want to get together. She . . . wasn't interested."

"So just for the coffee?"

"Yes."

"Did she tell you she wanted to have a baby?"

Tokey looks puzzled. "We didn't get very personal. We just talked about work and that was about it. I offered to take her to a movie, but she said she was seeing someone else."

"Did she say who?"

"No. There didn't have to be another person. She probably just said that. Look, you aren't investigating me, are you?"

"We're following the movements of people who might have known Margaret Brown."

"Wow. This was a long time ago. I almost didn't even recognize her on the news. Then I did. A person I had coffee with."

"Okay, so that's about that. Can you just tell us where you were this last Sunday? Six a.m. on."

"Here. Where else? Here."

"Anybody else working here?"

"That guy you see at the counter. He came in at eight."

"Thank you, Mr. Tokey."

Dolan goes out to the car while Potocki chats with the clerk. Yeah, the guy was at work on Sunday. All day. Potocki goes back and says good-bye to Tokey, who is hunched over, working away.

MATT CAN ALMOST hear through the door. Some words come through. *Grief counseling. Father.* What are they saying about his father? He plasters his ear to the door, but he can't make out anything more.

And then just in time, he sits again, as his new mother and father come out of the office and the lawyer stands at the door, asking him to come in for just a few minutes.

"Just me?"

"Yes."

He looks back to Jan and Arthur, who nod to him, and follows the man in and sits in a big leather chair in front of the desk.

The lawyer is old and a little bit fat. He doesn't say anything for a long time. The place is very messy. The chairs are nice chairs but there are papers everywhere.

"How are you doing, Matt?"

"I'm okay."

"Hmmm," he says. "If you wanted to not feel okay for a while, that would be all right, too. You've been through a lot. Most folks have to get old like me before they lose their mothers. Tell me, was your mother good to you?"

"Yes."

"I'm glad to hear that. That makes for a good start in life. Your new folks seem like very nice people. Is that right?"

"I guess."

"You should tell me if I'm wrong. If they have secret bad personalities they're hiding, you should definitely let me know."

"I just met them."

"Right. Make them take you places. Hockey games—you like hockey?"

"I guess."

"The park. The zoo. Do you have a bicycle?"

"No."

"You need a bicycle. A boy needs a bike. Activities. Friends. You have friends?"

"Yes."

"Now these people want to be your parents officially. So we're going to give it a tryout, see how it feels. Okay?"

Matt pictures climbing onto Arthur's lap and studying his nose hairs. He pictures Jan bringing him food. Two parents.

"Tell me something good. Something you have now that you didn't have before? Think. Something good."

"The play I'm going to be in."

"Excellent. The play you're going to be in."

"And the dog."

"Good. Have a lot of fun with those two things. Tell me, you have your own room at their house?"

"Yes."

"It has a bed?"

"Yes. But not mine. We're bringing my bed and dresser."

"Oh, excellent. I like familiar things myself."

Matt takes in his surroundings a little bit more. How can anybody have this many file folders and papers angled this way and that? What's in all those pages?

"What?" Blackman asks. "What's the question?"

"Do you have to read all of this?"

"Unfortunately, yes. But I cheat a little sometimes. Like a schoolboy." He slaps the desk. "Okay, then. Wow, I'm tired and it's only afternoon. Matt, I'll be on your side if you do one thing for me. I want you to go to this place downtown—your parents will take you when there's a session. It's for kids like you who have experienced the death of someone close to them. You go to that, and I'm totally in your corner."

"What do I have to do there?"

"Just go and talk a little bit and listen to people."

"Okay."

"Matt, one last thing. Is there anything you want that you don't have? Not that it's possible to have everything you want, but for the record, anything you want?"

His real mother back. His apartment back. "What do I call them? The people—" He points to the waiting room.

"What do you call them now?"

"Mr. Morris and Ms. Gabriel."

"That's what you call them until you feel like calling them something else."

"They said to call them Arthur and Jan, or Mom and Dad."

"When it feels good, do it. Don't force it."

NADAL IS HURRYING down Forbes to get something to eat when he has to fish around in his backpack for his ringing phone. The car ad?

His mother. "You sound out of breath."

"I'm walking. It's my lunch break."

"If you have a minute, I need to figure something out. Violetta down in Florida wants me to come and visit. I don't know. I don't feel confident about traveling. It's a plane flight—"

"Do it. Go."

"Do you have time to look up flights, Nadal? Because I'd want a good price."

"I'll find you a flight when I get back to work. I'll call you back and tell you when it would be and what it would cost."

"Probably from Pittsburgh, right?"

"Probably your best price, yeah."

"Thank you, thank you."

"Just promise me one thing. Don't turn into a servant for Violetta."

"I don't know why you say that."

Because his mother is always a servant. Always. But now that he's in front of the Qdoba, he hangs up. Students everywhere, moving without looking. They elbow past him and shove at him.

He buys a beef burrito and eats it walking back along Forbes.

That afternoon he finds his mom a couple of flights. Saturday, Sunday, and a Tuesday. He calls her back to report. She chooses Tuesday. She gives him her charge card number and he books the flight for her, promising to print out the boarding pass and everything.

When there is nothing more to do for his mother, he reads the *Post-Gazette* obituaries in case there is anything new about Maggie Brown. There are two new lines. Private memorial service to be held. Invitees only. Funeral arrangements by Freyvogel Funeral Home to be announced.

His pulse quickens. His son will be at the funeral. Whenever it is.

Late in the day, he gets out of work. He crosses the street to the same working pay phone in the dorm lobby. Using his higher voice, he calls Freyvogel Funeral Home. "I'm a friend of Margaret Brown," he says. "I wonder if you know yet when the actual funeral will be."

"There won't be a funeral per se. The people involved have chosen cremation. That date isn't set."

No date set. How can that be? "Are you sure? About not having the date yet?"

"The coroner sometimes won't release when there is an investigation. They delay it."

Delay. Investigation. He turns the words over.

JAN HAS MARINA onstage partnering with one actor after another reading the role of Bottom. All the while she's got one eye on Matt, who is beside her, and she's explaining her job to the student journalist for the *Pitt News*. Publicity is necessary, so she agreed to let the student come tonight, even though it's distracting.

The good thing is that Matt is alert, listening.

"Do you know who you'll cast yet?" the young woman asks.

"Well, Marina will be playing Titania, but I can't talk about the casting of Bottom until the cast list is published."

"Pick that guy," Matt says, pointing to the stage.

The student journalist laughs.

"Who's the Titania woman, Marina what?"

"Benedict. She's a pro. A teaching artist."

"She's funny," says Matt.

"Good. The role is funny. The character is sexy, selfish, foolish—a lot of things. It's Shakespeare."

"Who's this cute little boy? Related to you?"

"My son."

"Oh, wow, you should put him in a play one day."

Jan winks at Matt.

"When you watch actors, you're looking for what?"

"Voice and movement and all that. Understanding. But also there has to be a lot of exchange, a lot going on. Between actors. The right combos."

"Tell me about the next step after this. The rehearsals."

Jan give a quick definition of blocking rehearsals and how long that takes, then work-throughs, then polishing rehearsals and run-throughs and tech rehearsals and dress rehearsals.

The student writes furiously.

Marina and Martin leave the stage chatting, but then they part and Marina approaches Jan and her companions.

"Oh my God," the student reporter says. "You were great."

"Thanks."

"I already interviewed Dr. Gabriel. She said you'd have a head-shot I could use?"

"Got it," Marina says. She digs into her bag and produces one of her professional résumé shots.

"Could I interview you, too?"

"Sure."

Jan is relieved when Marina leads the young woman to the marble-topped radiator in the lobby, where they sit. All publicity is good publicity, as they say.

6.

FRIDAY

"**I CAN RELIEVE YOU,**" he said to the girl behind the desk. She looked surprised. He wasn't due at work until noon. "If you want."

"You kidding? Really?"

"It's okay. If you're tired."

"Well, all right. Thanks. I'll get you back sometime." She grabbed her backpack uncertainly. "You're sure?"

"Yep."

Work was better. It just was. He heard her on her cell phone saying, "I guess he didn't have anything better to do."

Fuck her. Unappreciative type.

But . . . ha. She was still logged on.

He looked up Arthur Morris in the course catalog online and saw that Professor Morris taught Victorian Poetry in a graduate seminar on Wednesdays and that he taught Shakespeare on Monday and Wednesday mornings. He went to faculty profiles and learned Morris wrote books—another professor, just like Old Arne.

And Janet Gabriel—articles, plays directed. Busy, busy people. Yes, he knew about people like that.

Now he wasn't breathing well at all. He went to various weather sites. Pittsburgh, Miami, Rio, Puerto Rico, Los Angeles. Then national news. Then YouTube. Covering his trail. Nobody would notice, nobody would care.

"Hey, it's you."

He looked up. It was the woman he helped the other day. "Hey, how's it going?"

"Better than I thought. You were right. I'm not the only old person in class. And I'm not the dumbest either."

"What classes?"

"I have a writing class, anthropology, sociology, and planetary science. I was afraid to tackle more than four."

Yes, she was very good looking. She didn't have a scarf on her hair today.

"I don't know where to work, though. When I go home, I get distracted and nervous—I don't know why, just other associations with home, I guess. If I sit in the lab here, I take up a computer for too long. The library isn't quiet anymore. People talk."

He didn't know what to tell her. "Try . . . maybe try the study areas in the hallways at Posvar. Or. There's, like, that little restaurant on the second floor. Or like today, when it's nice, you can study outside."

She laughed, a nice burbly laugh. "Believe me, I tried that. All the tables and benches were already taken. One girl was stretched out trying to get a suntan. And the cell phones! I couldn't hear myself think."

Again he didn't know what to say.

"Thanks for the counsel. And adieu. I hope you have a great day."

He wasn't a terrible person. She liked him.

CHRISTIE TELLS HIS SMALL GROUP of select detectives, "Keep at the Corolla registration and purchases. It's not a strong lead but it's all we have. The kid is smart. He's visual. Let's go with it."

The detectives look at him hopefully.

"Potocki and Dolan. Toyota dealers. Any maroon car sold in the last five years. The rest of you, fresh eyes on the surveillance tapes. And the DMV lists. Just keep spelling each other. Give it one last go."

They stand and go to their posts. Colleen holds back a bit, then begins to move to her cubicle, then comes back to him. "You like Matt."

He shrugs.

"Well, you won with the judge. Kept him out of the system and got him into a good home."

"Yep. I have to do something else today," he tells her. "Actually this is prompted by the judge. I guess she thinks I'm frivolous. She wanted to know if I've been back to see the Philips kids."

"Oh, wow. Like you're supposed to be taking care of eight families at once."

"No, she's right. I should have been back regularly."

"That's expecting a lot."

"Let's go see them now."

"You want me to come?"

"Yes."

THE DAY STARTED OUT cloudy but the sun is breaking. There are a few children on the streets since the elementary and secondary schools have yet to start; these are the last precious days of summer. So maybe the Philips kids will be home.

They were supposed to call him if things were bad and they haven't so maybe, hopefully things are okay—but then, they are proud.

He pulls up in front of their house, a small four-room place. A front window is open and there are sounds of pots or pans being put down inside.

The door is opened by a kid in a ponytail and glasses. She pushes the glasses up. "Oh. Hi."

It's Laurie. Christie still remembers their names. "Just visiting," he assures her. "Nothing to worry about." The kids fell in love with a guy named Nick who is now in witness protection. Before that *they* were his protectors. They were marvelous kids, all of them, generous and good to Nick, who was lost. "You're all home?"

"Well, no. Just, just two of us."

"Busy? You seem busy."

"I was just finishing dishes and I was going to take Susannah to the park. She likes the jungle gym."

"You don't?"

"I'm getting too old for it," she says.

"Can we come in?"

"Oh my gosh, I'm sorry. Sure." She opens the door hesitantly. The place is pretty much the same. One new chair. A tablecloth in the kitchen. An old iMac on the hall table with a stool in front of it.

"Where's your mum?"

"Alison went shopping. Then she has work. She starts work at twelve."

"Food shopping? Will she be back before work?"

"No, I think it was some other kind of shopping. And then straight to work."

"Where's your brother?"

"Basketball, I think. I'm not sure. He took a book. He might be at the library. He likes the computers there."

"How's this one?"

"Slow. We have dial-up. Meg's going to order Wi-Fi."

"The computer might not take to it," Colleen murmurs.

"I'd like to look into getting you guys a newer computer in the house."

"Wow. That would be great!" Laurie says in her gravelly voice.

"Mind if I look around? I need to make sure you're all doing okay."

She steps nervously aside. "Susannah," she calls. "Come on down." Her sister is at the top of the steps. She wears knee-length pants and a T-shirt. The clothes are clean, Christie notes. But that was the case before. Clean kids.

"Where's Meg?" he asks.

"Working. At Doug's Market."

"What are her hours?"

"Days. Like nine to five."

Not the typical teenage summer.

He opens the refrigerator. Not much, but more than before. Bread and milk and eggs. He opens a cupboard. Again, slender. He opens another. Crackers. A carton of cigarettes. He opens a lower cabinet. A bottle of whiskey. So Alison, their stepmother, was still not big on prioritizing food. Once more he wishes he'd been able to place them with Jan and Arthur.

He tries to keep his voice light. "What *do* you eat? What's for lunch?"

"Oh, we go to Doug's when we're done in the park. Meg buys us the special of the day. She gets a cut rate because she kind of makes the special."

"That sounds good. And dinner? Who cooks?"

"We all do."

"Very impressive," he says. "Four good cooks."

Laurie shifts from foot to foot, no doubt fretting that their *coping* won't be seen as good enough, wondering, is he here to ruin their lives?

"Maybe see you over at Doug's," he says lightly when he leaves. He and Colleen walk slowly to the car. "I don't like it," he says.

"Are we really going to Doug's?"

"Yep." But he drives down to North first and then up Arch, stopping in front of the library. "In case."

It turns out Joel *is* in there. He's at a table, head in his hand, reading. He, too, looks nervous to see them.

The library is brand new, everything ultra-blond wood and modern. The shelves . . . not very full.

The detectives sit down. "We're just visiting."

"Is this about Nick?"

"No. He's okay last we heard. Sober. We have to hope it lasts."

"He called us a couple of times."

"Did he?" Witness protection. Not supposed to call. "And?"

"He sounded okay. But I got scared when you came in something bad had happened to him."

"He's okay. I just wanted to check on your family. Schools working out, food in the house."

"School doesn't start again until next week."

"I know. Still on scholarship?"

"Yeah. Shadyside Academy. And Meg is going to CAPA."

"That's fantastic. That sounds right."

"Yeah."

"But lots of transportation to work out, I'll bet."

Joel allows himself a grimace. "You said it."

"So everything is going fine? Alison comes home. Stays at the house?"

"Yes."

"Good. What are you reading?"

Joel holds the book up. *When the Air Hits Your Brain: Tales from Neurosurgery.*

"Uh-huh," Christie teases. "A little light reading, eh?"

Next they go up to Doug's Market.

Meg sees them right away. Her face brightens excitedly before panic sets in.

Christie hurries to assure her, too. "Everything is fine. Your friend is fine. We're just visiting."

"Oh, good."

She wears an apron and she's ladling chili onto a hot dog for a park vagrant who smells to high heaven.

"You work long hours."

"It's okay. I like work."

And she gets to feed her family.

"I think we might need a couple of your chili dogs."

"Oh, great." She blushes and busies herself making them. "With cheese on?"

Colleen says, "For me, yes," and looks surprised when Christie adds, "Give us the works." He's going to need pills.

"Does Laurie still babysit?"

"When she can."

"And you?"

"The same."

"That's a lot of working."

"Sometimes babysitting is almost fun, like not working."

"Did you see the news by any chance about a woman who was killed last weekend in Squirrel Hill?"

"Yes. We saw that."

"She has a little boy."

Meg wraps their hot dogs carefully and presents them. Christie pulls out his wallet. "You have to pay up front," she says.

"You think you or Laurie might be able to babysit when the new parents need someone?"

"If we could get there."

"I'm sure something could be worked out. They might even come for you or drop him off."

"Okay."

"The boy I'm concerned about needs to talk some . . . be encouraged to talk. He doesn't have any family left, and he's a bit stuck when it comes to talking about his mother or his feelings."

"I could try."

"That's all anybody can do."

He and Colleen sit in the car eating their lunch. After a while, Colleen says, "I thought Matt was going to grief counseling."

"The next session doesn't start until October." If the idea is to put a kid with other kids who have had losses, he figured, why not arrange a little something himself?

"What are you thinking about the Philips kids?"

"They'll get by. They keep managing. It's lousy, lots of lemons, lots of lemonade."

Colleen pretends to punch at his arm. "Getting creative," she says, "with the words."

ABOUT THIRTY PEOPLE HAVE BEEN invited to Sasha's house in Highland Park. It's a worn-down brick off the main drag. Most people have brought food. Because the day is muggy, windows are open and flies are at the food. A video of Maggie on a camping vacation with Matt and Sasha's family plays endlessly on a loop in the living room where a computer shoots the images to a screen. Sasha has been pulling all of this together for days. All around the three rooms that hold the memorial party are still photos of Maggie; propped against the walls are Maggie's paintings. The mourners (or *celebrants*, since the current terminology used is a *celebration of her life*) wander from one image to another as if they are in a gallery.

Arthur and Jan sit quietly in the living room, watching the video. Jan leans forward at times, thoughtful, studying certain moments. At one point, she gets up to follow Christie who is touring the paintings with Sasha. "Tell me about these," he says to Sasha. "I'm not much of a gallery goer. They remind me of something."

"In the end, she didn't think they were working."

"I don't know how to judge these things. They're pretty."

Jan smiles encouragingly at him.

Sasha says, "Mag didn't want pretty. She was trying to overlay images of people with tile patterns from the Middle East. She liked the art of the Middle East and the music and the people. She thought she could see the angles and colors of the faces and bodies in the mosaic patterns."

"I can see what she was after," Jan remarks.

Christie is squinting at something that looks like a mosque spire and also like a face.

"She didn't think she caught it. She said all she'd managed was Omar Sharif in a bathroom."

The three of them laugh spontaneously, and other people look at them, both surprised and pleased that someone has found something to laugh about.

"Does Matt paint?" Jan asks. "Should we be getting him—"

"Never showed any interest."

Out of the corner of his eye—and Dolan does this too—Christie watches people who have alibis and no motive and don't seem in the least suspicious—a mark of just how desperate the police are.

They have run all the prints through AFIS Local and State and then National and cannot get a match. They have canvassed the neighborhood and questioned all of Maggie's friends, asking about everything, including the maroon Corolla. They have checked all Toyota dealers in the area. They are following up on the owners of maroon Corollas with the DMV.

They have looked (talk about a hopeless task) for anything with a Dal or Dol—among auto registrations.

"Nothing for us here other than some decent eats," Dolan says several minutes later. Christie—everyone—envies Dolan his metabolism. He is always thinking about food and somehow still trim and tidy and muscular.

Someone has provided a ham, someone else a poached salmon, and there are spinach pies and pasta casseroles. Lots of breads.

"Colleen and Potocki should have some of this," Dolan murmurs. "About the only reward we've had all week."

But those two detectives are at the office, working. Earlier today, Potocki lugged boxes of handbags and shoes and even some clothing to the office from Maggie's apartment and asked for a chance to look through them.

Colleen has stayed behind to help him.

Christie's phone buzzes after an hour. It's Colleen. "Got the name of the clinic," she announces. "And also a calendar with appointments on it. And a name. Danilo. You might want to find out if any of the friends knows of a Danilo. Potocki checked on the computer to rule out hairdressers and the like. That's it. We're about done."

Christie's jaw drops. It's so amazing to get good news—he can hardly believe it. "Where did you find these names?"

"Papers. In the bottom of a box of shoes and handbags. She was hiding them. Sort of about six months of stuff from when she decided on the clinic, I think."

"Good work. Give me the name of the clinic."

He pulls a notebook from his pocket and writes it down. He also writes down Danilo and Dal. He tells Dolan, "Ask these people about these names, Dal again and Danilo. I'll ask the kid."

Matt is sitting on the sagging sofa, half watching the video. He kicks his leg up repeatedly as if illustrating being a kid. Christie takes a seat next to him and is surprised when Matt speaks first. "I think I made a mistake when I told you all that stuff about the Toyota and Dal. Or Doll. Remember?"

"Yeah, I do. The name?"

"No. I think it was a Pontiac."

Christie takes a deep breath. "What makes you say that?"

"That long badge thing on the front. The line that goes down.

131

I think . . . I mean I saw it in a magazine and then I looked on the street and it seemed more right."

"Thank you, son." He jumps because he didn't mean to use that word and because Matt comes alert when he hears it. "Thank you for coming forward. A Pontiac, huh?"

"Yeah."

"And you're talking about the chrome on the front grille?"

"The other cars don't divide in front. Pontiac does."

"Good, good. I have some other questions for you. Ready?"

"Yeah."

"Can you remember the man's voice? High, low, accent, no accent, quiet, loud?"

"He was angry."

"Loud?"

"No, quiet. He had some . . . accent I think."

"Did he?"

"I think. It was a little bit of an accent."

"One more question. Did you ever know anybody named Danilo?"

Matt frowns. "No. I don't think. Is the part about the Pontiac important?"

"Yes, I think it is. We'll keep a lookout for a Pontiac. Anything else you remember, you tell me."

"Okay."

"Nobody named Danilo?"

Matt appears to think. He shakes his head.

"Okay, good."

Then, moments later, Christie goes outdoors to the scrubby front lawn and places a call to the number in New York that Colleen has given him. He hopes they're not gone—it's Friday at four. The phone keeps going to voice mail. So, the place exists at any rate.

He clutches the piece of paper, wondering how to proceed. Through the open window, he can see Dolan talking, pretending casualness, and Jan and Arthur following Matt hungrily with their eyes. He tries the number again. Voice mail again.

Greer and Potocki walk up the sidewalk, not touching, and wait at the door for him to escort them in and introduce them around.

Then he goes back outside and tries the number again.

Four thirty. The phone rings for a long time, but eventually there is a harried-sounding person on the other end. He introduces himself, explaining quickly to the woman the particulars of his case.

She says stiffly: "None of that matters. We assure donor anonymity."

"Right, right. I've seen the movies—"

"What Hollywood does is not of interest here."

"You do understand that things are changing with some clinics. Also that the law allows for extraordinary circumstances?"

"Here we have a policy. It's a strict policy. I would get into serious trouble if I went against it."

He wants to keep her on the phone. "How about letting me have the pertinent medical information for the donor. I've met the child and we're concerned about . . . about his health."

"I can't do that."

Before she hangs up, he blurts, "Your address, let's see, is 15 Bleecker Street? Correct?"

"Yes."

Man, he's not absolutely sure this is the service that got Maggie Brown pregnant. And Maggie might have had a flesh-and-blood lover during those months. "Did Margaret Brown actually specify wanting any sort of anonymity?"

"It wouldn't matter," she says. "It's just our policy."

"You understand she's been murdered?"

"You said that."

He thinks, *Keep her answering, break her down.* "Did she indicate why she chose your clinic? That's an interesting factor that might help us. Did she say?"

"I wasn't working here then."

Damn. Damn. "Thanks for your help and just one more thing." *Elaine Eselvetro.* He's written her name. He underlines it three times. "Ms. Eselvetro?" He calculates the risk, the time—a drive to New York. Not too terribly long. Marina has been wanting to see *South Pacific.* That's two birds. "I'm actually in New York on business right now. I didn't listen very carefully to your phone machine. Are you open tomorrow, Saturday?"

"Um. Only until one. But nothing is going to—"

He lets her say her spiel again while he watches Colleen and Potocki getting plates of food. Then he calls Marina and asks if she has a Saturday rehearsal.

"No," she laughs. "I think I told you only about eight times! We start Tuesday night. After Labor Day."

"Pack a bag. We leave tomorrow before dawn. We have to be back Monday because I promised us to the Morrises for a Labor Day thing at Lake Arthur. Meantime, see if you can get tickets to *South Pacific.*"

7.

SATURDAY

NADAL'S AD RAN both Wednesday and Friday.

Friday, he got the first of his inquiries. A woman came to see the car in the late afternoon. It was a good day, a sunny day, and the scrubbed-up car gleamed. The woman, unkempt, smelled of smoke. "Would you take five?"

"Five what?"

"Five thousand."

"Uh, no."

"It's all I have."

"Sorry."

Today, he gets a call and closes the door to his little room. The caller is male, aggressive, sounds middle aged, and asks how many miles are on the car, when the oil was changed, if all maintenance has been done on schedule.

Nadal answers everything.

"You're asking nine thousand dollars?"

"Well, okay, yes."

"Forget it. A Pontiac." But the man does not hang up.

"What is your best price?" Nadal asks.

"At the most, seven thousand dollars. If I like it."

Nadal almost takes it, but gritting his teeth, he says, "I'm going to wait for a better offer."

"Good fucking luck!"

He's shaken and thinks he made a mistake. But another person calls moments later. That person sounds like a middle-aged Indian man. He speaks carefully, precisely, and explains that he would like to buy a car for his son. "I have studied the Blue Book," he says. "May we see your car?"

"Yes."

"We would wish to drive it on a city street and a highway for approximately twenty minutes. Is that permissible?"

"If I go too."

"Very good. We will come to see it. We will come now."

Nadal gives his address and paces back and forth, waiting. He works not to make any noise. He hasn't told his roommates he is selling. They still aren't awake—which is good. It's only a bit after ten in the morning. He walks outside to wait.

The father is formal. The son is young, a freshman at Duquesne with a friend at Pitt who saw the ad.

"My son wishes to come home every weekend," the man explains. "And so we need a car that is big enough to be safe."

"I understand."

The father drives the car with his son in the passenger seat and Nadal in his own backseat for the first time, a position that makes him a little road sick. But the trip is short and they end up back at his place on South Neville.

"Would you accept eighty-five hundred dollars?" the man asks. "As I said, I have studied the Blue Book."

Nadal nods. "Yes."

"May I ask why you are getting rid of the car?"

"I need the money more than I need the car. Graduate school."

"Very well. There is a notary in Oakland but not open today—correct?" The son nods. "There is a AAA office open until five. We would like to make the purchase today. Do you have the paperwork?"

It's not in his control. He's afraid of AAA, the record keeping they must do and all that, but he does have the paperwork, and a buyer stands before him. He has to do it.

In his room, there is a brown envelope that has everything he needs. He tiptoes to get it and then he drives the father and son to AAA. When the paperwork is completed—interestingly, the father produces a money order for eighty-five hundred dollars that the clerk pronounces good, but Nadal has never had a money order and it makes him nervous.

"There's a PNC down the street. You could deposit it—are you at PNC?" the clerk asks, seeing his uncertainty.

"We will wait for you," the man buying the car asserts calmly.

Nadal walks to the bank. A deep breath escapes him when the teller stamps the money order. "Cash? Are you sure?" she asks.

He races back to AAA where the father and son sit exactly as he left them. After he hands over his two keys, father and son drive him back to his apartment where Seung, Shin, and Gab-do are now awake.

"Where you go?" they ask.

"Just walking."

CHRISTIE DRIVES HIS CAR UP THE RAMP and, reading the signs, stops, puts it in park. He hands his keys over to a sleepy-looking, unwashed man with an accent he can't identify.

They started out around four this morning. He drove fast and here they are.

A fortune to park—he's forgotten that about New York. "Let's hoof it from here," he tells Marina. According to the map in his mind, the fertility clinic is only two blocks away. Marina has an acting assignment. If she gets a phone call from him in which he pretends to be calling one of his other detectives, she is supposed to go into action.

They pass the office walking briskly. "I want to choose my moment," Christie says. "When she's close to closing."

"Let's eat there," Marina says, pointing back to tables on the sidewalk in a café next door to the clinic they just passed. "We can sit outside anyway. And you can see who comes and goes."

The place they land in is Frenchified, crowded with breakfast and brunch eaters. At neighboring tables they see crusty white bread, cloth napkins, expensive bottled waters, and lots of coffees. An omelet and bread seems to be the standard order.

Marina looks like she belongs here. She is five eight and looking gorgeous these days. He's seen the costume renderings for her for the role of Titania. Earthy, sensuous, and more than a little bit revealing. Almost naked.

Waiters flutter. She studies the menu, oblivious to admiring glances.

Two people leave the clinic. He taps his foot nervously though he has almost two hours to choose his moment. Ah, the whole thing is a crapshoot, but he has to try. They could get subpoenas and go into a long legal battle. But, say they do, then what happens to Matt while they're stalled with the courts?

He breaks off a piece of white bread and butters it, checking his watch from time to time.

"What are you thinking?" she asks. "It's making your face look really fierce."

"That stubborn woman—how to get her to break the law."

"Oh, you're good at that," she says blithely.

An hour later, he has chosen his moment and is in the place. The office is orderly, clean enough, though inelegantly furnished. In the waiting room there are four hard chairs, covered in a diamond-patterned cloth, 1960s vintage, meaning they were manufactured and sold before the craze for sperm and egg donorship. One tall, sad-looking woman with long, lank hair sits in one of the old chairs waiting.

There are stacks of brochures and one blown up on the wall. *We can help*, it proclaims, as he moves forward and stands before Elaine Eselvetro. She does not look up for a long time. Finally she does.

He sees that on her desk is a file marked Margaret Brown. Oh, how he wants that file in his hands. He smiles his best smile. "Christie," he says, showing his ID. "I know you guessed. I won't take much of your time. There are two things I need to know. One. What I'm not clear on is your contract. Did the sperm donor sign something that says he has given up parental rights?"

"I don't know."

"Legally, it's called a TPR—Termination of Parental Rights. Is it anywhere in the files?"

"I didn't see it."

"Is it in your advertising material that this is a given?"

"No," she says. "Not in the advertising."

"Okay. Second thing I need to know is if you do a medical work-up on the donor. I mean how much medical screening is there?" He adds, a little superstitiously, "Could he have had a serious disease?"

"We don't do a formal screening, no."

Suddenly she blushes. Out of the back room comes a scruffy, bearded student, strapping on his backpack. "Left the vial in there," he says in a booming voice. "Have a good one."

"Thank you." She flushes harder.

"Students are your donors."

"Mostly. Yes."

"How about—just take a peek for anything that could help me. I know you're not supposed to, but there's a child's life . . ."

She purses her lips. He takes out a small notebook from his

breast pocket. A pen. He thinks of the small notebook as unthreatening.

Out of another back room emerges a white-coated man of indeterminate age. He is slight and pale. "Send in Mrs. Vale," he says.

Eselvetro stands and peers into the waiting room. "You can come on in," she says.

The tall, sad woman whose hair curtains her face enters and passes right by Christie.

"No," Eselvetro says to him. "The answer is still no."

He looks at his watch. "Sorry. I have to make a call and then just one more thing. He consults a piece of paper and punches in several numbers instead of using the speed dial for Marina. He makes up a bunch of stuff off the top of his head when Marina answers. "About the stepmother. Is she working again or not?"

"Okay. I get it. You want me to come over," Marina says.

He continues with his little act. "Well, is the judge *there*? I mean can you see her? I expected as much. I plan to petition the courts, that's what I plan to do! Oh, we'll get her all right."

He hangs up, as if angrily.

Eselvetro waits. "What is the one more thing?"

He continues to invent. "I'm sorry. I have to make calls about this family I'm worried about. The children—"

Marina bursts into the room. "Excuse me. I saw the sign. This is some kind of medical office? I really need some help. I could hardly make it down the street. It's my foot," she says to Eselvetro. "It's my foot. Something's terribly wrong with it. I can hardly walk. I don't think I broke it, but it's so painful, I can't even manage half a block." Marina limps in from the door and holds on to the back of Christie's chair.

"This is not that kind of office," Eselvetro says. "You need an emergency room."

"Oh, I can't. I have an important audition. Do you mind if I sit down over there?"

"We'll be closing in a little while."

"That's all right. I have to get to my audition." She whimpers. "I'm trying to flex my foot and it won't move at all." She limps to the chair. She's very good—distraught face, close to tears. "My best audition yet and I can't walk. Oh, man."

"Is it letting up?"

"No. I need an Advil or Aleve."

Elselvetro nods. "What's the audition?"

"For a film. They have Johnny Depp. It's a thriller."

"Wow."

"Is there a pharmacy in the area?" Marina asks, wincing mightily.

"About two blocks."

"I'll go to the pharmacy for her if you just tell me . . . " Christie realizes as soon as he's said it that he's made a mistake. The way he related to Marina was too familiar.

Eselvetro looks hard at them. She appears to make a decision. "I might have an Aleve." She takes her handbag, which is right there on a chair beside her desk, and she walks with it in the direction of the doctor and the sad patient.

When she's out of the room, Christie turns the file folder around.

Marina gets up, continuing her act of limping, and reads over his shoulder.

He memorizes. Senior. Goal: grad school. Born in Lebanon, 1981. Guitar and piano. Jazz. Second Avenue address. *Thomas Zacour.*

"Thomas Zacour," Marina breathes.

By the time Elaine Eselvetro returns with a glass of water and a blue pill, Marina has hobbled back to a chair, the Margaret Brown file is where she left it, and Christie lets her see his notebook sitting open, blank page.

BUT WHERE CAN HE KEEP THE MONEY? Nadal wonders. He left the bank with the bills in an envelope and he stuffed the envelope inside his shirt. Eighty-five one-hundred-dollar bills. He will have to break them up. The roommates are honest, so far as he knows, but it would be wise to hide the cash, not tempt them. He separates the bills into three envelopes, and puts one under the mattress, one in a pair of shoes in a plastic bag, and one—he is looking around when Shin calls into his room, "Nate? Do you want some tea?"

"Yes. In a minute." He stuffs it into the inside pocket of his winter jacket.

When he has tea with Shin, who is especially happy today, telling Korean jokes and trying to explain why they are funny, Nadal works to keep his body from making restless moves. He tries to laugh appropriately, but all the while he orders himself to check the money each time he returns to his room.

"You are a funny guy!" Shin says.

"Funny?"

"Like the expression they say, 'a character'!"

"You think so?"

"I think mysterious."

Nadal shrugs. "Just quiet sometimes."

"Yes, good, very good," Shin hurries to add, realizing he has insulted his roommate.

Nadal goes back to his room to study for his course—the first day of which was Thursday night, two days ago. He has to read the same paragraphs over and over because they keep blurring before him.

Here at school and with the Koreans he is Nate. It sounds more American. His mother is the only one who calls him Nadal. For a while he tried just Dal. It's what Maggie called him. The last name Brown does not suit Nadal. He never quite owned it, mostly because he hated the man who had given it to him, but sometimes thinks of himself with his mother's family name, Medina. He plans to take it on one day. And he likes his grandfather's name, Danilo. Once Maggie asked him what Dal was short for. Danilo, he said, and she accepted that. In class the other night, the computer professor called out his formal name, his whole real name, Nadal Brown, in a booming voice. It was strange to hear it called out like that.

He eats a can of soup when the others are busy talking. He is at loose ends. When will he get his son? When will he change his life? Finally he checks his money one more time and announces, "I'm going out."

"Work?"

"Yes." He doesn't have work but now that he's blurted "yes" isn't sure how to get out of his lie.

A holiday weekend. Everybody's schedules are off; tomorrow and Monday many things will be closed.

He begins walking.

He walks down Fifth Avenue and when he gets to Wilkins, he turns onto it and begins the long stretch to Squirrel Hill. He has the address for R. Arthur Morris burned into his brain. The day seems odd, the traffic light, as if everyone, almost everyone, is away somewhere. He finds what he wants, Beacon Street.

He fingers his bus pass in his pocket, wondering if many buses are running today, and he keeps walking on Beacon until he finds the address. In there, somewhere, his son is there.

A large house. A nice house. He passes it and is almost at a street called Shaw when something tells him to look back. A car is pulling into the driveway. A square car, a foreign car. Lexus, Volvo, he can't see from where he is. He has to keep moving. He turns toward Darlington, but from his sideways glance he can see, yes, his son and then a man and then a young girl getting out of the car, going into the house.

THEIR HOUSE IS REALLY NICE—Meg knew it was going to be. She's seen it from the outside before; Commander Christie drove her and her siblings by because he wanted to place her whole family with these

143

professors. When Professor Morris picked her up today, she met him at the door so he wouldn't have to come in to her poor little place. Now she's in the land of Oriental carpets and shiny floors and things on the walls. Her eyes skim over wall sculptures that are like masks, paintings, small sculpted figures, decorated boxes—interesting things.

Meg wears jeans and her very best top. On the way here Professor Morris asked her about CAPA, what she was studying. And then he talked about books, Shakespeare, what he was writing about Shakespeare, and she got memories of how she used to listen to her father talk about Dickens.

She's supposed to spend three hours with the boy. She's brought a deck of cards and two books in her backpack. And he'll have his own books of course. So—

"This is Matt."

"Oh, hi." He's Susannah's age. He should meet her sister sometime. "You kind of ready to go?"

"I guess."

"Your father said you'd show me the way to the park."

"I googled it. It's really close. Just near where I used to live."

She says good-bye to Professor Morris and she and Matt start out.

Meg is afraid of silence. She thinks Matt might get lost in it and not be able to find words, so she asks him all kinds of things—how many steps to his old school, who the class bullies are, what he does when he can't get to sleep at night. Everything and anything. They keep a good pace, reaching Beechwood and then turning onto it.

"Are you going to be my babysitter?"

"Sometimes. When the times work out." They walk for a few moments. "I understand you've been through a lot. My mother died, too," she said. "And then my father a couple years later. It's hard at first. Then you start to get better. Pretty soon you want to do all kinds of things."

"What kinds of things?"

"Just regular things."

"Who do you live with—friends?"

"No, my stepmother." Meg sighs. "She's kind of odd, not too motherly. Here's the park. Do you know where the jungle gyms are? Do you like to climb?"

"Yeah."

"Well, let's do some of that. Do you know how to play poker?"

"My mother said that was a grown-up card game."

"It is, kind of. My brother likes it a lot and he's younger than I am. You have to have some strategy to play. I'll show you later."

Whatever they did, she was supposed to keep an eye on him at all times. "How's everything working out with the professors?"

"Okay, I guess. I don't know what to call them."

"Oh, that would be hard. I see what you mean. Nothing seems exactly right."

"The lawyer said I should take my time."

"That sounds like good advice."

All afternoon as she spends the three hours with him, she winds in talk about the recent events of Matt's life. She thinks maybe he is edging toward dealing with his feelings, but that he isn't quite ready. About other things, he gets more and more talkative. "I'm going to be eight in October."

"Oh, terrific. You know what kinds of gifts you want?"

"Definitely. I want *Red Dead Redemption*."

"I heard of that. It's good?"

"It's the best. They have prairies, caves, bars, shootouts, every-thing."

"Hmm," she says. "Do you play other games?"

"I have some, not the best ones, but some."

"Want to show me later?"

"Yeah."

So it seems to be working. She is making friends with him.

CHRISTIE AND MARINA SPENT the afternoon questioning people all around the area of Zacour's old Second Avenue address. Not one person knew him or where he'd gone. The boy might have given a false name to the clinic. They found a local post office, but no forwarding order on record. The way people disappear! They worked all afternoon and Christie couldn't help noticing Marina was energized by the task.

They had hardly any time to make love in the big hotel bed, and when they did, it was all right, but just that. Then they had to hurry to dinner. And through dinner. "Wife of a policeman," he said, taking her hand. "I warned you. Not easy."

"Well, what else can you do?" she teased. "You're not an actor." She'd ribbed him most of the afternoon about his faulty performance as a stranger to her at the fertility clinic.

"Right. What else can I do?"

Once upon a time he thought it was going to be social work or the priesthood. He knew he'd work *with people*. It was all he knew how to do—talk to people. He hadn't thought *police* until Will Stilton, a friend at the time, proposed they both go to the police academy. By then he was living in Pittsburgh, pushing papers for the Pittsburgh Diocese and not very good at it.

The bill arrived at the table, but Christie was thinking of things he could do to help Matt, and Marina had to say, "Richard? Are you okay? We should go soon."

"Sorry. Yes." His own father had left when he was seven. Never came back. Died somewhere in some other town when he was nine, or was it ten? So Matt's plight gets to him.

Marina gives his hand a squeeze. "Thanks for this. Today."

Good. He's done right. Something she wanted.

They sit in the theatre, in the back, perfectly good sightlines—he knows about sightlines from Marina. Christie is trying to remember what he knows of *South Pacific*. Like most folks, he saw the movie once a long time ago and that was that. Beaches, war, rousing music. He reads his program as if studying for an exam.

She apologizes. "This isn't cutting edge. It's old, you know, dated."

He frowns. It cost enough. She wanted to see it.

"It's romantic." She taps her heart.

The music begins and the lights dim and then the play begins. Ah, yes, old-fashioned good stuff: resistance to love, differences, can't live with, can't live without. Exotic man, American woman. Prejudice. Children needing love.

The music insists on his attention. The world is full of this story tonight. This is the story. It seems the only story.

NADAL WAKES FROM A DREAM that is so delicious and lush, he does not want to open his eyes, or get out of bed, or go to work, or ever attend school again. In the dream, he was how old? Not man, not boy, something in between and he was back in Puerto Rico, out on the land his grandfather owned, out of the city, one of the last rural outposts, a place with cows, goats, chickens, and . . . beans—oh, other things in the garden, too, but beans he remembers. In the dream, he felt the sunshine, the itch on his skin from spending his time outdoors, and he ate something in the dream. He could almost smell the food.

This is where he wants his son to be. The farm doesn't exist anymore, but there'd be other ones.

He could live, he could work, he could do away with school happily. Computers he'd miss, yes, for a while. He sits up in bed, confused. He needs both—the country, the home base, the real life in Puerto Rico plus a city with its traffic and wires and computers.

He has done a terrible thing to the mother of his son, he knows this. The temper that flares up in him sometimes, the temper that made him turn the knife on Maggie—how can he explain it? Nobody will ever understand him or know the real Nadal, a good person.

If they catch him, he will go to jail. He will never get to know his son.

If he can get his son to Puerto Rico, they can disappear. He knows exactly how to do it. Get down to Florida, get to know some fishermen, pay them or, better yet, get work on the boat, and when he's home, disappear from the docks into the city and then into the country.

The more he thinks about it, the more possible it seems. His prof couldn't care less if he never showed up in class. People bail out on a class all the time. His roommates—they might report him missing unless he left a note. He can say he has a sick relative in Florida and that he must give up his room. No. He'll say Texas.

He could go by bus.

No. His mother's car. He'll have it. What to do with it is a problem he can't solve. Think, think, think.

He gets up out of bed, puts his feet on the floor, tentatively. Yes, the floor is solid. He's awake.

He stumbles to the bathroom, confronts himself in the mirror, surprised to see that he is not the whiskerless youth in the dream, but a grown-up who needs a shave and whose face is creased with worry.

The police don't know who to look for; that's the positive thing to keep in mind. He reads the news every day now. They have no idea.

He starts running the shower, but by the time he gets in, his face is wet with tears, his body weak and trembling again. More than anything now, he is aware of how a human being can control thoughts. If he tells himself he is all right, if he wills himself not to think of what he has done, he moves through a day like an ordinary person, and he feels almost okay. If he lets it in, if he says the words to himself, *I am in trouble*, his stomach drops, his hands shake, his knees buckle, his eyes slam open wide, and his breathing feels like gasping through a fog or a net.

The sweet, familiar smell of the shampoo assaults him when he pours it into his hand. *Scrub,* he thinks, digging into his head, rubbing, as if he can clean out the inside. *Think, calm down, be logical,* he instructs himself. *Keep everything normal while you figure things out.*

Puerto Rico. Grandfather dead. Nobody he knows there. So it will be hard.

But then he gets the image of his son. The perfect child. His. And more than anything in the world, he knows they are meant to be together.

8.

SUNDAY

MATT IS DRESSED, BUT sitting on the edge of his bed, kicking his feet up. Breakfast is going to be pancakes because he said he likes them. Mrs. Morris—Jan—standing at the door, says, "I haven't made pancakes in ages. I'll take you out if I botch them. Give me ten minutes. You want to come down and watch?"

He nods but says, "I want to play with Felix," because the dog has just come into the room.

"Okay. That's fine."

The dog gets happy every time he sees Matt. Once Felix even stopped eating to come and sniff him. "You and Felix are going to be a great team," Mr. Morris said. Arthur.

His room is okay, but still without his own things. They don't want to give him his TV and video games, he can tell. They look at each other when he mentions them. They don't like to leave him alone much either; they take turns doing stuff with him. They have put up a big calendar in his room so he can write on it and keep track of what's happening when. Today, Sunday, he gets to go to the zoo with Mr. Morris. It's on the calendar. And for Monday, Labor Day, it says, *picnic!* And *new school* on the square for Tuesday. And *rehearsal* below that. His new father, Arthur, promised to drive him to his school today so that he can see it from the outside. It's for real; it's on the calendar, penciled in: *Drive by Falk.*

The picnic tomorrow is at Lake Arthur because he mentioned having a good time when his real mother took him there a couple of times. The plan is to meet up with the detective and his kids. They're going to rent a pontoon.

The rest of the week is school and rehearsal, all week long.

He asked, "Is there going to be a funeral?" because he looked and looked and it wasn't on the calendar.

"Not exactly," Arthur said. "The memorial party we had at Sasha's house was in place of a funeral. Sasha was sure it was what your mother would have wanted. Right?" he asks Jan.

"Yes."

"Does anything else happen?"

"We'll be able to say good-bye to her when we have the cremation."

"When?"

"Next Saturday. We think. Should we put it on the calendar?"

"Yes."

Jan wrote it down for Saturday, September 8th.

Now he hears Jan's footsteps in the hall. He's not playing with Felix, just petting him.

"Look how Felix loves to be with you," she says, coming into his room again. She hugs him. Felix licks his hand. "I'm just now starting downstairs in earnest. Come down in a couple of minutes, okay? We'll have those pancakes."

"Okay."

He studies the calendar, all the empty spaces, wondering what will go in them.

NADAL, IN HIS ROOM with the door closed, hears whispers. "He's not in there."

"Yes, he is. I know he is. Shhh."

"Okay. Yeah. Don't talk."

Then a bunch of stuff in Korean. Then they laugh. Are they talking about him? He is afraid to move, to make noise.

MR. MORRIS, ARTHUR, SAYS, "COME SIT WITH ME. I'm almost finished. Then we go see your school and go to the zoo."

"Can I play with the laptop when you're done?"

"Sure. I've ordered you one—your own. Should be here Tuesday."

Mr. Morris, Arthur, hits SAVE and hands it over. Matt sees words. *Joy. Final act. Tri-bu-la-tion.*

"You can just close that out. It's the red button."

"I know."

"Aha. You do?"

"Is this work?"

"It's a book I'm writing. I'll try out some ideas on the students."

He can read the top line. *Final Acts.* "It's a book?"

"Oh. I hope. Someday, yes."

Matt looks up at him, aware of whiskers, nose hairs, ear hairs. He closes out Mr. Morris's book.

"I'm looking forward to today," his new father says. "It's been a long, long time since I went to the zoo."

Matt nods. But right now he's worried about seeing his school, and he's not sure how he gets there tomorrow.

"You can play with that later. We should be off."

His new mother comes to the door, followed by Felix.

"Are we taking Felix?"

She smiles at him. "No. Unfortunately dogs aren't allowed at the zoo. It . . . I guess it confuses the other animals. But, he'll be here with me when you come back. He'll be waiting for you. We'll both be waiting."

She kisses Mr. Morris and then she kisses Matt on the top of the head and walks with them to the car. She smells nice, like food and soap.

Arthur. Jan. They like him.

"She's going to work on the play today," Arthur explains. "So she can come to Lake Arthur with us tomorrow."

"Rehearsal?" he asks her, getting into the backseat. "The calendar says Tuesday."

"Tuesday is right," she answers. "I'll be getting ready for rehearsal. Blocking in my head and on paper. Blocking is how you move the actors around. I'll make some plans and then see if they work when I have the actual actors. You'll see. It's fun. It's hard work, too, for everybody."

They get into the car, which is black, a Volvo. Through the screen door, Felix yips, wanting to come along.

And they're off.

"What's *Final Acts* about?"

His new father looks at him, blinking, surprised looking.

"Was that a bad question?"

"It was a wonderful question. It's . . . about Shakespeare and about the feelings at the ends of the plays, some of the plays anyway, a feeling that not too many other playwrights can master."

"What?"

"Joy. Not exactly happiness. But *joy*. It's bigger than happiness. Maybe more temporary, but also more spiritual. But here's my question for you. You could *read* all that on my computer?"

Matt shrugs. "I'm a good reader."

"Wow."

"I didn't know *tributation*."

"Tribulation. Troubles. Suffering, woe."

Suffering, woe.

They drive down several streets, then past the university where Mr. Morris and Ms. Gabriel teach. There are students everywhere, a big party on the lawn. A rock band playing. It seems they go up one hill after another, and then when they are surrounded by mud and cranes, Arthur announces they are at his school, a square building behind a lot of construction vehicles.

"And do I walk here?" he asks, trying to remember the way.

Mr. Morris puts an arm around him and hugs. "Never! We will drive you and pick you up. Every day. Rain or shine. And we'll go in with you on the first day, Tuesday, and help you meet everyone."

He is relieved even though he doesn't *want* to come up this hill to this square building with big construction tractors and mud all around.

They start out for the zoo.

SUNDAY AFTERNOON, hardly anybody at the office except Potocki to search out info on Thomas Zacour for Christie. Boss and his wife are continuing to ask questions in New York, going to places where musicians hang out. The universities are closed, so they can't do much at the schools, but he is supposed to work on the school connections when things open again on Tuesday—unless he finds something before. He sets up his computer and then calls Colleen.

"Just reading," she says. "I'll come in. Keep you company."

Potocki gets a lot of praise from Christie for finding needles in haystacks. Praise is addictive. So . . . Thomas Zacour.

He uses plain old Google at first out of curiosity, adding and subtracting *piano* and *jazz* and *music* and *CUNY, NYU, Juilliard.* No. Nothing. He messes around for a while with searches for *jazz* and *New York music* and then address databases, but nothing hits him as the right Thomas at the right age to be Matt's father; finally he gets serious with Lexis.

If this were an older guy, Potocki would go straight to the Social Security death index, but this guy, unless he was heavy into drugs, is probably still alive. And probably, possibly, long gone from the country.

With Lexis, he tries the last name, reading bios, listings. Sixty-five years old, forty-two years old, two years old. Nobody looks right.

Colleen arrives, gives him a squeeze from behind and goes to her cubicle.

He tries the public records search. Real estate. Unlikely that the guy bought a house or apartment if he was a student from another country, but on the other hand, if he stayed in the States, maybe he did. Some foreigners have a lot of money and New York apartments were the way to go for a while, until all buying fell apart. Still, a person who sells sperm is probably not rich. On the other hand, who can guess all the motives?

He eventually looks for court filings and finds himself looking for jury verdicts, applications for professional licenses. Thomas Zacour doesn't show up.

Voter registration? Did he perhaps become a citizen and vote? Or more likely—did he go back to Lebanon? It sure looks like he's gone, but Potocki checks seven years' worth of voter registration just to be thorough and finds no Thomas Zacour of the correct age.

Colleen comes up to his cubicle again. "Anything?"

"Not yet."

"You'll find something." She wanders back to her own work-station.

He logs on to Westlaw and he's reading through Criminal Records. There is a John Zacour, thirty, who robbed a few grocery stores in Connecticut. He traces this guy back a bit. Nah. Born in the country. Registered to vote.

He stops to consider. Who's to say anything in the guy's folder at the Family Fertility Clinic is the truth?

Back to Lexis and the public records wing of the engine. He remembers a menu item he saw there once and locates it again—the Watch/Risk List. He types in Thomas Zacour. The name comes up. Listed in early 2002, New York. No evidence of crime or wrongdoing, just a name on a list. He messes for a while longer. Things were crazy in 2001 and right after. But what does it all mean that, after his efforts, he can't trace the guy beyond that? A young Middle Eastern man with a New York apartment in the East Village on the watch list. Big news. That's it.

COLLEEN SITS IN HER CUBICLE during some of this, typing, thinking. In the victim's apartment, there was a lot of music—CDs, and a good number of them were Middle Eastern. The police haven't confiscated any of the CDs. She could go back up to the apartment. Or . . . she taps her foot restlessly . . . she could go out and find an open music store and look through the racks. Did Maggie Brown know the donor was a musician?

Colleen calls out, "Taking a break." After she gets a grunt of acknowledgment from Potocki, she drives into Shadyside because that gives her the funky record store above Pamela's, home of world-famous hotcakes. The guy behind the register upstairs in the music store knows every CD ever made. The second option is no longer—the large Borders, now defunct, where nobody knew anything but there were plenty of plastic cases to examine. Colleen heard some Middle Eastern jazz in her car once and liked it. Worst-case scenario, she'll have some new music.

The slender, goateed man at the store lifts himself from the low hassock where he sits reading a trade paper. "Traditional? Contemporary?"

"New stuff." What she saw in Maggie's apartment seemed contemporary.

"Play you some," he offers. And soon he does. "This the kind of thing you're looking for?"

It is. "Could I see the sleeve?"

He hands it over, saying, "The group is made up of a piano, oud, drums, and guitar. But sometimes the guitarist plays French horn."

The sounds are fresh, new—the whole influence of the Middle East in contemporary music is training American ears to hear something different.

Colleen studied Maggie Brown's paintings at the memorial. Maggie liked Middle Eastern looks. Her son is a beautiful example of the look. Now as she listens to the music on the store's system, she examines other CD sleeves that promise Middle Eastern sounds. She reads about duos, trios, quartets.

"What are you looking for exactly?"

"Not sure." She feels foolish, about to give up.

She almost misses it. A duo—piano and bass. She is about to put it aside when she notices the piano player's name. *Ziad Zacour.* She feels a huge stir of excitement. A tiny photo in the corner of the sleeve shows two men. One looks the right age to have been a student some eight years ago.

The man slides up from his hassock to ring her up, asking, "You don't want to listen first?"

"I think I'll just get it. You know this CD?"

"That one I don't know."

She has it opened and on her car stereo in minutes. Traffic is light. She is able to zoom to the office where Potocki is still working.

"Ziad Zacour," she tells him. "Let's try that name. See what you get. Duo with this other guy, Tom Tremont."

"Wow."

"Gut feeling." She shows him the sleeve of the CD. "Tremont looks sort of colonial."

Potocki sits up, starts typing. Colleen leans over and reads *Ziad Zacour piano Tom Tremont bass.* The CD comes up. But better yet, down the list of Google entries, an ad for a duo: "Parties, weddings, bar mitzvahs, reasonable rates." With photos and brief bios. *Tremont. Born in Connecticut. Attended CUNY. Ambition: Jazz musician.* Phone number for the duo. Email address. *Tremontt58420.* Yahoo! Might still be good.

Then the other, the one that thrills them. *Ziad Zacour.* "*Thomas.*" *Born in Beirut, Lebanon. Music student at CUNY. Piano. Ambition: Jazz musician.* Phone number. Email address. *ZTZACOURZT.* This one is EarthLink. Might still be good.

He is the one. A real heartthrob of a guy, too—deep, dark eyes you could drown in. Biological father, yes, yes, was her guess. Killer?

"You did it," Potocki exclaims, "you did it." He searches the directories for Ziad Zacour in New York. But he doesn't find him there. Not until he does a national search does he find a Ziad Thomas in Baltimore.

"That's it. I know it. I feel it." Colleen kisses him. "Let's call Boss and tell him we have a line on the supposed father. At least his last address in Baltimore."

They get hold of Christie who is just getting ready to make the trip back home.

"Wow," he says. "Both of you. Wonderful. Amazing work."

"We didn't try to call him. We didn't want to warn him."

"You did right."

MARINA IS STARING OUT the passenger window at the cars in the next lanes. "Pontiac," you said.

"Maybe Pontiac. He's a seven-year-old. I don't know." Christie wonders if he might be having an attack of some sort. He doesn't feel right. It isn't exactly dizziness. More like a lightness, a removedness.

"Lots of maroon cars . . ."

"You said it."

She makes a game to occupy herself as they negotiate the tunnel and get onto the major highway: to find maroon cars and study their drivers. Good, good, she's entertained.

This morning, she wanted to work, too, said she wanted to go back to canvassing the kid's old neighborhood. Christie was still deep in sleep and she woke him, whispering, "You need me for anything right now?"

He simply could not come awake.

She was worried he might be sick. She felt his forehead. "Just sleep, honey. I'm going out."

He groaned. "Where?"

"Just out."

He didn't care. He just wanted to bury himself back down under. He had dreams that were more like thoughts, glimpses, little commas. He was a boy, young, seven maybe, wandering streets, yards, playground, alone, no parents. Easy to see where that dream came from. Though indeed he'd once been seven. And he had had a mother, but felt alone.

Now, in the car, he rouses himself to be a companion. He told her when he got the phone call earlier, as they were climbing into his car, how Potocki and Colleen, working on Sunday, had found the next lead. He said, marveling, "Greer just went to a music store and found us a name."

"That's what I wanted to do!"

"What?"

"When I went out this morning. I walked up and down the streets, looking for a music store. Same idea Colleen had. A computer, a clerk who knew things and could also look up musicians by name."

He felt irritated that Marina so much wanted to do this work, his work. "You are a good detective," he said, knowing she craved the compliment.

"See, I mean I knew Tower Records was dead, closed, but I thought there'd be *something*. You know, there wasn't a music store that was open wherever I walked or I might have found your guy, the supposed father of the kid."

He told her that she could have, with a little luck and a headstrong will, been the one to find him. Or the next step in finding him.

Traffic getting out of the city was choked up. He wished he could climb back into that hotel bed and sleep again. Find that dream again. What was it trying to tell him?

"So there's somebody out there somewhere," she says now. "And I guess, in a way, we're lucky Maggie Brown didn't simply tell her son and everybody else his father was dead. It's like she wanted to keep the hope out there, in the mix."

Christie feels a wavering dizziness. He remembers the miniature dream, the thought, the comma.

He shakes it off. It was just a dream.

There is a misty rain on the road, the dusk is falling, and the glare from all sorts of lights hurts his eyes.

Marina runs a hand along his thigh. "Want me to drive for a while?"

"Yeah. I'm drowsy." He veers too much to the left. A passing car lays on the horn. "I'll look for a place to pull over. Keep talking to me."

And so she talks.

IN THE QUIET, SECRET, DARK cell of his room, Nadal counts his money.

He hears the sounds of the three Koreans coming and going, eating this and that. He can tell a little of what they're saying. "He's not here. I saw him go out." He's right because Shin repeats in English, "I saw him go out."

"Nate?" Gab-do calls. "Are you in there?"

"Shhh. Maybe he has a girl in there."

Gab-do laughs. He says something. Nadal guesses it means, "No. I don't think."

For a long time, Nadal lies still, afraid to move.

After a while he hears the others saying good-bye to Gab-do. Odd. They are almost never separate. But someone is still in the apartment—footsteps. Gab-do, he supposes.

Nadal still doesn't move.

Then he hears the tiny beeps of a phone being dialed.

Gab-do's voice is loud and clear. "Claire. Is this Claire? Hello. This Gab-do."

She says something because Gab-do replies, "Yes. Good to have holiday."

Again there is a silence while she apparently speaks.

"No. Better you come over here. Nobody here. I cook Korean for you." Gab-do pauses. "How quick? What time? I am here now. Good."

Pots and pans clatter. Gab-do's footsteps shuffle hurriedly. He could come out now, say he's been asleep. The more time he allows to go by, the more awkward it will be when he does his sleepy act. Yet he can't move, lies there as if dead, until a blessed thing happens, and he falls asleep for real.

When he awakens he can't tell how much time has elapsed, but there are two voices in the kitchen and also the smell of food. Rice and chicken? He begins to sit up but his creaky bed makes the slightest whisper and moan, so he lowers himself back down.

The sound of conversation comes through and he can hear and understand everything this time because Gab-do speaks English to the woman. "We think we will ask him to find other place. We have other friend who wants come to this apartment. Better with all Korean. He don't talk. He don't eat sometime. Very strange. Maybe not student."

"You mean you don't know?"

"We try to be nice. He very . . . I don't know."

"Weird?"

"Weird. Okay. Weird."

"Does he pay his rent?"

"Yes."

"Oh."

"But nobody feel okay, not relax, not . . . comfortable? Comfortable."

"You should ask him to leave then. I'm for cutting bait."

" 'Cutting bait?' I don't know what—"

"Oh, right. Fish or cut bait? It's an expression. It means like to just do the damned thing you came to do or change your mind and get out. It means make a decision without dawdling." She giggles. "Without waiting. Man, how does anybody ever learn English?"

"Not easy. Cutting bait? You think yes."

"Kick him out. You have to live."

"We try to be nice. We ask him out. Go to club."

"He sounds hopeless. Don't stress yourself. It's a small thing to change a lease."

"Don't have lease. Not for him. Extra room. Extra cash."

"Just tell him then."

So fuck them all. He planned to leave anyway. Now he will for sure. He hears the way things get quiet, hears kissing, then murmurs. Still he doesn't move. He hears the girl say, "I don't know. Three beds in the room. It feels icky."

"Icky?"

"Not right."

"Okay, okay, other room," Gab-do says.

That can only mean *his* room.

"I think okay this time." He can hear that Gab-do sounds uncertain. But footsteps approach and the door opens anyway. Nadal rolls over away from them, feigning deep unconscious sleep.

"Oh my God," she says.

"Close door. Hurry. Close door."

He listens to their sounds, their whispered entreaties and negotiations. Because he's not sure how to pull off his sleepy act, he lies there through Claire's departure and through dinner when the others return. His stomach growls, but he's missed meals before. He listens to the hushed conversation in Korean, trying to guess what they are saying about him.

9.

MONDAY

POTOCKI HAS IT TOGETHER. He's got a clean shirt at Colleen's place. Later he will pick up his son, Scott. They'll grill together in Colleen's yard, watch a flick, and then he'll take his son back to Judy. A nice, long Labor Day together. Like living together. They have it backward, he and Colleen. She's supposed to want marriage; he's supposed to be the edgy divorced guy not wanting to get stung again. But he loves marriage, no matter the troubles, the stresses; he sees mainly the warmth and reliability of it. He wants it again.

And today—because she feels good about finding Ziad Zacour, perhaps—she is all softness, warm and pliable, sweet with kisses. He doesn't want to get out of bed. Ever. "Too bad I have my son today," he jokes.

"Too bad," she sings.

CHRISTIE WAKES THAT MORNING FROM a dream so deep and dark, he again does not want to get out of bed. The dream was an old one, recurring, the one he had as a boy, though it has several variations.

This time someone whispers to Christie that his father is living down in the bad part of the city. This person, a stranger, tells him his father never really died, but only had people put out the word that he was dead. In the dream it turns out to be true; his father is alive, still living in the same town as Christie—Akron, Pittsburgh, wherever the dream maker sets the dream.

His father is very sick, looks to be on the point of death throughout the dream film, but does not die. He greets Christie hesitantly.

His father wanted to get away and be unknown. That becomes clear somehow, and Christie, understanding this, finds him anyway—in the dream, he finds him—and usually in spite of understanding that his father is trying to run, he asks him to come home for a day, for a meal, and his father grudgingly accepts. In last night's dream, as usual, the dinner didn't turn out well. Christie sat at a table knowing his father didn't really want to be there. They talked hopelessly, falsely, about another visit in the future—Christmas, birthday, something.

His mother told him when he was nine, or was it ten, a little more than two years after his father left, that his father had died in some other town. There was no funeral. She showed him no newspaper notice. No insurance checks ever arrived.

Had she wanted to free Christie of longing?

He climbs out of bed, heavy with the dream, unable to shake it.

He shaves, showers, sits down to breakfast. Marina is packing things for a picnic. They have to pick up his kids.

He thinks, *I'm a detective. Why did I not ever look?* He swallows a piece of toast, scratchy.

He almost laughs to think it. Is his father still alive, a phantom in a seedy part of some city? His mother passed on a long time ago, so he can't ask her.

"You could help a little," Marina says, frustrated, trying to lift a heavy cooler from chair to floor.

NADAL SLEEPS LATE and when he wakes he lies in bed for a long time. Then he walks to Squirrel Hill and past the Beacon Street house. There are no cars in the driveway. He goes up to the door, walks around the house. They are out. He can tell. It's a nice house, but those things don't matter. Blood matters more.

It's after noon. He wonders where they are.

He doesn't miss his car. He doesn't miss anything.

AT ELEVEN WHEN THEY GOT to the park, they found a picnic table that was unoccupied with an outdoor grill next to it. Marina brought fried chicken, potato salad, green salad, and drinks of various sorts. Jan Gabriel brought Fritos and dip, a couple of pies, the hot dogs and hamburgers to grill, buns, mustards and ketchups and onions. It was quite a classic picnic.

Christie liked to hear the women talking. About the play, about clothing, about teaching. He was aware that Jan's eye kept going to Matt, who held himself apart from the other kids.

Finally Christie's daughter, Julie, got Matt to play badminton. The boy played hard, almost angrily. He needed to win, and Julie, sensing it, backed off from trying herself and played without commitment.

Matt won the game.

Christie doesn't want his daughter to cave in like that. He plans to talk to her about it later, but at that moment, Christie flags Matt down. "Let's go look at the water. See the boats."

A whole fleet of rental boats bobs on the water. Christie points out the pontoons, one of which, at that very moment, Arthur is plunking down his Visa card to rent. In front of them, two young men wearing yellow vests and sporting bare feet, are towing in boats of various sorts and sending other ones out. The workers are good at gauging docking speed—they know right away when they have to reach out to pull a boat in the last couple of yards or slow it down.

"Make sure you wear your life vest," Christie says. "Very important."

Matt doesn't say anything.

Christie asks, "You understand about the life vest."

"Oh. Yeah."

Christie says, "Talk to me, Matt. Tell me what you're thinking."

"Nothing."

"I know you had some time with Meg Philips on Saturday. Did you like her?"

"Yeah."

"That's good. You seem angry today. I just wondered if there was something specific."

"No. Just everything."

"Everything is a good enough reason."

There is some noisy shouting from the workers to a motorboat that is coming in too fast. Christie shakes his head at the show-offs steering it. The motor is loud and the workers keep shouting, "Slow it down!"

The boaters, no doubt drunk, laugh as they bring the boat in too fast with an eighth of an inch to spare. Criminal material. Criminals in the making. Unfortunately, Matt seems to like their daredevil act.

"You like picnics?"

"Yeah."

"Boats—they can be beautiful, don't you think? Those guys were being jerks, huh?"

"Um-hum."

"Which pontoon do you like best?"

Matt points to a red pontoon nodding like a big-footed red frog. Marina and the kids and the Morrises all walk toward them.

"Just so you know. You can tell me anything. I'm totally in your corner."

"What do you mean?"

"Any questions you have, anything you want . . . if it's in my power to help, I will."

"Can you find out if that man that . . . did it . . . is really my father?"

Christie is caught off guard. He answers slowly. "That's something I hope to find out."

"If he isn't, can you find out who is?"

Christie feels as if he's on a boat, tipping. "I will try."

"I remember once my mother said he was a musician."

Now the kid tells him! Corroboration. Better late than never.

10.

TUESDAY

THE HORN TOOTS lightly once and Colleen is ready. She agrees with Christie that five a.m. is a good time to start a trip. They'll be there before ten in the morning, giving them a whole day to find this Ziad "Thomas" Zacour with time to get back home.

If they find him. If he's home.

She tosses her satchel into the backseat—requisite overnight kit—and takes her place in the passenger seat. Nice and early and they are on their way.

"Spent the day with Matt yesterday. He's a tough little bugger."

"Mind some music?" She holds out the CD.

"I mind it. I'm sorry. I can't think when there's music on."

"Oh." And no iPod to entertain herself. She digs in her bag. "Here's his picture. We printed it out from an ad for a music duo. It's a couple of years old. But he doesn't look like a nut."

Christie studies the photo as well as he can while driving. "He looks okay. Not that I'm banking on one photo to tell me. He looks . . . like Matt."

"Yeah. Good looking, both of them."

She twiddles her thumbs for a while, thinks about this and that. "Do *you* think they're the same guy? Zacour and the killer?"

"Don't think so but hopefully we will know more today."

"Right. I tried to come up with some wild scenarios about how he knew, how she knew, and all that. Didn't quite work."

They drive in silence for a while. "Take a nap if you want," he says.

She reclines her seat and tries. Light glances off her closed eyelids, giving her something close to a hallucinatory light show. She throws an arm over her eyes to block the light. What she'd really like is to stop for a nice big breakfast, because that's how she thinks when she travels. She digs in her bag for a cereal bar, a poor substitute for pancakes and sausages. She's brought two bars. "Want one?"

"Yes. Thanks."

"How are you feeling lately? Do you get your checkups?"

"I'm doing well. They think I'm a miracle."

"We all think that."

"Don't flatter me, I hate it."

She feels herself flush. She puts her seat back up. "I wasn't trying to flatter. You have that look again, jumping over mountains, and I'm trying to understand it."

He waves her aside. "Something's going on with me."

Are they over it, their attraction to each other? She thinks they are. She hopes so. But she's always one for diving right in. "Are you and Marina okay?"

He's surprised and then not surprised. "We're good. Very good. She's all up and excited about work. She has enough stuff right now, the play and the teaching. It's filling up her life and it makes me see she has to have a lot of work to do in addition to taking care of the kids and indulging me. She's smart. She needs to have challenges."

"Smart people do."

"Right. But the teaching is time limited, so when it's over, she might be pretty down."

"You know what the folks at AA would say? That you're living the future problems instead of staying in the moment. You need to do the one-day-at-a-time number."

Christie laughs. "You always have advice."

"I thought that was good advice."

"It is."

"So there. Take it, Boss."

How things change. She was in love with him and now she isn't but she still sort of *is* in a muted way, as if there is always that old dream under the surface.

THE OFFICE MARINA USES is small, practically two by four but with a glorious window, a great view of the lawns and university buildings. And because she has time and privacy in this small place, she types in inquiries again about the police academy. No sense bothering Richard with it before she's sure. He will just say no, no, too dangerous. But she can't go on envying his work and the weekend has whetted her appetite again. She'd be good at it, and it isn't as if she is going to have one role after another. And the two things might not be mutually exclusive.

She brings up the site.

Just reading it gives her butterflies. She would have to drive north for the academy. But it's doable. She fits the requirements: US citizen at least eighteen years old, high school diploma, able to pass a physical exam, valid Pennsylvania driver's license, pass a personality test (ha!), pay a fifty-dollar fee.

Okay, that's the easy part. A bit harder is coming up with tuition, but she can use what she makes from teaching plus a bit more. So the big commitment is $3,123 and twenty-three weeks of her time, from eight in the morning till five thirty in the afternoon. Richard would have to make adjustments. Meals on the table—not quite as easy, but she's organized, so she can probably do it.

She can start in January or July, full-time training.

Her secret.

"UPSCALE BUILDING," COLLEEN SAYS, toeing the hall carpet in front of Zacour's door. They had to slip into the building behind a resident, but it worked fine. They took the stairs to the third floor like old regulars.

Christie nods, knocks on the door. There are sounds of someone inside moving toward the door. Finally the door opens to a man in a T-shirt and pajama pants and bare feet. He is running a hand through his hair.

Christie shows his ID. "Police. May we come in?"

The man looks as if he will cry. "My visa is good. I have papers."

"This isn't about the visa."

"Oh? Not the visa? What? Is Kate okay?" He looks around them to the hallway.

"Not about Kate," Christie says. "We're from Pittsburgh."

"Pittsburgh."

"Sorry to wake you."

"No, no, I was working." He indicates a table stacked with books and papers. A thin thread of steam rises from a coffee cup there.

"We need to ask you some questions. Please, can we all sit down?"

"Yes, I'm sorry, yes. Here." He indicates a seriously nice living room, very adult, chairs and sofas with throws, beautiful reading lamps, small objets d'art on the tables.

Colleen cannot deny it—there is a pleasure in being around a beautiful man. This one is very beautiful. This one is . . . Omar Sharif in a bathroom. She watches him move to sit across from them as she and Christie take seats on the sofa.

"Would you like—?"

"Please don't trouble yourself. This is about Maggie Brown."

He shakes his head slightly, frowns, waits.

"Do you know Margaret Brown?"

"I can't think—student? Colleague? The name doesn't come to me."

"I see. What kind of car do you drive?"

"A Nissan."

"Year? Color?

"White. A 2000."

"You live with someone here—there was another name on the mailbox."

"My fiancée? Kate?"

"Kate McCauley?"

"Yes. Is she okay?"

"So far as I know she is fine. She works?"

"She's a doctor."

"She's at work now?"

"Yes."

"What kind of car does she drive?"

"A Nissan, but newer, 2007."

"Color?"

"Silver."

"We're homicide detectives."

He freezes.

"We need to ask you where you were weekend before last, Saturday and Sunday of ten days ago. Can you tell us where you were?"

"Saturday? Last Saturday? Here in the daytime. Working . . . on my dissertation." He points to the books and papers. "Are you—is this about an alibi for me?"

"We need to know your movements. Take your time."

Christie lets him worry out the whole day, though daytime isn't much an issue from the police point of view; Saturday night and Sunday morning are.

"My God. Oh. Let me think. Supper here with Kate. At night, a club. We played until maybe two. That's the usual."

"Then what?"

"Came home."

"Anybody see you?"

"Kate."

"Anybody else?"

"I don't know—it was late. You're scaring me. Did someone accuse me of something?"

"Just think of this as clearing the decks. Sunday morning?"

"Slept until maybe ten. Then we went out to brunch."

"You went out?"

"Yes. To brunch. A place we like. Please tell me what this is about."

"People saw you at brunch?"

"Yes."

"Good. Can you write down the name of the place?"

Colleen can see the poor man's hand shaking as he writes.

"This isn't about my visa?"

"I could care beans about your visa. If this alibi checks out, you're clear."

Ziad shakes his head. "Margaret Brown, you said. Who is she?"

"A woman who was killed last Saturday. Murdered."

He catches his breath. "And you think I did this?"

"We have to do a few things to clear you in the case. Are you willing to give us a DNA sample? It's easy. Just a swab."

Zacour shrugs. "Yes. But I don't even know who she is."

"We think she's the mother of your son."

He shakes his head. "I don't . . . what are you saying?" Realization begins to dawn.

"Did you ever hear of the Family Fertility Clinic on Bleecker Street, New York?"

"Yes. I went there three times. When I needed money."

174

"We think you have a son. We're going to check to confirm it. This is a complicated situation. The mother of the boy has been murdered. The boy is being adopted. They've engaged an attorney. What they're going to want to know—the courts, the lawyer, soon as we clear you of any suspicion and should you turn out to be the father—is whether you have any medical conditions they should know about that would affect your son. And second, whether you will sign a paper giving up any claim to the boy. They want to make sure everything is legally smooth."

"I never knew."

"Right."

"I was a student. I needed money. I'm . . . I'm sorry now that I did it, now that—"

"Well, it made a woman happy. She wanted a child. Nobody could have guessed she'd be killed."

"She has a husband?"

"No husband."

"I see." Ziad casts his eyes down and pushes one fist into the other. "And you have papers to sign?"

"I don't have them. If I make a phone call, they'll be sent to you tomorrow."

"There are people who will take care of this boy?"

"Yes. People who want to adopt."

"And they're . . . all right?"

Christie says, "I would call them upstanding, yes."

"Medical—there is nothing bad except the bad arteries that all people from my country have. High cholesterol, I mean. Otherwise, I'm healthy."

There is a long silence.

"What are you writing?" Christie asks, indicating the table full of books.

"A dissertation."

"What subject?"

"Music. Composition. Disharmony and harmony."

"And you have a fiancée? A medical doctor?"

"Yes. We're getting married . . . when I finish—" He points to the table.

Colleen pulls out a kit and takes the swab quickly from the open mouth of the nice musician named Zacour. He's a fellow young in spirit, yes, maybe perpetually young, which fits with his chosen field. No track marks on his arms. Embarrassed, nervous. He wears it all well.

"THE LIBRARY," NADAL told his mother. "Right in front. I'll be working. I'll cut out."

"Will that be all right?"

"Oh, yeah, yeah."

Today he doesn't really have work. He only wants to keep his mother away from his roommates. "Noon," he told her. "You remember where the library is? No place to park usually so I'll be waiting for you."

And he's as good as his word. He asks her to go around to the passenger seat and he gets behind the wheel. Her car is a red VW Bug, small and peppy, even though it's old.

"Don't I get to see your apartment?"

"Not today. I'm going to have to get back."

"We should go have lunch together."

"I don't think I have— Never mind. All right. Let's." He drives to Atwood Street and, miracle of miracles, finds a parking meter. He takes her into the dark restaurant with the painted sign out front. Mexican food. She'll like that. Though she'll get plenty of it in Florida.

"Two weeks," she says, looking around the place as if her vacation has already begun. "I can't believe I'm doing this."

"It's okay. People take vacations. Enjoy."

She studies him for a while. The restaurant is a noisy one, making talk an effort. She keeps asking him how he is. He keeps smiling and telling her he is okay. The food comes and he pulls out his wallet.

"I wanted to treat *you*, Dal."

"My treat, Mama."

Then he feels both impatient and sad as he drives her to the airport where he says good-bye at the curb. "You have anybody taking care of the house?"

"No. I don't want to bother anyone. I hope it rains though. For the garden."

"I'll check on the place. Water your garden."

"Oh. Oh, that's wonderful. Thanks."

"Did you lock the top lock?"

"Yes."

"Better give me that key. I don't have that one."

THE WHOLE DAY IS ABOUT NAMES, LISTS. "Attention please. My name is Ms. Conti." She points to a list on the board. It says: *1. Interview. 2. Schedules. 3. Reading. 4. Recess.*

All around the room are lists. Tons of lists. How to behave. Names of animals. Names of people in the class.

"We'll go alphabetically today just to make remembering names easier. Other days we won't do things alphabetically." She points to the girl in the first seat. "Come up."

The girl is staring openly at Matt.

"Tell us your name."

"Sharon Abo."

A, B. That's why she's first.

"Tell us something about yourself."

"I have a little sister."

"Okay. How old?"

"Two months."

"So still pretty new to the family. Anybody in between?"

"No."

"Thanks. Sharon Abo, everybody. Next. Matt Brown."

"Can I wait?"

She considers it. "Okay." And the class proceeds.

Anita Buhpalla says, "My father is a lawyer."

Lee Chang says, "I play baseball in a league."

Johan Friedman is a big kid who gave Matt a cross look when he first sat down. Johan says he spent the summer in Germany, where his father had a research project.

"Germany!" Ms. Conti says. "That sounds exciting."

She asks Matt if he feels ready. He goes up to the front of the room. "Matthew Brown," he says.

"And tell us something about you."

He can't think of anything to say. The other kids get restless.

"Like where did you go last summer?"

She puts her fingers to her lips. "Can you tell us just anything?"

"I'm in a play."

"Really? What play?"

"*A Midsummer Night's Dream* by Shakespeare."

"Oh, that's a good one. Who's doing it?"

"It's at Pitt."

"Terrific. I'm definitely going to come see you in it. Maybe we can all go."

The rest of the day isn't so bad, not quite a nightmare, and then it's over. Arthur and Jan pick him up in the afternoon. Arthur says, "One down. Your first day."

He still wants his old school. Why does everything have to be different?

The new parents smile at him with eyebrows going up, up. "I really want to know everything you did," Jan says quietly.

Arthur nods. "Anything you can tell us. We're going out to dinner so we'll have time to talk."

"I introduced myself. I did best in the reading."

"What do you mean, 'best'?"

"I knew the most words."

"Did it feel good?"

"Yeah." He doesn't know what else to tell them. At recess he was afraid of Johan but then later Johan was his math partner and he wasn't mean.

He eats a burrito and it's okay, spicy, something Jade would like.

Then they go to the first rehearsal.

Arthur comes into the auditorium to wait for him because he's only allowed to stay for the first part. He knows people are looking at him. The one named Beattie comes up to him, smiling broadly. "Hello, again."

"Hi."

"What we do here is we sit in a circle," Beattie says, "and read the play. And learn everybody's name."

More names. He feels panic rising. He can't remember his old life. He can't remember his mother's face.

HE SITS IN THE LIBRARY, reading the *Pitt News*, an old one in his backpack with his ad in it. He turns a page and freezes. Why did he not look at the whole paper before? One picture of a beautiful woman is labeled *Marina Benedict*. She's an actress in a play. But the other picture next to it is labeled *Janet Gabriel*. The caption says she's the director. He studies her face. Then he reads every single word she said to the interviewer about the Shakespeare play she is directing. The student journalist has focused on the long hours it takes to do a play. First the mind work of preparation, then weeks of blocking, then revised blocking, then work-throughs of scenes, then the polishing of scenes. At the end there are more run-throughs for getting the flow of the play. She rehearses four hours a night, six days a week.

How can she take care of his son?

When he leaves the library that night, he passes the theatre where the rehearsals take place. It's right on the way to his apartment and it's a public building. People are coming and going from it. A couple kids go in with drinks. Some come outside to smoke. An old woman comes out carrying a shopping bag.

And then the thing happens that proves fate is on his side. A man comes out with a boy. And Nadal, afraid to look closely, turns and hurries up the steps that lead to the patio above the theatre level. He sits on a bench and opens his backpack, practically putting it in front of his face as he does, even though he's up a level, not particularly in the line of vision of anyone walking below. Yes. It's his son. It's Matthew. He can see him getting into that black car.

His mouth goes dry. He licks his lips. Waits.

They drive away.

11.

WEDNESDAY

LATER TODAY ZIAD WILL have to go in to the office to teach his piano students. He's hardly moved away from the table and his work since the detectives were there; he didn't even go for a run yesterday. Or buy food. The refrigerator sat almost empty, cooling a quarter bottle of milk, some soda, a few limp vegetables, and an old chunk of cheese until last night when Kate went out and filled it up again.

"What's the matter with you?" she asked as she unpacked the groceries.

He's never kept a secret from Kate before. He couldn't tell her. How could he tell her?

Outside the window of this place, Kate's condo, is a city garden, crowded with plants, the blooms going or gone. The gardeners keep after it daily, but sometimes he catches that moment when the bloom dies—like a head tilted to the side.

This morning he carries his coffee outside to the deck. The sun is not visible today. The air is moist. Even though his feet are cold from the cement deck, he doesn't want to go back inside.

He will defend in November. They will marry in December. She's pregnant, three months, but she doesn't want to deal with a wedding until the dissertation is done.

The cold of the cement deck—funny to call it a deck—seeps through to his bare feet. He steps back in, goes into the bedroom, and, forcing himself, puts on socks and shoes and gets the set of house keys he takes when he goes running. It's a gray day with clouds moving in toward his neighborhood. Pushing himself, he takes the stairs, passes his mailbox, but then goes back to it, checking. No, of course, nothing. Not yet. What did he expect? It will take time. It will come when he's not watching. Or it will be a special FedEx package. He puts everything back into the box and heads out.

As he runs, he gives in to the comforts of routine: slow speed until he gets to the fountain that marks ten minutes of running and the spray hits him in the face, on the shoulder, invigorating him. He picks up speed, circles the fountain twice and moves on to the running path. Ten minutes on the circular path and back to the fountain. He'll do two more laps on the path and then the ten minutes back home.

During the first lap he thinks about how and when to tell Kate about the form he will soon sign, about his history. He imagines her listening, speaking in that logical way she has—kindly—about the emotional upheaval it must cost him. By the second lap, she has become cold and frosty, disappointed in him. She says terrible things.

He thinks perhaps he can't tell her after all. How can he undo the miracle of her loving him? The image that will remain with him forever is the night he was playing music and she sat in the club with friends. She had such a confident manner, he assumed she must be rich and privileged. He was dead wrong. She'd come up from poverty.

He runs and runs, doing a third lap, trying to put the whole sad circumstance out of his mind. Just tire the body, he tells himself, but, starting on a fourth lap, the thoughts creep back, images of Kate, shocked at first, then unable to forgive him.

By the time he reaches the fountain, he is soaked with sweat and wrung out emotionally.

Back around the fountain, slowly this time. He lets some of the spray hit him. And then he canters home slowly, thinking how strange it is, the way people change. He needed money eight years ago. He listened to a friend. He wishes he'd washed dishes, dropped out of school.

He picks up the mail, reads the paper, eats breakfast, showers, and dons clean, decent clothes.

He sits down at his computer. He must work. He must.

But his email is up on the screen and he sees immediately that there is a message from an unfamiliar person. It's flagged red—important, urgent.

Mr. Zacour. I represent Arthur Morris and Janet Gabriel. The following is a formality. You have already terminated parental rights at the Family Fertility Clinic. However, should it turn out as we expect, you will be shown to be the biological father of Matthew Brown. The prospective adoptive parents as well as the judge in the case wish to have your signature on a TPR so that they can proceed swiftly through the adoption process. In the interest of celerity, I am taking the liberty of attaching the TPR by jpeg. Let me know that you have received it. Are you able to print and sign, then scan and send it back and follow by sending the hard copy? In the meantime, I will start the other paperwork on my end.

Jeremy R. Blackman, Attorney at Law

He rereads the message several times. That simple? Print out, sign, scan, and send back.

He clicks out of his email and into his dissertation—which includes both a symphony he has written and an exploration of the balances between harmonic and nonharmonic elements from the composer's standpoint.

The hard part for him is not the composing, it's the talking about it, the qualifications, the analysis, the saying exactly what he means and not something else. The dissertation is the last of several difficult gates: the Peabody audition—terrifying enough. The prelims, the orals, and now just this monster project to finish. And then, if God wills it: employment, marriage, happiness, time to play music, a healthy baby with Kate, a life, a future.

AT A BIT AFTER LUNCHTIME on Wednesday, the cheerful woman comes into the computer lab, waves at Nadal, and takes a station. He watches her, flushed to think she's interested in him. She is typing fast, looking sure of herself.

When she prints out, he figures out who she is by studying the log. Her username is ALA21. A few more keystrokes and he learns that she is Angela Anderson. He delays taking her printout to the table—girding his courage. She stands patiently, hopeful looking, waiting for her anthro homework. Finally he snatches up the papers and goes to her. "How's it going?"

"Very well. Thanks."

"You're Angela?"

"Yes. Oh, I see. You have my name there on my paper."

He hands over the papers with the pink ID page on top. She smiles at him. "Thanks. And you know, I've been studying up in the restaurant in Posvar—your suggestion. It's good. Just enough people moving around to keep me awake, but nothing too intrusive."

"So I helped."

"Oh, yes, you did."

"When will you be up there? I could take a break, come up, and buy you a coffee."

"Oh . . . well . . . I'm going up there now. But if you're up there, let me treat you instead. You got me through the first day. When do you have a break?"

"In about an hour. Will you still be there?"

"Yes. I expect to be. And if for some reason I leave before your break, I'll treat you another time."

Breaks come only every two hours and are only ten minutes—and he's just had a break. He fiddles at his computer, trying to do the homework for tomorrow night's class. The reading is boring. He won't stick with it anyway. With luck, he'll be gone.

"Did something go wrong with my paper?" a man asks. "I put it through a good fifteen minutes ago."

So, all right, he's late, he's late. He grabs up the new pages, alphabetizing by username as he walks to the shelving table. What he guesses are the angry man's pages are fourth, but he tucks them back at the end so they will be the last he gets to.

Students flock around like hungry hens at the feed.

Suddenly it's as if he has cornmeal in his hands; he's a boy in Puerto Rico, barefoot, on a small farm, his mother pushing him to feed the chickens, pick up the eggs. The hot sting in the air. Humidity and earth and shit, waste from all creatures.

When the distribution of pages is done, he tells the other worker, a young woman who is at one of the lab computers troubleshooting a problem of some sort, that he is taking a break. He grabs his backpack and leaves.

Yes, Angela is still there at the café, studying with just a bottle of water in front of her. *Angela*. He likes her name.

"Hello, there," she says, looking up from her books. "I realize I never got your name."

"Nate."

"Nate? Nathaniel?"

He shrugs an assent.

"My treat. What do you want? Espresso? Latte?"

"Plain coffee, black."

"Okay." She gets up to get it. Very neat hair, very neat clothing. Takes care of herself.

He watches her order, pay, and carry back a latte and a plain coffee. She places both carefully on the table and slides into her chair, managing to return change to her wallet in her open handbag. "There," she says. She sips her latte. "Lovely. I'm hooked. You're sure plain coffee was what you wanted?"

"Yes."

"Well it's a small thank-you for that first day. When I think how nervous I was! I still am, sort of, but things change so much in a single week. It's amazing. I think I'm going to be able to do this school thing. I love it."

He can't think of anything to say but "Good."

"Your classes? Going well?"

"Excellent."

"So you balance school and work . . . very impressive. You must be busy all the time."

He nods slightly.

"Do you have a long commute?"

"I live in the suburbs."

"Oh, like me. Which?"

He picks a direction. "North."

"Ah. And you have a girlfriend, I'll bet."

"Not at the moment. I'm available."

"Best to take your time."

"And," he blurts, "I have a son. I take care of my son."

"Oh. Just by yourself?" She sips her latte.

"Yes. It's a lot of work, but worth it. He's my pal."

"Of course. Fathers and sons. It's enviable, that bond."

"I can manage to go to a movie. If you'd like to go to . . . a movie." Before he finishes saying it, he's aware she's stopped moving. "My mother can watch him."

"That's very kind. I appreciate it. But I don't think it's a great idea. For your sake, for one thing."

"My sake?"

"You need to be with people your age. I believe that. I have a son who's a freshman—at another school, he's at Dartmouth, thank God, and I don't have to run into him crossing the lawn, when I'm looking panicked about this or that—but even in a couple of years I wouldn't want him to spend time with someone older. I want him to be with people his age."

"I'm not that young."

"Still."

"My son is eight."

"I see. I'm sorry if you took something I said wrong. I'm very appreciative of you and your skills and your complex situation, the way you handle it all."

It wasn't a marriage proposal. It was just a movie. She must think an awful lot of herself. "I ought to get back," he says, standing.

"Please don't be angry. It's my fault. I come across as overly friendly—I know that about myself."

"Yeah, well, you seemed interested."

She's biting her lip; she doesn't look so attractive now. "I have an awfully full life. I'm seeing a man I like."

That classic thing they say. The dust off. The brush-off. Whatever the hell it's called.

He doesn't look back. He just walks away.

He doesn't go back to the lab either, but finds himself outdoors, heading to one of the benches to open his textbook and his laptop and to try to get hold of his class assignment.

He's sitting with his head in his hands when his phone rings. It has to be his mother, the only person in the world who has his number. He lets it go to voice mail.

It's only a few hours until he can watch the theatre to see if his son is there again.

187

COLLEEN HAS SPENT the afternoon in the Strip District, following up on a tip about a stabbing there three months ago.

Her mind is much more on the visit she made yesterday with Christie to Baltimore.

"What did you think of him?" Christie asked as soon as they left Zacour.

"He's lovely."

"Funny word, but yeah, he is." They started toward the hospital to find Kate McCauley, but they decided to spare Zacour, if possible, the embarrassment of having his partner questioned at her place of work. So instead they went to the restaurant where he said he'd had brunch.

It was easy. The manager found Zacour's charge slip from that day and he also remembered him.

They got into Christie's car and started back to Pittsburgh. "Talk to me. More of your impressions."

"About Zacour?"

"Yeah."

"Well, he's a musician. An artist. Lots of feeling. He believes in feeling. He lives by feeling. He's sweet-natured."

"You liked him."

"You didn't? I thought you did."

"It's just that he threw me for a loop."

Colleen knew why. She understood Christie. They both saw the same thing: Zacour was the right father for Matt—but it was too late to try to persuade him. The machinery was already in motion for the other folks, Jan and Arthur.

Now Colleen hurries back to Headquarters and to Christie's office. She makes her report of zero progress on the Strip District stabbing. "And what's with the Zacour situation?" she asks almost breathlessly.

"Jan and Arthur contacted their lawyer right away. I mean right away. He got out an email to the guy. They want to expedite."

"Email?"

"In lieu of fax. A form. Termination of Parental Rights. It should be all done in matter of hours. A week before we even have the definitive DNA."

"But we know. The boy *looks like* Zacour."

"He sure does."

"Boss. I know what you're thinking. You got an idea yesterday. I got the same idea. But you can't control everything."

"I don't want to control everything."

She smiles. "Okay then, let it go. Don't you think?"

"Sure. Of course I think that."

CHRISTIE HAS HEARD the criticism about playing God before. All right, all right. He has to let it go.

There is nothing wrong with Jan and Arthur. They're great. Zacour just seemed . . . right.

His heart pings in his chest—little twinging pains that remind him of how closely the body listens to the mind.

In spite of his promises to himself, an hour later he gets into his car, telling himself he must check on the Philips kids again now that school has started. Are Shadyside Academy and CAPA working out? Is Alison Philips home at all?

It's Laurie who answers the door again. She seems less frightened than before.

"I came to see how school is working out."

"It's okay. Kind of like last year for me. The same."

"My teacher is better this year," Susannah says. She has a tumble of golden brown curls that he loves to look at.

"And your stepmother is where?"

"Working. At Peanutz." Laurie gives the name her signature comic sound.

"Does she get home soon?"

"She works through dinner. They feed her."

"What will you have for dinner then?"

"I think meatballs and pasta. Meg is getting good at that."

"I'll bet. What did she say about the kid she babysat last weekend?"

"Oh, she liked him."

Just then the door opens and Meg herself comes in, bustling, calling out, "Change your clothes. Tell me what you—" Then she sees Christie. "Oh. Oh, hi. Is everything all right?"

"Yep."

"Matt is all right?"

"This is just a visit. To see how you are."

"We're pretty good. Alison is working," she hurries to say.

He wishes he'd thought to take them along to Lake Arthur last Monday. He feels sure they never get to do anything like that. He'll have to come up with something else for them. Something. "How do you think the job with Matt is going to work out?"

"We got along," Meg says.

"Will you be working with him again?"

"Actually, yes. Saturday. After the . . . cremation. Mr. Morris wants to pick me up. I said yes. The idea is that I talk to Matt."

"Mr. Morris must trust you."

"I guess." Meg smiles, her hopeful look.

When Christie leaves the Philips kids, he goes to Peanutz. Alison is working. She looks both little-girlish—something about the way she's pinned her hair back—and old, too, tired out.

"How's it going?"

She makes a face. "This is my life."

He sits in his car for a long time. He's made mistakes. He's moved too fast and not been vigilant enough.

He sits back in the car and closes his eyes. And thinks about things. He goes back to the office and calls Potocki to him. "I'm leaning on you a lot. I know. Nobody beats you at the computer stuff."

"I'm okay. I've made contact with folks in Ohio and West Virginia to help with the DMV searches. This guy . . . we don't have anything much. I'll keep at it though."

"I know you will. Close the door."

Potocki closes the door.

"I *want* you to keep at it. But when it breaks, if it breaks, when you have time, I want you to do something personal for me and to keep it confidential. Can you do that?"

"Yes."

"Well. Sit. This is a bit odd. Would you do a comprehensive search for Richard Christie—" Potocki almost says, "You?" Christie hurries to say, "It was my father's name. We lived in Akron many years ago. I don't know where he went. My mother told me he died. I realize I never saw anything—obituary, place of the burial. I've been thinking about it lately. I want some details. When you have time. Not while you're searching for Maggie Brown's killer. I don't know anybody who can do it as well as you. Would you do that for me?"

"Yes."

"John . . . ?"

"I'm not a talker."

Christie thanks him and lets him go.

NADAL CHOOSES A different place, across the street from the theatre, at the tables in the plaza where he buys a bagel sandwich and sits with his book open. The evening gets cooler. He doesn't have a jacket. He sees his son go in with a woman. Some people want the chairs from his table to add to another table.

"Take them," he says angrily. He buys a cup of bad coffee, so he can keep sitting there. He tries to work out how he can do what he needs to do. At one point, his son comes out of the big doors walking with two college-age students. The students talk to each other and also to his son—one of them puts a hand on the boy's head. He watches them cross the street. They go into the 7-Eleven. After a while they come out, carrying drinks and bags of something. Food, candy? He puts his book in front of his face and waits. At eight thirty the black Volvo parks outside the theatre building, with emergency blinkers on. The man goes into the building and comes back out with his son. So. That's the pattern.

12.

THURSDAY

NADAL'S CLASS, which he is not prepared for, starts at five forty-five. That's done, that's dead, he's not going to go; he has more important things to do. It's five thirty. He chooses a different table, from which, unfortunately, the view isn't as good because of heavy foot traffic. Still, he pretends to work, opens his backpack, takes out his laptop. Cash. He keeps all of it with him now. He's broken five of the big bills down to twenties and tens. He's ready. In case.

He is getting glowering looks for having commandeered a whole table to himself. He glowers, too, not wanting anyone to take a seat and block his already limited view. The other tables are full. He's not moving.

The Volvo has pulled up while people were passing in front of him. The woman gets out of the car first and goes around to the back door for the child. There are moments of talk, kissing between the adults, before the car pulls away.

The woman laughs at something and takes the boy's hand. A college-age person comes up to them. All of them talk together and then they walk toward the theatre, stop, talk some more, and reverse their steps. They cross the street and go into the 7-Eleven. After a few minutes they come out, holding candy, drinks.

His phone rings, and he picks up because it's so loud.

"Didn't you get my voice message?" she asks softly.

"I have class right now."

13.

FRIDAY

LEAVING FALK SCHOOL, Jan tells Matt, "Watch all this mud. What a mess!" But her voice is happy.

The backseat of the car is warm from the sun. Jan smiles at him and makes sure he gets his seat belt on before she gets into the front seat. After she buckles up, she reaches back and squeezes his leg. "Your teacher tells me you're doing well."

"School isn't hard yet."

"That's good. If you need more of a challenge, let us know."

"What will you do?"

"Get you more things to read. Talk to her about other assignments."

"Are we going home?"

"No. Next we go to my office. I'm having a session with one of the actors. She's panicking she can't do the role. Then we go to dinner. Then rehearsal."

"Why is the girl worried?"

"Thinks she doesn't have enough experience to get Shakespeare's language right."

"What will you do?"

"Help her, talk to her. For a little bit, an hour."

Soon he is up at Jan's office, reading one of the new books they've bought him. It's for ages eight to twelve and it's called *Powerless*. Arthur is in a corner, reading a manuscript bound in black, like a binder, except without rings—it's a dissertation. Matt can almost hear Jan working with the actress next door. He can hear her voice, then the actress's voice, though he can't hear what they are saying. It's called a coaching session. It means working one on one.

"She always finds time when someone is worried," Arthur says.

They're okay, Jan and Arthur.

He misses his mother. Sometimes when he turns a corner or drops something and hears her voice, it's as if she's right there, saying something she said to him. *Oh, Matt, pick that up.* Or, *Nothing for dinner in the house, not a thing.*

He dreamt about her once. He dreamt about that man, too, who says he's his father. In the dream, the man wasn't mean, just talking.

A funny sound surprises him. He stops reading and realizes it's the sound of snoring. Arthur has fallen asleep sitting on Jan's office couch, reading. At first he looked dead, but his head bobs. His chest goes up and down. Sleeping.

Matt reads.

Still sleeping.

His new laptop is at home, but Jan's computer is on. He'd rather mess around with that. He could play a game if he mutes the sound.

He goes to the computer.

Arthur doesn't move. He's out.

Ping goes the computer sound and a new message comes up on email.

It says: Forward: Matthew: TPR.

He doesn't know what *TPR* means. Maybe it means . . . he doesn't know.

Arthur twitches, snores. The dissertation falls to the floor. Arthur jumps in his sleep. Matt waits, pretending to look away from the computer out the window to the buildings across the way. He turns back. Arthur is still sleeping.

The message on the screen is about him. It's from the lawyer. He knows how to do email because he messed with his mother's. He clicks, reads. *Good news. I have heard from Matthew's father.*

His heart stops. *Matthew's father.* What does that mean? He keeps reading, stumbling only briefly, making out all the words. *I'm forwarding his note. See below. The TPR is attached.*

He reads what's below.

Dear Att. Blackman,

This situation has upset me greatly, but I realize I must give up my parental rights to Matthew. I was a very young man then and a good deal has happened to me since. I have signed the form for Termination of Parental Rights. I hope my son will be well and well cared for.

> *Yours sincerely,*
> *Ziad Zacour*

P.S. Please send any hard correspondence to my office address:

> *Ziad (Thomas) Zacour*
> *Peabody Institute*
> *Music A 120*
> *1 East Mount Vernon Place*
> *Baltimore, MD 21202*

He looks to his new father. He can still hear his new mother's voice next door. He reads the letter again. And again. He stumbles only over *termination* and *parental*, but he gets them. The other words are easy.

The person who wrote the letter is his father. He has a name. He works in a music building, and he doesn't want him.

He stares at it for a long time. A funny name. Two Zs. Is this his father? *Ziad. Zacour.* Two Zs. Baltimore.

Is this the man who hurt his mother? Why is nobody capturing him, putting him in jail? Only writing letters back and forth?

Matt's heart is beating wildly. He wasn't supposed to look, but he's glad he did, even if they hate him for it.

Arthur is snoring regularly.

He wants to read it a fourth time, but he thinks he hears Jan coming. He closes the message. But Jan does not come and he hears her voice again at a distance. He opens the message again, about to click on the attachment. Jan's voice changes. Now it *is* coming from the hallway. He opens up Google. He asks Google for games. And when some games come up, he chooses the first one he sees: *Rescue the Little Hero.* It's loading, loading. Jan's voice is still in the hallway.

His father doesn't want him.

Matt is staring at the screen when Jan comes in. She takes in the scene, Matt playing, Arthur asleep. "I guess he's tired," she says with a laugh.

"I guess."

Arthur starts to move, coming awake.

"And you, Matt? What have you been up to?"

"Games."

"Aha. Games again."

Arthur comes awake. "Oh, man, I was out. Sorry."

"Let me shut down and then we can go to dinner."

Matt watches closely as she shuts down her computer without reading anything.

"Let's go eat."

At dinner he is supposed to order anything he wants even if it's eight packs of sugar. He feels like he's going to cry, but he doesn't know exactly what everything means. Why are Arthur and Jan being so nice to him? Why do they write notes about his father? A cushiony softness surrounds Matt, and he can't think.

He tries to smile so they don't know what he saw.

THAT SAME AFTERNOON, Potocki comes to Christie and says, "I have something—if you have a moment."

"I have a moment. You don't mean . . . ? Already?"

Potocki closes the door and sits. Somewhat reluctantly, leaning forward, concern on his face, he says, "I believe I've found him. All the particulars fit. I took the liberty of making a few calls. Look, Boss, I'm so sorry, but straight out, the news is bad. He's in a hospital—well, a nursing facility—but it's terminal care. They don't give him long; he's *non compos mentis* according to them. I don't know how hard they try to make him sentient, but he's on heavy drugs, so that could be part of it."

Christie tries to stay calm. His dead father not dead, only almost dead. Like the dream. He slumps in his seat. "I feel very foolish that I never checked before."

"I can't see any reason to. A boy believes his mother."

But I'm a detective, Christie thinks. I'm trained to be naturally suspicious. Potocki, he sees, isn't sure what to do. He sits patiently, waiting, looking occasionally at the papers in his hands.

"Where?"

"Ohio. Akron."

"I grew up in Akron and then Canton. He didn't go far away, did he? She might have known."

"Maybe. Maybe she didn't want to know."

"Do you have the name and address of the place?"

"Yes, Boss. Here's everything I have. I wrote it up."

Christie didn't have time to go, and yet, time was everything now. He took the sheets of paper from Potocki. Overnight? Friday to Saturday? "Anyone know you worked on this?"

"I did it mostly early this morning. I told no one. Absolutely no one."

Christie studies his face, hates and loves the compassion in it. And he believes him.

JAN ASKS MARINA to lead the warm-ups. She's worried for Matt. The cremation is tomorrow and he's very different tonight, more distracted than usual. Sad.

Marina runs them through vocal exercises and some physical exercises. She moves to the meditative part of the warm-ups and Jan participates, gets down on the floor, too, next to Matt.

Marina takes them through the details of practicing diaphragmatic breathing. Soon Jan and the students are working to relax a foot, ankle, leg, calf, thigh.

After about five minutes, they reach the part of the exercise where the mind is supposed to put the day's cares aside. Not so easy. Jan will try. They are breathing deeply—she is, anyway—and Marina instructs them to choose a place where they were happy. And then very slowly they are to let in smells, sights, sounds until they are— and without computers—*virtually there*. Jan eases herself into the exercise. A gate. She presses in a code. It creaks open. She unlatches the second gate—just a farmer's back gate latch—and starts down the steep dirt path, careful to get a decent purchase in her sandals. Another gate, the slow opening, the groaning sound it makes. Steps going downward, downward, brick, dirt, plants everywhere. Suddenly she is in the house without having walked to it. The house is full of everything—eight hedge clippers, fifty dinner plates, twenty-five jugs, books on every table and in every corner, and who could count things, really? It is also full of photographs, some of old folks, clearly ancestors, but mostly, mostly of children. Then memory makes its way in. Jan smells ripe bananas, oranges. "You can hear children's laughter here," Arthur says. "In every corner."

She climbs the steep stairs as she did the first time she visited the place. Oh, yes, one whole room with bassinets, cradles, toys— evidence of children and grandchildren and those cries of laughter and excitement that Arthur was able to hear.

They thought they would not have a child. And then they got Matt.

"You'll have to begin saying good-bye to this place," Marina tells them. "One last look. One last smell or sound. Enjoy it. Let yourself love it. Keep breathing. When you feel ready, open your eyes. Slowly. Slowly. And when you feel ready, move a little until your body wants to get up."

Jan wants to joke that her body creaks like the gate did. She sits up and beside her is Matt. His eyes are wide open. "Did you do the exercise?"

"It was okay."

Careful with him, careful. "Can you tell me where you went?"

"Jade's house."

"Good, good. We're due for a visit. I'll tell you where I went too, later."

"Where?"

"France. A place with a pool and a big house. We were just there, and it's beautiful. I want to take you."

He frowns.

"Think you'd like it?"

He wags his head.

She hates to turn from him but she has to work now, the actors are waiting for her. "We should talk about it."

She starts rehearsal because she has to. It's the fourth night of rehearsal. They're on their way.

CHRISTIE CHANGES INTO A comfortable polo shirt and jeans, and then puts his dopp kit and a change of shirt into an overnight bag. He's hardly eaten dinner, a cold chicken breast and some vegetables Marina left him. Can't eat. Can't think. He'll get something on the road, maybe, if it isn't too greasy. One way or another, his stomach is going to act up.

He doesn't know why he couldn't tell Marina the truth when he called her. "An old case," he said. And she didn't question him because she was busy starting warm-ups.

The "old case" was very old all right.

Oh, he has been full of error lately, he can feel it, and perhaps the stars have lined up in his disfavor—what they call sand in the works, or Mercury in retrograde. He jumped the gun with Jan and Arthur, wanting to give them what they wanted and at the same time to make Matt safe *right away*. He never counted on seeing, only days later, the person who should be persuaded—and, oh, Christie can be persuasive when he needs to be. He could have worked on Ziad Zacour. The right age, the right look, the right personality for Matt. Instead, he thought of the disapproval of Judge Gorcelik and toed the line like a miserable schoolboy.

He tried to tell himself all this week that Zacour was young, dreamy, irresponsible; but he knew perfectly well that young and dreamy and irresponsible often snapped to in a second and revealed a mature human being capable of love. Of . . . naturalness.

So here he is, lying to his wife and sneaking out of town. Even though it is too late, probably, to speak to his father, reportedly near death in a nursing facility. End-of-life care. And what can he get out of this visit except to look at someone he hardly remembers, a person absent in his presence those first seven years.

He checks the back door twice, the windows, the front door as he leaves. Then he goes back in and writes a note for Marina. *Shouldn't be too late home tomorrow. Supper with you. Love you.*

As he drives off, he wonders what he will say to the figure in the bed.

Photos, the few he has seen, showed a semi-ragged-looking

young man, not bad looking, medium height and weight, but in each photo not any hint of a square gaze into the camera, so somehow unseeable.

His plan is to find a motel that's not too horrible, rest up, watch some TV, maybe order in something to eat—maybe a drink, too, a tribute to the old man.

He'll try to sleep, get up early, and spend a good part of the day at the nursing home, looking, talking to the nurses, finding out if there are any other contacts, any other family hidden away, any other people in his father's life.

He'll talk to doctors if they come in on a Saturday and he'll find out if his father is getting good care.

He imagines the way they will question him with their eyes— why has he never come before? Is he here at the final hour, hoping for money?

He gets out of his neighborhood, Bloomfield, and to Fifth Avenue, and he passes the theatre where Marina is rehearsing. He looks toward the building, guilty about his lie. Out front are three kids smoking. They all smoke, Marina tells him. They feel invincible.

He keeps going through Oakland, catches the ramp to the parkway off Fifth Avenue and is soon on his way toward Ohio. Place of his birth. Place of his father's imminent death.

MATT IS ALLOWED TO STAY later tonight because it's Friday. A couple of the actors find a corner and do homework when they're not onstage, but not too many of them tonight. They clump together talking about where to go after rehearsal. From where he's sitting in the back of the auditorium, he notes that a lot of them slip outside the big doors to smoke when they're not needed.

Matt pretends to be reading, but he keeps thinking about the email, reciting it to himself.

Some of the actors whisper that they're going to the 7-Eleven, but they forget to ask him if he would like to go. After a few minutes, Matt moves from the back of the auditorium to the lobby. The floor there is made of large stones, kind of like in an old castle. He stands at the side door, his favorite door, because it's smaller than the others and nobody uses it, so it seems like a secret door. It leads out to the grass around the theatre building. The door, like the larger ones, is decorated with big black metal straps and bolts. He opens his secret door. Nothing happens, nobody stops him. Jan is inside working, so she won't know. He sees a few actors walking back and using the main entrance. They don't notice him at the side door. He exits the building. Students who have nothing to do with the play walk up and down the sidewalks ten, twenty feet away, busy talking to each other or talking on phones. He has money in his pocket, and he knows where to go.

It would take him two minutes to get to the 7-Eleven. Less. He stands for a while, deciding, then . . . three steps. Three more. Just do it. Who cares? Everybody lies.

He makes a dash to the sidewalk and then walks at a more regular pace to the store. Jan wouldn't let him buy spearmint leaves the other day. He thinks a swear word about her, then another.

They know who his father is and they won't tell him. Nobody tells him anything.

There are customers everywhere in the store, so that he can hardly squeeze in to the shelf that has the bags of candy. One big guy bumps him without even noticing.

"That's it, little fellow?" says the woman at the register. "No cigarettes?"

"No."

"Way to go," she cackles.

He's not sure if it's five minutes or more that he's been gone. Maybe less. He hurries out of the store with his candy in a thin plastic bag. He crosses the street and steps onto the lawn.

"Hi. Hi, Matt. I was looking for you, hoping to catch you."

It's the man who killed his mother. Matt's legs and arms freeze.

He should tell someone, he should run, but he can't make himself move. He tries to grab his phone, but switching his bag of candy from one hand to the other, he finds his hands don't work right, and a second later he drops the bag on the lawn.

The man picks it up.

"Woops. Here you go." But instead of handing it over, the man holds on to it. "I was looking for you. You know who I am?"

"You hurt my mom."

"No, I did not. She's okay. I admit I argued with her. Over you. I'm your father."

Matt tries to grab at his candy. "You hurt her. And then she died." He hates the way his voice sounds—frightened. But he can't think. He grabs again, but the man holds the bag of candy away.

The man shakes his head. "No. She didn't die. Look. If you run, you're never going to know what happened to her."

"I don't understand. You stabbed her."

"I did not. I argued with her. I wanted time with you. Then I left. Then I went back and I found her that way. I ran out again. I called an ambulance."

"Who stabbed her?"

"Somebody. I don't know. But we got her. We saved her."

"What do you mean?"

"We saved her."

"How?"

"Blood transfusions. I gave blood. Lots of my own blood. The doctors said my type was just right for her. It's B positive. She wants to see you."

"Why didn't somebody come for me?"

"I did. Just now. She wants me to take you to her. She's still going to be . . . pretty weak."

"Oh. Where is she?"

Someone on the street blares a horn at another driver. Matt jumps.

"Hospital. We could be there in no time."

It's okay. He has a cell phone with him. Besides he keeps studying the man's face and thinks they look alike. So maybe it's true. "Are you really my father?"

"Yes."

"Is your name Ziad?"

The man pauses. "Yes."

"You wrote that you didn't want me."

"Who told you that? I never did."

"But I saw it."

"I'm trying to think what letter it was." The man frowns. "I do want you. I want to take care of you. I want to give you things . . . and a good life. We should get going. This is my car." He points to a red VW Bug. It's not a maroon Pontiac, not what he thought. How many things has he been wrong about? He gets in. Front seat. No booster.

"Seat belt. You have to learn to obey. Rules are rules. Why are you out at night?"

"Rehearsing. Why does my mom like you now? She didn't like you."

The man looks out the side mirrors and the rearview mirror. "I know it seemed that way. Grown-ups fight and make up. You'll see." He pulls out and drives smoothly, then fast through traffic. "Just around this truck. Good to have a little car sometimes, huh? What's in your pocket? Another candy bar?"

"No."

"What?"

"Nothing."

"You can't do that. You have to answer me when I ask you something."

"Why?"

"Because I'm your father."

"It's just something that belongs to me."

"Then it belongs to both of us. Let me see."

Matt inches the phone out of his pocket.

"Aha. Now that is useful. Your mom definitely wants to hear from us. Hand it over."

"I want to talk."

"We'll see how she is. Give me the phone. That's a rule: I ask, you give."

He hands over the phone all the while thinking of ways he can grab it back. "You're passing the hospitals."

The man, his father, presses several numbers. Matt tries to hear ringing, but doesn't and yet the man starts talking. "Mrs. Brown," he says. "Okay. Tell her then we're on our way. It won't be long. Tell her to rest."

"Where are you going? Which hospital? She was in Shadyside."

"Not anymore."

They pass another hospital—Montefiore. Then yet another one. "You passed Magee."

"Smart kid. But they needed to put her someplace where she could rest. Someplace special."

"Why?"

"Blood supplies."

"But you said you—"

"She needed a lot of blood. Mine and much more. She's coming along, though. You want to play with my laptop?"

"Yeah."

"You like computers?"

"Yeah."

"Me too. It's what I do."

"Your job?"

"My job is computers."

Like father, like son. That's what his mother always said about people.

"Somebody is going to be looking for me."

"No. I wrote them a note, an email. I'm angry with them, you know. They tried to take you away. From me."

"They're supposed to adopt me."

"That's not going to happen. You need your real parents, right? That's the right thing. Play with the computer. Take a nap. We'll be there soon enough."

Matt does not take a nap. He pretends to. Mostly he tries to watch his father through almost closed eyes. He recognizes some of the road signs for a while and then he doesn't.

This is far, this is very far. This is not twenty minutes away. He's missing rehearsal. He doesn't know what to do, but he is sure he wants to see his mother again.

His phone rings and rings in the man's right jeans pocket.

"Aren't you going to answer?"

"No."

"It's my . . . my foster parents. They'll want to talk to me."

"I'm not going to let them at you. They don't have any real right to you. They snatched you away from me."

Matt wants to grab at the phone but he doesn't want to touch the man. After a while a different phone rings. The man curses and reaches for his left pocket, but seems to change his mind. He begins to hum. And they drive for a very long time. He hums and Matt watches him.

Much later they have taken an exit and slowed down enough that Matt could almost jump out, but he doesn't. There is nothing here, just bushes. The man pulls out both phones, turns them off, and slips out the batteries while he drives. Then he tosses the batteries out the window and, later down the road, the phones, before he gets back to the main road.

"Why did you do that?"

"We don't want to be bothered just yet. I'll get us a new phone. We have family business to attend to."

Matt watches the clock on the dashboard clicking off the minutes. He doesn't sleep but he goes away in his mind, like in the floor exercises. He goes back to the old apartment and sees his mother. He sees her robe that hung on the bathroom door. The way she sat and drank coffee with her head in her hand.

After a very long time, they stop in front of a house. The dashboard clock says it's after eleven.

"Where is this?"

"Where we'll be with her. Out of the hospital. Home Nursing Care it's called."

"This is your house?"

"Yes."

"Why is she here?"

"Bring the laptop. I'll explain."

The house is not big or rich, but it's a neat little thing with a small lawn bordered by hedges. There are purple flowers in the yard. Some kind of front patio with two chairs. It's not a scary place, but as soon as he steps inside there are smells Matt can't identify. Metal? Something medical. Also spices.

"She's here?"

"Up the stairs. In one of the bedrooms. To the right. The little one. Hand me the laptop."

He does. "They carried her up?"

"Yep."

Matt hurries up the stairs.

"To your right."

He opens the door to a darkened room. Small. Completely dark. Black. The door clicks behind him. He hears the sound of a key in a lock. A small light clicks on, almost as low as a night-light. The man stands, holding a key.

"Until we become used to each other. You have to be good. You might want to fight and I know that. Believe me, I was like that. When I was a kid. Just like you. So I know. I'm not blaming you or any of that."

"Where's my mom?"

"I'll bring her home tomorrow."

"I have to talk to her!"

"On the phone they said we shouldn't bother her anymore tonight."

"Then you lied."

The man sighs and moves into the room. "You make a person lie. By being bad and—and headstrong. You need to learn to listen. To follow rules. Didn't your mother tell you that?"

Matt moves the other way, toward the door. He feels behind him for the doorknob and when he finds it he tries it every which way. "Let me out."

"No. You have to learn discipline."

"I'm hungry."

"I'll bring food."

"I have to pee."

"Use that thing." The man points to some kind of metal thing on the floor.

"I don't understand."

"It's a hospital bedpan. You pee in that, and I will empty it."

That means the man will have to open the door. When the door opens, Matt will run out. He looks around the room. The bed he thought was a cot at first is some kind of hospital bed. It has only a thin spread on it. In the corner is a table with a sewing machine. There is one small window. If he could fly . . . if there is a roof under the window . . . He inches toward it.

He has to be super smart. He will escape. If he thinks, if he thinks, he can always figure things out.

"Are you really my father?"

"Yes. Absolutely."

"Turn away. I have to pee." He is shaking. Can he do it, get the zipper down, let the water out?

"Why would you doubt me?"

"She said you weren't."

"She was just angry."

He manages to get the pee going. "She's in the hospital?"

"Coming home tomorrow. You're going to be a good boy, right?"

"I guess."

"Here's the rules. No running, no yelling, no crying. Be patient. It will take time to get to know me. I understand that. To answer your question, we'll live here for a while. She wants that. If you're good, everything will work out."

"But school."

"We're going to put you in school here."

"Really? Where are we?"

"A small town. A nice small town, good for raising kids. A couple of days and you'll like it."

He starts to cry even though he knows it will get him in trouble.

"What is it?" His father's voice is kind. "What is it? I thought I said, 'No crying.' Hey."

He turns away to hide the crying.

He hears the key in the lock again. The door shuts and makes a turning sound from the other side, locked.

"Wait!"

From the other side of the door he hears, "Look. Hey, I'm sorry about this, but until we're used to each other and you totally behave . . . "

Matt pulls himself together and thinks hard. The door will have to open if the man brings food. "I'm hungry," he calls.

"I'll get you a good breakfast in the morning. I left the candy."

Footsteps retreat from the door. He starts to shout for help but in seconds there is loud music playing, so loud he can't hear himself.

He tries a wall switch, but sees soon enough there are no bulbs in the ceiling fixture. He backs up, trips on something—the pot, the bed pan. He's looking for a phone jack, a phone, something. He tries to open the window. It doesn't budge. Painted shut.

He has to find out about his mother, if she's coming here. If she's not, he will jump or run or . . .

He opens the spearmint leaves and eats.

He spies papers on the sewing table under pieces of cloth. Old envelopes. He can read them, pretty much. They say *Home Nursing Care.* He opens one. *Paid by insurance. Owed by member.* It's a bill for medicine. Is that the smell in the room? Medicine? The envelope is addressed to Arnett and Mala Brown. *Brown.* He looks at other envelopes and stray papers. All of papers are addressed to Arnett and Mala Brown. That's not his mother's name. And nothing says the name Ziad Zacour.

He cries for a long time before he goes to sleep.

BACK AT THE THEATRE, at eight thirty, the stage manager had called out Matt's name. Jan kept working. They were in Act II, scene i. Marina's scene had been blocked, she'd been doing her long debate with Oberon, and Jan and the cast were now ready to do the section where Titania and Oberon fight openly about the boy child he wants.

In the scene Oberon asks of Titania a price to fix their world in which everything is upside down—he wants the beautiful changeling boy she keeps with her. Titania does *not* intend to give up the child. She is committed to rearing him. She tells him, "Set your heart at rest. The fairyland buys not the child from me." Marina was especially potent in that part.

Jan Gabriel now needed to weave Matt into the scene. Her idea was to reveal him gradually. He would start out a little behind Titania's entourage, and then come more and more into the scene as they fight over him.

The stage manager, a tall youth, came back to Jan. "Matt must be napping someplace. Can we take a break? It's time for ten minutes anyway. I'll find him." Jan heard a trace of panic under the stage manager's upbeat assurances.

By eight forty-five, panic was in full order. The stage manager, assisted by a couple of actors, had looked under seats, in the balcony, in the dressing room, outside on the steps, but nobody could find Matt. Jan was looking everywhere, too. Earlier in the evening, Arthur had gone home.

Jan speed-dialed Matt's cell phone, but there was no answer. She punched the number in manually, so she could see the numbers come up, one by one, to be sure. No answer.

Her breath came in short, sharp jabs. *No, no, no, no, no.* Lost him. How, how? Then she reminded herself, *He runs away. He's done it before.*

She called Arthur to tell him what had happened, and like the stage manager, she tried to say it calmly, but she could not keep the alarm out of her voice.

"You looked everywhere?"

"Everywhere."

"Who saw him last?"

"Some of the kids, sitting in the lobby."

"I'll be right there. His phone?"

"I tried, I tried. You go ahead and keep trying. I'm calling Christie. Bring . . . bring pictures."

When she called Christie, she could hear a radio and the hum of a motor. She told the story quickly. "We don't know if he ran, you know, if he's hiding. You remember, he . . . "

"I'm coming," Christie said. "I'll be there. I'm on the road, but I'll turn around and be there in . . . about thirty minutes."

She told the cast, "Everybody, everybody, split up and examine this building top to bottom and the lawns outside, and the streets. Start from a small core and then widen the circle." By then she was crying. She hadn't been watching. She'd been working, trusting everyone, and she didn't see the signs that he was going to run.

Beattie took over, gathering everyone in the lobby, giving assignments. Three to the basement, four to the bathrooms, four to the balcony again, four to the dressing rooms. There were so many nooks and crannies in the building that it would take serious searching, so she put the bathroom people on nooks and corners once they had done the lavs. She sent the others in pairs to the outside in tight circles, wider ones, wider ones, and even wider. She had twenty people at work before eight patrol cars and Colleen, in a different car, got there. They consulted with Beattie and dispatched patrolmen to do much the same thing.

Colleen sat Jan down and made her tell everything from the beginning. "What was different today?"

"Nothing. He had a good day at school. He seemed a little vague tonight. I thought he was tired. That's why we thought he was napping somewhere, in a corner somewhere."

Colleen nodded. "We'll get Dolan to trace your call to his cell. We'll get a location."

"Can you do that?"

"Dolan can. Yeah."

Arthur came rushing in from home. "Anything?"

Jan shook her head and he went to her. She got up and fell into his arms.

"It's not your fault," he said. His voice lacked conviction.

Colleen told them, "Don't worry. We have all systems in place. We'll find him."

THE WHIMPERS FROM UPSTAIRS drive Nadal to pace from kitchen to front door. Even with his mother's Cuban CD playing, he can hear his son. He wants to comfort the boy, but the kid is a tough one, Nadal can tell that much. Better to let him cry himself to sleep and then Nadal can make him a proper breakfast tomorrow and get around him and talk to him until they connect.

He knew what his son needed to hear—but the lie . . . it's going to be in the way.

He flicks on his mother's TV in the living room and in an

instant his world falls apart. Of course, of course what he did is all over the news and there's even some idiot kid describing him. He can't think what to do next. He paces back and forth, hardly able to watch the news, unable to stop.

FINALLY AFTER MIDNIGHT, the actors drift away. But not Marina. She has four identities, four roles here. She is an actress and she searched the building with the others. She is Jan's friend and she has offered words of comfort as she could. She is Christie's wife, able to see his stress, the determined way he works. And she is a woman who thinks she could do this work, too. Her husband is sweating with the tension of the last hours. He's called in Dolan and Potocki and by now the police have questioned at least a hundred people. By now they have searched every corner of the theatre building multiple times. And she knows he has sent officers to search the Cathedral of Learning. He's sent Dolan and Potocki to Jan's house for Matt's laptop. And they have nothing. The laptop only shows that Matt looked up his new parents, his mother's obituary, and various games.

Richard catches Marina's eye. Shakes his head slightly. Nothing yet.

"Please tell me something I can do," Jan Gabriel pleads. "Please. I have to do something."

"I understand. Let's go up to your office. Let's have a time to talk—us and the other detectives and Marina if you are okay with that."

"I want Marina there, yes."

"Okay, let's go."

The Cathedral of Learning is a big faux-Gothic building with an institutional ground floor, and for thirty-six floors above it, flights of stairs, corners with stone arches and nooks. There are enough Gothic hidey-holes, offices, classrooms, and restrooms that hundreds of people with suspect intentions could be hiding out. The numbers of thefts each week of computers and audio components and handbags prove that. Marina finds the building very frightening at night, the way it offers odd noises to the easily frightened. Thumps. The occasional voice. Footsteps on stairways.

But tonight there are a group of them moving together.

The ground floor elevator doors open and they get in—Christie, Colleen, and Marina with Jan and Arthur. It's an old elevator. Even with paneled refurbishing, the age shows in the size, the grid above, the rattle as they ascend.

Then they get out and go around two corners to Jan's office.

Richard takes Marina aside. "You can get into the main office, right? The copiers?"

"Yes."

"Make more flyers."

Marina hesitates at the door. She whispers, "We don't need more yet. Let me stay."

He nods briefly.

"Sit, everyone," he orders. "We need to think. Quiet and calm." They take their places on chairs, sofa. "Matt was up here today, you said?" he asks the parents. All the while his eyes are searching the room for anything, any kind of sign.

"Yes," says Arthur. "Together, we were together, waiting for Jan. She was working next door."

What is there to look for? What else can they examine?

Jan lets out a cry and Marina comes to put an arm around her.

Richard says levelly, "Help me. Think. How was Matt—earlier today? After school? Anything could have happened at school. Someone contacted him, maybe?"

"Things seemed normal when we picked him up," Jan answers.

"No," Arthur interrupts. "Remember at dinner. I looked over at you and we both felt worried. He seemed vague, different. I thought it was because I fell asleep in here when we were waiting for you, when I could have been keeping him company."

"He used my computer," Jan offers. "He was playing a game when I came in."

"Turn it on."

She does, grateful to have an assignment, and Richard moves closer.

"I was logged on all day. I left it on and when I came in he was playing."

"What about your email?" Marina asks. "He might have used it."

"Yes, email was up." Jan types several keys fast, curses at her trembling hands, restarts the password and it goes through.

"Did he—?"

But Marina and the rest of them become aware that Jan is sitting very still. "This . . . this is my inbox. There's something I didn't see. I mean it's been opened but I didn't open it." She doesn't even turn around to look at them. "It's from Blackman, our attorney. I've never seen it." She clicks it open then tells them, "It's the letter from his birth father. It's the TPR. It means . . . I think Matt saw it." There is a moment's silence. "He was different at dinner. Sad. This . . . this explains it. Maybe he's angry, right?" she asks. "Hiding. Run away. Could it be?"

Marina knows that's it. The kid saw the email. Just then her husband's phone rings and he takes it. He listens for a while. "Bring the guy up here."

"What? What is it?" Jan asks.

"Someone saw a man and boy talking."

Dolan and Potocki who have been canvassing since their search of the Morris-Gabriel house arrive at Jan's office moments later, ushering in a ragged student. Torn T-shirt and torn jeans, though the tears have a touch of fashion about them. The boy is about nineteen, with unevenly cut hair. He is wearing flip-flops that look cheap and in danger of tripping him up. He comes face to face with her husband who is studying his face.

"You saw something?"

"Maybe." His voice is light, frightened. "I just saw what looked like a father and son arguing on the lawn and these detectives showed me a picture and I told them, 'Yes. That's the kid.' I don't know what this is about."

"Tell us what you saw. What you heard."

"Didn't hear anything. I wasn't that close and I had my earbuds in. I thought, like, the kid is eating junk food and the father doesn't want him to eat that stuff and he takes the bag from him. Then they walk off together. That's what I saw."

"What junk food?"

"I don't know. It was like a little white plastic bag. But the kid started out with one hand dipping in it so I figured chips or candy."

"Where'd they go?"

"I didn't see where they went."

"Describe the father."

"Late twenties, early thirties, maybe. Dark hair. Not fat or anything. Jeans and a T-shirt I think, yeah. Regular clothes."

"Tall, short?"

"Medium. Like what is this, one of those domestic snatches?"

"Oh, God," Jan cries out.

Richard grabs the kid's shirt. "Get serious here. The man may be dangerous."

"Didn't look it."

Potocki says, "The news teams are out in the hallway. They want a piece of something. This guy's story could help."

Richard says, "Go ahead. Take him."

Arthur bursts out. "Tell us what we're up against. You think this Zacour drove up here after all?"

Richard shakes his head slightly. "We look at everything, of course. But it isn't my first thought, to be truthful."

He gets another call and then he says impatiently to Marina, "More flyers. Then join us on thirty-six."

Marina hurries off to do her other role, whichever one it is, wife, grunt-work cop.

CHRISTIE, POTOCKI, DOLAN, and Colleen take the Morrises up to the thirty-sixth floor where a security officer is waiting to play them the DVD from the security system that captured the time between seven and nine that evening. It's a wide swatch of time, wider than they need perhaps, so Christie asks if first they can focus on seven thirty to eight thirty.

The scan is slow because the camera makes a full 360 degrees around the Cathedral. It takes in part of the lawn on Bigelow and part of the Student Union and then moves up to get some of Fifth Avenue, focusing fairly tightly on the walkway into the building. Then there's more lawn, after that the Heinz Chapel, after that the Forbes Avenue strip, then back to the lawn around Stephen Foster Memorial. The whole scan takes ninety seconds so what happens in between at any single location is lost. Still, they are hopeful.

What they see are many people in sweats, shorts, jeans, T-shirts, backpacks, a little army of learners and procrastinators. "Everybody looks so alike," Colleen grumbles. "Jeans and T-shirt, our witness said!"

"Except we're looking for a little kid," Potocki reminds them.

They watch for a full ten minutes without recognizing anything. Marina arrives with five hundred more flyers and is caught up on the routine. "We're looking for anything that helps," Christie tells his wife, taking the flyers from her.

Marina points. "That's James, our assistant stage manager, and that's Beattie," she says a split second after two people come into view.

"They left rehearsal?"

"They go to the 7-Eleven; they take orders for other people who get desperately hungry or thirsty but are onstage."

"They've taken Matt with them once at least," Jan explains, "but they would have told us. They're wonderful kids."

"Okay, then. You trust Beattie."

"Totally. With my life."

The camera panned maddeningly slowly. The security guard, hearing their frustration, sped it up. He said, "We can always go back."

How much there was to see. Hundreds of cars.

"Also," Christie reminds them, "anything that looks like it might be a maroon Pontiac."

And finally at the camera's 7:52 they see a slip of a boy crossing the street. "That's Matt!" Jan cries. "He's alone. Oh, my God, he just left and went out alone. How did nobody see?"

"Is it possible he was meeting someone?"

"I can't imagine it. He's . . . going to the 7-Eleven I think. See, the way he hopped to the crosswalk? That's where we cross."

"Are you able to zoom in," Christie asks. The guard does so quickly. "Is he using his phone at all?"

They all lean forward. They watch him, arms loose, head cocking forward crossing the street.

And then the camera moves toward Fifth Avenue and all the rest of the circle—maddening, maddening when what they wanted to see is the boy and yet they concentrate, looking for twenty-something and thirty-something men in the pictures. When the camera comes around again to the Foster lawn, the boy is not in the picture.

"Ninety seconds. Would he still have been at the store? I think yes," Colleen says.

Jan whispers, "It's usually busy. It could take easily three minutes, four."

They begin to jot notes on the cars parked around the Cathedral. No Pontiacs. Lots of Jeeps and SUVs. People seem to come in waves, too many of them sometimes to examine anyone well.

Another ninety-second sweep and no Matt.

Then another ninety-second sweep. What they feared most is what they see next coming into view: man and boy walking away.

"Oh, my God," Jan cries.

Marina goes to her and puts an arm around her.

It is hard to see much about the man. T-shirt and jeans, that's accurate. Medium height. Dark hair. Four seconds. The two walk, the boy looking up, inquisitive; they walk toward the park and the library while the camera is busy moving off toward Fifth Avenue.

"Shit," Dolan explodes. "Damn."

"Back up. Slow it down. Blow it up."

But the security guard doesn't need to be told. He is already doing it. Then he pauses the video and zooms in.

Back of the man's head. They can see the boy's face but not the man's face. The clothing is clear enough. From the back the man is totally ordinary.

"Go back to the beginning. Study the cars," Christie commands.

Dolan goes out to the hall to take a call. He comes back in to talk to Christie. He does so in an almost whisper. "I got my pal at Verizon. They're checking on the kid's phone. I want to leave for when they have an answer. I want to go back to canvassing the 'hood. My eyes aren't good on the DVD."

Jan and Arthur are frozen, listening.

Christie knows Potocki and Colleen are both better at the video screen than he is. He needs to be outside, directing the available cops. "Call me," Christie orders Colleen, "if you find anything."

COLLEEN FEELS the warmth of Potocki's hands on her shoulders as he moves behind her to watch the DVD, which the security officer reversed by two minutes as soon as Christie stood to leave.

221

Colleen asks to have the DVD totally stopped for a second and turns to Marina and the Morrises. "We're going to find him. I know it's hard to wait but the routine investigations will work. Would you like to go get some rest?"

"I don't think rest is possible," Jan says sadly. Arthur kisses the top of her head and rubs her shoulders. It makes Colleen think how alike couples are, the ways they physically touch each other, the roles people adopt—the worrier, the comforter. Not that there is much comfort to be had here.

"I'll stay for as long as I can be helpful," Marina says. Then when the video starts running again, she asks, "What does this guy want from the boy? We need to know that."

"To win some bout with the mother?" Arthur tries. "He killed her after all."

"I think he wants love," Marina says. She says this line simply. "The tilt of his head, the rhythm of his walk. That little nod. That's my guess. I hope I'm right."

Colleen doesn't say anything. Love takes many forms, and sometimes it turns to hate in a second.

NADAL HAS SPENT HOURS at his computer, going to news sites. He looks up information about Amber Alerts and learns that word about Matt's disappearance is going to be just about everywhere, even at construction sites or anywhere on a highway or in front of a store where there is programmable signage or an LED billboard.

There are rules for Amber Alerts. The police have to believe an abduction has taken place and that the child is in danger. Okay, that's how they think of it, but they are wrong. His child is now *safe*. They also have to have descriptions of the child and the captor and the vehicle. Nadal keeps checking every fifteen minutes. The news websites describe him as a man of about thirty with dark hair.

Aren't there a million men who look like that? There is nothing about a vehicle. And no name.

They don't know who he is. They don't know the car.

Good, good. He will stay holed up here until he has won the boy over. He can imagine a perfect day unfolding. They'll have breakfast, watch TV, play games on his computer, talk.

One day here, calm, holed up and getting to know each other, and three days more and they can be in Florida. Then he has to figure out what to do with the Bug.

Hope blossoms, too. He has all his money, cash. He can do anything that needs to be done. He'll buy food supplies on the road, get his son some clothes, buy himself a new phone.

He wants to be a good father. He wants the day to start.

POTOCKI, STILL AT the video, jiggles his foot nervously. Colleen asks him, "You want to go check? Go ahead."

He shakes his head.

He has his son Scott at his place this weekend, and he hasn't even been home yet. He's *called*. Multiple times. No doubt drove the kid crazy.

Scott, only fourteen, insisted he would be all right on his own. Now it's almost three in the morning and Potocki doesn't want to call again to find out if his kid is sleeping. It doesn't look like this case is going to wrap up anytime soon, so Potocki is going to have to give in and call Judy and have his ex pick Scott up tomorrow morning. Judy will get a perfect reminder of why she hated police work.

Scott is going to turn out okay. He is utterly normal. Cares what his friends think, worries about how he looks, pretends he isn't totally occupied by sex, needs movies that allow him to laugh at idiocies of all sorts. Are there teenagers who *don't* crave the satirical?

"You can hate me," Potocki told his son not long ago. "You can hate Colleen if you want. Just promise me you'll stay alive."

"I don't hate her," Scott said. "I like her."

Potocki tries to remember how an almost eight-year-old boy thinks. Why is this boy on the video screen walking off with a man he thinks killed his mother? Could a boy want a father so much that he would forgive murder?

By now Potocki knows all of the extras in the movie, how they walk, where they are going, what cars they park or drive away. But he has no more on Matt.

A few minutes ago, Colleen urged the Morrises to go home as well. She suggested they could wait for the boy there. She said he might find a way to call, and finally that persuaded them and they went. Marina left then, too.

Now it is just three of them—the security guard, Potocki, and Colleen—studying the screen.

Colleen takes a call. She listens and when she hangs up, reports. "They talked to Verizon. They pinpointed the tower where the last call came. It's on Route 22, near Blairsville. So it sure doesn't sound like Zacour. It also sounds . . . pretty alarming. Boss said he's going to wake up this guy Ziad Zacour, make sure he's in his condo, clear him. He just has to arrange it with some police in Baltimore. But first he has to get police searching along Route 22."

"This is bad. The phone."

"I know."

For the hundredth time, they watch the guy in the tape.

Colleen says, "You know, the head just a little forward. . . it's a disturbed posture. Marina was right about the walk, the psychology behind it. I give her credit. She learned it in acting school. I learned it in counseling classes."

A security guard brings in a fresh pot of coffee.

The tension, the night, the caffeine make everything zingy. Potocki feels himself bouncing off the walls.

Colleen stands, restless. "It's so weird. Boss went off on a case earlier tonight. An old case, he said."

"Why is that weird?"

"He's my partner. Why wouldn't he tell me?"

Potocki shrugs. He knows perfectly well where Boss was going tonight—and he knows how much Boss had to give up to come back here to the case of the missing boy.

Everything is strange. The coffee tastes like black acid.

14.

SATURDAY

THE BOY SITS UP GROGGILY.

Nadal says, "Let's just sit together and have breakfast."

Matt doesn't say anything but his gaze goes to the window. It is still dark out.

"It'll be daylight soon."

The boy nods.

"Still sleepy?"

The boy nods.

"Good boy. Now to eat a little. Cereal?"

Another nod. Matt sits on the edge of the bed.

Was it going to be this easy, this wonderful? Nadal brings the bowl of cereal over to him. "It's Cheerios. Do you like Cheerios?" There is no answer but Matt picks up the spoon and makes an effort. "There's toast and egg, too. Do you like those?"

A shrug, a slight nod.

"Okay. I like to see a good appetite. Have you ever had plantains?"

His son frowns and makes a slight shake of the head.

"They are fantastic. And *bacalaítos*. Wow, I want you to taste a bacalaíto."

The boy doesn't eat much. He tries to look around him. His eyes go to the metal urinal and Nadal waits a moment, then gets up to see it has urine in it. He is suddenly embarrassed that he's made his son use the old man's piss pot. His first impulse is to go empty it, but he doesn't want to open the door or leave Matt. He is making headway, though, the boy is behaving. Now he needs to make him talk. He brings over the plate of egg and toast. "Eat."

Matt stares at the egg and toast.

"You should eat."

His son dips the toast in the egg and takes a bite.

Nadal is so afraid Matt will run. He fishes around in his pants pocket for his mother's packet of Benadryl. "I have something for you. For safety, in case you're allergic to anything—if you know of anything you have to tell me, like peanut butter, some people can't eat peanut butter—anyway, take this pill for safety. It's Benadryl. Good for all kinds of things."

Matt sighs. He puts down the toast and takes the pill with milk. He sits still, not trying to eat.

Nadal remembers a time . . . eating *mofongo* and *masitas* and a humid breeze, almost wet on his face. "Let's talk about things."

Matt looks up.

"Things we like. Tell me what you like to do, you know, what subjects you like in school, what games you play. I want to give you the best."

Matt's face registers an expression of distress and Nadal knows, knows, there is going to be a question soon about Maggie. Though he thought for the last several hours about how to handle that whole subject, he has no solution. He has control of his temper now and, in fact, he can hardly remember the moment he *lost* his temper. It's happened before—a rage so big he didn't feel it coming and didn't understand it after. "Don't be angry," his mother would say to him when he was a teenager. He would challenge her: "What are you talking about?" She would tell him, "Your face. Your face is angry."

Is his face angry now? Is that why Matt is quiet?

"Don't want to talk about school?" he asks.

Matt shakes his head.

"I think we need a good rest, both of us. A nice, long, easy day." His son shuffles his feet to balance the tray on his lap. "You like TV. You like games."

Matt looks up. A slight nod. Progress. Good. Good, good, good.

MATT KNOWS HIS MOTHER is dead. He wonders why the man wants to talk, to feed him, just like his mother did. She always told him, "Eating makes the brain work." He forces down another bite. He would ask his mother for pastries—scones and Danishes, and sometimes she got them for him. Jan and Arthur told him eggs were good brain food. He needs to work his brain.

Only trouble is, he's still sleepy. He would like to lie down again.

"Let's watch some TV."

He knows everything in this room—the desk, the papers, the clothes in the closet, the metal pee pot. There is no TV in here.

"Come." The man opens the door and they step out into a hallway that he hardly noticed last night. They stand there for a minute, the man in front of him, watching him closely.

Matt touches a banister that is decorated with little lace circles. When one of the circles falls to the floor, the man says, "Damn these *tapetes*," grabs them all, and tosses them to the wall. Matt stands still for a second before allowing himself to look toward the bathroom. Will he be allowed to use it? Is the window open and, if it is, if he yells, will anyone hear him in the middle of the night? If he calls out and nobody comes, what punishment will he suffer?

"You have to go?"

He nods.

The man takes him by the hand inside. The room has a bunch of smells from soaps and perfumes and sprays. It has a window, but the window is closed. Even so, the man goes to the window and tries it, as if to make sure it is well locked, then looks at Matt as if to say, *This is the test. Are we going to get along? Are you going to behave?* Finally he steps aside, walks to the open door, and turns his back so Matt can do his business, which right now is just a pee.

Is this his father? He wishes he knew for absolute sure. The names on the papers he saw are all wrong.

"We'll watch a little TV."

Matt knows every program that is on TV from early in the morning but he's not sure what's on in the middle of the night.

They descend the stairs slowly. Matt would like to lie down. He walks to the sofa and the man doesn't stop him, but the man asks, "Are you sleepy? Television is nice when you're sleepy." The man flicks the button and something comes on.

After about five minutes the man goes to his laptop, which is sitting on the snack table next to a chair. "I'm looking things up," he says. "I'm always looking things up."

Matt hopes that if he is very good, he will be allowed to use the computer.

Soon he feels himself falling asleep. In this haze, he asks, "Are you Arnett Brown?"

The man jerks and seems worried. "I am definitely not Arnett Brown."

ZIAD GETS UP FOR THE THIRD TIME, trying not to disturb Kate with his restlessness, but it's hopeless.

"What is it?" she asks.

"Sorry. I didn't want to wake you."

"Can't be helped."

He goes to the bathroom, thinking, hoping she will get back to sleep. It's still dark, night, only the little bit of light coming in the window, but it's only hours before she has to shower and start out for the hospital. When he was sound of mind, two, three days ago, he could sleep right through her showers and her leavings. Now nothing seems to work.

They are having a baby, he and Kate. He's wanted to get married since he met her and all the more once she announced the pregnancy. She insisted they wait until his dissertation is finished—as if she's *testing* something, his worthiness.

He is hardly finished in the bathroom when the phone rings. Kate's voice comes through from the bedroom in a groggy, almost querulous hello.

A wrong number, surely, at three in the morning, but she doesn't hang up. She's listening to someone. He opens the bathroom door.

"Yes, he's here. Just a minute. Police?" she says, handing the phone over. She flicks on the light and sits up, studying him.

He turns slightly away from her with the phone. "Yes?"

"Commander Christie here. I have an officer at your door. I'm sorry, but it's important. Will you open the door to him? He needs to do a search."

"I don't understand."

"Have you been at home all evening?"

"Yes."

"You'll be all right, then. Stay calm."

"I don't understand. I'm . . . I'm going to the door. This is . . ."

"Terrible. I know. The boy is missing. The boy we believe is your son. We have a report of a man taking him away—"

"My God. Oh my God. Not me. I was here."

He puts on living room lights and opens the front door to a sour-looking detective followed by an open-faced younger man. Both come in. He feels himself backing up, as if guilty, and bumps into Kate, who is already robed and behind him.

Yet on the phone, Christie's voice is kind. "If you think about it, you'll understand the investigation. Please just cooperate and feel free to call me back. Take down my number."

"I don't have . . . it'll be on my phone. . . . No, wait." He backs up to his dissertation pages and jots down Christie's number. "I'll call back. I need to know."

Kate says, "What is this about?"

"Detective Olson." The sour one shows his card. "Cooperating with the Pittsburgh Police. If my partner can do a quick search of your premises?"

Ziad says, "Okay. Kate. I'll explain."

She stands, hand to her mouth.

Olson asks her, "You were home tonight?"

"Yes. I got home from work at seven."

"And Mr. Zacour?"

"He was here."

"All night."

"Yes."

"This is routine, then. Just hang on till my partner does his thing. On an Amber Alert, we have to check everything." He seems not sour at all now, but almost nice. "We're sorry, but—"

Good, Ziad thinks, no more secrets. He turns to Kate and touches her arm and says, "I have a son. I . . . just found out, just days ago. I've been . . . I knew I would tell you, but . . . He's gone missing. The detective in Pittsburgh had a report that he was taken away by a man."

"Young man, tall, dark hair," says Olson. He gestures to Ziad.

"I was here."

Minutes pass in which Ziad is aware of Kate's watching him, nothing else.

The other detective comes back to the living room. "Everything looks totally normal."

Olson has picked up on the division between Ziad and Kate. "We'll leave you two. It's almost morning. Soon."

And just like that, the police are gone.

They sit quietly, facing each other. "A relationship you can't tell me about?" she asks.

"Not a relationship. Almost nine years ago, I needed money."

She frowns. "Oh."

"I didn't think ahead. I went to a sperm bank. I just found out a couple of days ago about this boy. His mother was murdered, and I guess I was a suspect. But I didn't know her, and I didn't know I had a son."

"He's yours?"

"They took DNA but they won't have results for a couple of days yet. They showed me a picture. It's almost certain."

Kate gets up, goes to the kitchen, and presses the button that will start the coffee. She pulls her robe more tightly around her and comes back. "I don't understand why you didn't tell me."

He wants to say this right, accurately, so he takes a long time. The coffee is the only sound, gurgling as it boils and drips. "I haven't been sure what to say. You puzzle me, putting off our marriage, and . . . I'm embarrassed that I sold sperm for money without thinking of the consequences. And then I thought things were settled. There's a couple—nice people, professors—who desperately want Matt . . ."

"Matt?"

"Matthew. It all came to me because those people needed me to sign a termination of rights so that they could adopt him. It's the first I knew. Three days ago. The lawyer sent the form. They told me this was the right thing for . . . for the boy."

"You signed?"

"Yes. It seemed a done thing, the way it was presented. And you're in residency. And you want me to finish that—" He points to the pile of papers. He can't hide his anger. "And we're having a child in six months."

"But your son—you have a son, I'm getting my mind around that—and the boy is in danger?"

"Yes."

"Is there anything we can do to help?"

"I can't imagine what."

"Ziad, are you afraid of me?"

That he couldn't think of how to tell her his secret—did it mean the relationship was no good?

"I've done something wrong," she says, "if you're afraid. This thing has happened. And you can't talk to me."

"Yes."

"You've been torn up, right?"

"I have."

"Do you want to call that detective back? See if anything is happening?"

"Yes."

"When you heard, did you wish you could know him?"

Ziad begins to cry. He cries copiously. When he finally manages to look at Kate, she is crying, too.

THE AMBER ALERT HAS CHANGED. Police are seeking a man who spoke to seven-year-old Matthew Brown before he disappeared. The abductor may be driving a maroon Pontiac.

Nadal can't breathe. Can the Pontiac he thought he was rid of be traced to him, to this address? He tries to figure out the police. Why did they not mention the Pontiac before and mention it now?

In his mother's freezer are all kinds of things. He finds a package of store-bought burritos, two frozen dinners, a loaf of bread, crackers, cereal. He puts these things in two shopping bags, moving as fast as he can. No milk left. No juice to be found.

He's got to get out before daylight. He knows where to go. He'll go where Arnett Brown took him a long time ago. Nobody will find them there, in the middle of nowhere.

In one trip he takes his backpack and the shopping bags of food to the VW. He goes back in and wakes Matt enough to help him stumble to the car. "Backseat," he says. "Lie down."

And then the motor rumbles and the tires crackle branches and they are on the way.

"THIS TRIP," THE MAN SAYS, and he keeps turning toward the backseat while he's driving, "this trip is for you. A Saturday trip."

Matt has lain down in the seat as he's been instructed, with the seat belt fastened around him in an uncomfortable way, something that reminds him of a Boy Scout belt across his chest, and he's trying to figure out what he needs to know, but he is having trouble staying awake. A part of his brain is saying, "Think, notice," but another part of him doesn't care. It's dark out, still night. He doesn't care . . . about anything.

"This kind of trip is what my father took me on. And so I'm taking you."

Saturday, yes, the day his mother is to be cremated, but he's not there. Think, notice. There's a town outside the car windows, street lights, the sounds of other cars. He lifts up a little. Big empty parking lots. Walmart.

"What do you usually do on Saturdays?"

TV. All morning on Saturdays. But he doesn't say. He is trying to think of what he needs to do.

"You have to answer me when I ask a question. That's a rule. Do you hear me?"

He can tell the man is upset, even scared, by the sound of his voice. He can usually pretend to be asleep, but since he's fighting to keep his eyes open to notice things, since the man keeps turning and tilting the rearview mirror to see him, he can't pretend. "TV," he manages to squeak out.

"Ah. Well, today you'll have an adventure with your father. Two times my father took me to the woods. Three times. Once when I was little, then when I was grown up. We didn't hunt. It wasn't for that. It was for looking. And learning. He was a zoologist. You know what that is? Answer me."

"The zoo?"

"Animals. He studied animals. The first woods, forest, was in another country, a beautiful country, and the woods were . . . you can smell them, very rich soil there, and . . . and plants that are different from here and . . .the animals are different, too. Lizards. You like lizards?"

Matt shrugs.

"Couldn't hear that."

"No."

"Well, they're important there. Where I come from, there are almost five hundred different kinds of animals and birds and almost three thousand kinds of plants. In one little country. Lots of places have beauty if you know how to look. The plants here and the animals . . . I'll be honest—I don't know the numbers." He turns slightly. "You have to talk. Ask me a question."

Matt can't make his voice work. "Will we camp out?" he manages.

"No, there's a place. We won't get rained on. Ask me how I know about this place. Ask me questions."

How can he think, notice, when he is falling asleep. How can he ask questions when his voice won't come up. "Your father," he murmurs.

"Answering. That's right. Questions and answers. The other guy who has this place—he won't be there. . . . If he is, we won't bother him. He owns it. I mean, his grandfather owns it. They get some kind of deal, gas and mineral rights, and so they just keep being allowed to own it. Never have to sell. My father was a good friend, so he was allowed to go any time he wanted. He went because of the animals. Not to kill them, right? He studied them. He used to put up cameras to scan the woods—yeah? Can you imagine? Slow action, huh. Just so he could watch what went on when he wasn't there. The cameras might still be up, I don't know. When my father died, my mother told the owners they could keep the cameras, like, as a gift. Infrared. For nighttime pictures. Are you listening?"

"Yes." He doesn't care.

"Good. I want to teach you things. What he would say, my father, is, 'I want to watch the woods coming to life.' That's early morning. That's almost now. We won't get there in time this morning to get those first noises. We'll have to watch the woods going to bed tonight. And coming to life tomorrow. And all that while, time to talk, time to just . . . have a chance to be quiet and think and eat and talk."

The man is still talking, talking, still very nervous, what Matt's mom would call *hyper* and Matt knows enough to know that's not good, but he can't stay awake. It's still dark out, just getting light, the motor humming, nothing much to see out the windows, so his eyes keep closing. "McKean County," he hears and, "thickest woods you ever saw."

McKean County, he thinks, remember that.

ARTHUR AND JAN haven't slept—it's six in the morning. The coffee hits Arthur as a dry taste, or the aftertaste at any rate leaves him dry mouthed. Not even two small weeks ago this started. Their lives have rollercoastered since. He wonders about fate, wanting things too much. The stars, Shakespeare would have said, the explanation for everything, just everything.

He can't bear to think about what his son must be going through, but the DVD image haunts him. The boy walked willingly it seemed. Was he not afraid of the man? Did he know the man? His head was tilted up. He was *listening*.

Christie and the whole police force have no idea who this man is. How can it be—that a man could kill Maggie Brown, take her son, and leave no trace?

The circles under Jan's eyes are dark smudges. She looks like tragedy, like madness, Judith Anderson playing Medea, Helen Mirren playing a drunk. "Maybe if you try to lie down."

"Can't. What about the babysitter, Meg? We should talk to her. He liked her. Maybe he said something."

He tilts his arm to look at his watch. It's six now. They'll be waking Meg's family up on a Saturday morning, but they have to go. In case he said something. Arthur nods. "Let's wash up and go."

"If only he's okay," she says. "I'd give up everything."

And he? Trade a healthy Matt for a healthy heart? Yes. Done.

He picks up his car keys, puts them down again, and goes to the kitchen sink and washes his face with a bar of hand soap, finally dunking his head under the water where he gets a brief refreshing memory of a waterfall, and life, and happiness.

MARINA CAN'T SLEEP either. Tomorrow if there's no news, she has to run the rehearsal. Oh, who can watch a boy every minute? Even a rebellious, grieving boy. It's nobody's fault.

She walks up to the small desk she uses in the room they keep for the kids. They're going to need a new house—the kids are getting bigger, need separate rooms. And there is no place for her and her papers.

On the desktop is the newspaper she carried around for a week in her bag—the one that contained the article about her and Jan. She kept planning to show it to Richard, but what with one thing and another, it never got from her hands to his. Well, it was just a student paper. Just an article.

Then she does the thing that is her signature mix of logic and inspiration and spookiness—the way she wins Jotto games by simply intuiting the word her opponent is thinking of. Maybe the guy who took Matt read *this* paper, maybe he knew about Jan Gabriel somehow and knew where the boy was going to be. If he read the paper, he was local. Okay. Student, faculty, staff possibly. Of course, her husband and his colleagues are already considering that. She turns pages, as if an answer will come to her, thinks about members of the student newspaper staff—the girl who came to interview her and Jan, a nice kid, not a likely suspect. Keeps turning pages.

Want ads.

She reads them beginning to middle. She doesn't have to go past the middle because she sees the ad for a maroon Pontiac for sale. She knows in her gut she has it.

She dials the number in the ad. No answer.

She calls Richard to tell him what she found.

"Wow. Wow. That sounds— How did you do it?"

"Can you and Artie . . . ?"

"You bet." But even while he is on the phone with her, he is alerting Artie. Then she dictates the number and hears him dictate it to Artie in turn. All the while she is near tears. She listens carefully to be sure Richard and Artie have the number right.

DOLAN GETS THE CALL at six thirty. He listens carefully, says, "Got it, got it," and looks at his boss. "This is a weird one. Guy named Nate Brown owns the phone. Bought it a year ago. Address on Dawson Street. *Brown*. Like Maggie Brown? There's something we don't know about going on."

"A relative after all?"

"It sounds like, doesn't it? Why did nobody know?"

By six forty in the morning, Christie and Dolan are knocking on doors on Dawson Street.

The name Nate Brown does not appear anywhere on the door of the rundown building that Dolan has been told was the address for Nate Brown when he purchased the cell phone. The detectives rouse the occupants of apartment 4 anyway. The students who live there trip over computers and pizza boxes and remote controls and beer cans as they let the detectives in. One of them was up early, three have been asleep.

They are nervous, probably looking around for roach butts left about.

Christie makes a lightning-quick speech about the earliness of the hour and the importance of an Amber Alert investigation. "Which one of you is Nate Brown?"

They look at each other confused. "Never heard of him," one says and the others ditto him.

"Anybody know him?"

They all say no.

"He once lived here. How long have you been here?"

"Just moved in like a week ago," the spokesman answers. "Like maybe two."

A fairly good mess has been made in two weeks. "Need to see your IDs," Christie insists.

Finally he shows them the rough photo printed from the clip of video.

"Can't see anything in this," the mouthy one snaps, as if the police are totally inept. "I mean, like, that could be anybody."

Three of them yawn in unison.

"Get some sleep."

Dolan and Christie then check all the students in the building. Mostly it is the same routine—waking people up, getting curious stares from windows and doorways, drivers on the street stopping to see what the flashing lights are all about.

They go to neighboring buildings.

"This is not—" Dolan begins.

"*Pitt News*," Christie says. "The ad."

"Anybody there at this hour?"

"If we yell loud enough."

By then it is seven. They call ahead to get a security guard to open the *Pitt News* offices. "And get me somebody in student records."

As soon as they get there, the door to the *Pitt News* office is open. They ask the officer to get them the number of the faculty adviser so they can call him.

"Meanwhile, look the other way," Dolan tells the security guard. The guard nods and turns to the hallway to make his inquiries. Dolan starts looking through file cabinets and loose file folders. "Can't find it, can't find it. Shit."

Meanwhile Christie has another security officer on the phone going through student records. "Nate Brown," he tells her. "Nathaniel or Nate. Used to be on Dawson Street."

"Pitt has hundreds of Browns. Nathaniel?"

"We think so. Or another possibility is something like *Danilo* or *Dal* in the name."

"I'll keep looking. Can I call you back?"

"Yeah."

Christie takes a call from Ziad Zacour. He tells him he has no information yet and will call him when he does.

"Watch it," the security guard in front of him says. "Somebody's here."

The student who walks in to the office looks about suspiciously. He takes in their clothes. His expression suggests they do not look like thieves.

Christie shows his ID. "Police investigation. A seven-year-old boy is missing. We think the man who took him placed an ad here. To sell a car. A Pontiac."

Miraculously—it felt like a miracle—the student said, "Pontiac. Yeah. I'm Josh Hansen. I remember the guy and the ad. He placed it online. Then he came over and paid cash, wanted to get the ad in right away. And we did."

"Did he fill anything out, give an address?"

"He skipped the address and we didn't press it. But he did say he could run right over, that he was working in the computer lab and got a ten-minute break."

"Working? A job?"

"Sounded like."

"Where's the lab?"

"There are several. There's a main office, though." Hansen looks up the phone number for them.

"You don't write about this, you understand?" Christie warns. "Or talk. There's a boy's life at stake."

"I saw nothing going on here," Hansen says, hands up. "I am dumb as a doorpost."

By seven twenty they are in another office, waiting for a secretary to arrive to look up employee information. She gets there at seven thirty and when she has consulted a few pieces of paper, says, "Looks like you're looking for Nadal Brown." She pronounces his name just as the call comes to Christie from the security officer studying student records. She says, "I found a part-timer in student records. A Nadal Brown."

"Bingo."

Both women give the same address on South Neville.

Things happen this way, all at once, and when they start rolling—well, Christie hopes it will be this way from now on.

Without intending it, he's in the field with his old partner Dolan, though Greer is his current partner. To finesse what amounts to a kind of infidelity, he calls her and is pleased to find she's awake.

"Slept?" he asks.

"Two hours. It helped. You?"

"Not yet." He tells her what to do next and that she can keep working with Potocki this morning. He feels like a man having an affair.

WHEN JAN AND ARTHUR arrive at the Philips house at seven twenty, they do awaken everybody, but the girl Meg is polite and invites them in. She pulls a robe around her. "Let me put some clothes on. I saw the news," she says. At seven thirty they are seated at the kitchen table with Meg, who is making coffee. She says she doesn't know anything, but she advances the theory that Matt has been doing his best to adapt to his new parents. She doesn't think he was acting out.

Jan looks about at the sparsely furnished little house and the two chipped cups on the drainboard. Somehow Meg has found two cups with saucers for their coffee.

"Can I make you toast?" she asks. "And we have some hot cereal, too. I could make oatmeal."

Jan hastens to say, "No thanks," but Arthur says, "Yes, I'm ravenous from staying up. Oatmeal would be . . . "

Jan looks at him, surprised. "Shouldn't we . . ."

"And do what?" he asks in a voice so loaded with failure that Jan stops herself.

She wanted to go up and down streets with flyers. Asking. Now she watches the girl pouring oatmeal into a bowl, then water, then a pinch of salt. How can Arthur eat? "Tell me anything Matt said."

"He talked about video games he liked, he talked about school a bit, and he talked about trying to figure out what to call you."

"What do you mean?"

Meg pauses. "He didn't want to use formal names, you know, Mr. and Mrs., and yet he wasn't quite ready for Mom, Dad, or anything like that, and he said first names felt funny."

Soon after the oatmeal is microwaved and eaten, Colleen Greer and John Potocki arrive and ask the same questions of Meg all over again. But the detectives have one new item. They have a name to ask about. "Did Matt ever mention a fellow named *Nadal*. Nadal Brown."

"No," Meg says. "Never."

"A relative?" Arthur asks.

"We don't know."

"He's who was walking away with Matt?"

"We think so. You've never heard of him?"

"No," Meg tells them.

Arthur shakes his head. Jan feels tears begin again. Who is this man? "Marina said he looked disturbed. I thought so too. His walk."

Colleen nods. "Matt is smart. Right? Let's rely on that."

NADAL IS NOT CERTAIN he can find the cabin. He looked it up, Google-Mapped it, but he had no printer at his mother's house, and when he gets into the wooded area, no Internet, he has to rely on memory of the time Arne brought him here. Twice. Not exactly a good memory and yet . . . somehow it's turned into a good one. The woods are deep, so thick that he feels comfort just in knowing the bright-red car can disappear from view. The boy won't be able to run. There is no place to run.

What he thinks he remembers is a deeply rutted road, then a gravel road, then something that is more like a weeded path. One such muddy, deeply ditched road seems to be the correct one, until he follows it to the end and sees two hunting cabins side by side—he's in the wrong place. It's difficult to turn the car around, briars every-where. He watches, fearful that someone with a shotgun will emerge.

His father's friend's place—where the hell is it? Why can't he remember?

His heart thumping hard, he gets himself away from this wrong place he's ventured into. Soon the pumping blood gives him a headache that feels like a tight band across his forehead. What if he can't find the right camp? What if he drives and gets lost and the boy wakes up? What will he say?

Studying Matt through the rearview window, he is pretty sure it's a real sleep, maybe deep. The boy's mouth is open.

Those are white pines, these are hemlocks, he will explain. When we get farther in, there will be oaks. They have the distinc-tive big leaves.

Oh, if someone is there at the cabin, it's no good, no good at all. Just . . . just leave is all he can do.

Puerto Rico is only four or five days away once he gets on the road south. He can make Florida in two or three days. His thoughts jump and weave, knitting uncertainty with images of a calm, good life. Confession, at some point, about the accident, the error that took the mother's life. Explanations. Assurances about the love he feels for his son, felt from the moment he saw him in that parking lot.

The boy has not asked about his mother.

Nadal is thinking, thinking, when he finds himself on another rutted road. This one jostles his mother's car just the right amount. The ruts are deep, just the right depth. Then some gravel, crunching and spitting. Could this be it? His breath catches. The gravel path seems longer than he remembers, but he keeps going, no backing out now, he has to find out if this is it. Then the branches of trees reach over and swipe at his windshield. He doesn't want to think about what they're doing to the paint on the car.

And there it is, his father's friend's cabin. No smoke curling from the chimney. No cars parked in front. He pulls up close to it. The boy does not move. Suddenly and without warning, a panic about his son hits him so hard he cries out. Still nothing from the boy. Oh, God, oh, God. He jumps out of the driver's seat and leans over the backseat, holding a palm to his son's mouth. There's breath, steady even breath.

When he's calmed himself, he approaches the cabin, a tidy thing, almost like a house, this one of logs, real logs. *Pretty place*, his father used to say. *Graceful*. The door is locked. *Not that it matters*, his father would say. *When thieves want to get in, they get in. The trick is to expect it.*

Nadal hurries to the carport at the back of the cabin. The truck is there. Same truck. Old. Must be a 1980 or something. At the top of the carport, stuck into the slat, used to be a key. Yes, still there. He pulls it out and hurries around and opens the door.

A safe place. Two rooms. A bunk bed and two other beds in the small room. A kitchen and a rocking chair and an old sofa in the main room. Running water. A battery radio. And other than that, silence, peace.

He goes out to the car and carries in his son, who is heavy, much heavier than he would have guessed. Back arched, arms already weary, he lays the boy on the bottom bunk. He pulls up a wool blanket that's folded at the foot of the bed and covers Matt, who stirs, murmurs, but doesn't come awake.

Nadal goes out to the main room and looks about. Is peace overrated? He does not know how to exist without a computer connection. He opens the refrigerator. Beer. Lots of beer. A couple of beef jerkies.

CHRISTIE AND DOLAN MAKE it to the address on South Neville where they come face to face with three Korean grad students. One wears jeans, two wear pajama bottoms, all three, like the undergraduates the detectives have awakened on this Saturday, struggle not to yawn.

"Nadal? Don't know Nadal. Nate? We know Nate."

"He's here?"

"I don't think. This his room."

Christie opens the door to a room that is so small it must have originally been meant for storage. It has no window. There is a cot in it, and—he draws on gloves he's carried in his pocket—he finds a few clothes in the closet, mostly winter things, boots. Some school texts.

"What's missing?" he asks one of the young men.

The student pokes his head into the room. "Computer. Some clothes maybe. Backpack."

"He brought a child here?"

They shake their heads.

"Ever?"

"No."

"Did he talk about a child?"

"No."

"How long was he here?"

"From . . . May," says one of them.

"We only know Nate. No last name," says another.

"Where would he go?" Christie asks.

"He have car," the one says.

"I don't see car this week," another says.

They identify themselves. Dolan makes them write it all down while they are saying excitedly, one overlapping the other, all they know about the suspect—which isn't much. A first name: Nate. Had a car. A Pontiac, yes. Was mysterious and not friendly. Worked at the computer lab. Was often absent.

"Did he want to be in that storage room with the cot? Did he *ask* for that? No windows?"

"No. Yes, I mean. We put his bed in big room with ours, but he say no, this room is good for him."

"Four people here?"

"Lower rent."

"Landlord's idea?"

"Was not official on the lease," Gab-do says. He looks embarrassed. "Our idea."

"Ah, I see. A source of income." So they had little contact with him and didn't know his last name. How much help could they be? It's not likely Matt was ever brought here, but they must print the place anyway. At the very least, they'll have DNA and Nadal's prints.

Dolan is already on the phone to the lab. "We need a mobile unit. Prints, trace, DNA. Yes, I kn—" Dolan is interrupted by a call from his contact at the phone company. Christie pauses in his interrogation of the students to listen to Dolan's end of the conversation.

"What do you see?" Dolan asks. Then he listens and repeats

what he hears. "No calls since day before yesterday. Most calls from a number in State College belonging to a Mala Brown. A series of other calls . . . almost all incoming, seems he never calls the numbers back. Okay, couple of calls a week ago. He writes down names. Angela Piero, James Grogran, Nalin Patel."

"The car ad," Christie says.

"That it? Can you get me a location? ASAP?" Dolan hangs up. "Bless Sprint for fast answers."

"State College," interrupts the one named Gab-do. "State College is his mother."

Dolan calls Nalin Patel first, gets him, and learns the car was sold last Saturday, a week ago, which makes sense as to why it is not yet on the DMV listings. It takes two weeks, generally. The purchase price was eighty-five hundred dollars and the guy cashed the money order right then because he wanted to make sure it was good. So Nadal Brown no doubt still has cash and the maroon Pontiac is gone. Shit.

Christie is on his phone asking cops he knows in State College to help them by going to Mala Brown's house. He tells them everything he can, frustrated that he wants to be there himself. On the other hand he wonders if he can manage a three-hour drive.

Dolan, reading his mind, says, "I'm okay, Boss. I can drive."

Dolan's phone rings. "Sprint again," he says. He listens. His face looks sick. Ending the call, he tells Christie, "Last location for the phone was near a tower in Blairsville. Same as the boy's phone. Shit."

The Koreans watch them intently. "You don't talk to the news," Christie orders them. "This is serious. You hear?"

Soon Dolan is beginning the long drive to Mala Brown's house. The State College police call back a half hour later when Dolan has gotten to Route 22. At the house: no Mala Brown, no anything. A light left on, a bed rumpled—it's everything and nothing.

"Get your guys in there ASAP," Christie says. "Print the place. We'll be there to see what we can see."

NADAL'S FATHER, after the first trip to the woods, had insisted upon therapy. "You're too quiet, Nadal. You don't talk. You have to talk." Nadal didn't want to see a shrink, but he went, thinking he could quit right away, after a session or two. He told the therapist he didn't talk because he didn't have anything to say. He did have secret thoughts, though. He wished he'd never come to the United States and he didn't like his father.

Now he sits in the main room of the cabin, trying to imagine the conversations he will have with his son. He will have to be clever, like a therapist, to get his son to talk. Dr. Solar, whose name was like the word for sun, was clever enough to get *him* to talk. Solar even understood things that weren't said. Once he smiled and said, "You don't much like it here and you don't much like your father."

"That's right," Nadal said, surprised. "You got it."

"In fact, it doesn't seem you like anyone. Well . . . except your mother. You say positive things about her except for the fact that she took up again with your father."

Nadal found himself talking, telling, then. "I lost respect. He's using her. It's just because he's sick and he wants a nurse."

"Can you think of other reasons?"

"No."

Nadal looked out the window to a large tree, all the branches full, but the leaves starting to get yellow. He tried to concentrate on the tree instead of the question.

"No other reasons?"

"No. Well, his first wife died. So there was a job opening there."

Dr. Solar laughed a little. "A job opening, huh? But, to stick with your mother, is it possible she genuinely cares for him?"

"She's nuts if she does."

"But her feelings might not be your feelings. That's all I want to point out. I guess they both *know* you have these negative feelings. So it must get tense. I just want to ask if your father has shown you any care, any warmth. Has he done things for you?"

"He thinks he has."

"Like?"

"Sending me to college."

"Paying?"

"Not very much. He gets tuition benefits. His colleagues think I'm his stepson. He doesn't tell them otherwise."

Solar grunted as if this made Nadal's negative feelings make sense, but he asked, "Anything else he's done for you?"

It was his third appointment, and he was only just calm enough to notice things at all—the shiny tables, the rug with vacuum marks, the little gold clock. Nadal tried to think about what his father might have done for him and how he could explain to Solar that what drove Arne Brown wasn't love. "Clothes. Food. A room. Sending me here. He wants to make me fit in. He wants to control me so he's not embarrassed."

Dr. Solar touched his mustache, which is what he did between thoughts. "I see what it feels like from your perspective. I take that seriously. Does he talk to you?"

"He took me to a cabin in the forest to show me plants and animals. He said it was a time to talk. We went two times, but I couldn't think of anything to say. He wanted to go again, but I had a . . . trip I had to make. Out of town."

"To see friends?"

"Sort of."

"So there are friends, people you talk to?"

Nadal shrugged.

"Are there people who comfort you, women in your life?"

"Why do you ask?" He wondered if shrinks could spy telepathically. This meeting was right after Maggie had dumped him.

"Have these women understood you?"

The plural threw him off. Maggie was the only one. But he didn't plan to tell Solar any of that. Some things were off-limits. He would never tell anyone how desperate he had been, the way he hitchhiked to Pittsburgh and got dumped. And when he got back, old Arne and his mother studied him, trying to figure out what was wrong and where he'd been.

"Any drugs? Drug usage?"

"That's prejudiced."

"In what way?"

"Because I have Puerto Rican blood."

"That has nothing at all to do with my question. Drugs are a common occurrence. People with Russian backgrounds and Italian backgrounds and Irish and British heritages get hooked on drugs. People with totally American backgrounds for five generations or more get hooked. In each case, they think the drugs will help them cope and the trick is . . . the opposite happens. They end up coping less well. So it's always a possibility. With anyone who is hurting."

"I'm not hurting."

Solar nodded.

Nadal thought how Maggie was like a drug. He got hooked and he got worse.

"What were you thinking just now?"

"Why?"

"Your face got angry."

"Nothing. Just how rotten it all is."

He watched the little gold clock ticking until he could get out. "I feel better," he told Arne and his mother. "Yeah, I feel better. I'll concentrate on school. I'll talk more." And he quit Solar after one more session.

He hated Solar, but when he thinks about it now, he can't figure out why.

He walks around for a bit in the small main room and finally opens up his computer. He boots up in the wild hopes that somehow he can get the latest, but there's nothing doing. And of course he knew there would be no signal out here. The little arches don't show up, the dialogue box tells him he is not connected to the Internet, and he stares at his laptop . . . thinking of all the waste, even including the paper for class that he began—wasted tuition money. But he's leaving his old life behind.

Luckily this cabin is more substantial than most. Two rooms instead of one and a generator-driven refrigerator and a two-burner stove. Electricity, anyway. Almost enough food for two days—counting the beer and beef jerky and what he brought, the two frozen dinners, plus his bag with cereal and wrap makings and crackers. No milk. No juice.

He goes into the bedroom and makes various noises, testing. The boy doesn't move. Asleep. Now is the time to go. Get it over with.

He's pretty sure he remembers where there is a general store. If the boy wakes when he is gone . . . he can't think it. He has to believe in luck. He hops into the VW and drives as fast as he dares, up over the bumps like a kid riding something at Kennywood Park.

WHEN MATT WAKES, he is not sure why everything looks so strange and it comes to him slowly that this is not his bed or the one he had at Jan and Arthur's or the one in the strange room in the house the man took him to, but something else entirely. This is a bunk bed, and he doesn't know who or what is above. He peels a rough gray wool blanket off him and sits up slowly. There are no sounds. Nothing. He shakes himself—trying to get rid of the fog that envelops him, noting each detail. He is still wearing his clothes, even his shoes. His feet feel a little buzzy, so he flexes his toes. The door to the room is a wooden thing—up and down boards and then one that goes on the diagonal. He is sure it will be locked. Finally he gets the courage to stand and look to the top bunk. Nobody. He is alone.

Still, it's as if the air around him is fuzz, cotton, something soft. If only he could feel better. He tiptoes to the door and pulls. It's heavy, but it opens, making a scraping sound on the floor where he can see a groove has been cut by just this thing, the opening and closing.

The next room is like a kitchen but also has a chair and a couch. There's a little stove and a refrigerator. Where is the man? He walks from wall to wall—all logs, the insides of logs, but there is only one door. And two windows. He looks out the front window to see woods for as far as his eye will take him. And out the back window is some old truck and otherwise just more woods. There is the man's laptop on the single table. The man's backpack is on the floor.

His mother's voice says, *Think, think.*

But he isn't sure what to think. So he sits on the sofa. His mother is dead. Today will be her cremation, and he is not going to be there. The man who brought him here is a liar, because his mother is not alive.

For a few minutes he lets himself think perhaps his mother *is* alive and the man will bring her here. But then he knows she isn't because in his mind he hears Christie's voice. Then Jan's voice. Then Arthur's. They all said she was gone, and they did not seem like liars, any of them.

The names he saw—Arnett and Mala—make no sense to him. The email he saw—it feels like a dream. There's something he needs to know but he can't figure out what it is.

He waits for the man to come back. To give him rules.

But nothing happens. So he gets up to study the room, looking for a phone. The man threw away their cell phones, but maybe . . . No. Electrical outlets but no phone outlets. He peers out the window. No sign of the man.

His heart begins to pound. He knows it's wrong, but he opens the backpack, hoping for something, another phone. But there is only a T-shirt and . . . envelopes. In the envelopes, money. Lots of money. His heart sets up a wild racket. What is all the money for? Where did it come from? What is it for?

The computer is sitting on a small table, open. He approaches gingerly and presses the power button. It hums to life. He can hardly use his hands, he's so nervous. He recognizes the little *e* and the other thing, the flames around the world. Selecting one, then the other, he gets the same message each time: *You are not connected to the Internet.*

He goes to the window again. There is nobody in sight. No sounds except rustling and maybe something croaking—a frog perhaps, if there's water. He can't tell.

Back at the computer, he clicks on an icon.

Nate Brown
Comp Sci 2003
Changes in Firewall Protection Systems
There are significant changes being made in firewall protection.

Nate Brown, Mala Brown, Arnett Brown. Are these relatives? He clicks on other icons but nothing makes sense even though he sees the name Nate Brown several times. He suddenly feels his stomach drop. The man (Nate?) will probably be angry if he catches him. He powers off the computer and goes back to the sofa, waiting.

After a while, he tiptoes to the refrigerator and looks in. Beer and little brown sticks, maybe cigars. The label says beef jerky. That sounds like food. He opens one and smells it. Then he takes a bite. It makes him chew, like licorice, but more so. He opens a cupboard and finds cereal—the same kind he was given this morning. Cheerios. He takes a handful of cereal and eats it like candy, surprised at how good it is.

How long is he supposed to be alone?

Matt opens the door to the outside.

Now is the time to run.

The air is chilly. The forest sounds are unfamiliar, but he can figure out what he's hearing: animals, leaves rustling, birds chirping. There's forest and more forest as far as he can see.

He begins to walk into the woods. Just go a little. Find a path, he tells himself. The old good feeling of wanting to run won't come to him. His heart knocks hard against his chest.

He begins to walk down the path that the car probably used to get them here. It's hardly a road.

He misses his mother. *Think, think, think,* she says.

In the distance he hears something new. An engine, a noisy motor.

"HOW'S GREER ABOUT SPLITTING duty with you?" Dolan asks. He's driving well for a man who hasn't slept, skirting potholes, timing lights.

"She's okay. She's a pro. No information from the Philips kids so she's back to the office, waiting for word from us. I'll call her as soon as I have something she can do." Christie feels like he's on heavy drugs—sleep deprivation makes him almost hallucinate. Light hurts his eyes. There's something that feels like a heavy lump at the back of his skull.

Route 22, part of it, is a nightmare as usual, but they aim to get to State College in record time.

Christie has been on the phone almost nonstop with the team up there. He wants them to take samples but not to disturb anything until he gets there.

Lights flash up ahead. Parked on the side of the road are two police cars. One is State Police, the other Johnstown Police.

"Stop," Christie says. But Dolan, who always understands what to do, is already pulling over.

Christie doesn't have to introduce himself to the other cops. He's known, from TV mainly in any area that picks up Pittsburgh stations. As soon as he exits his vehicle, the others do, too. They're eating a take-out breakfast. They hurriedly stash food wrappers on their car seats and turn back with the look of guilty children. "You have any news, Commander?"

"We think he took the boy to State College. They're not there now, but we're going to look around."

Christie knows these guys are on the road trying to locate the cell phones. The Johnstown patrol cop gestures to the State Police officer. "He has one of those metal detectors. We haven't given up."

The phones will help, no doubt, when it comes to a trial, though the Pittsburgh Police also have the phone records to go on.

And moments later he and Dolan are back in the car and on the way again to State College. He has asked the folks up there to use an unmarked car and to have at least two officers in the house, hidden and armed. Also, they should hide their lab car. And even more importantly, he wants two cars at each end of the street in case this guy, Nadal Brown, is on his way back and gets the willies and the thing ends in a chase.

"We have to put it on the news, his name," Dolan says.

"I know. I have this hope that he just went out for breakfast and is coming back with the kid. If we can nab him before we scare him . . . "

Most of the phone calls to Nadal Brown from Mala Brown originated from a landline at the house in State College. And where is she? Is she involved?

"His roommates say he was strange. But what version of strange?" Dolan taps at the wheel.

Christie bargains silently. Get the kid back and he'll quit trying to arrange everyone's life. If it's Jan and Arthur as the parents, then all right, that's it. After all, it's what he wanted to begin with.

MATT'S EYES ARE WIDE. He sits on the sagging sofa, an old mohair thing. He's breathing rapidly.

"Did you go outside?"

"A little bit."

"Why?"

"To see the woods come awake, like you said."

But the boy can hardly breathe and Nadal's own heart begins to pound. He reaches behind him for the door lock and slides the bolt. "I thought we were okay."

"No," Matt blurts. He seems as surprised by what he has said as Nadal is by the show of spirit. "You tried to tell me my mother is alive." He waits, open-faced, hoping to be contradicted.

Nadal knew this moment would come, but he thought it would come differently, gradually, with sideways questions. He sits down in the chair across from the sofa, thrown off at first by how it sags and the way the springs poke up at him. Leaning forward over his knees, he tries to hold Matt's eyes.

"I'm sorry. It was an accident. Nobody can understand how much of an accident it was. I thought she was going to kill me."

"If it was an accident, you would get help."

"It was an accident. But I wasn't thinking clearly about what to do. I wanted you, to take care of you. So I looked for you. And then I left. All I knew was, if they took me to prison, I couldn't take care of you."

"Why did you want me?"

"Because you're mine."

For a long while, Matt doesn't say anything. Then he says, "I got hungry. I ate cereal."

"That's okay. That's fine. That's good. I went out for milk. Would you like a bowl of cereal?"

Matt nods, biting his lip. Not speaking again.

Even Nadal's hands feel the tremors of his terror. He has made big decisions and now he has to make them right. With delibera-tion, he opens one cabinet after another, finds a bowl, washes it out, finds a spoon. He's hungry, too, his stomach is growling, but he is too shaky to eat. He holds the cereal box with two hands and pours a full bowl, then adds milk. His boy is lean, not sloppy, and that's good. "You burn it off," he observes. "That's a good thing. Come to the table. It's easier."

Matt comes to the table.

"Where would you go if you left? I just want to know, to understand."

"The people I was with, I guess. They wanted me."

"I want you. It's going to be all right. You'll forget them. Everything will fade. It takes a little time."

Matt takes up the spoon and begins with tiny bites. He doesn't seem as hungry as he said he was. "I had friends, too. And a dog. And a new computer. And I was in a play. I should be going to rehearsal."

Nadal sighs raggedly. "I'm sorry about that but . . . we've cut ties. We can't go back to anything we had before. It's all new from here out."

Matt pushes the cereal away. "I was getting used to things."

"I'll get you a dog."

The boy's face changes, interested.

"I'll buy you a computer."

"Really?"

"Yes."

"I like games. Video games. I like *Red Dead Redemption*."

"I don't know much about that."

"It's hard but it's good. It's an adult game, but I play it."

"I see. Are you going to eat your cereal?"

"I think I changed my mind."

"I'll eat it then." Nadal pulls the bowl to him and takes up the spoon, working to control his hands.

"That's my spoon. I mean, I used it."

"Well. There aren't many here. And your germs are my germs. I mean, you're my son."

Matt's face furrows.

Nadal studies him as he tries to get his hands to hold still. "What? You frowned."

"Just . . . she said you're not my father."

"Why would she lie about that?"

"Who wrote to . . . my other parents from the music school?"

"Somebody. Somebody lying. Look. After . . . I have something to eat, we should go into the woods, see what we can see. It's beautiful here. People come up here to study the animals."

"Are there bears?"

"We'll be careful."

"Can I use your computer later?"

He thinks about this, wanting to get the balance right between rules and generosity. "Okay."

15.

THE COFFEE IS COLD NOW. Earlier, Kate turned off the pot without thinking—she's vague and thrown off course, too. He's never seen her like this. She sat alone for a while. She went out for an early walk. Now she's in the shower. She was supposed to work early today, but she called and arranged to go in later. He does not have to go into Peabody because it's Saturday—he was supposed to sit at home and face his dissertation, not that that is going to happen now.

He pours himself a cup of coffee and heats it in the microwave. It took him seven years to get used to American coffee. Even his mother, who had been American born, had stopped being able to drink it. Now he actually likes it, finds himself craving it. There are practical reasons for Arabic coffee, as there are for espresso. A daintiness, yes, a fit in a crowded place, yes, a punch of vitality all at once—and, best of all, no need to find a bathroom ten minutes later.

He looks about the place he shares with Kate—a condo in a large building, hardly a stick of furniture that is his. Before this, before her residence assignment, she lived in an apartment, which was small, cramped, and smelled like other people's food. She drove him by it once. He wasn't used to anything better, either, only surprised that she'd been so poor. But the bank thought her a good risk; every city needs its doctors and she's at the top of her class.

He remembers, as if it happened last night, the way he found her. He was playing in a club in DC—a group that's disbanded now, but one made up of compatible cronies. He was on piano and two of the other three members were trained in Arabic melodies and rhythms. They took in a gringo on guitar, but he was okay, a nice kid, except when he goofed off in rehearsal, adding vocals that mimicked Middle Eastern singers who, to this kid, sounded woeful and whiny.

"That's our sound," Ziad told him. "It's not meant to be whiny. It's a series of progressions we grew up with. The singers are singing about buying houses and falling in love."

"Not, 'We are lost in the desert and everybody hates us'?"

He'd had to walk away from the kid. Albert. Very blond, Swedish the family was, he thinks. But Albert went off to Juilliard, and Charles, whose real name is Marwan, went to be with his wife, who did not want him out nights in the clubs. That left him with John Aboud, who could add drums to his piano, not very exciting. However, John was ambitious—always looking to pull other musicians, strangers, in for a gig.

Then, just when they needed them, two brothers arrived in town. Word went out that they were good. They'd been living in California. A certain ripple of excitement went through the four of them the first time they started playing together. They had found one another as if they had all been looking.

He was with the old group the night she came into the club. When he looked up from the keyboard, Kate, sitting with a big group of friends, totally distracted him. She seemed so . . . confident, so American, so tall, healthy looking, happy.

At one point, she got up to go to the ladies' room. She had curly light hair. He watched her move around the small tables. Marwan was watching him and laughing as he started the riff that suggested a break. It was a few minutes early for a break.

He turned from her to give the piano all his concentration. He closed his eyes to feel the music.

"So you are normal after all," Marwan said when the applause died down and they began to move.

"What do you mean?"

"You never look at anything except your piano. Go meet her."

He shook his head. He had been seeing a woman named Theresa for the last six months, a new grad student at Peabody. "Do you want a beer?" he asked Marwan.

"Sure."

"I'll get them."

He stood at the bar. And there she was beside him.

"Hello," she said.

A light fragrance of some sort wafted his way.

"I like the music."

"Thank you."

"I've never been here before. I almost never get out for things like this. It's really fun."

"You seem to be having a good time. With your friends."

"Friends and family. It's my birthday. They dragged me out."

He guessed she must be a runner or a tennis player. She stood straight. Her eyes were blue.

"I mean I saw you laughing," he said lamely.

"Laughter. The cure-all." She smiled. "When does the next set begin?"

"We take fifteen minutes. I'm getting a beer for my friend. May I get you something?"

"A water? I've had enough of the other. Do you have a card? For your group?"

"I don't. But my friend does. He's the business head."

The two beers arrived. He asked for a bottle of water for her. He slid a twenty across the bar, and waited for change. The water arrived, a bottle, then a glass with lime. She tipped the bottle to her lips before pouring some into the glass. He couldn't make himself move away.

"Do you have a day job?" she asked.

"I teach music."

"Full time?"

"No. Part time. Peabody."

"Oh. Peabody."

"You know it?"

"Yes, yes, I know of it. Very well respected. You're faculty?"

"In a sense. Graduate student. I'm finishing a degree."

"Which?"

"Doctor of music."

She beamed. "I like that. Doctor of music. I'm a mere doctor of bodies."

Ziad got distracted by the galumphing approach of Marwan, who said cheerily, "I will never get my beer."

"Sorry. Here it is."

"Hello," Marwan said to the woman. "Is he talking your ear off?"

"Hardly. He's very modest."

"Not inside. Not where the ego grows."

"Marwan, do you have a business card? She would like to have one."

"Yes. Just a minute." Marwan put his beer on the bar to dig in his wallet. The move established him as a part of a conversational triangle.

"Doctor of the body?" Ziad asked her. He wondered if it would turn out to be something new age and flimsy. "Do you mean a medical doctor?"

She nodded soberly, then opened a small black purse he had

hardly noticed hanging from her shoulder. Both men paused as she searched it. "I didn't put any cards in this little thing," she said.

Marwan said, "I have two. Write your name on the back of this and give it back to our boy."

She shuffled the two cards, studied the one on top, and accepted a pen from the bartender, who stood nearby. "I'll try to catch the group again," she said as she wrote. When she finished writing, she handed the card to Ziad. "If I don't make it through the second set, please don't be insulted. My friends are already talking about going, and I almost never stay up this late."

She walked away. He looked at her card. Marwan took a long drink of beer and watched him.

"Why didn't you give her your phone number?"

"It seemed too bold. And besides . . ."

"But you're in love. It's already happened."

And that was true. He knew only these things about her: Her name was Kate McCauley. She gave two phone numbers, one with *cell* before it and the other with *hosp* before it. So she truly was a doctor of the body.

The next day he worked harder on his thesis than he had in a long time. Theresa came over to his place with a cooked meal—he can't remember what it was. She was a guitarist. Classical. And smart. He told himself to stick with her even as he knew for sure he would not be able to.

She put an arm around his waist as she brought him to the table. "I'm so glad you're working again. I've been . . . so afraid you'd let it go."

"Everybody lets it go. It's the doctorate disease."

"*I* won't."

"Your head starts to do tricks."

"What tricks?"

"If I finish this, I will never make it as a musician. I will be all head, all theory, and I will lose the . . . physical part of myself."

"The gut connection?"

"Okay. Gut connection. Yes. A fear that the cerebral will take over."

She looked at him. "I understand."

She was terrific, but he couldn't pretend. He told her he had become interested in another woman last night, even though he wasn't sure Kate would so much as remember who he was.

Theresa was devastated. He felt awful.

Then, the next day, he called Kate and there was no disguising her joy when she heard his voice.

Now the shower stops. He's turned Kate, who's near perfect, into a mess. It's already ten o'clock and she's still home. He wishes he could erase what he did eight years ago, almost nine, when he sold his sperm for spending money.

He carries his coffee outside to the deck. The sun is good today, the air is dry, but it's a bit brisk. Even though his feet are cold he doesn't want to go back inside, to face her and whatever she's been thinking during the shower.

He makes a deal. If I work today, concentrate on my work, act in good faith, my son will be found. He will be okay.

Kate comes out to the deck and touches his arm. "If you don't want to wait, some people at work told me it's possible to drive to a place in Virginia where you need only a pulse. Nothing else. They marry you on the spot."

He turns to her, confused. "Why now? I don't understand."

"I've been too obsessed with work." She pauses. "And also making a show of my independence. Pregnant and proud. Don't need a wedding band. All that. Stupid."

Is that what it was? She's never stupid.

"It's a two-, three-hour drive to this town in Virginia. Winchester. I could take off Tuesday."

"YOU SHOULD MOVE BACK HERE," Violetta tells Nadal's mother. They are drinking fresh orange juice and sitting on her small balcony, one of some eight hundred tiny balconies in the apartment complex. "The good life, don't you think?"

"It's possible I might." Mala Brown looks out over the concrete jungle—the jutting balconies, each with plastic chairs and a grill, the parking lot below, cars baking in the sun. She's lived so many places in her life, each different. There is everything to recommend the small town of State College—she has a house and a yard big enough to garden in; the shops are all only a short drive away; food and clothing products are of good quality, though she can't always find the foods she grew up with. But for the first time in her life, she's desperately lonely. There was family, for better or worse, in the early days in Puerto Rico. There were fellow countrymen in the years in Florida—plus she was working then and made friends easily with the other cleaning women. And then, because her life tended to be run by others and their needs, when Arnett Brown called her to tell her he was widowed, she thought perhaps he would come to see her more often. And he did—but only for a few months before he announced two things. He wanted to marry her and take her with him to his place of work. He wanted to be a father to Nadal, who he thought was badly in need of *something*. The boy was odd, he said. Too *inner*. He needed help. He needed a father. For Nadal's sake, she had agreed to move. It tore her away from her friends and from familiarity. Because Arne didn't want her working, certainly not cleaning houses, she got to State College and for a while had no contacts other than Arne and Nadal. It was hard. She applied for various jobs in spite of her husband (they had married) and she worked at the Target for almost two years, but when Arne needed her, when he was really ill, she gave the job up. The timing was bad for being rehired. People were out of work everywhere and desperate. She didn't so much need the money—she had enough to live on—but she needed people around her.

Now, being with Violetta, she remembers the comforts of work and friendship. "I've got to get a job," she says.

Violetta laughs. "Didn't we always say if we had enough to live on, we wouldn't be at some terrible job?"

"We don't always know ourselves."

Hardly a tree anywhere, but the birds don't appear to care; they hop along the balcony walls no doubt looking for crumbs. "Not here," Mala tells the birds. "Violetta is very clean."

They laugh.

"How's the boy?"

"I don't know."

Violetta raises her eyebrows. "He's not a boy anymore. I forget. You said not married yet. Do you see him?"

Not married yet. The least of her worries. He's not right, not calm, her son. He chose that strange small room at their house when he had a choice of a better room; he put a lock on the door. Why? Always keeping himself apart from others. Arne didn't know what to do with him. He tried everything. Except of course being a father for the first nineteen years. But did that account for her son's strangeness? Plenty of boys didn't have fathers. Mala was rock solid—other people became calm around her. So, no, it was something else, something from birth, a curse, a dent to the head, a punishment for some ancestor's sins.

"He visited me one Sunday, not even two weeks ago, and he drove me to the airport. So I saw him."

"Good boy, then."

Good. She's not sure. She got an idea a while back that froze her blood, but it was a crazy idea, and she doesn't know why it keeps coming back to her in the form of fear, a small underlying daytime version of a bad dream.

MATT HAS TROUBLE KEEPING HIS BALANCE over the bumpy ground. He keeps turning around hoping to see the red car. "Should we be marking trees?" he asks.

"Marking? I don't know what you mean."

"To find our way back."

The man stops and looks about. "I guess we're getting kind of far. I think I have it, though, what we've done."

"I don't want to get lost. People mark trees."

The man smiles at him, but the smile is tight, almost angry-looking. "Would you like to do that?"

"Yes, I would. Crayon would be good, but I don't have my back-pack."

"Right, right, the backpack. What do we have?"

"Nothing." He holds out his hands. He doesn't even have other clothes or the book he was reading. Just . . . nothing.

The man pats his pockets. "I have this." He comes up with a pen. He frowns. "I don't think we'd see it."

"I can use that!" Matt says excitedly. "It's good because it's a felt tip." It will take time to mark with it, then time to see the blue ink.

"Plus, I'll try to remember."

"And if we prop up a twig or branch against the trunk to point to it, to point to the blue mark . . . "

"I knew you would be good at things. I knew." The man seems excited and also angry at the same time.

Matt *is* good at things, but he doesn't want to be here, thinking them up. He marks the first tree, low down, changes his mind, and makes a mark at eye level. It's a small mark, hard to see, but he finds a fallen branch and makes a pointer of it.

"Very good."

"What are we looking *for*?"

"We're looking just to look. To be in nature. To listen to sounds. To see the tracks."

"Are those tracks?"

"Looks like it."

"What kind?"

"Bear . . . could be elk."

Matt never studied the woods before, and everything is beautiful, but he doesn't want to be here. "Can't we go back?"

"Just look. Take things in." For a moment it seems the man really *is* his father and Matt almost doubts what he read on Jan's computer. But then he reminds himself he read it three times. So who is that other person—with the Z names?

Hesitantly, he asks, "You liked coming here with your father?"

The man stops, considers. "I didn't think so at the time. I thought he was always pushing me. But now, now I think it was a good thing to see something different, to get out of the city. I wanted to give you that."

Something scatters in the distance. "I think that was a groundhog," Matt says. "The shape."

"Smart boy."

Matt marks a tree and finds a branch.

The man stops. He leans on a tree and does something like push-ups, straining. Then he slumps with his head on his arms, then drags his head to the side, crying, trying to wipe off the tears on his sleeve without using his hands.

Matt pretends he doesn't see, stoops down, and studies a plant, hoping it's not something poisonous. He thinks, *Mark the trees, keep him calm.*

He can hardly remember his mother or Jan and Arthur or the play he's in or his new school. He can hardly remember anything before this.

THEY ARE NEARING STATE COLLEGE. They already have some information because an hour or so after Christie and Dolan passed the police on the road, he got a call telling him some of the prints looked small, possibly a child's prints.

"Any blood?"

"No blood."

"And the owner of the place?"

"Not in sight. We've been asking the closest neighbors, like you said."

"And?"

"One lady said, 'I haven't seen her this week. Is she okay? She's usually out in the yard, weeding.' Another lady said, 'She was here last night. I saw her car.' "

"What kind of car?"

"A red VW Bug. Nobody else knew anything."

"Keep it up. We're almost there."

Christie got the call back from the DMV minutes later. The car registered to Mala Brown was a red VW Bug. He updated the Amber Alert to look for a man and a boy and possibly an older woman in that car. The Pontiac was history, and this was the likely vehicle.

"No blood," Dolan said. "That's good."

"Hope so."

Finally he and Dolan enter State College and spot the address for Mala Brown, a modest brick house of the three-bedroom variety bounded by a well-kept yard, like most others on the street.

The State College team is still there. Even though Dolan parks on the street, even though the forensic van is several doors away, any smart looker-on would guess something is up.

Christie enters a brick house not unlike his own. He is led to a room with a lock on the door. He studies what are probably the boy's prints.

"Any other child's prints?"

"Nope."

"We still have to match these. Point me to the neighbors with something to say."

They show him the house next door and one across the street. It is the woman across the street, a frazzled type, wiping her hands on an apron, who says, "I know she was gone somewhere. I mean, I could tell, not just from the car being gone, but because of the lights. Just one little light on in a downstairs window. And the drapes almost completely drawn."

"Did you notice her car last night?"

"No. I wasn't looking, but no."

"What time did you go to bed?"

"Ten. Or so."

Christie and Dolan hurry to ask the neighbor next door. She appears angry that there is police activity in her neighborhood and that her next-door neighbor belongs in the undesirable category. Touching her molded hair, she says, "I was up, baking for a group I belong to. Then I locked up. I saw her car."

"What time?"

"Midnight. After."

"You were friendly with her?"

"We said hello. She was from Puerto Rico. I don't think she spoke much English. I was friendly with Mr. Brown's first wife. She was a nice woman."

Right. A first wife and not foreign. "And, for our records, what time do you get up in the morning?"

"Five."

"See it then?"

She shakes her head.

"Were you looking?"

"I wish. But I wasn't. Is this about that kid on the news?"

"Who said that?"

"The other police."

Christie says, "We'll comment on the details soon." So much for keeping leaks out of the case.

They are about to start down the street to talk to more neighbors when the State College detective, Sam Taylor, waves him over. "We ordered you guys coffee, figured you might need some." He is kind looking, with a big mustache.

Dolan says, "I do. Thanks."

Christie says, "Very kind. Would he send it after us? I want to talk to a few other neighbors."

One block over they find a woman who says she knows Mala Brown fairly well. This woman, who might be Thai or Filipino, says she walks her dog for long hours and often saw Brown in her yard. "She was going away. She was excited. A vacation."

"With her son? Did she say?"

"Nothing about him. To see a friend in Florida. She was nervous about flying because even when she first came up here from Florida, she came in a car."

"I see. This is helpful. Did she say the friend's name? A city?"

"No name. Just Miami."

"Very helpful."

"Is she all right? Was there some kind of accident?"

"Nothing like that."

"Because she was the nicest woman. Very kind."

"Thank you."

And back to the house. They go through papers. And Dolan has already put in a call for her phone records. But they don't need them. They find a piece of paper with *V* and a phone number with a Florida area code.

"Call?" Christie thinks aloud. "Send someone?"

He wishes he could plop down in Miami and knock on the door, but this time, there is no time.

STEPPING OVER FALLEN BRANCHES, Nadal tries to think of things he'd heard about how to wear out an active kid. After a two-hour hike in the woods, Matt does not seem tired, while Nadal, not having slept last night, not used to rugged activity, badly wants sleep. When he sees the log cabin in the distance, he feels immense relief. They have found their way back; at two points they could not find the code on the trees, but eventually they did. And now they approach the cabin, and nothing seems different, nothing amiss.

Nadal knows the owner used to set up a trail camera in one of the trees. He looks about but doesn't see it. If there is one, he needs to remove it.

He lets Matt open the door to the cabin, aware of the boy's energy, and also of his restlessness. Nadal wants to go to sleep now. His laptop sits on the only table—useless for getting news.

Matt doesn't say anything. He sits near the computer, looking toward it hopefully. Nadal says, "Go ahead." He watches his son open it up, scan the buttons, find the power button, and get booted up. All the while, Nadal walks about, tries to eat a spoonful of soggy cereal, and finally ditches the rest in a garbage pail.

He comes back to look over Matt's shoulder. Matt quickly tries to close the lid of the computer but Nadal pushes it open. "No secrets from me. That's a rule. You understand?"

The screen says, *You are not connected to the Internet.* The request in the box was for *hotmail.com.*

"I thought you were smart," he says. "I thought you were a smart one."

"I am."

"And you thought I would let you mess with the Internet?"

"I'm sorry."

"Who did you want to write to?"

"My new . . . my other parents. To tell them I am all right."

"I told you I wrote to them."

"You told me my mother was alive. How do I know when you're telling the truth?"

"I did write to them. Are you worried about them?"

"Yeah."

"They aren't worth your worry. But I did write to them. If they don't mess with the police, you'll be safe. We'll both be safe."

"What if they called the police?"

"That makes our lives more complicated. Not impossible, but harder. You can't mess around with things without telling me."

"I just wanted to do an email."

"Can't. We're deep in the woods."

"I know."

"Look, don't you want to sleep?"

"I just got up."

"We both need to rest up. Me too."

The boy's face lights with interest. He isn't won over yet. He will run.

"We're going to take something to help us sleep."

"I don't want to. I'll just sit."

"There's nothing to do here. You'll get bored."

"I'll go out in the woods again."

"No. Not alone."

"I'll just sit."

"I already said no. We're going to rest up, so we're ready for anything. I'm going to give you something."

"I don't want to."

"You don't have a choice. It's all right. Everything will be better after. You'll see."

Matt starts to cry. "I don't believe you. I try to believe you, but I don't."

Nadal fetches his backpack from the floor and from it he takes the box with the packet of Benadryl. The backpack is almost empty except for the packets of cash and a T-shirt to cushion any blow to the laptop when he carried it in there. Nadal goes to the kitchen to pour a mug of water for his son, but when he comes back to the boy, the boy is sitting with his arms folded.

"No, please, I don't want to sleep."

"This will help. You'll want to. Sleep is the big cure for everything. That's what my mother always said."

"Where is your mother?"

"I'll tell you where if you're good. And maybe we'll find a way to visit her. Just take these."

"Two?"

"Two is better."

There is a long pause in which he holds out the pills which he's pressed from the packet wrap and he waits until his son takes them up.

"Everything will be better if we're rested. You'll see."

Finally his son sighs and takes the pills.

Nadal longs for eight hours of oblivion, but he has other things he must do. When the boy is asleep, he carries him to the car and puts him in the backseat. It's not particularly cold out now, but he goes back in for the wool blanket on the bed Matt used and he covers the boy. Then he puts his backpack on the passenger seat of the red VW Bug, but he sits there for a long time, unwilling to leave the safety of the woods.

His head drops against the headrest. He's so tired he wants to sleep, but there's Wi-Fi in Bradford and he's not going to rest until he checks the news.

COLLEEN AND POTOCKI are back in her house in Squirrel Hill in front of her personal computer. Waiting. The police in Miami proudly announced they use Skype and Christie told her to go ahead with it, even though he can't be there for the session. Instead he is on the open phone line while driving back with Dolan. She can hear both of them talking; they can hear her and Potocki.

The mechanical recorded ring that is her Skype alert interrupts both conversations. She leaves the cell phone on speaker and accepts the Skype call. In a living room setting, a face comes into view. Not Mrs. Brown, but a worried-looking detective who identifies himself as Detective Tinsley. "We're here with your witness. And her friend. For the record, here is the friend."

A woman sits down in front of the computer. She has long hair pulled back and fastened at the neck. She is middle aged and probably stocky from the look of her face and arms. "I am Violetta Santos. I live here. My friend Mala Brown is here for vacation. I did not see her for nine years."

The woman moves away from the camera and another, the same age, but leaner, takes her place. "I am Mala Brown." This woman's voice is almost a whisper; she wipes a tear. "You want to talk about my son."

Colleen says, "I am Detective Colleen Greer. Behind me is Detective John Potocki. We're working a case in Pittsburgh. We have to ask you a few questions. Your son is Nadal Brown, is that correct?"

"Yes." The image disappears for a second—Mala Brown has moved away from the camera for a tissue and then comes back. "Yes."

"Your son is a person of interest in our investigation. Can you tell us when you last talked to him?"

"He drove me to the airport. We talked then. We had lunch. That was last Tuesday. I called him to tell him I am here. Tuesday. I called Thursday but he didn't answer. I called last night but no answer. Where is my son? Do you have him"—she consults with her friend—"in . . . custody?"

"We would like to speak to him," Colleen says levelly. "Do you know where he is?"

"No."

"What car was he driving when he took you to the airport?"

"My car."

"The red VW?"

Brown seems surprised. "Yes."

"And you left it with him?"

"Yes."

"When did you last see him, previous to the trip to the airport?"

"He came to visit me. It was a Sunday. Not last. The one before."

Colleen looks quickly to Potocki. He gets it too. "What was the reason for the visit?"

"I don't know . . . just to see me. He just came. We watched TV."

"What did he talk about?"

"Nothing. Very quiet."

"What car was he driving?"

"His Pontiac. He likes it."

"Did you know he sold it?"

"No, I didn't know."

"Did he do anything unusual when he visited you, anything to make you suspicious that something was wrong?"

"He washed his clothes." She begins to weep. "Please tell me. Please."

But what can she say to comfort the woman? Potocki gives her a quick shake of the head. "It's all right. It's hard, I know, but I just have a few more questions. What is your relationship to Margaret Brown of Pittsburgh?"

"This is the woman who died? Who was killed?"

"Yes."

"I saw about it on the news. It . . . made me sad."

"Was she a relative?"

"No. I never saw her before. She had our name, but she was not a relative."

"Did your son Nadal ever mention her?"

"Only when I said about the news on TV."

"What did he say?"

"He said, 'It's a common name.' And he said, 'What will happen to the son?' "

A shiver goes through Colleen. "He mentioned the boy?"

"I think. Yes."

"Did he ever tell you he had a son?" Or believed he did.

"No." Brown looks toward her friend, clearly distressed. "Please tell me what is happening? Are you saying . . . Is this his wife? His son?"

"Mrs. Brown. It's important that we have your cooperation if your son gets in touch with you. Do you understand?"

"Yes . . . but tell me . . . "

"He may be in trouble. We believe he has this boy now. He's disappeared and the boy has, too."

"He has a son. . . . I didn't know."

"We are almost certain this is not his son. He may, however, think it is. And so we need to ask: Has he ever done anything like this before?"

"No."

"Has he ever been accused of hurting a child?"

"No."

"Clearly you know things about him that would help us. Can you tell us where you think he would go, who his friends are?"

"I don't know any friends."

"Why is that? Did he keep friends away from you?"

Mala Brown cries openly. "No. No."

"Did he seem to be alone a lot?"

"He had roommates. I was happy he had roommates. I thought they would be his friends. I wanted to meet them when I came to the airport. But he said we didn't have time."

"Do you know where he would go if he needed to be alone or, say, with the young boy, for a while. Where would he go?"

"My house? The police here told me my house."

"Yes, other than that. After that?"

"I don't know."

"Tell me, what kind of trouble he has ever been in? Anything about him, anything about why . . . he has no friends."

"He is sad. Always. From when he was a little boy." Her friend Violetta hands her a fresh tissue and puts an arm around her, then half on camera herself and half off, Violetta says, "She took good care of him. She was wonderful with him. It's not her fault."

"We're not talking about fault at all. Believe me. We think he's a man in trouble. And we're worried about the boy he believes is his son."

"I know he was always hurt," says Mala Brown. "Always worried, wishing to make friends."

"Just a moment, Mrs. Brown. Anything else, Commander?" Colleen asks Christie.

"Ask her if she'll help us. For her son's sake."

But Nadal's mother can hear the question before it's asked. "I will help. Please don't hurt him."

"He may contact you. It's important that you let us know immediately."

"Yes."

"And if you think of anything, a place he might go . . . let us know that."

When Colleen ends the Skype call, Christie asks, "What did you see?"

"Clean, neat, takes pride in herself. Speaks clearly. Good grammar. Truly broken up. Doesn't appear to be lying."

"So where is he?" Christie groans.

He could be anywhere eight or ten hours from State College or still in the town. He could be on the move or hiding out somewhere. They just don't know.

NADAL FINALLY FINDS a parking space outside the library in Bradford. He reaches back and touches his son's leg. No reaction. Then he panics again and gets out of the car, putting his hand in front of Matt's face. There is breathing. Yeah, there is breathing.

He climbs back in the front seat and opens his laptop. He is able to log on. Man, it feels good to see the computer working. He googles "Pittsburgh news." And he chooses WTAE news again.

Police report that the child abduction in Oakland last night . . .

He clicks. He reads quickly. The story is different from last night. They have his name. They know about the car. He reads again more slowly.

Police are searching for information about Nadal Brown, a person of interest, in the abduction of the child Matthew Brown, who is not believed to be a relation. Information about the relationship is still forthcoming. Police believe the man and boy may be using a red VW Bug and that they may be in the State College area. For a video of the suspect and the boy, go to . . .

It's their pictures. Somebody took their pictures as they were walking in Oakland.

Not believed to be a relation. What do they know?

Slowly, as if in a dream, as if walking naked in a dream and hoping not to be noticed, Nadal closes his laptop, starts up the car, and begins driving back to the woods.

He is still so tired he can hardly think. If they know about the car . . . they will be able to trace the car to his mother. How long will that take?

Once more he's shaking badly. He can't keep dosing his son to sleep. He has to get Matt's cooperation. He reaches back to touch his son's leg. No response.

He must get them further south, where nobody will be looking.

He can hardly steer the car though. Nothing looks quite right. Perhaps he missed the path to the cabin. He backs up in a small patch of brush, and backtracks. Still nothing looks . . . He turns again and drives more slowly, so slowly he can hardly touch the gas pedal. And then he sees the clearing that signals the way in. Even with his errors, it's only been under an hour getting back to the cabin. He lets his head drop against the headrest and goes to sleep in the car.

ALL AROUND POLICE HEADQUARTERS the detectives move through the space with an insect-like, constant buzz. When the two civilians appear at the door, everything stops. Jan Gabriel and Arthur Morris.

Potocki goes to them, and although Colleen can't hear what he says, she can guess it's something like, "We have plenty to go on. The car. The . . . general location. We'll find him."

Colleen, knowing the profs need something to do, has decided to put them on television. They have language—and dignity. The news team will be here, ready to go in twenty minutes.

Colleen joins Potocki, Jan, and Arthur, and they all walk into the conference room. "Do you need to write anything down or practice?"

"No," Jan says. "I know what I want to say."

They don't rush to the restrooms to comb their hair. Colleen can understand why Boss wanted to help them have a child. They're straightforward, decent. They spend their twenty minutes asking each other. "Okay?" They are very much in love still after how many years?

Then the cameras come in. A mike is set up on the table.

"I thought those little clip-on . . . " Arthur murmurs.

"Sometimes. We had the table mike handy and we're at a table," one reporter explains.

"We're rolling," says the guy on camera. "We can edit out. Just speak normally. About how you want—you know—the boy to be safe and all that."

Jan is not wearing her reading glasses. Her eyes show her fatigue and sorrow. Even so she appears quick-witted—she's the person you would go to in an airport if you thought you were going to faint or if something terrible happened and you needed someone to understand right away and do something sensible.

She says, "We're Arthur Morris and Janet Gabriel. A couple of weeks ago we began the adoption process for Matthew Brown. This child has already suffered one trauma with the death of his mother. He is now missing. We are pleading with the person who has taken him to keep him safe, to calm him, and to return him to us. It's our wish to take good care of him for the rest of his life." She turns to her husband.

Arthur says, "Please keep him safe. We hope anyone who has knowledge of where he is will come forward. Matthew is a wonderful child who . . . deserves to be cared for."

Jan breaks her gaze from the camera to ask, "Do we need anything else?"

"I think that will be fine," says the reporter. "By the way, where's the big guy? Christie?"

"He's on the way back from State College."

"What's in State College?"

Colleen explains. Everything they know is on the news now anyway. No secrets.

NADAL WAKES IN THE CAR after only an hour because his neck is cramped. He lifts the boy in his blanket and carries him inside the log cabin to the bunk bed he used before. Then he drops himself onto another bed in the room and falls asleep. When he wakes three hours later, it's four in the afternoon.

His son lies in the position he put him in, mouth open. Nadal gets up noisily but nothing budges the boy. No more pills. He has to win him another way.

Nadal shakes himself awake and goes to the kitchen leaving the door to the bedroom open. Again, the noise doesn't wake Matt.

Abruptly Nadal begins to pack the food, anything that doesn't need to be cooked. Right in front of him is the answer to what he will do next—a long string on a nail behind the microwave. He remembers. The string leads to the key for the truck that's parked out back, the same truck that was here nine years ago. First he searches the two narrow kitchen drawers for anything that will help him. He finds a hunting license from 2003. He folds it into his pocket.

Then he fetches up the key and goes out to the truck. It's an old thing, but somehow not terribly noticeable. It's black with scratches in the paint from all the trees and bushes it's rubbed up against. On country roads, there are plenty of old trucks like this.

The old monster starts up. He searches around inside it, finding bits and pieces of everything—rope, wire. There is a kind of backseat area without an actual seat, a small and narrow area, but big enough for a kid. So that's where the kid will be. The rest of the truck is a pickup, open bed.

The glove compartment opens so easily it's as if it wants to yawn on its hinges. There are papers: Bill of sale for tires. Hunting license 2012. Truck registration for Stanton Adams with an address in State College. A map.

He should have thought of this right away. Nobody will be looking for the truck.

Two days to get to Florida. One if he doesn't sleep.

He goes inside and peeks at the boy, who remains in the same position.

He packs the remaining cereals and crackers and in spite of his hurry, puts the TV dinners of burritos he got from his mother's kitchen in the microwave so they'll be cooked.

Once he has everything in the truck, he drives his mother's car into the woods where there is plenty of tree cover; then he goes back for the boy, who continues to sleep soundly. He carries his son to the truck and puts him on the chipped rubber floor behind the driver's seat, not comfortable surely, but it's the best he can do right now. He covers his son with the gray wool blanket, and grinds the engine into life.

Up in the truck's cab, he feels like a different person, more rugged and practical. He drives a hundred feet and studies the map. Back roads. Old back roads all the way.

IT'S SATURDAY. FIVE O'CLOCK. They've been at this for under twenty-four hours and it feels more like two weeks.

Colleen cannot remember her life before Potocki.

He's now doing Internet searches for Mala Brown, her husband Arne Brown, and her maiden name, Mala Rodriguez, but all he finds is a clean slate. And he can't get anybody at Nadal's schools to check on behavior problems. It's the weekend. Sometimes it feels like they are the only people in the world working.

The way Potocki keeps at it, she loves that about him. Just as she's trying to figure out what to order them to eat, Christie, who is just back, comes up to her cubicle. "Go home. Get some rest. I'll call you if there is anything more we can do. Right now it's a matter of keeping all the other troopers and police aware. He could be holed up. He could be on the road. We don't know. All guesswork now."

"I hate guesswork."

"It's odd about the names, isn't it?"

"Totally. Totally. Browns everywhere."

Christie sits down by wheeling the adjacent chair over to her. "Any thoughts?"

"I'm just making guesses. A troubled person, a loner, a person who doesn't connect . . . gets ideas, fantasies. Could he have felt there was something between him and Maggie because they had the same last name? It might be the way his mind works. Your wife profiled him pretty well when we looked at the video. The way he leads with his head. I'm not ready to say schizophrenic, but it's a troubled person's posture. He might be given to creating his own realities."

"And what makes him violent?"

Colleen is often asked such questions, having been a therapist in her former life. "No fixed answers, but I'd say if he's crossed, that would do it. If he's stepping delicately through his fantasies and if he's . . . thwarted, crossed."

"Go home. Rest," he says abruptly. "Potocki, too."

Potocki looks up from his work.

"Go home. Call me tomorrow morning if you don't hear from me."

Christie walks away so unsteadily he looks as if he's had a few bourbons. He hardly ever takes a drink, so it's surely fatigue knocking him off his pins.

"Your house? Mine?" Potocki asks.

"Your son is gone?"

"Long gone to his mom's. I failed him this weekend. At least he watched the news and knows the reason is good."

"My place then. I need to be in my place."

They don't argue about his shirts. A calm settles over them. Food, shower, bed. Together.

"TELL ME," KATE SAYS, speaking of the time he was an undergraduate, living with seven roommates in New York. She is taking dishes out of the dishwasher, and he is putting them away. "This was when you were broken up with your sophomore girlfriend?"

"Junior/senior." He sighs. "I had no money. My father wanted me to come home to Lebanon." He tries to explain bit by bit. "I didn't want a fixed marriage. I wasn't sure I had enough talent to keep studying music. I was . . . yes, I'd say I was sad. Confused. Having those blues that people get in senior year on top of everything else. What's next, what do I want, all that. Half the time not enough money for food."

She settles a pot on the counter, too hard. "Again, I don't like your father. How could he not send you money? Was he trying to starve you out?"

"He forgot. He was simply not thinking about me."

Her arms drop. "God help us from ever being like that. I don't think it's possible. Do you?"

"My mother had died. He was . . . dating. He was very self-involved."

"Damn."

"And I thought he didn't like me very much. What I was doing. Music. It seemed frivolous. He didn't understand. So he closed off."

She begins to stack plates again, waiting for him to find the way to tell her about that time in his life.

"One of my roommates brought home groceries one day, and he said, 'Compliments of the fertility bank.' I didn't let myself think much about it. The language is . . . about the people you are helping. And it *does* help people. But it also divorces you . . . me, the donor . . . from your own body. It's just this thing you do. You can't think about the consequences. They don't *want* you to think about them. They tell you you are anonymous. Nobody will ever know. And that was that. I went three times."

"Only three."

He thinks. "Yes. Underneath I felt worried but I didn't let myself think why."

She begins unloading glasses and cups. For a while they are silent, but she isn't so much angry as thoughtful. She's just begun to show, just the smallest swelling of her belly. Tuesday he will have what Americans call a "shotgun wedding." The good news is that Kate still wants him. The bad is that he comes to her ragged, unknown even to himself.

There's a barrier between them now, something that wasn't there before. Will it dissolve?

MARINA TOYS WITH THE ENVELOPE that contains the letter that tells her she is accepted into the academy. Now is not the time to break it to her husband. But soon she has to answer, sign papers, send a check. When a stage role comes to her, fine, she will take it if possible. When it doesn't, which she assumes is most of the time, she will do this other thing she's good at.

THE MAN BEHIND THE COUNTER looks up, hopeful. "Room?"

"Yes."

It's chancy, but when he got off the back roads a while back, thinking he needed to see something, anything, what he saw was the VACANCY sign outside of this place and under it the WI-FI sign and then he drove around the lot, checking it out. There weren't many cars in the lot, maybe five in front but only two on the side and, driving around the lot that outlines the place, he saw no cars at all in back, only scrubby woods bordering the lot.

"Fill it out." The man turns a piece of paper around so that Nadal can read it. Name, address, phone, automobile, credit card.

He puts a hundred dollars in twenties on the counter and begins to write.

"One night?"

"Yeah."

The man behind the counter eyes the money. "Seventy-nine, that'll be. Plus tax. We don't do breakfast here, just coffee. But there's a breakfast place down the road. It's good."

"Okay."

Where the form asks for the number of occupants, Nadal leaves it blank. He also leaves blank the credit card. He uses Stanton Adams' address.

The man turns the pad around. "You're from State College?"

"At one point."

The man continues to read. "I saw your truck through the window. I've been wanting a two fifty forever."

Nadal has to think what to say. "I've had it for a long time." What the registration shows is that it's a 1979 Ford F-250. He hopes he doesn't have to talk about trucks because he doesn't know a thing about trucks.

"You aren't selling by any chance?"

Nadal shakes his head.

"So I need some ID."

Nadal hands over the truck registration and the hunting license.

"Driver's license?"

"It got stolen, along with my credit cards."

"I could look up the credit card if you want."

He turns and studies the coffee machine with the stack of Styrofoam cups and powdered creamer beside it. He hopes the Wi-Fi works. He says, after a while, "The card was maxed out."

The man hesitates, takes his money, and makes change, then chooses a key from the many hanging behind him, all of them chained to burgundy plastic ovals.

"Could I have a room around back? I like looking at woods."

The man puts the key back and chooses another. "Knock yourself out, as they say."

He can hardly believe it. He did it. A room.

Rest, regroup, then more back roads.

He drives the truck around back. All the other drapes are closed; all the other people are in their rooms or out to dinner. He does everything slowly. Parking, going to the door, trying the key, propping it open. He carries in the bits of food first. Then his backpack and his plastic bag of clothing. Nobody is around. He tucks the gray blanket around his son and carries the boy in. Until this morning, he didn't know how heavy a boy could be. His son smells like sweat, like fear, and like some kind of food, maybe sugar from the cereal. He carries the boy, staggering.

The room has two double beds. He puts his son on one of them and leans over, and yes, he's breathing.

Nadal sits on the edge of the other bed, thinking, noticing everything around him. There is no refrigerator. Okay. TV, good. Alcove to hang clothes. He doesn't need that. Phone. He mustn't leave his son alone in the room with the phone.

Around the corner is a bathroom. Shower. Good.

This is the moment to find out what's happening. Dragging his backpack toward him, he wonders when he will ever feel calm again. He opens the computer and boots up. He finds the Amber Alert. Nadal Brown. Red VW Bug. Good. They still want the Bug. And nobody is looking for Stanton Adams.

The Pittsburgh news shows no updates except a plea from those two people who tried to adopt Matt.

His jaw tightens, watching them. Professors. Probably like his father, they think they know it all, they think *brains* are everything. But they'll never guess where he is.

He's gotten away.

He digs out his power cord and plugs the laptop in. This way it will be good for six hours tomorrow.

He uses both MapQuest and Google Maps to check out where he is and where he's going. There are more woods on the way, and he likes the idea of being in deep woods, but the kid wants things like the TV and the computer. He's going to have to chance it soon and get onto 95 where there are endless connections with the world. So long as he's got the truck and can be Stanton Adams, he ought to be able to get them to Florida.

Next, googling Benadryl he learns that some people have slept for eighteen hours after taking it. Wow. Eighteen hours for Matt would take it to . . . tomorrow at six in the morning. He misses the company of his son, but he needs sleep, too, so maybe now is the best time. It's only seven thirty in the evening, but his eyes are closing.

The laptop slides out of his hands. He catches it and places it on the floor. With the last bit of strength and will he has, he opens the covers, takes the phone off the nightstand, and tucks the phone into bed with him. In seconds he is asleep.

THE OUTLINES OF THINGS. A TV. Two beds, not bunks or cots. Drapes closed. They are somewhere else. Another place.

His head feels funny, like when he has a cold and a fever and has to stay in bed. It's so dark. Everything is dark, but he can see more and more, so light is coming from somewhere, a crack in the drapes, yes, and from the tiny green power light on the computer, which he spies on the floor. And also from a clock radio turned around to face the man. Soon Matt can see the shape of the man asleep in the other bed. Or pretending. He listens for breathing.

Matt moves his leg, his arms. No, he is not tied up. He peels the wool blanket off him and realizes only then that he's sweating. But he doesn't get up. He has a kind of tiredness—muscles don't want to move. He tests his body by trying to lift a leg up in the air. He can do it, but it feels heavy.

Is he sick? Is he going to die?

His stomach lets out a large growl, so loud he is sure the man will sit up in bed, but it doesn't happen. He presses on his stomach to keep it quiet. It works for a few minutes, but then there's rumbling and growling again.

And he has to pee.

By now he can take in most of the room. The backpack, two grocery bags. Is he allowed to eat?

If he takes one step at a time . . . He sits in bed, aware now of how much he wants a bathroom. It must be around the corner. First it's one leg out of the bed and nothing bad happens, then the other leg. He is sitting facing the man, who is under the covers. The room is warm.

Feeling brave, Matt leans forward to turn the clock around. 11:37. Nighttime. Often in summer his mother let him stay up to watch TV. He would keep an eye on the clock, wanting to make it to midnight. With the clock turned around he can see the other wire—that would be the phone—and he can see that it goes under the covers. The man is holding on to something, both arms together. He's holding the phone.

Matt thinks about this. He must not make the man angry.

If he's really my father . . .

He's not my father. The names don't match.

Then another voice, his mother's voice, so clear to him it's as if she's here. *He's not your father. I swear to you. He thinks he is. Your father is far away finishing school. He's a good person.*

Why can't I see him?

Some things you can't do even if you wish. Lives are complicated. There are all kinds of circumstances. We're okay, just the two of us. We don't need anybody else.

But you always say, "Like father, like son. When Grady hits me."

Right.

So, who am I like?

A man. He's smart. Very smart. And kind. A good man. That's the important part. He's good.

But he's not here. He ran away.

You scamp. She laughs. *He didn't run. He has a different life.*

What's a scamp?

Somebody who tries to get me bothered. Somebody who wants to scare me when he gets angry. You!

Somehow every time he asked about his father she would talk about other things. And hug him and kiss him. It wasn't so bad being with just her, better than this.

He stands. Nothing happens. He waits in one position for what feels like a long time. Then he walks to the bathroom. It has a shower. A sink. A door he can close. And a light switch. He turns on the light, not knowing if it will get him into trouble and quickly closes the door. He has a nice long pee. Flush? He thinks no, too noisy. Wash hands? He turns on the tap—slowly, carefully.

He doesn't want to sleep again. He's determined not to take any more of the pills. To make him calm, the man said. And safe from allergies.

Once the water is running—and it's noisy so he expects trouble—he hurries to tear plastic off the plastic cup at the sink. Impatient, he fills it to the brim, drinks, fills it again, drinks most of it. Nothing happens. Maybe the man is standing just outside the door.

But when he opens the door, even with light illuminating the room, the man doesn't move. So, closing the bathroom door partway, he tiptoes over to the dresser. Cards and papers from the hotel are propped in a plastic tray. On the floor, there is food in the two bags. A burrito in a package. A package, like it, empty. Crackers. Cereal. Milk. He grabs the bag of food and the papers and goes back into the bathroom, where he closes the door and puts down the toilet lid and eats the cold burrito and reads.

Where he is, it's called the Excellent Motel. He makes his way through the brochures. Free WiFi. Cable television. That's good. Another brochure tells him attractions are: nearby Raystown Lake, also ten miles to Snyders Run Boat Launch, fifteen miles to Seven Points Marina. Things to do are: Lincoln Caverns, Penn's Cave, the "Thousand Steps" walk, IMBA Mountain Biking.

The burrito has only managed to make him want more food. He begins on the crackers, wishing he had jelly or butter. Then he gets an idea. He pinches bunches of cereal, this time bits of Special K, and puts the flakes into a drinking cup. Then adds milk. The milk isn't cold at all. He uses his fingers to eat the cereal. Three cupfuls.

The fact that he could eat and use the toilet and wash his hands without being punished makes him more comfortable. He wonders what else he can explore. What's outside the motel?

He tiptoes out to the draperied windows and looks through the crack. It's deep nighttime, but there are lights in the parking lot, and what looks like woods in the distance. He can't see the red car anywhere, only a black truck.

He hears a sound behind him, like a hum.

"How long have you been awake?" the man asks.

IT'S MIDNIGHT. CHRISTIE DROPS into bed next to Marina who is reading. "I thought you'd be sleeping."

"I was up all night and then I napped and now my sleep schedule is as screwed up as yours. It was worth it, though."

"Colleen told me you were dead on, profiling the guy." There are dark patches under his eyes. He fumbles absently with the covers. "I hope I can sleep a little. I've been calling everyone I know about the searches on the roads. But . . . this is a big country, lots of roads."

"Or he could be holed up."

"Yeah. The mother didn't know of any friends."

"I would have guessed that. No friends. The guy isn't close to anyone. Childish to childlike. Connects with his mother, but that's about it. Not exactly autistic but needs a solo occupation. A golfer, not a tennis player. That is, competitive, but needs to be alone."

"Not bad. Makes sense of the computer stuff in his life. I had Potocki at Pitt for a while today, trying to trace his computer activity from when he worked in the labs, but it seems he might have logged on with another name. Tomorrow they're going to try to use Spyware to get at something." He kisses her. "I'm going to put the covers over my head so long as you're reading."

"I'll turn out the light."

She does, but there's a full moon and the room still holds a good deal of light, the kind of night that thwarts sleep even when you aren't working an abduction case.

"You could do this job if I ever buy the big one."

Not that. It isn't a bargain like that.

He continues, "Tell me, if he needs to be alone, why did he assault the mother of the kid? And what does he want with the boy?"

Marina considers this question, not for the first time. "Maybe he also hates being alone."

"Okay. And what next? Give me an answer."

"I don't know. But I'm glad you said I could do this job . . ." She winces and backs off from saying anything about the academy. Why risk an argument at this time of night, with him so depleted?

"You can do just about anything. Doesn't mean you should. It can be lousy."

"But useful."

"Sometimes useful. I sure don't feel useful right now."

COLLEEN AND POTOCKI both wake up after midnight, near one o'clock. They are at her place. "Damn," she says when she realizes he's awake, too. "That's what we get for going to bed early."

"They say you can't catch up, but I don't believe it. Let's go back to sleep."

"Well, food would make us drowsy again."

"Let's eat something then," he says. "What's in the larder?"

"Frozen tortellini. Or eggs, sausage, toast."

"Breakfast is my vote. Let's just hope it doesn't tell our brains we need to drive to Headquarters."

"Move slowly. Try to stay sleepy," she whispers.

In a moment she starts four sausage patties cooking, attempting to take her own advice, moving slowly, as if in a dream. She places bread in the toaster and cracks four eggs.

Potocki flicks on her TV. He finds a black-and-white movie where everyone is shooting everyone. Eventually she brings food to him. They eat on trays in front of the TV.

Potocki is in boxers and a T-shirt. His hair is sticking up. His eyes are hooded with fatigue. He's so . . . real. And he loves her. She's never been this close to anyone.

She slips down beside him, then drops to one knee. "Marry me," she says.

"Don't joke."

"I'm not joking."

MATT IS WATCHING an old black-and-white movie. The man—he doesn't know what to call him—holds on to the remote control, but he has promised to find something else when the movie ends. He isn't exactly watching the film himself; instead he's working on his computer. "You like that movie?" he asks.

"It's okay." After a while Matt turns to him and asks, "What are you looking up on the computer?"

"Maps and maps and maps."

"Because we're going to Puerto Rico?"

"In time. Yes. I think so. We'll see."

"I like it to have a TV."

"I realize that. I'll get you any of that kind of thing. So long as you're good." The man is calmer now, not shaking so much.

"I couldn't see the red car anywhere."

"We don't have it."

The truck is the only vehicle out there. It must be the truck from that place in the woods. "I never heard of this town. They have camping and biking and things. Are we going to do that?"

The man's eyes narrow. "You like that?"

"It's . . . okay." A sinking feeling goes through Matt. He did go camping with his mother. She wanted him to like it and he didn't. "I like video games the most."

"Then I'll buy you some of those. In time. In time. Everything in time."

For a while they both watch the movie.

"For my birthday maybe."

"When is that?"

"It's next month. The twenty-sixth."

"You'll be nine!"

"No, eight."

"Nine."

Matt frowns. He forgets to watch the movie. He knows how old he is.

"What . . . what makes you think eight?"

"School. And it's written down. I'm in third grade."

"There can be mistakes. Like, what year were you born is how you figure it."

"I know. It was 2004."

"That's the mistake." The man is getting angry.

But Matt saw it on papers his mother filled out. He presses himself to watch the movie. The man doesn't know anything important. Plus he's still hiding the phone. Plus he did something with the red car. Matt gets up abruptly to go the bathroom. He doesn't want to cry. He should run, but . . . they're in the middle of nowhere and it's black night.

He comes out of the bathroom after a few minutes. "My mother had cremation today. I was supposed to be there."

The man hangs his head. A silence goes by. He doesn't try to say she's alive anyway. He's shaking again.

Matt says, "If you take me back, you could just let me off."

"No. You don't understand at all." The man goes to the window and just stares out of a crack in the drapes for a long time.

"Can I use your computer now?"

"Okay."

Are people looking for them? On the computer are maps and maps. "I know how to do this," Matt says. "Maps. I'm good at it. I can even do a city, like how to find a building."

The man—is he Nate or something else?—sways, then sits.

Matt studies the map. He tries to see where they are. With two fingers he types in his address in Pittsburgh. The man comes over and stands behind him. "We're not going back."

"I saw that. We're going . . . south."

"More or less."

Matt studies the screen. He types in *Peabody Institute, Baltimore.*

"What's that?"

"Just a place." He presses directions and search, trying to see how far away it is.

"No. Come on. What is it?"

"That's where the man works who said he was my father. On the email. You said it was you. Ziad Zacour. Are we going there?"

The man is very angry now. "I'm not that person."

"I don't know what to call you."

"You call me *father*. That's enough with the computer." He grabs his laptop and jerks it away from Matt.

For a long time they watch TV. They even laugh at some of the antics on screen in a new movie.

Matt closes his eyes and pretends to sleep when he loses interest in the movie. He does not want another pill. He pretends so hard he falls asleep a little, but every time something happens in the room, he wakes again. Still he keeps his eyes closed. He knows to let his arm hang limp. He fooled his mother every time with pretend sleep. Through slitted eyes, Matt watches the man go to the computer, where he clicks and clicks, searching, studying something. Then he paces to the window, seemingly disturbed. Matt almost falls asleep a hundred times and brings himself awake every time, watching.

16.

SUNDAY

CHRISTIE IS UP AT FIVE, having surprised himself that he slept at all. But he feels invigorated. Only . . . there is little he can do now but wait or call people.

The morning papers aren't here yet. He releases the automatic timer for coffee and presses the manual START button.

He knows what Marina was trying to say last night, but he doesn't want to tangle in that argument right now. Yes, she is good at searching, figuring, yes, she helped them yesterday . . . but their lives, the kids, the total disruption. No, he can't tangle with that today.

There's hardly a cup of coffee in the pot yet, but he pulls the pot out and pours what there is into a mug.

He sent Denman and Hurwitz to watch the State College house along with the police from up there.

What else, what else?

He sips the too-hot coffee.

A part of him wants to take off for Akron, to meet the man lying in a nursing home, but he can't indulge his own life in the midst of this crisis.

He will go to church today, early mass. Sometimes he can find himself there.

He has still not told Marina the old man has been found. His father will be dead by the time Christie gets there, and it's going to turn out as if he never found him at all. Too late is too late.

He shivers, takes up the coffee, gulps the rest of it.

Suddenly—without warning—he's crying quietly.

THE KID SLEEPS WELL, that's good. Nadal carries his few bags of things—a grocery bag with some crackers left, and his backpack with computer, the wool blanket—to the truck. He puts those things on the passenger seat. Then he goes back in, making sure he has left nothing. He pokes his head outdoors and seeing no one, goes back in for the boy and lifts him. Once more he's aware of how heavy the kid is; who could have thought a boy could be so hard to carry? At first, having lifted him like a baby from the bed farthest from the door, Nadal lurches toward the door, but he can't keep his balance and stops to put his son down on the bed near the door.

He catches his breath. The boy doesn't move. Good. Next Nadal tries the fireman's carry and that works better to distribute the weight as he makes it to the car. It's hard from this position to get the boy down on the floor of the truck's cab, and he's almost tempted to put him in the passenger seat, but he doesn't. He looks about, almost circling to be sure no one sees him. Then, moving awkwardly, he manages to get Matt down on the floor. The boy stirs, moans, and curls up in the fetal position. Nadal stretches for the wool blanket and covers him, watching to see that he doesn't wake. He doesn't. Okay. Done.

Nadal never knew anything about trucks, but this one is a lucky find, with this space behind the driver's seat. Maybe that's what the motel owner meant when he said he wanted a truck like this.

The way he figures it, he probably has a week before the truck is reported missing, because the cabin is a weekend place and if Stanton Adams didn't come to the cabin yesterday, Saturday, he probably won't come until next weekend—if that.

Nadal gets in and starts driving. It's Sunday morning and very early and so almost nobody is out and about. His only goal is making his way via rural roads toward 95 and then paralleling 95 on his way south.

Around seven o'clock in the morning he realizes he needs food.

For a long time there is nothing indicating a restaurant, but after eight o'clock he sees a sign for a Burger King in a nearby town. Drive-thru is the best bet.

The kid still sleeps.

Eight years old, he says. Third grade. A huge canyon of doubt opens up.

If he's eight, if there is this person with a strange name who wrote the email . . . what was that name the boy used? And the places he was looking up? Nadal's heart is making a clatter. He can't bear the thoughts that are coming to him. The boy is his. It's clear. They look alike. They are alike. He won't let himself doubt it now.

Up ahead is the Burger King. He turns to see his son is not moving from the curled position. He will be hungry eventually. So at the window Nadal orders the breakfast bowl and three breakfast sandwiches, a large coffee, and a large milk. This will keep them going until suppertime, probably.

He pays cash and then picks up a huge bag at the second window. "Have a good day," says a teenage boy.

The smells of fat and salt and meat fill the truck as Nadal forces himself out on the road again until he sees, a full forty minutes later, a place to pull over.

He grabs at the bag. It rattles. The kid sits up, rubbing his eyes.

WHEN IT WAS STILL DARK NIGHT IN THE HOTEL ROOM, after they had watched TV and Matt could hear the man moving around in the night, he tried to make plans while pretending to sleep.

With his eyes closed, trying to calm himself, he called up his mother's voice, the way she always told him to slow down and think and figure things out.

More than once she sat him down and told him, *If a man should ever capture you and try to make you do things, kick, run. Do you understand?*

What she meant was about body parts.

Run, yes, he needs to run, but where can he run that the man can't run after him or run the truck after him. When he sits up at the smell of food, there is nothing but a field on the one side and some woods on the other side.

"Where are we?"

"On the way to someplace good."

"There are no buildings around."

"Farmlands. Are you hungry? See what you like. I got milk for you."

He starts to feel bad for the man, to like him a little. He digs into the bag and pulls out a sandwich and milk.

It's awkward trying to find a sitting position in back on the floor. There's no place for his knees. "Can I sit up front?"

"I have stuff on the seat."

"I can move it. I'll use the seat belt."

"Not yet."

"Can I sit up front sometime?"

"Sometime."

Matt finishes the sandwich in silence. It's good, the kind of thing his mother fretted he shouldn't like, the kind of thing his new parents wouldn't let him eat at all. But good. It's as if the man can hear him thinking.

The man says, "Those people you were living with. Tell me about them."

"They were supposed to adopt me."

"They were teachers, right?"

"Yes."

"I don't like teachers. They weren't taking care of you. They kept you out at night."

"I was in a play."

"I don't care. It wasn't right."

"Are we allowed to have the truck?"

"Yep."

"I thought it belonged to the guy with the cabin?"

"I wrote him a note."

Will the police be looking for the truck? "Can we stay in a motel again? With a TV and Wi-Fi?"

"Sure."

"How far will we go today?"

"Far."

"What if we have to use the bathroom?"

"Side of the road."

"I have to sit up front because it hurts my body back here." Matt reaches forward and starts to move things off the passenger seat.

"No! I said no!" On the last word, the man slams Matt in the head and Matt is crying before he knows it.

"You went too far. You understand? You went too far."

Matt slinks down to his position lying in the back of the cab. Soon they are moving again. Outside he sees trees and sky and every once in a while he hears the sound of another motor. He can't imagine yelling in time to alert some other driver passing, or if he did, the other driver wanting to get involved.

AT HEADQUARTERS CHRISTIE, Dolan, Colleen, and Potocki gather behind Colleen's computer. It's Sunday morning at eleven. Colleen has engineered another Skype session with Nadal's mother, Mala Brown. She's in silhouette at first because there's a glass door to a patio behind her, but when they ask her to move, she is totally cooperative. Soon there is a wall with a TV behind her and her face is more visible.

Christie asks Colleen to begin the questioning.

"Have you heard from your son, anything at all?

"No."

"Even a hang-up phone call?"

"No, nothing."

"And you knew nothing of Maggie Brown?"

"Nothing. My son said many people have our name."

The police have run the fingerprints found at Nadal's apartment and at Mala Brown's home in State College. "Mrs. Brown. The news is not good. We have evidence that your son knew this woman or thought he did. And that he believed her son was his. And that he now has this boy. This is a very serious case."

Mala Brown claps her hands to her mouth. She is shaking her head. "I don't know about this." She does not appear to be lying.

"We will of course be checking student records from all his schools, but you can be very helpful in telling us everything you can about his life. Small things that don't seem important might be crucial."

"I don't know what to tell."

"How about when you came to this country? Did he adjust well? You weren't always in State College, correct?"

They listen carefully as she explains that the adjustment was difficult and that indeed she did once live in Miami where she is visiting now. She had cleaned university apartments in Puerto Rico and she cleaned in Miami. Her son had been quiet, a bit difficult in Puerto Rico, but much more difficult in Florida.

"What kinds of things set him off?"

"Other kids bullying him." She pauses. "His father."

"Tell us about that."

"His father . . ."

"Was this Arne Brown?"

"Yes. His father was . . . married to someone else. He only came to see us sometimes. Like maybe once a year or not even. He was decent to Nadal but Nadal hated him."

"Friends. Likes, dislikes in school."

"Nothing much. He kept to himself."

"Girlfriends?"

"He always wanted but he was not . . . successful."

"Do you know why?"

"Too nervous, I think."

"Did he ever show interest in children in a sexual way?"

She sinks back into her seat, shaking her head. "No. Never. Please. This is so terrible."

"Did he ever get violent? With you? With anyone?"

For a moment, she lowers her head. "Not with me. With things, yes. He threw things. With kids at school."

"He had a temper?"

"Yes. Please, please. Help him. He is not a bad person."

"We want to help him. Just . . . just a few more questions. You eventually moved up to State College. He came with you, right?"

"Yes."

"When was that?"

"Nine years now."

"And how did he adjust?"

"He was unhappy."

"With school?"

"He didn't like college, but my husband . . . a widower then and we got married . . . he believed college would help Nadal, so he insisted. And Nadal did it, but he didn't like it. Always nervous."

"Did he fight with his father?"

"More . . . sarcastic."

That, Colleen thinks, covers most boys but most boys grow out of it.

"Where did you go on vacations?"

"No vacations. Always working." She hesitates.

"What? You thought of something?"

"Not a vacation, but my husband would take my son to a cabin where he would study animals."

Colleen's heart quickens.

"Study? How?

"Cameras. It was my husband's work to study animals."

"Do you know the location of this place?"

"I went once, but I don't know."

"Your husband rented this place?"

"Oh, no. A friend had it and let him use it."

"I see, I see," says Colleen.

Christie murmurs almost inaudibly, "Good, keep going."

"About how far was it?"

"About two, three hours."

"Do you know if the friend still has it?"

She frowns. "I don't think Nadal would go. He never liked it. The woods."

"Well, we should check it as a part of routine. Do you have a phone number for the place?"

"They didn't keep a phone. Just two rooms, very rough."

"I see. Name of the owner. Just in case."

"I can't think—"

Colleen closes her eyes.

"Adams. Stanton."

"Adam Stanton?"

"Other way around."

"Did this man stay there year-round?"

"Oh, no. He teaches at the university, too."

But Potocki is already at his computer.

Colleen stays on Skype asking questions but the others peel away, excited. A place to look. One little clue to give them hope.

NADAL HAS LOST TIME by taking a wrong turn and dizzying himself driving in circles. The dock he wants in Florida seems suddenly years away instead of days away. He's beginning to think the highways might have been better. Nobody is looking for the black truck. "Matt," he calls. "Matt? I'm sorry I hit you."

No answer.

"Are you going to be difficult?"

No answer.

"Okay. Not answering when you're spoken to. I'll have to show you what that costs."

"What?"

"No restaurant, no new clothes, no TV."

"Where are we?"

"Just some woods." He'll pull over for a while, rest up. "I want to tell you something," he says, opening the take-out food bag, but not wanting anything he sees. "Everything can be faked. Even a birth certificate. Just so you know."

BY THREE O'CLOCK Christie, Greer, Dolan, and Potocki have joined some state troopers and Stanton Adams at the cabin.

Adams wasn't supposed to get there before they did, but he didn't honor their request. He wasn't supposed to touch anything, but Christie guesses he probably did.

"I'd say somebody ate or took a couple of beef jerkies. Don't think they hit the beer. My truck is gone. That's the main thing." Adams doesn't look or sound much like a professor. He is squat and muscular, bald-headed by choice, and talks like a blue-collar toughie.

"Description of the truck?"

"Ford 250. Black, 1979."

Potocki is on the phone in a second, updating the Amber Alert. Dolan and a trooper take some quick prints of the place, the others stand outside the doorway so as not to contaminate the scene further. Adams points out where he has two cameras fixed to the trees to catch the movements of elk. They're both disguised to look like tree bark.

"Hope those cameras are working," Dolan mutters, but Christie can't help being excited by the luck of possible camera evidence.

"That Nadal was a problem kid," Adams says as he takes out the memory cards from the cameras.

"Tell us anything you know," Christie says.

"Nadal? Didn't like anything. Didn't like anyone."

"His mother described him as hurt," Christie says.

"Well, maybe. I always felt bad for him. He was, you know, far away, not in the here and now. I brought my laptop. I can play clips from these cards. There might be something. They're motion-activated."

And, moments later, there it is. Man and boy walking into the woods, boy reluctant.

Christie sweats, mops his brow. Please, not dead, he thinks. We'll get through anything else.

The films show the man and boy went into the woods but also that they came back. The films do not show the red Bug, but it has to be somewhere since the truck is gone; so the assembled party sets out scouring the woods and pretty soon the car is found.

"Perfectly good car," says Adams.

"He must have known we were looking for the VW. He's a computer geek. Where does he get on the Internet?"

"Not here," Adams says. "This is my refuge from it."

Potocki says, "He could be anywhere. I mean he'd know how to nose up to a house or a business and borrow web access, so to speak. Filch. Warjack. Or he might have gone to a motel and gone legit."

The troopers agree to keep someone there to watch the cabin.

Christie and his people take turns walking in the woods, seeing what they can see, and in spite of their panicking hearts, noting the astounding beauty of the place.

"I followed a path," Colleen says. "Some tree markings. Very tiny. They appear to stop. Like they went so far and returned. It would make sense of what we saw on the camera, the timing. Matt came back with him. That's good."

"They're gone from here," Christie murmurs. "They have the truck. They won't be back." And so he and his crew get in their two cars to drive back to Pittsburgh.

Christie drives with Colleen in the passenger seat. "Someone will see the truck," she says. "Surely."

But he's thinking about the boy's predilection for running and he's thinking if it hasn't happened yet, that's a bad sign.

THE BOY IS CRYING. He's trying to do it quietly, but he's crying. Nadal wishes he could undo the fact that he hit him. "What's going on?"

"I'm sick."

Nadal is pretty sure it's just an excuse to stop the truck, but he does anyway. When they get out, Matt throws up everything he's eaten. He's bent over, heaving, and Nadal touches his head, because that's what his mother used to do when he was sick. Matt jerks away, frightened.

When they get back into the truck the boy looks for napkins and tries to remove a splash of vomit from his shirt.

"We could use some water," Nadal says.

The boy nods.

"Wonder if there's a stream around."

And now the boy starts crying in earnest. He's used to showers and TVs and full refrigerators. Can they risk a meal in a restaurant? No, they can't, no. When Nadal sees a sign for a motel, he thinks, *Yes, all right, let's have a calm day again—TV, order food in, check the Internet, get showered up—everything calm.*

He can't stand the crying.

"What do you like to eat? Just tell me. Look, I'm not going to hit you again."

"I don't know."

"What feels good on your stomach? Soup?"

"I don't know. Maybe soup."

"I think you need a nap. We were up most of the night."

"I slept a lot."

"Sleep is good for us. Try to sleep now."

"Okay."

"If you stay in the truck, if you behave, I'll get us a room. Can you stay? Behave? You have to stay lying down. Okay?"

"Yes."

Some twenty minutes later, he pulls up at a Red Roof Inn. There's a restaurant next to it, not much else to see. On his way inside, he turns back to the truck. Can't see the boy. He's staying down. Nadal pulls out his money and Stanton Adams' registration.

But the young woman at the desk says, "We're not allowed to take anybody without a driver's license and a credit card."

"My wallet was stolen. I'm getting replacements for everything."

"I'm sorry."

"Well, I have other ID and I have money to pay."

"I'm sorry, I can't."

He leaves, slamming the door. He didn't like her at all. She thought she was somebody special because she stood behind a desk.

The boy is curled up still.

He drives for another hour and decides on another motel, this one with a name that means nothing to him. Everest Motel. It's hard to find these lone ones that are not part of a cluster of chain motels. All he knows is he, too, wants to stop, regroup.

At the desk, an old fellow looks to be half-asleep and gives him no grief. Doesn't even watch him signing in. Nadal turns from time to time to look at the truck. All is still.

"You have any food delivery in case I don't feel like going out?"

"Mostly pizza. Pizza okay?"

"Might have to be."

"You're bushed?"

"Yeah."

He drives around the side. The room he was given is not totally out of view, but he didn't want to make a fuss. He carries his things in, watching the boy, who doesn't move and who almost looks like a baby, curled up, his thumb toward his mouth—not in, but like a memory.

He will be a good father. He will be better than he has been.

He carries the boy in. Nobody seems to notice. He trips twice, manages to get the kid on the bed.

"You're not sleeping?"

The boy's eyes open. "No."

"You want TV?"

"Yes."

"You like pizza? It's about all they have."

"I like it."

"Pizza it is. Take off your shirt. I'll wipe it off."

"I might need clothes."

"I know. It's on the list."

"What list?"

"All the things we need to do."

He puts on the TV and hands the remote to Matt. "Anything you want to watch is okay."

He finds some papers on the bureau and those include the pizza places, two, one of which he chooses. He orders an extra large pizza and two Cokes.

Matt is channel-surfing.

Nadal opens his computer and boots up. The dialogue box keeps telling him he is not on the Internet. He calls the front desk.

"We don't have Internet in the rooms, but you can get on my machine here in the lobby."

Lobby. He might have to do it. Eventually. He can't leave the boy now.

They watch a Steelers–Ravens game. Matt starts to talk to the TV. "Come on. Get him. Stop. Grab it." He does all this quietly, but still, it's something. It's nice to see him interested. Things get calmer.

The pizza arrives. The delivery man sees father and son watching TV. "Go Ravens," he says.

Matt looks up, surprised. When the man leaves, he asks, "Where are we?"

"This is Ravens territory, I guess. Here. Eat."

The motel is not as empty as Nadal thought. He hears cars pulling in, doors slamming. He keeps watching the boy.

Nadal realizes what he can do with the phone. He unplugs it where the wire meets the instrument and puts the phone under his bed. Matt appears not to notice.

THE ACTORS SLOG AROUND, worse than they are on an ordinary Sunday, this time both hungover and aware they may be bumping up against a tragedy. So after Marina, who is taking over the rehearsal, has done her best to rally them, after she has reviewed all the blocking they've done so far, she calls Jan Gabriel to offer what comfort and assurance she can.

It turns out it's Jan who catches her up. "Your husband called us. They're trying to trace another car now, a truck, I mean. It seems this man took Matt to a cabin in the woods . . . " Jan's voice cracks. "But no blood. He's hopeful, he says, that Matt is alive."

"I have hope, too," Marina says softly. "Please try to do something to comfort yourselves."

"What? There isn't anything."

"Watch TV?" Even at rehearsal, one of the kids has tuned in the Steelers game on his iPad and the others gather around when they are not onstage. "Everything is going well here."

"Good, good."

"Someone will see him. Stay hopeful," Marina says in as bright a voice as she can manage. She and Jan don't hang up.

The Steelers play. The kids manage to cheer every so often.

"Try to watch football," she tells Jan. "Really, it's very occupying". Even she wanders over to the iPad.

Marina pictures back roads, fumbling at motel desks, a man going backward in his life: becoming a young man in the woods with his father, becoming a kid in Florida with his mother, then a child in Puerto Rico.

He's going to Puerto Rico, she thinks.

FOR NADAL AND MATT, it is a calm day, just what Nadal wanted. They watch TV all day. Both television and pizza make them drowsy. When they get a little hungry at ten at night, they order another pizza. Nadal looks for comic movies on the TV because they make his son laugh. When it's midnight and he's pretty sure Matt is really tired, he puts him to bed.

"I'm going to need another shirt," Matt says.

"I know. Tomorrow. I'll take care of you. I'll get you anything you need."

Matt nods and closes his eyes.

Nadal sits up. Just sits on the bed, worrying. He's tempted to go to the front office to use the computer there when Matt is asleep. He opens the drapes to look out. Too many cars. Too many people.

He must sleep. Tomorrow he will start in earnest for Florida and he won't stop until he gets there. He starts to pace, uncertain. He can't go back. Ever again. What's done is done. He has to go forward. Even if . . . he has doubts. He wipes them aside. He looks out the draperies at the cars in the lot. Everything is still, so still now, just glaring lights. He cries for a long time, quietly, so as not to wake the boy. He knows about men who step up and take care of a child, not asking, not wanting to know if it's theirs. He's seen it in movies. They're the good guys.

17.

MONDAY

MATT IS HALF-ASLEEP WHEN the man comes to him in the morning, saying, "Here, take this." Matt tried to stay awake all night, but he slept some of the time. To keep himself awake, he watched the clock numbers changing. He also watched the man sniffling, maybe crying at the window. He had to remind himself that the man hid the phone, yelled, hit him. He had to remember those things.

He pretends he doesn't hear the "take this." He groans and rolls to his stomach.

"Son, take this. We're going to get going soon. We have a long way to go today."

He opens his eyes a bit. The glass of water. The pill. The pill that makes him sleep.

He takes the pill. He drinks the water.

"Another," the man says. "Here."

He takes it, afraid it will go down. The first one is in his cheek. He squirrels away the second one, afraid to swallow.

The man gets up. He must pretend to sleep. He must pretend to be almost dead.

A long time goes by. He watches the clock. When the man goes to the bathroom, he gets the pills out of his mouth; yes, two, he can feel them, and he stuffs them in his jeans pocket.

When the man comes back, Matt tries to look like he's in a deep sleep while the man attempts to put his shoes back on him. He's awkward enough at it that he smashes Matt's toes, and Matt lets out a sound.

"Easy. Easy. I'll get them on."

He groans. His heart starts to thump hard. The man will know he's awake.

He is lifted up over the man's shoulder. He feels the gray blanket over him. It's the truck again. He hangs limp. Today is the day he will do something.

The truck starts up, but moves only a few feet. The motor is running, but Matt can hear the man get out.

Matt lifts his head. The man is in the front office. It's not quite light out. Nobody is up in the other cars. Nobody is walking. If he runs now, the man will snatch him up.

IN THE FRONT OFFICE the man behind the desk says, "Sorry, bud, our Internet connection is down. It's so iffy out here."

Nadal curses, kicks the counter. "This is a lousy place."

"Hey, it's not my fault. It's the damn company."

Nadal realizes he's going to have to go into town, find a Starbucks or something.

The kid is sleeping.

After an hour he finds a Caribou Coffee. He pulls in and shuts off the engine. He opens his laptop. Only one bar. Inside it must be better. Plus . . . coffee, milk, some pastries, some Internet, and he can be on his way.

He checks the back of the cab. It's okay. The kid is still knocked out.

There are lots of people around here, though, so Nadal needs to make this quick and get away.

He goes inside. He plunks himself down at a table and logs on. Okay, yes, the bars are coming up. He checks the Amber Alert.

Oh, God, oh, God.

They've changed it. They aren't looking for a red VW Bug now. He almost shouts his alarm. They're looking for the truck. The black truck. They even say the truck belonged to Stanton Adams. He can't use the truck again; he can't use the *name* again. He's got to get out of here.

He looks up to see the boy climbing from the back of the cab into the driver's seat, opening the door, and running, running to a corner. He grabs up his laptop and sees the boy hail a passing school bus.

The bus stops.

The boy gets on.

He's not his son. Can't be, not if he—

He slams out of the coffee shop to his truck, door still open. He starts it up and follows the school bus.

THE DRIVER SAYS, "WHAT'S UP, KIDDO? That's not the bus stop."

"Um. I didn't know."

"What's your name?"

"Matthew Brown."

"You're not on my manifest."

"I know. I'm new."

The other kids watch him curiously. He walks to the back of the bus. The driver turns to look, keeps going.

"Do you have a cell phone?" Matt asks the kid next to him.

"Not allowed."

"Does anybody?"

"The driver."

The bus stops. Two more kids get on. The doors close and the driver walks to the back of the bus.

"What's up?"

"I need a phone."

"Are you in trouble?"

"Yes."

The driver hands over a phone. "Hurry. I can't be late."

For the third time in his life Matt dials 911. "I need you to call Detective . . . Commander Christie in Pittsburgh. Tell him I got away."

The driver takes the phone from him. "Look. I don't know what's going on. This kid was running. He got on my school bus. I should keep moving. I gotta keep moving. I have a schedule." He listens. "He told me Matthew Brown."

All around the kids are getting out of their seats, excited.

"You run away from home?" one asks, wide-eyed.

"No."

The driver is saying, "Hillcrest Elementary."

Outside the window the black truck zooms past and keeps going.

CHRISTIE AND COLLEEN ARE IN A car in minutes. "Four hours to get there," he says. He'll drive eighty-five, of course, and though she would, too, Colleen feels her hands knuckling.

He hasn't called Jan Gabriel yet. He doesn't even mention picking them up. Colleen knows what he's up to. She can't hold her tongue. "Boss, don't we have to at least *call* Jan and Arthur? They're devastated."

"I know. I will. I just want make sure we get there first. Find out what condition he's in." He begins cursing at the morning traffic. "Come on, come on."

"I know what you're up to," she says quietly.

"For God's sake, look where he landed. He must be twenty-five, thirty minutes away at the most from—"

"I get it, but you're still arranging lives."

"I'm a monster. I know."

"Not a monster, Boss. Just, I hate to see you get hurt."

"Me? Christ, it's hardly about me."

He's going to hurt Gabriel and Morris who are a good match, not a perfect match. They're B-plus in this instance.

The phone rings. Christie flips it open, reads the screen, and taps the speaker button, telling her, "Somebody at the school." The voice says, "This is Detective Don Bolden. We have your Matthew Brown here. He was definite he wanted me to call you."

"Matt seems okay?"

"He's going to be okay. I'm out in the hallway here. We don't think there's been any sexual contact. He admits to being hungry. He needs a shower. He's in shock. The boy showed me two Benadryl he was supposed to take. The guy who took him wanted him doped up or sleeping."

"Is he talking?"

"A little. We have to take him to a hospital first thing of course. He doesn't want to go, but of course . . ."

"I don't know Baltimore. Is the hospital anywhere near Peabody Institute?"

"About fifteen minutes. Why?"

"Huh. I know somebody who works there who—let me talk to Matt? Is he there?"

"Down the hall in the nurse's office. I'm walking toward it now. I see him. There's our brave fellow. Here he is." Then Bolden says, "This is Detective Christie on the phone. He's on his way here to see you."

"Hi?"

"Hey, Matt. You got away. How did you do that?"

"Pretended I was sleeping."

"Smart. Good. Did he hurt you?"

"He hit me once."

"I'm sorry."

"Sometimes he was nice."

"That must have made it hard to figure out what to do."

After a second, he says, "Yeah."

"You did right."

"You said to call you if I needed anything. So I asked for you."

"You did right. I'm going to be there soon. Let them get you breakfast and all that. They have regulations to examine you at the hospital. Just . . . put up with it. It won't be awful. It won't take long. Then I'll be there." Color rises on his neck and face.

When Bolden is back on the phone, Christie asks, "Your men are looking for the black truck?"

"You better believe it."

"Nadal Brown might dump it. Might already have."

"We're looking for it with or without him."

When they terminate the call, Christie says, "We got a good one, Don Bolden."

Colleen agrees.

Finally, Christie calls Jan Gabriel and Arthur Morris. "Good news. Very good news. We found him."

Colleen can hear them shouting, weeping in the background. If Christie has his way, if he does, oh, man, their joy will be very short-lived.

"How? Where?" Arthur asks.

"He ran away from his abductor."

"Was he hurt?"

"He's rattled. He's probably okay. He's near Baltimore."

"Baltimore?" There is the faintest whisper of suspicion in Morris's voice. "Should we—"

"Sit tight if you can. If you can't, call me back and I'll tell you where to go."

So the would-be parents will get there thirty minutes or at most an hour later than she and Christie will.

As soon as he terminates the call, Christie says, "You have Zacour's number?"

"In my phone."

"Call his house."

She presses in the number. There is no answer. She puts on her speakerphone so Christie can hear the series of rings and then an answering machine.

"Could be out running, but, wait, he teaches today," Christie says. "Did you keep the number for the Peabody Institute?"

"No, but I can get it." She takes the shortcut and calls Information and is rung through.

After she is transferred several times, she is told, yes, he teaches there and will be in session this afternoon, from noon on.

"Better slow down, Boss. We need to live."

"You're right. Okay. I'm going to call Marina." He turns off the speakerphone but his volume is loud enough that Colleen can pretty much hear the whole conversation. He tells her, "Good news. Matt ran away finally. He's safe. In Maryland. We don't have Nadal Brown yet, but somebody will get him. Colleen and I are on the road. Irwin exit. An hour to Breezewood."

Then it's something like, "You're looking for Nadal yourself?"

"I'm leaving that to others. But believe me, I see a black truck on the road, I'm going to be on it."

Colleen hears words she can't make out and then something about Florida, and something about Puerto Rico.

Boss smiles. "You've talked to Brown, eh?"

She's pretty sure Marina says, "In a way."

"Catch you later." He closes his phone. "Marina being a profiler."

"She's very good."

"I know."

NADAL PARKS THE TRUCK in a strip mall, which he realizes soon enough is the wrong place to get the license plate off. There are maybe twenty people coming and going, hurrying to their own tasks or their vehicles. He doesn't know what to do. He rattles around in the glove compartment. Christ, no tools. He gets out and places his backpack in the bed of the truck and tries to use a dime to get the plate off. His fingers fumble hopelessly. He needs a Phillips-head screwdriver.

"Everything okay?" a young, maybe teenage, guy asks.

"Need to put my new plate on and I forgot to bring a Phillips-head."

"I think I have one. You need a toolkit in your truck. I thought truck people always had tools." The kid laughs. "My father wouldn't be caught anywhere without a kit."

Nadal tries to think of light responses but he can't. He murmurs a thank-you and waits. The kid brings him a kit and takes out the screwdriver he needs. Trembling hands again—do they show—he removes the plate and hands back the screwdriver.

"Where's the new one?"

"I have to pick it up," he says lamely. "My mother has it. In the . . . store." He stuffs his old one in his pack and mumbles, "Thank you. It's nice you helped," and before the boy can point out that he's going to need the screwdriver again, Nadal walks to the first store he sees, a Dick's Sporting Goods, where, once he's inside, he wanders agitatedly through the aisles.

"Help you?"

"You sell phones?"

"Walmart. Up the hill."

He hurries out, doesn't see the kid, and drives his truck up to Walmart, up at the end of the mall but not in it.

"Need to buy a cell," he tells the first clerk he sees, a man who appears to be a senior citizen, a bit slow.

The man says, "Well, okay. Let's see." He picks one off the shelf and begins reading. "This one . . . okay. Charge for a minimum of six hours . . ."

Nadal, caught off guard, drops his backpack on the floor. "Damn, damn, damn. I forgot it had to be charged. I—"

"Be my guest," the man says, pulling a phone from his pocket.

"It's long distance."

"Doesn't matter. All goes in the same pot."

"I have to call Information. They charge for that. Unless, unless you have Wi-Fi here. I could use my laptop, maybe find it."

"Go ahead. I can afford two fifty. I can see you need to make a call."

Nadal accepts the phone and walks aside down an aisle. He first gets his mother's friend's phone number. Then he makes the call, breathing so hard he doesn't know if he can speak when Violetta answers. "It's Nadal," he manages. "Is my mother there?"

"She's . . . right here. Just a minute."

"Nadal? Are you okay?"

"No. I think . . . I think some police think I did something."

"Where are you?"

"I don't know. I don't know."

"I'm all packed to go back home. I was just about to start for the airport."

"Your ticket isn't until next week."

"I got my flight changed to leave today. Violetta helped me. Nadal. Can you . . . get back home?"

"I can't."

"Are you far? I could meet you somewhere?"

"How will you get to State College, Ma? Your ticket is to Pittsburgh."

"Oh. Yes. I know. I was going to take a bus home. But I could meet you in Pittsburgh. Just say where. You can drive me and . . . I'll take care of you. I'll make sure you're safe. Where can you meet?"

He can't think where.

"A restaurant?" she prompts.

He can't *think*. Mad Mex near Pitt? No. Might be recognized. "There's a Mad Mex in the North Hills. But you would need a cab."

"That's fine. I'll get there. Are you . . . driving?"

"Yeah. Yeah. Why?"

"Just be careful. Take your time. I'll be there in four hours, five hours. I get in at four twenty-one. Then, time for a cab. Where are you again?"

"Not sure exactly. . . ."

"If you think you can get to the restaurant, I'll wait for you."

Is she sobbing? He can't tell.

Nadal rushes to the truck, thinks better of it, and begins walking toward the entrances to the strip mall.

On the road he gets his first ride right away from a guy in a truck that looks a lot like the one he abandoned, only red and silver. The man asks no questions. He's a grubby sort, looks like he hasn't had a shower in seven days, but he behaves with utter calm and kindness. Nadal is so grateful he's afraid he'll cry. Somehow he manages to ask for Route 70 back to Pennsylvania.

"Going that way but only so far." The man takes him as far as he can and then leaves Nadal on the road.

DETECTIVE DON BOLDEN turns out to be a tidy, agreeable-looking man of about forty. He shakes Christie's and Colleen's hands and says, "Nurse reports all vital signs are fine." He gestures to the nurse who is approaching them. "Psychiatric social worker is in there now, talking to the kid. Very low pressure. We have to let her at him. Give her fifteen minutes?"

"No abuse?"

"Doesn't look like it. We had a bit of a struggle with him about his clothes but he's like, what, eight years old? Almost? He doesn't believe in taking his clothes off."

"At that age they do not like *naked*," says the nurse. She introduces herself. "Stella Hammer. Anything I can do for you, just say."

"Is there a vending machine?" Colleen asks.

"Right. You guys drove straight through of course. I can order something from the cafeteria. What kind of thing are you up for?"

"Anything," Colleen says, handing over two twenties, which Bolden waves aside, with a "We got this."

"Sandwiches, Cokes."

Stella Hammer, while making a phone call, goes to a kitchen area and comes back with crackers and juice, the hospital staples. "Until he brings the sandwiches," she says, handing them to Colleen, whose stomach is actually roaring.

Bolden takes a phone call, listens carefully, and explains to Christie and Colleen, "I'm going to have to go outside. We have reporters and cameramen practically climbing over the walls to get a picture of Matt."

"Need me?" Christie asks.

"You sit tight and have your sandwich."

Their sandwiches arrive in record time and they are halfway through them when Colleen's phone rings. As soon as the speaker identifies herself, Colleen immediately switches on the speakerphone. "Mrs. Brown," she says. "Yes. Do you know something?"

"Can you hear me?" It's noisy on both phones.

"Yes. Sorry about that, but I can hear you. Do you know something?"

"I want to persuade my son to turn himself in."

"Has he called you? Don't hang up. Where are you . . . ? It's noisy there, all right." *Sounds like an airport*, she mouths to Christie.

"I'm at the Charlotte airport. I flew from Miami but I had this stop to change planes. I'm coming back. Would you be able to meet me at Mad Mex in North Hills?"

"Mad Mex in North Hills. Pittsburgh. Sure can."

Where is he? Christie mouths.

Colleen puts a hand up and says, "He called you then?"

"Yes. I told him to go there."

"Good. That's a good plan."

"I told him to get himself back to Pittsburgh and I would meet him. I won't get there until maybe six o'clock tonight, six thirty if the plane is late."

Colleen looks at her watch calculating. If Mala Brown is in Charlotte, she might get there earlier than six. She says, "If I can't get there, and I'll try, I'll send someone I trust. I promise that. Someone good who will be gentle. Where was your son when he called you?"

"He said he didn't know."

"Did he call a cell phone? What number did he call?"

"My friend, Violetta."

"Good, good. The number we had. I'm glad he had a way to contact you. And I'm glad you called me."

She raises her eyebrows at Christie, who is now on his phone, already playing all the angles. Whether they find Nadal long before the appointment at Mad Mex or not, he's going to probably send Potocki and Dolan to do the snatch. Potocki who will be kind and Dolan who can sweet-talk confessions out of anyone.

"Mrs. Brown. How are you holding up?"

"Me? I have these thoughts like it would be better to die."

"No. You're doing the right thing. Your son needs you. What time is your flight?"

"Pretty soon. I need to go to the gate."

"Please take care of yourself. Remember you're going to be needed."

When she gets off the phone, Christie is alerting Headquarters to put people at all roads coming into Pittsburgh from the south. And Dolan and Potocki to trace the phone call for a location, but he definitely wants them at Mad Mex from four o'clock on.

The psychiatric social worker comes out and tells them they can see Matt.

The door is ajar and they push it in. "*Heeey*. There he is," Christie says. "Man, am I glad to see you. We both are."

There's something different about the boy. He lets them hug him, both of them. He seems calmer than before.

"Are you hungry?"

"No. I ate."

"You remember Detective Greer, right?"

"Yes."

"Now's the part where we both want to know what happened. Can you fill us in?" They all sit as if this is an ordinary conversation. "What—first—what did you call the man who took you?"

"Nothing. He said to call him *father*, but I never said it."

"Did you know to meet him outside the theatre?"

Matt looks surprised, confused. "No. Was I supposed to?"

"We're wondering how he found you. Had he called or anything? Phoned you?"

"No."

"And then what? He just came up to you."

Matt thinks. "Yeah. I got scared at first."

"I would think so. How did he persuade you to go with him?"

Matt looks at the floor. "My mother's dead, right?"

After a long pause, Christie says, "Yes."

"Is she buried? I mean, cremated?"

"No. We wanted to wait for you to be there, so we postponed. Was that right?"

Matt nods.

"Why did you ask me that when I asked what the man said to you?"

"He said she was alive. He said he saved her and he would take me to her."

"Did you believe him?"

"Kind of. Then I didn't."

"Where did he take you?"

"To a house. A regular house. He locked me in a room."

"Did he hurt you?"

"Sometimes."

"How?"

"Hit me once. I think once. Kept making me sleep."

"How did you spend your time?"

"We kept going places. A place in the woods and two motels."

"Did you try to run?"

"He kept watching me. He threw our phones away. In the hotel he put the phone in bed with him."

"Were you near the phone? In the same bed with him?" Does Matt register the bladed questions?

"No. He always put me in the other."

Christie looks up at Colleen, who nods to him that she believes the boy.

"Do you know where the man is now?"

Matt shakes his head. "He was coming after me in the school bus, but then he passed it."

"How did you . . . how did you get to the school bus?"

"I pretended I was asleep. He went to a coffee shop and he went inside. Then I ran out of the truck, looking for somebody to help and when I saw the bus I ran hard and the driver picked me up."

"Very smart. Very, very good. Tell me. When you were lying there, trying to sleep, pretending to sleep, who did you think about? Who did you wish you could talk to?"

Matt shrugs. "My mom. You."

"Really."

"I thought you'd know what to do."

"Did you miss anybody?"

He shrugs. The question stumps him. "My mom?"

THE WAY IT HAPPENS . . . Christie calls the Peabody Institute and a secretary confirms that Zacour is teaching. He checks his watch.

He asks if Zacour can be interrupted.

"Is it an emergency?"

"It's . . . yes. Tell him Commander Christie is calling."

Three minutes later, Zacour comes to the phone. His hello is raspy.

"It's good news. He's found. We're right here, practically around the corner from you. You didn't know he was coming this way?"

"How could I?"

"No, of course."

"Is he all right?"

"He's doing very well. Considering. He's untouched but it was rough."

"And you've caught the man?"

"No. Not yet. We will."

Christie pauses. He holds his breath.

"Would I be able to see him?"

"Yes. Yes. That would be possible. We're here for, oh, another hour maybe. We're at the hospital. Johns Hopkins."

"Oh, but that's—"

"Yes, it's quite close. We're in a consulting room off the emergency ward."

"I'll cancel my session. I'll be there. Give me, give me twenty minutes."

Christie raises his eyebrows in answer to Colleen's silent inquiry.

Then fifteen minutes later Bolden comes in to tell Christie that Janet Gabriel and Arthur Morris have arrived. The photographers have recognized them and the reporters are asking them all kinds of questions. Bolden has sent two cops to bring the couple through the crowd. "Do you want to make a statement? How do you want to do this—let the photographers in?"

"No photographers yet. Would you make a careful statement for me—you know the 'we are still determining what happened but the boy is safe' kind of statement."

"Fine." Bolden goes out as his men usher Jan and Arthur in. They are flushed and ragged and in their ways *beautiful*—full of joy.

They rush to Matt and hug him hard. Jan's eyes are closed and she holds the boy tight while he looks surprised and a little bit pleased.

Christie sighs and goes to the door. Colleen is watching him.

Soon after there's a voice in the hallway, insisting, "Yes. I'm allowed. Please. I talked to Commander Christie."

"Don't push. Wait a minute. How do I know who you are?"

Christie can hear in the cop's voice that he's frightened and he's probably thinking, *Oh God, oh God, this might be the man who took the boy and I'm . . .*—

"I can show you identification. Do you need identification? I have it. I'm—"

Christie goes out to rescue Zacour. "He's Ziad Zacour. He's the boy's father."

And then he brings him in and everything in the room stops. Everything. The man and boy stare at each other. Jan and Arthur can't move. Zacour is biting his lips tight and tears well in his eyes. "I wanted to see if you are all right? Are you all right?"

"Yes."

I ought to say something, Christie thinks. *I ought to explain.* But still nobody, including him, says anything. They can't be interrupted, those two. They're onstage in the greatest scene of all, two people falling hopelessly in love.

THE WAY IT HAPPENS, Potocki goes to Mad Mex and Dolan to just outside the parkway exit to Pittsburgh. Both take backup with them. Dolan wins the prize. A man in a rattletrap pulls off onto the berm just short of the exit and his passenger hands him a fistful of money.

Then Nadal Brown gets out of the old car and begins walking

327

toward the tollbooths, looking uncertain about the best way to avoid scrutiny. He needs another ride. He is no doubt thinking this was not a good place to get off. Then he stops in his tracks. He sees the cop cars. In moments they are on him, handcuffing him.

Dolan strolls up and speaks quietly. "Nadal Brown. I'm going to ask you to come with me. Quietly and calmly. I'm arresting you for the murder of Margaret Brown and for the abduction of Matthew Brown. You have the right to remain silent. You also have the right to an attorney. You should know that anything you say may be held in evidence against you."

Brown looks as if he will not say anything. They begin to walk to the police car. Brown walks oddly as if the arms behind his back make his balance unsteady. "There was someplace I was supposed to be."

"I know about that. We'll bring your mother to see you."

He frowns. "I don't understand."

"I'll explain everything. We'll talk. Especially when we can sit down and be quiet. Try to relax. We just need a little calm—it's a short ride."

They get into the car. Nadal closes his eyes.

"Tired?" Dolan asks.

Nadal nods.

Dolan calls Potocki first. "You can come on in."

"Got him?"

"Yep. But send somebody good, really good to deal with his . . ."

"I understand. I will. I'll brief Denman and Hurwitz for that. And have them bring her."

"Yeah. Good."

Then he calls Christie. "All is well. Suspect in custody. We'll be at Headquarters in fifteen. Anything on your end?"

"Oh. Messing up a few lives."

"That's our job."

Later, when Dolan gets to Headquarters he puts Nadal into a

room and leaves him alone while he waits for his partner, Potocki. When, not much later, Potocki is there, Dolan tells him, "We have Nadal's backpack. There's a ton of money and nothing else of interest in it except the computer. That's gonna have something we want. You up for it?"

"Yes. What's he like?"

"Quiet son of a bitch. Bad posture. I'm going to get to know him better." Dolan winks.

COLLEEN GETS A MOMENT aside with Zacour. Colleen likes the expressions that cross his face, moment to moment. They stand in the lobby of the ER before she is about to accompany the whole party back to Pittsburgh. "I'm glad you came," she says.

"I am, too."

"I thought maybe your fiancée would come, too."

"I called her. She's on her way, but they had another kind of emergency at her work. She's very responsible."

"She sounds like a person who would make a good doctor."

"Utterly."

Utterly, she thinks. *Utterly.* Wonderful word. "Will you see Matt again?"

"I arranged to visit on the weekend."

"Next weekend?"

"Yes. They were kind." He tips his head toward where the parents are taking Matt to the car. Matt is turning back looking at him. Ziad claps a hand to his mouth, then turns it into a kiss to his fingertips, followed by a hand up. Matt waves back.

"It's a shame he won't see Kate."

"She'll come with me on the weekend."

"Oh. Good. That sounds . . . right." She smiles.

"Tomorrow we're driving to Virginia to get married."

"Oh?"

"There's a place there—Winchester—you don't need anything.

Just show some ID and get married." He smiles ruefully. "We're like movie stars getting married after the pregnancy."

Colleen laughs. "They only made it fashionable. It was the way of the world for a long time. But I have to tell you, I don't agree with that as the reason to get married."

"I don't either."

"But you're doing it?"

"I've been trying for a year to marry her. Maybe longer. Maybe since I met her."

"Oh. Well, then. They're waving for me to come. I hope you'll have a wonderful day tomorrow."

Winchester, she thinks. Not that far.

THE WAY IT HAPPENS is that Nadal thinks, no, more or less *feels*, that if he remains silent, this arrest, this nightmare will go away. And the man who arrests him allows him to be silent. For what seems like two hours, he sits in a room, alone, except for when the man comes in to ask him if he needs anything—coffee, cookie, sandwich, ice cream, anything. He shakes his head no to everything, but nods when the menu gets to Coke. Later the man brings him a sandwich and a Coke.

His cuffs have been removed, his leg secured to the floor. He tries to think of nothing. He eats. If there were only a bed, he could lie down here and sleep. That would be all right.

After a long time, the man who rode in with him comes in and sits across from him. "I'm glad to see you ate something. You must be very, very tired. Now, I can understand you don't want to say anything much right now, everything being new, but I'm leaving the paper here in case you want to write out what happened. I mean I *think* I know. Well, I know the possibilities. If you say you did the things you are accused of, it gets pretty simple, pretty quick. No big trial, no reporters, just a jury thinking what would be the proper punishment. But my thought is the whole thing from the beginning is complicated and you want to explain all of that part, but man, it's a lot to explain. I'm not trying to put words into your mouth. I just want to tell you what I think I see. I mean, you knew this woman Maggie such a long time ago, and you were trying to live your life, and things . . . happened. Am I saying too much? I mean, my job is to make this . . . easy for you and at the same time to serve the law and justice."

Nadal looks at the clock on the wall, startled. "I need for someone to contact my mother."

"We've found her. She's a very nice woman, my people tell me, salt of the earth. You *do* get one phone call. You are permitted to call an attorney if you wish, or you could call your mother."

"Can I talk to her here?"

"Sorry. Not yet. It's just not allowed. She loves you. Some people aren't that lucky. You have a good mother."

Nadal stares at his hands. He hasn't looked at them for a long time. They don't look like his. He doesn't know what to think of this man, Dolan. He keeps expecting him to yell or shout questions or hit him, but Detective Dolan doesn't do any of those things.

"I think there are going to be mitigating circumstances," Dolan says in an almost whisper.

Nadal looks up at the small, neat man who arrested him. He would like to look away, but the man's deep-brown eyes almost mesmerize him.

"If you were my son, I'd advise you to tell everything and let the system and people start to take care of you. I'd say, 'Rest, you're pushing too hard. Just turn it over.' I know, I sound like a preacher saying, 'Turn it over to God.' But it is sort of the same thing, turning things over to some other system."

Nadal thinks, No, I don't want to talk.

The man asks, "Did you mean to hurt Maggie Brown?"

"No." The answer comes so quickly, Nadal isn't sure he heard the question.

"That's what I thought. That's what the blood evidence showed. If you don't feel like writing, can you tell me . . . just maybe in three or four words, what happened."

"She had a knife. I got scared."

"You fought?"

"She was yelling things at me, that kind of fighting."

The detective snaps to attention. "Insulted you? Were they insults?"

"Yes."

"That makes sense. And what? You grabbed the knife? Or . . . knocked her down or . . ."

"I don't want to talk."

"All right. I'm just trying to picture it. If you knocked her down—"

"I never knocked her down. All I know is the knife was in her hand and then I was turning it around and then she fell and there was blood."

"Which part of this is right: You were talking, she insulted you, you got angry, she had a knife, she was going to use it—was she going to use it?"

"I guess."

"You thought she might use it?"

"Yeah."

"And you were scared, of course. Angry?"

"Yes."

"I understand." The detective frowns. "If I were your father, I'd have to tell you you have to step up and admit you lost control." He shrugs. "That's what it sounds like to me."

Nadal closes his eyes. He did lose control. He knows he did. And he ran.

"There is nothing that can't be explained if you have patience. I can think of things, lots of things, but I need for you to say them.

That's what this is about. The law. You have to do right. If you did something, you have to make it right."

"How?"

"By explaining."

"I just wanted my son."

"I think we're getting somewhere. If you're saying you never intended to kill her, you didn't go there with that in mind. You wanted your son, you wanted to be a guy pulling his family together, doing right, but she fought with you, and you lost control when she had a knife. Is that at all correct? Tell me if it isn't."

"It's correct."

"Now we have your computer. You work with computers, right. And we saw you looked up this place called Peabody Institute. On your computer."

"I didn't look it up."

"But the page comes up several times."

"My . . . Matthew looked it up. I let him play with the computer."

"Do you know why he looked it up?"

"No."

"Oh. You let him keep bringing the page up?"

"No. I looked again to see what he was looking at."

"Makes sense. You have to keep after kids with computers. Did he tell you why?"

"He thought some guy who wrote a letter about being his father was there."

"Ziad Zacour."

They know the name. How—?

"We don't have the DNA back but we're virtually certain from other evidence that Zacour is the biological father."

Nadal puts his head down on the table. He wants to weep for days, weeks, months, just to be left alone to weep. Everything he does is wrong. Everything.

"One thing I find interesting. You kind of took Matthew there. Close anyway. You got him close to Peabody."

Nadal keeps his head down. "It wasn't on purpose."

"You ever heard of 'accidentally on purpose'? The mind does tricks."

Nadal lifts his head.

The man's eyes are kind, not mean.

BY THE TIME CHRISTIE GETS THERE, Dolan is able to say, "Got him. Getting him anyway. Not death row 'got him.' He'll do time, probably in the psych prison once a defender sees his history. He's messed up." Dolan sighs. "He's writing it down."

"You didn't force it?"

"No. I pretended I was his father."

FELIX IS ECSTATIC to see Matt again. It seems strange that certain things will happen normally now—normal seems strange. Jan and Arthur will teach tomorrow and the next day, Jan will hold rehearsals those days—this time with Arthur sitting next to Matt the *whole* time he is not onstage even though the danger is over. Matt will go to school. But this family, this new family, is temporary, as temporary as a play. In just the way a cast gathers together, lives a fictional life together, and then parts, this adventure will be over one day soon, with only photographs or digital recordings to show it happened. And memory of course.

Jan and Arthur put their son to bed. The dog sits at the bedroom door as if guarding. The dog won't be enough to hold him.

Jan knows that. She is already the good mother in the Solomon story.

"We've lost him," she says, closing the bedroom door.

"I know," Arthur says.

18.

FRIDAY

THE NEWLY MARRIED COUPLE, those two people who sit in the auditorium at rehearsal, have a glow and glitter about them. Everybody looks at them as they lean forward to watch the stage.

Matt swells. He can't stand still. He looks and looks and then walks offstage in the middle of a scene. He walks right down to the auditorium. Everybody stops rehearsing to watch the other play unfolding. Even Jan. She can't help it. It's like magic—the words are only partly audible. But she can read the bodies. "This is Katie, my wife. She wants to know you. She's a doctor."

"Can you stay?"

"For a while. This weekend. We'll be back."

"Can I come see you?"

"Anytime. We want that."

And so a new life is made and another one disappears.

CHRISTIE MAKES TWO VISITS before the week is out. The first is to the Philips kids. Laurie seems a little less afraid of him when he comes to the door this time. In fact, she invites him in, even though she asks, "Is anything wrong? Or just checking in?"

"Nope. Just checking in. Where's everybody?"

"Alison and Meg are at work, Joel is reading, and Susannah is folding clothes. They're just upstairs. Hey, guys," she calls, "visitor."

"I just wanted to come by and tell you all the good news. Matthew Brown was found."

"We *know*," Laurie says. "Meg was always watching. We even looked it up on computer."

"What time does Meg get home?"

"Couple minutes after seven."

"Hm. I'll say hello to her over at Doug's Market, right, she still works there?"

They tell him yes and he drives the few blocks to Doug's.

Meg is behind the counter helping an old woman count out her coins. She smiles at him. Her smile means, "I heard the good news." When she can speak to him, she says those very words.

"I was just thinking if you could do the babysitting as much as possible. I'm going to tell you a secret. It's a secret, a serious secret between us. Matt's birth father has been located, and he appears to be coming into the picture. If I had to take bets, I'd say it's a matter of months at most. Ziad Zacour is going to want the boy and vice versa. So Matt is going through a lot, a whole lot, not to mention what he went through, and Jan Gabriel needs a babysitter for rehearsal, not to use any of the people in the play because they have other functions. And Professor Morris, Arthur, really has a lot of work to do. Now of course Matt doesn't think he needs anyone, but we all want to make sure he, oh, I don't know, sits still, doesn't wander off. So how much of that do you think you could do?"

"A couple of nights a week?"

"That would be great."

"Would I be allowed to do homework?"

"Oh, yes. Yes. And another thing. Eventually the parents are going to be very sad when they lose Matt. They already understand it will probably happen. They already *are* sad. Give them a little attention. Talk to them when you can."

"When Dr. Morris drove me home, I could tell he needed to talk about his book he was writing, so I asked him questions. I drew him out."

Christie pauses, almost freezes. "Right, right. I'll let them know I talked to you."

When he leaves he laughs at his denseness. Of course, of course. Not to say it won't happen if the stars align—this other new family of his making. But who's taking care of whom? She *drew him out.* Of course.

He gets into his car and he drives out of Pittsburgh, out of everything Pittsburgh, to Ohio.

The next visit happens the next day. It's to the hospital in Akron.

An old man named Richard Christie lies in white sheets with oxygen tubes going into his nose. He has not been shaved, his hair is thin, white.

"He's not aware," the nurse said moments ago in the hallway. "We feed him intravenously. He's been out."

"Do you know anything about him?"

She looked at him curiously. He had told her he was the son.

"I didn't know him, not after the age of seven," Christie explained. "I just found out he was alive." They both almost laughed and said *not very.* "I'm catching up. As well as I can."

The nurse said, "I don't know much. A couple of people from the nursing home—the residence section—came here to see him a week or more ago. They said they'd liked him. They said he was quiet, minded his own business."

"And his illness?"

"His insides are a wreck. Liver. Everything, really. He was an alcoholic."

"They liked him?"

"A couple of people did." She backed up. "I'm sorry we had no way of contacting you."

"Nobody could have known how. I wasn't aware."

Now he sits next to the bed. Aware. A lie. Somewhere underneath what isn't known, all is known. He believes that. He believes Nadal let Matt go near Baltimore because he knew what he didn't want to know.

"Hello. Dad, can you hear me?"

There is no movement at all.

"I'm Richard. I'm your son. I just found out about you."

Nothing moves. The guy doesn't want him. Never did. Still doesn't.

But a nice man, pleasant, there's that.

He remembers a little. Images come to him of a sad, yes, quiet man. Never angry. Often . . . wobbly. Sedated. Didn't want to climb up out of it.

How does that happen to people?

He feels no anger at all, only puzzlement and sorrow that he's late.

He touches his father's hand. It's not cold but there is no reaction. "Well, I came here," he says. "Better late than never."

It won't be long now, the nurse told him in the hallway.

He has the day off, two days if he needs them. Somebody ought to be here when it happens.

Acknowledgments

My gratitude goes to several experts who helped me along the way in writing this novel. New contacts/consultants include Detective Christopher Jordan, Computer Crimes, Pittsburgh Police; Virginia Giannotta of The Caring Place, a center for grieving children, Pittsburgh; Lisa Bednarchik of Children and Youth Services, State College; Phyllis Smith of the Peabody Institute, Baltimore; the teachers at the Falk School, Pittsburgh; and directors of a number of funeral homes and crematoria in Pennsylvania.

As always, the usual suspects have provided valuable information with great patience: Marc Silverman of the University of Pittsburgh Law Library, shepherded me through cases of sperm donorship and taught me about databases used for people searches; and retired Commander Ronald B. Freeman of the Pittsburgh Police continued to teach me about crime investigation in a way that suits me—he cares about people and their stories.

I'd like to thank Otto Penzler of Mysterious Press and his wonderful staff, Alex Franks, Nina Lassam, and Rob Hart, for making this book such a pleasant and rewarding experience.

The University of Pittsburgh has provided me with a home for

ACKNOWLEDGMENTS

many years, not to mention a setting for much of this novel. I pass certain places every day and, in my mind, scenes happen in them.

I have a support system that makes my life rich. Let me thank here "The Seven," my writing group; my wonderful family; and my extraordinary husband, writer Hilary Masters.

MYSTERIOUSPRESS.COM

Otto Penzler, owner of the Mysterious Bookshop in Manhattan, founded the Mysterious Press in 1975. Penzler quickly became known for his outstanding selection of mystery, crime, and suspense books, both from his imprint and in his store. The imprint was devoted to printing the best books in these genres, using fine paper and top dust-jacket artists, as well as offering many limited, signed editions.

Now the Mysterious Press has gone digital, publishing ebooks through **MysteriousPress.com**.

MysteriousPress.com offers readers essential noir and suspense fiction, hard-boiled crime novels, and the latest thrillers from both debut authors and mystery masters. Discover classics and new voices, all from one legendary source.

FIND OUT MORE AT
WWW.MYSTERIOUSPRESS.COM

FOLLOW US:
@emysteries and Facebook.com/MysteriousPressCom

MysteriousPress.com is one of a select group of publishing partners of Open Road Integrated Media, Inc.